The Queen of Spades

or

The Imminent Possibility of Death in the Mind of Someone Living*

(*With Apologies to Damian Hirst)

A Fable

By

Peter Alexei

Copyright © 2013 by Peter Alexei Maradudin

This is a work of fiction. Any resemblance to any persons, living or dead, is purely coincidental.

All rights reserved. Except as permitted under the U.S. Copyright Act of 1976, no part of this publication may be reproduced, distributed, or transmitted in any form or by any means, or stored in a database or retrieval system, without the prior written permission of the author.

Bark! Books

Visit the author's website at www.peteralexei.com

First Printed Edition: May, 2013

ISBN: 978-0-9852354-2-0

Lyrics for *Defying Gravity* by Stephen Schwartz used by permission.

The Queen of Spades

or

The Imminent Possibility of Death in the Mind of Someone Living*

(*With Apologies to Damian Hirst)

A Fable

Also by Peter Alexei:

The Masked Avenger

*For Noah and Fiona, who would not let **me** rest
until this story was told.*

Fable *n.* 1. a short tale to teach a moral lesson, often with animals as characters 2. a story not founded on fact 3. a story about supernatural or extraordinary persons or incidents; legend.

I

The giant truck rumbled through the foggy, deserted San Francisco streets, coming off the freeway and moving slowly towards the city center from the south. After midnight there weren't many pedestrians – the town went to bed early and got up early – giving one of the world's greatest financial and cultural centers a bit of a small-town feel. But there were pockets of activity here and there South of Market. The Flower Mart was already getting ready for its day, the clubs along Folsom Street were still grinding away, and the staff at the San Francisco Museum of Contemporary Art were putting the finishing touches on their new exhibit of British Art of the Turn of the Century – the 21st Century, that is.

Thomas Bradshaw, the director of the museum, paced the marble lobby feeling something he rarely felt anymore – a sense of anticipation, mingled with excitement. It was truly hard to run a world-class arts institution without growing jaded and cynical, he thought. The art world was too fickle, too full of poseurs, too of-the-moment, too flash-in-the-pan to hold anyone's passionate interest or sense of romance for long - let alone thirty years. He had spent most of those thirty years working his way through postings at small to medium sized museums in Great Britain until he landed one of the most coveted and daunting positions within cultural America, the San Francisco Museum of Contemporary Art. At the pinnacle of success, however, he found, much to his despair, that little of excitement actually happened within his scope. His life had become filled with meetings that led nowhere, budget cuts that hamstrung him and his vision, and endless flagellations at the hands of his board. He had almost grown bored. But this new exhibit, and its star artwork, gave him a new thrill.

The truck was running late, and that made him antsy. The driver had radioed in a few minutes earlier, however, and the installation crew was standing by in the museum's loading dock. As Thomas Bradshaw stood in the center of his four-story central lobby, with giant posters proclaiming the upcoming exhibition, he looked up at the logo for the exhibit.

The Killer Whale.

It was a formidable graphic. It was, almost incontestably, the iconic image for a period in contemporary art that changed the way people saw art, or the world for that matter. Donovan Hirsch's seminal piece, The Imminent Possibility of Death in the Mind of Someone Living, a Killer Whale suspended in a tank of formaldehyde solution, had blown people's minds when it was first unveiled in the early Nineties. Almost twenty years later, it still had impact. And it was the central piece of the exhibition, newly acquired by the museum as part of its permanent collection through funding from a wealthy donor who had requested anonymity.

The truck maneuvered its way through the ever narrowing streets, finally arriving at the alley that led to the loading dock of the museum. A few homeless people stopped and stared as it negotiated itself back and forth with considerable beeping, until it could slide straight back towards the dock. The installation staff, along with an associate from Hirsch's atelier who would guide them in the final positioning of the piece, as well as a marine biologist and an art preservationist, waited patiently. All of them were used to waiting – giant sculptures and canvasses had to move slowly and gently. Art took time.

Thomas Bradshaw was still in his reverie when his assistant came to fetch him.

"It's here," she said.

"About bloody time," he replied with an exhalation of breath.

As they entered the loading dock, the giant crate that had been suspended within the truck's climate controlled interior was finally touching down onto the polished concrete surface. Straps were removed, and locks were unlocked. The obligatory crowbar was applied. The wood panels that encased the enormous tank fell away. Everyone held their breath, anticipating a face-to-face encounter with one of the greatest predators on earth.

As the dust settled, Thomas Bradshaw stepped forward and peered into the somewhat murky tank – the formaldehyde solution still agitated by over three thousand miles of cross-country transportation from New York. After a moment, during which he took off his glasses, rubbed them and put them back on, he said what was on everyone's mind.

"Um. That's not a killer whale."

II

She was flying. Swooping over a golden city surrounded by cobalt blue water. Bridges stretched out in all directions, gracefully arching into distant hills and across green islands. Towers rose up and touched wisps of fluffy clouds. Pyramids, columns, cathedrals. She accelerated as she dove closer to the ground, her arms outstretched like wings. Cruising through the avenues and boulevards, she wondered at the tall buildings around her. There was no one on the streets, the city was empty. But it was beautiful in the golden light of a sun setting to the west.

Is this what heaven looks like?

Somewhere in the back of her mind she knew she was dreaming, and there was a moment of lucidity when she recollected reading somewhere that dreams where you're flying had something to do with sex. She couldn't remember if it had to do with freedom or frustration...

"I think I'll try... defying... gravity..."

What?

Maddy awoke with a start, and stared at her cell phone which was singing away on her bedside table. A musical theatre aficionado, she had recently changed ring tones to her new favorite song from *Wicked*. Gone was Music of the Night. That had brought sad memories.

Defying Gravity.

She tried to make out the time on her alarm clock, her eyes stuck together with sleep. 3:29 AM. She then tried to make out the name of the caller on the backlit screen on her phone.

Jimmy.

"Hey, Good Lookin'," he chirped.

"Dude, do have any idea what time it is?" She had gone from being concerned that there was an emergency to being more than a little annoyed. Their regular "Miss-Me Nights," which had been born out of professional necessity had, over time, become somewhat sacred to her.

"I do. Exactly. I'm on my tenth cup of coffee. But you want to get over here as quickly as possible."

"Where's here?" asked Maddy, suddenly alert. The journalist in her kicked in.

"SFMOCA."

"Isn't it rather late – or early - to be at the museum?"

"Let's just say that if you want to see some cutting-edge art, you better come down right away." Jimmy paused for a second, reconsidering.

"Make that bleeding edge."

III

After being out of work for six months, Darryl Richards was grateful to have the job. He'd heard the stories, though. Night watchman at 580 California was, for the most part, a pretty simple gig – especially for a former cop like Darryl. Just no one held onto it for very long. People just up and quit. He had to admit, it was a pretty creepy building. Built in the Eighties, designed by the world famous architect Philip Johnson, it was a seminal piece of Post-Modern architecture. What made it creepy were the twelve wraith-like female figures that stood watch at the top of the building, twenty-three stories above the street. They were statues that had been commissioned by Johnson from a mysterious sculptor named Muriel Castanis. No one knew what they meant, and both Johnson and Castanis had died in recent years, taking the secret of their dark purpose with them. Called by some the Corporate Goddesses, they stood, three to a side, on top of the building.

Faceless.

Darryl Richards had seem them from reasonably up close. He had been introduced to them by his supervisor when he took the job. During the day they were disconcerting enough, but at night, lit from below by metal halide floodlights, they became spectral – their cloaked and hooded figures revealing just blackness where their faces should be.

Darryl Richards sighed. The alarm at the front desk beeped, and he put down his Stephen King novel. It was time to do the rounds. His shift started at ten at night and went until eight in the morning, four nights a week. He figured that just past the halfway point in the shift, 4:00 AM, was the time to stretch his legs and work his way from the top floor on down, checking the doors on all of the suites in the building. His cohort, Miles Watanabe, would hold the fort at the main reception lobby while he ate his lunch and caught up on the re-runs of SportCenter.

"See you in an hour," said Darryl to Miles as he turned his key in the elevator lock. Miles just grunted, his face already aglow from the television. It took an hour, because Darryl checked each of the twenty-three floors, and, to stay in some sort of shape, he took the stairs from one floor to the next. At least he worked from the top down – not quite the strain on his heart that walking up all of those flights would be. He'd had some surgery – a stent to open up an artery – and he wanted to be careful. Exercise was important, just didn't want to blow a valve. At fifty-five, he wanted to be around for a while. Wife would miss me, he thought with a rueful smile.

It took the elevator two minutes to reach the twenty-third floor. The lights in the elevator lobby, triggered by the motion sensor when the elevator doors opened, blinked to life. It was somewhat reassuring that they did so – it meant that no one else could be up there, or at least could not have been for a while. The elevator lobby was quite impressive – and strange. Dark marble floors and walls with ornate carvings of mythical creatures lurking and creeping around Corinthian columns – another one of Johnson's post-modern jokes, I'm sure, thought Darryl. A large, intricately carved wooden door at one end led to the penthouse and board room, which looked out over the city. The top two floors had been empty for a few months, the previous tenant having moved out after the implosion of their stock during the financial crisis. Not everyone received a bailout, thought Darryl with a knowing chuckle. He certainly hadn't.

A new tenant was rumored to be moving into the penthouse suite within the month, something to do with international imports and exports. A Russian firm. Sounded like something out of James Bond. Universal Exports. Wasn't that the cover name for MI6? Darryl whistled the theme from the movies and strolled over to the large door, confidently rattling the handle, knowing full well that it would stay fixed in his hand.

Except it didn't.

He almost fell over as the handle dropped downward and the door swung open. Inside, the suite was in mid-reconstruction, the floors bare to the concrete and the ceilings gutted. The lights were not yet on any motion sensors, so the cavernous room yawned darkly before him, an echo bouncing off the walls and windows from the sound of the heavy wooden door swinging inward and banging against the wall.

Huh. Must have been the cleaning crew. Except there was no point for the cleaning crew to have been up here. Darryl was instantly on his guard, but he wasn't such a chickenshit that he was going to call Miles over this. He entered the large, loft-like space. All of San Francisco splayed out before him, impressionistic in the fog. The room was lit by the floodlights from below softly illuminating the ceiling. Outside the windows the twelve Corporate Goddesses stood immutable and terrifying. It was said by some that they were placed as a warning to the denizens of the Financial District below them. Choose not the way of greed, or turn out like us. Darryl listened carefully. He could only hear the soft moaning of the wind outside, along with the distant sounds of the foggy city at night: fog horns, the odd ambulance, and the cooing of pigeons nested in the eaves.

He circumnavigated the space. There was nothing there. He went towards the windows on the east side, looking to catch a glimpse of the Bay Bridge and home on the far side. It was too foggy, though. He could just make out the first few lights on the Bridge before they were obscured by the mist. The fog was moving quickly around the building, and he felt a momentary sensation of vertigo. It was as if he were flying through clouds, or even worse, that the building was falling over. He shook himself and stepped away from the window. He turned towards the door of the elevator lobby.

What was that?

It must have been the fog…

And then his heart stopped. Over on the corner, the north-east corner, one of the wraith-like creatures…

Moved.

IV

I should be used to this by now, thought Maddy as she entered the loading dock of the museum. Used to the tape strung from between blinking traffic barriers with Police Line – Do Not Cross. Used to the glare of the floodlights that got set up by the Crime Scene Investigation unit. Used to the milling about of hardened people with their cups of coffee, making jokes and looking bored as they processed something horrible.

She should have gotten used to it, having a police detective as a boyfriend, but there was something about the disconnect between the cold efficiency of the police in their procedures and the often grotesque and arbitrary nature of the death they were investigating that still left her disoriented and disturbed.

I'll never get used to this. Still the sweet little girl from Newport Beach. Some tough investigative journalist.

"Hey, Damian," she said with a smile, recognizing a friendly face. The big black bear of a cop grinned at her.

"Hey yourself," he said, giving her a friendly squeeze on the shoulder. "Nothing like starting your Monday at the crack of ass in the morning. You're looking good, though."

"You're sweet to say so. Feel like crap, if you want the honest truth. I hate starting my day without a shower or a good cup of coffee." And with barfing, she thought ruefully. She'd lately not felt so good. Must be fighting off the flu.

"Well, your day's about to get a whole lot better. He's over there." Damian jerked his thumb in the direction of a tall, crisp-looking young Chinese man in a trench coat who was talking with a slender, close-cropped, nervous looking man in thick, designer-y glasses. Jimmy Wang looked up as Maddy approached, winked at her and raised one finger in a sign that he would be a moment. Maddy nodded and turned her attention to the scene on the dock.

There was something about the large, rectangular object covered in a tarp that filled her with dread. She knew that whatever was under the tarp was not for public consumption, and she wasn't looking forward to seeing it. But she had a job to do, and due to her "special relationship" with the police, she had first access to some sensational material. Suck it up, girl, she said to herself. What would Barbara Walters do?

Detective Wang finally broke away from his interview and came towards her. "Hey, good-lookin'," he grinned at her. This was the other thing that she never got used to. It was now instinct to turn her face up in anticipation of a kiss, but that would be *so* unprofessional, so she curbed the impulse with some difficulty. She just winked at him, and he winked back. Their mutual assurance.

"Now you're not supposed to be here," he whispered, "and the director of the museum would have a conniption fit if he knew you were press, so just try to look as much like you're on our side as possible."

"You could always get me a set of blues for situations like this."

"With some boots, a badge and a gun? Baby!" He gave her the raised eyebrow. "Impersonating a police officer, though… I would have to arrest you. I'm sure handcuffs would be involved."

Incorrigible, thought Maddy. She couldn't help giggling, though.

"So what have we got?"

"The photo team is just about ready, so if you're sufficiently braced..." He gestured and a man in a hazmat suit pulled the tarp away.

Ew, thought Maddy. It was all she could do not to barf.

It was a large tank, filled with some sort of liquid. Floating in the middle of it was a man's head.

Just a head.

Maddy closed her eyes, took several deep breaths and opened her eyes again. She did a little shiver and then put on her game face.

"This is art?" she asked.

"I suppose it would depend on who you ask," said Jimmy. "More likely, it's someone's idea of a sick joke."

"What was supposed to be in there... Oh." The light dawned. She had heard of the killer whale – banners and posters were up all over town. "Not what anyone was expecting, I guess."

"No, so there are a bunch of mysteries here. Not only do we have 'who is this?' but 'who's behind it?' and 'how did this happen?'"

"And, of course, um, 'where's the killer whale'?"

"Of course. Super fun."

"So is the artist here?"

"No, but his assistant is. Donovan Hirsch has been called. Even with the nine hour time difference, we woke him up. Must be nice to be a world famous contemporary artist."

"Last I heard, his stuff was selling for millions," said Maddy.

"This piece, according to Mr. Bradshaw, is, I mean was, worth five million."

Maddy exhaled through puffed cheeks. "Well, that's the start of a motive."

"Yes and no. What makes the piece valuable? Is it the killer whale? Is it the killer whale and the tank? Is it the artist's name attached to it? I would think it would be all of the above, so I'm not sure why anyone would steal just the whale."

The tank and its contents were photographed thoroughly from all angles. Finally, the gruesome moment arrived. The officer in the hazmat suit pulled out what looked like a net for cleaning a pool and, with some fishing about - which was oddly and grotesquely funny – the head was extracted. It was placed on a sheet of white plastic. As the photo team set up, Jimmy and the forensic pathologist snapped on some surgical gloves and bore in for a look. Maddy stayed discreetly to the side, working desperately to keep her gag reflex from kicking in.

"That's one ugly motherfucker," whispered Damian, who had sidled up next to Maddy.

"I'm pretty sure with that level of trauma, no one would look their best," whispered Maddy back.

The forensic pathologist was speaking into a small digital recorder. He had strapped a headband with a bright LED lamp onto his head and was doing a close examination. "Subject is male, Caucasian. Dark hair…" he peeled back an eyelid. "Brown eyes. High cheekbones. Possible Slavic ethnicity. Head cut cleanly below the fifth vertical vertebra." Almost as an aside he added, "And how that was done, tough to say… super clean cut, though." The forensic pathologist took something that looked like a wooden shoe horn and worked it in between the lips of the head.

That is one tough job, thought Maddy. You would just have to be wired differently to do that. The forensic pathologist pried the teeth open and peered into the mouth. "Teeth are in terrible condition, and wait... What's this?" He pulled out a pair of tongs from his bag, along with some tweezers. He grasped the tongue with the tongs and fished underneath with the tweezers. "Huh."

He held up, with the tweezers, in a small plastic bag, a thumb drive.

V

The Very Reverend Deacon Sergei Arkadin breathed a deep sigh. He could not be more tired. It had been an exhausting weekend, with the biggest week in the Russian Orthodox church schedule still ahead of him. Palm Sunday services had been packed, much to his delight and that of the Archdeacon. It was gratifying to see a resurgence in spirituality. There was something to be said for the Great Recession - people began to connect with the things that were truly important. They put less in the collection plate, however, Arkadin smiled ruefully. Still, he felt validated in his choice, in his calling, after struggling as a young man to find himself. Within the Russian Orthodox Church he had found his center, and his connection to his cultural and ethnic roots, something that had been sorely lacking in his upbringing. His expatriate parents had divorced when he was fifteen, not long after they had arrived in the U.S. after the collapse of the Soviet Union, and between their manic efforts to fit in to their new country's culture, and their general disregard for Sergei while they wrestled with their own issues, he was left rootless and disaffected. A chance invitation to attend a Russian Easter midnight service by one of his friends, and the event itself with its incense and mystery, caught him by surprise, however. The next thing he knew he was an altar boy, and then working his way through the Orthodox seminary. It was good to finally belong to something. Something deep and ancient. But supporting the burgeoning Russian expatriate population in San Francisco took an enormous commitment in energy, however, and by this point in the week he was desperate to go home and climb into bed. He had officiated three services the previous day, on Sunday, prepared sermons for the Great and Holy Monday, Tuesday, Wednesday, Thursday and Friday services, gone through the weekend's receipts, and now that it was almost four in the morning on Monday, he had only to lock up before a few hours of sleep would embrace him.

He shuffled out of his office – shuffled! he thought to himself, I'm still a young man – not even forty, just feel old tonight – turning out the lights as he did so. He peeked into the main chapel to do one final check and found himself wanting to sit for a moment, to take in the stillness and the darkness. There were no seats in the chapel - Russian Orthodox believers stood during the services – so he rested his weary bones on the step before the altar. The Church of the Holy Trinity was the oldest church of its kind in the Americas, and he breathed in its venerable air, steeped in over a century of incense, with deep satisfaction. On the corner of Green Street, the church was right on Van Ness Avenue, and the pre-dawn thrum of the traffic on San Francisco's main street was like the distant roar of the ocean. But it was still peaceful. The only lights within the chapel were the little LED candles that had been installed in front of the icons in the little red glass votives. Otherwise there was a faint glow from the streetlight outside that cast colored patterns through the stained glass window onto the ceiling, and the glistening through the lower windows of the passing car headlights.

Another big sigh.

One last duty – no, make that an observance. He slowly stood up, rubbing his sore back as he did so, and headed down to the sub-basement. Down to his holy of holies.

Few people realize that while Spain was colonizing California from the south, Russia was colonizing California from the north. Russians had been on the West Coast of North America before anyone else had been, and there were deep mysteries and faint echoes of their presence still. The Church of the Holy Trinity held one of them – one of the great treasures of Russian culture, hidden deep in the sub-basement, and away from the public. An icon painted by the immortal Russian icon painter, Andrey Rublyev, considered by many to be the greatest of them all. When the Church was founded in San Francisco in the 1860's, Father Nicholas Kovrigin was sent down from Alaska to become the first Rector of the Parish. He brought with him a Rublyev icon – a copy painted by Rublyev himself of his famous Annunciation, and which had worked its way across Siberia in the 17th Century and finally to Alaska in the 18th. Its presence in San Francisco was shrouded in mystery, and after the earthquake in 1906, it was rumored to have disappeared. It was simply safe, where it would come to no harm, deep in the sub-basement of the little church.

Sergei Arkadin unlocked the door to the little chapel in which the icon resided. He turned on the small electric chandelier that gave a dim glow to the room. On the wall in front of him was the wooden case in which the Rublyev was kept. He opened the doors of the case and gazed for a moment in rapturous wonder at the colors, the gravity of its subjects, the sureness of the hand, the gorgeous, almost Byzantine relationships of the characters.

Then he heard a noise behind him.

He turned in time to see the large candlestick come down upon his head.

VI

The phone jolted him from sleep. He was annoyed, but then realized, after glancing at the time on his phone, that he had overslept. Carlos Rodriguez slowly slipped himself out from under the arm of his boyfriend, tapped his iPhone, and took the call into his kitchen.

"Dude, where are you?"

"I overslept. I'll be there in ten minutes."

"Liar," laughed Maddy on the other end of the phone. "You take more time to get ready in the morning than any girl I know. Late night?"

"They're all late, these days," sighed Carlos. It was true. Now that he and Robert were an item, they were up late every night. Not that there was that much messing around - although they were still in the early sexual bonding stage of the relationship - it was just that Robert's job as the Maitre d' at a high-end sushi lounge kept him working late, and Carlos was just anxious enough to wait up for him each night. "He's been angling for more lunch shifts, but the money's much better at night."

"It's sweet that you wait up. Get over here as quick as you can, though. A lot went down last night. Some serious stuff."

"Order me the usual. No shower for me, I'm out the door."

"Just watch those pheromones," said Maddy, with a giggle as she hung up. Carlos sniffed himself, and decided that a small dash of cologne would get him through.

It wasn't ten minutes, but it was surprisingly fast for Carlos, even factoring in the quick smooch for his sleepy beau. Maddy was already clicking away on her laptop, but the barista at the Peets on Market had only just set out their coffees when he walked in the door. This was their daily routine. They met each morning at eight to compare notes and plan their attack for the day. Carlos was Maddy's office-mate at the Clarion, and her right hand. Or was she his left? They hadn't quite reached the status of Mather and Roos, the Clarion's famous (or infamous) muckraking reporters, but they had made quite a name for themselves in the investigative reporting game, and were now referred to as "maddyandcarlos" by their cohorts. The incidents surrounding the Masked Avenger the previous fall had catapulted them from lowly interns into reporters with bylines.

"I thought *I* looked like ass," said Carlos. "What happened to you?"

"I've been up since three something. No shower for me, either."

"Ew," said Carlos. "I hope we don't have to do any interviews today. The two of us put together..." He rolled his eyes. "So what's the scoop?"

Maddy told Carlos about her early morning escapade at the Museum. Carlos got less and less interested in his muffin as she went on.

"That is, hands down, the most gross thing I've ever heard," he said. "And the thumb-drive, what's on it?"

"I don't know yet. Jimmy is going to call me once they've finished the other forensic analysis."

"What more could there be?"

"Finger prints, micro-fibers, DNA evidence. It's amazing what you can find on a tiny swab of stuff."

Carlos looked doubtful. "And the killer whale? Where do you begin to look for evidence about that?

What about the driver?"

"Well, the driver of the delivery truck has been questioned, but he knows nothing that anyone can tell. The truck was fitted with a special electronic key, and it was sealed in New York. Only the director of the museum knew the code, so if the whale was stolen…"

"And the head replaced…" added Carlos.

"It must have happened before the crate was sealed in the warehouse in New York."

"I wonder…" Carlos looked thoughtful.

"What?"

"That truck must have stopped somewhere. The driver didn't just drive non-stop 3,000 miles. He slept somewhere."

Maddy typed it up. List of all truck-stops that the driver stopped at. Perhaps someone saw something. She looked up from her laptop.

"There's still the code," she said.

"Crackable. Maybe?"

"Maybe. Perhaps the code was known by more than just the museum director."

"Or maybe he's in on it. It wouldn't be the first time…"

They paused. There was something about extremely rare objects that could corrupt almost anyone. They'd seen it happen before.

"What about Bradshaw?" asked Carlos.

"He was in a complete panic. I don't think he was acting. He looked legitimately like he was going to have to do the biggest spin job of his career."

"No shit. Nothing like losing your big ticket item just before your show opens. What's the angle on the head?"

"Again, tons of forensic analysis. No clue as to his identity yet. The SFPD have already been in contact with the NYPD, looking for missing persons."

"Missing persons from New York? Talk about a needle in a haystack. There are probably half a million people missing on any given day from that town. That doesn't sound like the best use of resources."

"It's procedure. Jimmy didn't think it was a great idea, either, but as much as there's a book, he's got to go by it. What do you think?"

"I'm wondering. The tank. The one the head was in. Is it the same tank that the whale was in?"

Maddy smacked her forehead. "That is such a great question! I wonder if anyone thought to take a look at it like that..."

"You said Donovan Hirsch's assistant was there. What's his deal?"

"He's already on a plane back to London. There was nothing for him to do. He was not a person of interest."

"It's something to think about. I mean, who would know if it was the same tank?"

"So you're suggesting that not just the whale was taken, but the whole thing? That one tank was replaced with another?"

"It seems like that would actually be easier to do."

"That would take a lot of premeditation, especially with the tank on the move."

"And full specifications of the original tank. I wonder where one would get those...?" Carlos was looking upwards and to the left, pretending to think hard.

"You're a genius. Text to Jimmy to have what's-his-face stopped at Heathrow." Maddy started clicking away at her BlackBerry furiously. "They would want to test the formaldehyde solution to see if there was any organic material indicating the prior presence of the whale."

"It's simpler than that," said Carlos with that

infuriating smirk he had when he was quite sure he was the smartest guy in the room.

"How so?"

"Displacement. A man's head displaces a lot less liquid than a killer whale. How full was that tank."

Light dawned on Marble Head. Maddy's eyes grew really wide as she realized that no one had considered that.

"The tank was full. To the brim. Dang. That seals it!"

"It doesn't seal it, but it makes me think that we need to be looking in a certain direction."

"So why would someone do this? What are the possible motives?"

"You said yourself that the piece was worth five million. That sounds like significant motive."

"Yes, but, if what you're proposing is true, that's an extremely expensive operation to set up. Think about it: accessing the specifications for the original tank, constructing a duplicate, somehow transporting the duplicate tank in such a manner as to be able to do a switch at some opportunity, secreting the original tank away. This would take a small army of people to do. A small army of pretty highly trained people. I don't think money is the motive."

"What would it be, then?" Carlos looked out the window, squinting into the sun that sliced its way down Market Street.

"Maybe someone is sending a message."

"Um, Twitter would be easier?"

"It most certainly would be. That would mean that who ever is sending the message is interested in real impact, and money is not an object."

Carlos' eyes now got really big. "Shit. Just like in The Godfather. The horse in the bed."

They both shivered recalling that chilling moment in the movie.

"Just like in The Godfather." Maddy puffed her cheeks and exhaled. "This is some serious stuff."

She suddenly had that sensation in her stomach that she got when she knew she was in way over her head.

At that moment, both of their cell phones pinged simultaneously. Text message from Carey Portman, their boss.

"It's like Charlie's Angels. That's cool how she does that."

The message read:

580 California Street... 1520 Green Street... Divide... conquer... pick your poison

"Dude," said Maddy.

"Flip for first choice?" said Carlos.

"Can I do Green Street?" asked Maddy. "I can then cut over to the station on the other side of the hill and see what Jimmy's found out."

"So much for fairness," teased Carlos.

"Well, if you *want* to do Green Street..." Maddy gave her most generous look.

"Nah, I like hanging out in the Financial District – more cute boys down there. And I can stop at House of Nanking for lunch. It's okay."

"Thanks, Carlos," said Maddy giving him a hug as she headed for the door. "See you back at the office."

"Hey, maybe you could take a shower!" Carlos called after her.

As she stepped into the sun, and headed down Market towards Van Ness and the bus stop, Maddy thought that that might be a good idea. It would help get through what now looked like another really long day.

VII

Long day didn't begin to describe it.

Detective Jimmy Wang had been up for over twenty-four hours. It was time to take a walk, clear his head, and get some coffee stronger and better than the sludge that lurked in the office coffee maker.

I get it that bad coffee and police work have a long history together, but this is San Francisco… we, at least, should have better coffee than this, he thought as he stared at the half empty mug on his desk. He was tempted to stick a pencil into the mug to see if it would stand up straight, but thought that would be a waste of a perfectly good pencil.

He put his computer to sleep and grabbed his jacket. Outside, North Beach was basking in the warmth of an early spring sun, with just enough bite to the breeze to remind you that you were still in San Francisco. He squinted and stood for a moment, sighing deeply. I love this town, he thought. The air is perfect, and when the sun is out, the place sparkles. It had been a wet winter, so everything was green and crisp. And that morning there wasn't a cloud in the sky.

He headed down Columbus Avenue a few blocks to Caffe Greco to get a large cappuccino. He was tempted to sit at a café table on the sidewalk and watch the world go by, but he felt that if he was going to take a break from the office, he should make the most of it. He turned north on Columbus and walked towards Washington Square Park. Within a few minutes he was standing over a chess match being played with a furious intensity. One player was a grizzled old black man, Jefferson Rollins, a grandmaster of the game, and an habitué of the park. The other player was a short, stocky Chinese man with steel gray hair, who wore an expression of quiet agony on his face.

"Let the game come to you, Dad, let the game come to you," Jimmy said with a smile. James Wang, Sr. glanced up from the board for a moment without moving his head. If ever a look said Fuck Off, this one did. After a moment, though, he sighed, released all of the tension, and laid his king down.

"He was one wrong move from taking me this time," said Jefferson. "The day is coming soon that he's going to beat me. Very soon."

"After almost two years," said James Wang.

"Can't rush greatness," said Jefferson in that way he had that made him sound like a wise sensei.

"Yeah, but I'm seventy, and I don't have all the time in the world," said James Wang with that baritone growl of his that made him sound like an old bear. Jimmy just laughed.

"That's bull Dad, and you know it. You're going to outlive all of us. You're looking great."

"And you're looking really... really terrible, Jimmy," said James Wang, taking in his son. "Hey, Jefferson, let's take ten."

"I got all day, so take your time," said Jefferson. He pulled out a beat up copy of the New Yorker and re-lit the cigar that had been lying in an ash tray by the side of the chess board. He leaned back on the bench, and started to read a movie review from six months earlier. James and Jimmy strolled through the park.

"So what's up? Looks like you haven't slept in a while. That girl keeping you up?"

Jimmy knew his dad was teasing. James Wang,

Sr. adored Maddy, but he liked keeping Jimmy on his toes.

"I wish. Just a really interesting case that popped up in the middle of the night. Some really crazy stuff at SFMOCA."

"Crazy? How crazy?"

"Decapitated head, missing killer whale, that kind of crazy."

James Wang stuck out his lower lip, impressed. "Man, this town. In my day, it wasn't this weird, but it was pretty weird, all the same."

Jimmy's father had retired a few years back as Assistant Chief of Police, so he had known some seriously strange cases in his time. The Zodiac Killer, Jonestown, Harvey Milk's assassination – they all went down on his beat. San Francisco had a way with crazy.

"You can say that again," said Jimmy. Both men took in the scene. Sun-bathers, a couple of loose dogs, a homeless man sleeping on a bench. Another perfect day in the park.

"So what's the angle?" asked James Wang.

"No angle, yet. Waiting for forensics to do the voodoo that they do. I'm just taking a break to clear my head. I can't see anything in the way of a clue, yet. Jose's burning it up down in the lab, so he should have something soon."

"You kids rely too much on science these days. Takes some of the fun out of it, don't you think?"

"I like knowing that the guy I've busted is the right guy, Dad. I like having the tools. Besides, crime is just rougher these days, and criminals are that much smarter. Just trying to keep up with the opposition, that's all."

"Well, keep me posted. I live vicariously through you."

"You shouldn't do that, Dad. You've got lots on your plate. You're life is pretty full as it is."

"Yeah, but you get all the girls."

"Any time you wanted, Dad. I know how well you can dance."

"Yes, well, your mother would have something to say about that."

She sure would, thought Jimmy. She'd kick his ass.

James Wang clapped his son on the back. Damn that guy still packs a wallop, thought Jimmy with an internal grimace. "Coming over next Sunday for dinner?"

"Planning on it. I could use a dose of mom's cooking."

"Maddy doesn't cook for you?"

"No, not really. We do a lot of take-out, or, when we're lucky, we horn in on some of Angelique's cooking." Angelique was Maddy's apartment-mate, an expatriate French girl who worked at a French gourmet food import company. "We really don't have much time for it." He hesitated to say that Maddy wasn't much of a cook, but she was getting better all the time. Between Angelique, Carlos, and Pearl, Jimmy's mom, Maddy was improving by osmosis, if nothing else. Jimmy couldn't really complain – he could barely boil water himself, but his dad was old school, and assumed that Maddy should do the domestic work, and would tease him no end if he admitted that he was trying to do his part, too.

"Well, I should get back to it," said James, and they headed back to the chess table.

"I should, too, Dad. Great to see you. Go easy on him, Jefferson. Let him win, once in a while."

"He wouldn't dare," growled James as he hitched up his pants and sat down at the table. "I'm taking him like a man."

Jimmy was just heading back to the office when his phone rang. "Hey, Good-Lookin'," he said into the phone.

"Hey, Handsome," Maddy replied. "What's your 20?"

"I'm at the park. Just took a break to stir the blood. Why? Where are you?"

"I'm at the little Russian church on Van Ness, but I'm wrapping up here. I was going to come over and see what's up, but after what I just saw I need a shower." She sighed.

"Are you okay?" Jimmy could hear the tension and exhaustion in her voice.

"I'm okay, just… I need a small break from the world, I think." Jimmy could hear her shudder.

"Would you like some company?"

"In the shower?" Maddy sighed happily. "That'll help get me through the day."

Jimmy laughed. "See you soon, then.'

And Jimmy Wang turned and headed up Union Street towards the top of Russian Hill, a little lighter on his feet.

VIII

He had finally arrived in America. Not just arrived, but had entered an elite club.

Ivan Ivanovich Orkin now owned a basketball team.

He had bought it cheap, actually, but that didn't matter. The San Jose Orcas were perennial basement-dwellers, but with the money he had at his disposal that could change. If nothing else, he could make them entertaining. Some significant free agents were entering the market during the upcoming off-season. With the right coach and some time to gel, within a couple of years the play-offs could be attainable. Orkin thought about how much fun it would be to give Jerry Buss a run for his money. He didn't have Jack Nicholson to sit on his sideline, but there was a healthy contingent of Bay Area celebrities to whom he could offer courtside seats to amp up the energy. He wondered if Clint Eastwood or Sean Penn or Francis Ford Coppola liked basketball. He would have his marketing director make some calls.

He was sitting in what would now be his private box, watching his new team practice. Introductions had been made, the players obviously indifferent to who their boss was. They were polite enough, but their minds were elsewhere. Most were Tweeting away - when they weren't scrimmaging - and even the scrimmage was half-hearted. Ivan Orkin smiled to himself. A self-made man, he found it hard to understand how someone could be paid millions of dollars to put in a token effort. But he, as much as anyone, understood how to motivate a man. He had no problem replacing everyone on that court – or off it, for that matter – if they failed to perform. He liked to think that he was a quiet, dignified and gentle man, and he always began any negotiation with a smile. But if he didn't get what he wanted, for what he felt was a reasonable offer, he had no problem cutting his opponent's balls off.

Literally.

He sighed, and caught himself sighing. This also made him smile. Russians sighed. There was even the expression, "a Russian Sigh." What was it about the Russian soul that leant itself to this mode of expression? Perhaps, after centuries of disappointment with their government, their weather, their place in the world, their lives, Russians had developed a strong sense of accepting the vicissitudes of life with a certain equanimity. There was nothing in the Russian scheme of things that could be so terrible that it couldn't get worse, so get over it.

But he, personally, had triumphed over the traditional Russian acceptance of the "way things were." His life was a textbook on how to succeed at the end of the Twentieth Century. Much of it, he admitted to himself, had to do with being in the right place at the right time. But great men take advantage of the moment. He remembered his Shakespeare: "Some are born great, some achieve greatness, and some have greatness thrust upon 'em." His moment came when the Soviet Union collapsed. The August Coup, when several generals tried to place Mikhail Gorbachev under house arrest but failed to win the hearts and minds of the people, gave him his opportunity. A colonel in the Russian Army having risen through the ranks of the Corps of Engineers, Orkin was instrumental in keeping his men in their barracks, helping to shut down the ill-fated coup. He threw his lot in with Boris Yeltsin, and when the time came to receive his reward along with the other men who won that throw of the dice – the oligarchs - he took the one thing that no one else wanted: the rights to millions of tons of scrap metal that had been abandoned by the Russian Army at shuttered bases across the country. He parlayed this rough diamond of a gift into an industrial empire that spanned Europe, Asia and now, America. He had diversified his portfolio, investing in the odd, but essential technologies that no one really thought about, that had no glamour, but had unlimited growth potential. Giant tunneling machines that could build subway systems under existing cities, wireless communications networks that linked huge swaths of otherwise isolated areas of Siberia, Africa and the Arabian Peninsula, ore extraction facilities in Borneo, and just recently, micro-chip manufacturing plants in Finland. He had done well over the last twenty years, and now got to play a little bit.

All of his contemporaries had beaten him to the world of high-level sports franchise ownership. The first teams to go were the British football teams, like Chelsea. Then American hockey and basketball – baseball was still, for the moment, the sacred refuge of old-money white America. Orkin thought that he would never join the club, until the cantankerous owner of the Orcas died, his surviving family choosing to no longer deal with the headaches associated with the ownership of a mid-market franchise. Someone else had offered them more money, two brothers who owned a casino in Las Vegas, but Orkin had made them an offer they couldn't refuse.

Besides, he loved basketball, and saw it as more than just an investment.

He had also moved aggressively into the world of

contemporary art. He had envied the Charles Saatchis of the world, people who moved effortlessly through the exciting and compelling world of high-end art collecting. Art Basel, the Venice Biennale, auctions at Christies – there was a rush to these events that made him feel really alive, and he loved rubbing shoulders with the beautiful and the sophisticated. His own collection was becoming quite notable, and he looked forward to the day when he could make the kind of splash only having a wing of a museum named after him could provide. Soon.

He leaned back in his leather chair, the downlight overhead suddenly causing his face to reflect in the glass of the window of his box. He held still for a moment and took stock. He still wore his hair military crisp, and at 58 his face had the craggy good looks of a young Mikhail Baryshnikov. He was tall, and had maintained a level of personal discipline that kept his stomach flat. Unlike many of his countrymen, he rarely drank, or at least not vodka. He allowed himself a very nice Chateau Margaux every once in a while, though...

He patted his stomach as he stood up. All was good in his world. He even had a beautiful American mistress who was half his age, who enjoyed sharing that bottle of wine with him. His ex-wife, well, she had been beautiful, too, but she had been an evil bitch. He shivered momentarily thinking about it, but shook it off. She was out of his life, thank God.

The only true dark spot in his soul was his son. What had gone wrong? Orkin sighed. He hadn't been the best father. Building an industrial empire worth billions could demand a lot of one's time and energy. He hated to think that he had sacrificed his family to get to where he was now, but as Stalin had famously said, you have to break a few eggs to make an omelet.

He switched off the light in his box, and at that moment his cell phone purred. He tapped it gently, while looking out over the now empty arena.

"Yes?"

"It's gone," said the voice on the other end of the phone. The British accent told him immediately who it was.

"What do you mean, it's gone?" demanded Orkin.

As the voice on the other end of the line explained, Orkin began to feel a rare sensation.

Fear.

IX

Carlos knew something strange was up as he worked his way towards 580 California. He zigged and zagged down Market Street, then up to Geary, then down to Montgomery, then up to California. As he walked, he saw people starting to stream past him in the same direction. At cross streets, more people joined the flow – bankers, brokers, secretaries, bicycle messengers, the denizens of the Financial District. There was a weird energy all around him, and he couldn't put his finger on what it was, but he wondered if this is how it felt on Black Friday, when the Stock Market crashed in 1929. He then felt the hair on the back of his neck bristle, and he did something that few urbanites rarely do – he looked up.

On buildings all around him, people were standing on the rooftops. He could see people at windows looking across towards something – he couldn't yet see what. As he hit California Street, he was aware of a huge crowd gathered at the base of number 580, with police flashers and television news crews already in place. A police helicopter was circling overhead, with the Channel 5 News copter hovering at a discreet distance.

Carlos finally stopped an older, well-dressed man – obviously someone important at some nearby bank – and asked him what had happened.

"They've turned their backs on us. We're doomed."

"Who's turned their backs on you, I mean, us?" Carlos asked, alarmed by the spooked look in the older man's eyes.

"The Goddesses. Look!"

The man pointed skyward. At the top of the building, where the twelve wraiths had for twenty years looked down on the scurrying, ant-like creatures many stories below them, the statues were no longer gazing downwards.

They were facing the other way, back in towards the windows of the penthouse.

Carlos felt his skin crawl. He knew of the Corporate Goddesses, and had glimpsed them from time to time. They had been disconcerting before. But now, with their backs bent, as if they had fully abjured the world of men, they seemed to be saying that there was nothing left for them to watch. Carlos, for a moment, felt doomed, too.

And then he snapped out of it. Wait a frickin' minute. Statues don't just up and move. This isn't Ghostbusters. At least, not yet. He pulled out his press badge and worked his way towards the front of the throng. He arrived at the steps of the building just as an ambulance pulled away out of the underground parking garage. Carlos jotted down the ambulance company and its license plate. A second later a woman in a crisp police uniform, followed by group of men, came out of the main entrance to the building and approached the forming phalanx of journalists, whose microphones and cameras bristled in front of them. Carlos recognized Interim Chief of Police Fay Liu. The crowd grew quiet.

"Everything is fine," she declared. "There is no cause for alarm. As much as we recognize the bizarre element of what has happened, we have found, at this present moment, no reason to believe that any harm has been done, and that there must be a perfectly natural explanation for all of this."

"Which is?" called out a voice from the throng.

"We don't yet know," admitted Chief Liu. "But what we do know is that you should disperse, and return to your ordinary business. We shall let you know as soon as we understand what has happened."

"Who was in the ambulance?" Carlos called out.

"A night watchman, who suffered a heart attack last night. His status is critical, but stable. It is, as yet, unclear if the incidents are related."

"It's the end of the world!" screamed a voice from the crowd.

"Sell!" screamed another.

Suddenly, the crowd roiled as panic gripped them. Everyone, it seemed, felt compelled to get to their desk as fast as possible to make whatever last transactions they could make before their world came to an end. Those who had the wireless technology were pounding away at their phones and tablets like maniacal zombies, their eyes glazed.

It was bad.

Carlos, who had just learned of an equally bizarre, but not yet public event of the night before, squinted as he looked up towards the sky and reflected on his conversation with Maddy earlier.

Maybe someone *was* sending a message.

X

Detective Chen had told Maddy that there was nothing she wanted to see – it was not for the faint of heart. She told him that she had already seen a disembodied head earlier that day, so she thought she could take anything. He relented, albeit grudgingly. And Jimmy had told him that she was tough.

The body had been removed, but there was still a lot of mess. Bits of brain were still smattered on the wall, with an enormous red spray streaking across the doors of a now empty cabinet where once a priceless icon had been stored.

Maddy did get sick, after all. She apologized profusely to Detective Chen. "There's something about the sight of blood, you know? The head earlier, well, after the initial shock was, well, just a head. No blood." She had often had difficulty with blood tests, getting queasy at the sight of the merest drop.

There were more than a few drops here. Whew.

"What the heck happened?" she asked, after freshening up in the bathroom, and sitting outside on the porch to the church. Thank God for Altoids.

"It seems pretty simple. Russian priest in the wrong place at the wrong time."

"So this is a burglary."

"A theft. A heist. At least I think that's the right way to put it," replied Detective Chen as he sucked on a cigarette and blew the smoke out the side of his mouth. He was a pretty humorless guy, and, as Jimmy put it one day to Maddy in the strictest confidence, not the sharpest knife in the drawer. But he was relentless and tough, and in police work that was still worth a lot. "And, of course, a murder."

"And the item or items in question?"

"A painting. A Russian religious painting..."

"An icon."

"Yeah, that's what they're called. An icon."

"There are icons all over this church." It had felt, when Maddy first entered, as if hundreds of eyes were watching her. "What was so special about this one?"

"According to the church secretary, during her few moments of lucidity before we had to take her home, this painting – icon – was quite old, and extremely valuable. By some famous icon painter. Andrey somebody."

"Huh." Maddy had no clue. Some time spent online later. "And who knew of this painting's existence? It's down in the basement of a little Russian church that maybe fifty people know about. I mean, I live just up the street, and I had barely any idea what this place was."

"Only a few people, actually. It was a pretty well-kept secret. Only the higher-ups in the church. The secretary, the deacon, the arch-deacon. But there's an enormous congregation. A lot of Russians in San Francisco." Detective Chen pulled one last pull and tossed his butt into the gutter.

"And the deceased?"

"One of the deacons. Poor guy. Jesus. What a mess. He must have been locking up, and just had a bad encounter with a candlestick."

"More than a bad encounter, judging by the leftovers. That was a really violent crime scene."

"Yeah," said Detective Chen, making a face. "As bad as I've seen."

"Do you have any thoughts about what happened?"

"The victim's head was completely destroyed. The secretary identified him by his clothes. He was struck more than a few times. As if his assailant was not just interested in incapacitating him. Really violent."

Maddy shuddered. "Sounds psychotic, almost."

"Yeah. Just what we need in this town, another psycho." He looked sour. "Well, back to work."

"Can I take another look? I mean, before the cleaning crew gets here."

"If you want to. Just no more barfing, okay?"

"Okay. I promise."

They went back into the church and down the stairs. Maddy steeled herself and took in the little room once again. The trick was not to focus on the walls or the floor with the white chalk outline, or anything that had red on it.

"What an odd little place to keep something so valuable," she wondered out loud. She scrutinized the little cabinet on the wall. It had only a latch with a padlock on it, no sophisticated security system or anything. The latch was undamaged, meaning that it had been unlocked at the time of the murder. "Do you know how much the painting could be worth?"

"No, not yet, but from what we've been told, there aren't many of these in the world. I guess you could say it was priceless." Maddy just took a note. More internet research.

"And the time of death?"

"We're estimating about 4 AM. We'll know for sure later today. Busy day for old Bones."

It occurred to Maddy that it would be, indeed, a busy day down at the lab.

"I guess there's not much left to do here," she said, taking one last look around. "Hey, what's that?" Something had caught her eye.

"What's what?" asked Detective Chen, suddenly

alert.

"Up there." Maddy pointed to the little lantern that hung from the ceiling on a gold chain. There was something that was not gold hanging just under the lantern. It glinted silver, and would have gone unnoticed by anyone. Except Maddy, who had been trying desperately to not look at anything with blood on it.

It was a thumb drive.

XI

The shower worked miracles, in more ways than one. The temptation to snuggle afterwards, and take a nap, was profoundly strong, but they both decided on professionalism. Maddy was the one to say first that they should just get dressed and head back down to the station, but was annoyed when Jimmy had agreed so readily. She had hoped that he might talk her into doing what she really wanted, but he didn't.

There really was a lot to do.

But it felt good to be clean, and given the second wind that twenty minutes under hot water with your boyfriend can give you. As Maddy brushed out her hair she thought that, all things considered, it was better to have days this full, than to be bored, sitting at her desk, scrubbing around for the next story.

Crap, I've got to get to my desk, she thought. She needed to post something about both the museum mystery and the murder/heist at the Green Street church, and do so before it got too late. She wondered how Carlos was doing. She had seen the panic on the streets in front of 580 California on the Clarion home page video as soon as she had flipped open her laptop. She tried to call Carlos, but he didn't answer. She hoped he was okay. Knowing Carlos, he was just fine.

But first, down to the station on Green Street, to see what was going down.

"Can I write anything about the missing killer whale? I mean, this is as big a story as it gets." They were hiking down Union Street towards Powell, Coit

Tower rising up ahead, gleaming white in the crystal clear air of the spring day.

Jimmy ran his fingers through his hair and sighed. It was hard having the press so close, although both Maddy and Carlos had been more than useful to him and the SFPD in the past. But there was always a negotiation regarding the balance between the people's right to know and police procedure, and it was complicated by his feelings for her and his desire to see her succeed. He understood that she felt the same way regarding him and his success, and it did often help to have someone on his side who didn't think like a cop, or have the same issues of legality or liability that a cop did.

"Let's figure it out. We don't know much yet, but even if we did, we need to weigh how much we want anyone on the other side to know how much we know. Can we keep it really simple for now? You'll still be the first one out of the gate. It was a pretty tightly controlled crime scene, and it would seem to be in no one's best interest, at least on the museum's side, to be letting anything out of the bag this early. I'm sure Bradshaw is scrambling, and won't release any announcement until he's got a backup plan."

"So how much *do* we let out? This one's sort of all or nothing. We can't just say that a piece of art has gone missing, can we, and leave it at that?"

"Why not?"

He could be so dense sometimes... "Well, fundamental story-telling. No one cares that a piece of art has gone missing. People care that a Vermeer has been stolen, or a Rembrandt, or, in this case a Donovan Hirsch. If I say how big the piece is, then anyone who has a clue will know what I'm talking about, anyway. I think we're saying that the killer whale has been stolen..."

"Has gone missing..."

"Okay, has gone missing… and that the police are following various leads."

"No mention of the head, yet."

"Okay, no mention of the head."

"And we don't go to press until the plane lands in London and Hirsch's assistant is held for further questioning."

"Why wait until the plane lands?"

"I don't know, maybe just being cautious," sighed Jimmy.

"It can't make any difference – he'll be in a secure area, won't he? No way he could get wind of our suspicions. What's his name, anyway?"

"Richard York. He graduated from the Royal Academy of Art ten years ago, and has worked at Hirsch's studio since."

"I wonder what more we can find out about him…" Maddy suddenly had a vision. She wasn't sure if her boss, Carey, would go for it, but it was worth asking.

"Not much, probably, until he's in custody. But we should start building our list of questions for our friends on the other side."

"Happy to help," said Maddy, thinking that this his how she could leverage further disclosures.

"Okay, run your story as soon as you can, then." Jimmy was silent for a moment, and looked serious. Maddy hated that.

"What's up, Big Guy?" asked Maddy, taking him by the arm. He *was* a big guy, actually, standing almost a full head taller than her. He was quite tall, for being the son of Chinese parents - something that always made Maddy smile when she saw him together with his mother, who was even shorter than she was.

"I'm just trying to figure out the whole 'message' thing. If your theory is correct, then we're doing the perpetrator of the crime a favor. We're delivering the message for him."

"Then maybe there's a way we can work the media coverage of this to the investigation's advantage."

"Exactly what I was starting to think."

"Do we let on about the whole tank being switched?"

"I don't think so. I think it's just about the whale. And the cost of the item."

"Speaking of which, you said that the museum had acquired the piece through the gift of an anonymous donor. Can we find out who that donor was?" They were just entering the police station, and Maddy was starting to get nervous – something about the first time she ever met Jimmy there, she had thought for sure she was going to go to jail. It had been a memorable evening.

"Why?"

"Well, whoever it was, wouldn't they be the most impacted by the news of the theft? Maybe they're the ones for whom the message was intended."

"I'm all over it. I have an appointment with Bradshaw at four."

They arrived at the station, and moved into Jimmy's office. Jimmy had barely taken off his jacket to roll up his sleeves when his BlackBerry buzzed. He took in the message, and put his jacket back on.

"You up for a drive?" he asked Maddy.

"Sure, I guess. Where are we going?"

"Building 606, down at Hunter's Point."

"That sounds mysterious – sort of like Area 51. And Hunter's Point. That's a pretty rugged part of town."

"You don't know the half of it," said Jimmy with a grin. "Let's just say it's the Dead Zone."

XII

Settling into his first-class seat on Virgin Atlantic, Richard York had felt overcome with exhaustion, and longed to sleep. He was wary, however. Not in the clear just yet. It wasn't until the doors had shut and the jetway pulled back from the plane that he finally exhaled and relaxed into the soft leather. He started to munch on his warm cocktail nuts, and even though it was seven in the morning, the gin and tonic was exactly what the doctor ordered.

"Tough day?" asked the young man in the seat next to him, who had been flipping through a Wired magazine. The young man looked at his watch, then at the two little bottles of gin, and gave a wink – the day being only a few hours old.

"I'll say," replied Richard York with a deep breath. He was tempted to leave it at that, and put on his headphones and zone out to some Coldplay – he had read recently of a survey in which Coldplay was named as the number one band to fall asleep to and believed it – but there was something about his companion in the next seat that piqued his curiosity. First class travelers could, for the most part, be divided into two groups: those who felt they belonged in first class and were comfortable there – as he had become in the employ of Donovan Hirsch - and those for whom first class was a rarity and a stroke of luck – a chance upgrade, a glimpse of how the other half lived. His seat-mate was neither. On one hand, he radiated a quiet, but grungy, wealth. The clothes were obviously extremely expensive, but perfect for their wearer - mid-twenties with a carefully neglected beard, and a certain mumble-core movie, leading man quality – a cross between a young Ethan Hawke and Colin Farrell. On the other, he looked almost as if he didn't belong. Richard York couldn't put his finger on it, but the other man seemed almost as if he would have been more comfortable on a private jet.

There was the slightest hint of an accent. Couldn't place it.

And he had the most remarkable eyes. Pale green.

"My day started yesterday," Richard York continued, after gulping down the remainder of his first gin and tonic and cracking open the second little bottle of Bombay Sapphire.

"Mine, too. I had a lot to do before I could go on this trip. You know, all of the little things that need to be dealt with before leaving town for a few days."

Richard York laughed. "I flew all the way to San Francisco, showed up for work, and there was nothing for me to do. So I'm going home."

"London?"

Richard York nodded. "It'll be good to get home. California makes me nervous. Too much sun, or something. Give me the gothic climate any day. You – business or pleasure?"

"A little of both. I've got a little bit of work left to do, then I can enjoy a couple of days in London."

What is it about this guy? He looks so familiar... thought Richard York. "Only a couple of days?"

"Yes. But it should be a good time," said the other man with a smile. "I'm going to an auction."

"An auction? An art auction?"

"Yes. I could have done it all over the phone, but this is more exciting. Nothing like the live theatre of it. The smell of sweat, the looks of desire and despair. Worth the trip."

"Modern, Contemporary...?" asked Richard York.

"Impressionists. I like old things."

"Contemporary Art man, myself," said Richard York. He was starting to get drowsy. He yawned. "Sorry to fade on you, my friend, but I think I'm going to need to take a nap."

"You'll get plenty of rest on this flight," said the other man, again with a wink.

The engines were gearing up for take-off, Richard York sinking deeper into his seat. There was something about the white noise of the engines that made everything seem to fade away. As he drifted off he noticed the young man next to him return to his Wired magazine, flashing the cover as he did so.

The cover. It was the cover of the magazine. Shit.

And then nothingness.

XIII

"Where are you?" asked Maddy.

"On the roof of 580 California," replied Carlos, taking in the view.

"Holy crap! How did you get up there?" Carlos could hear the disbelief in Maddy's voice over the phone. She had called to check in, having heard from Jimmy and the police band what had happened downtown.

"I haven't outgrown my deviousness. Where are you?"

"I'm on my way to Hunter's Point. Building 606."

"That sounds mysterious. A good lead?"

"I think so. Jimmy's being a pill and not giving me any clues, though." Carlos could just imagine Jimmy being poked at that point. Those two.

Carlos looked at his watch. It was just after ten in the morning. "Rendezvous at noon? I'm buying."

"Where?"

"House of Nanking. I've been building a jones for Kung Pao shrimp since breakfast. Bring your boyfriend, if he's free. I think we need to triangulate."

"10-4," said Maddy, and hung up.

As he adjusted his safety harness, Carlos reflected that it took complimentary talents to make a good team. Maddy was relentless and forthright and athletic and friendly and open. She won hearts everywhere she went, going by the old adage that you catch more flies with honey than with vinegar. Being bubbly and blonde didn't hurt. Carlos, however, was, in fact, devious. Had a real talent for misdirection and slight of hand. He relied on his instincts, and was a classic inserter of his foot in the door. He was super smart, but could play dumb with the best of them. Often he took advantage of the racism that was invisible to most people, and the dark color of his skin – his father's side of the family, he reflected ruefully - and let himself "hide in plain sight" – a tactic he had just used to gain access to the roof of the building.

After the panic on the street, he had tucked his press badge into his jeans and wandered into the parking garage of the building through the service entrance. He found a crew of painters and sheet-rock men, milling about next to a couple of vans by the service elevator, being held at bay by the police from entering the building. He sidled up to the crew, all of whom were Hispanic, and milled around with them.

"Perro! What are you doing here?" asked one man in Spanish, clearly the foreman. Suspicious, but not entirely unfriendly.

"I was told to report here," replied Carlos, also in Spanish, with the accent of the Central Valley. "I wasn't expecting to come in today, but the dispatcher said you were a man short."

"Where are your whites?" The foreman gestured at Carlos' clothes, referring to the white overalls that distinguished painters everywhere.

"I wasn't expecting to be here. I had already left home when the call came." Carlos waved his phone.

"There's some spare whites in the van."

"Can we get in?" Carlos gestured towards the cop standing in the elevator lobby.

"They told us that we'd be clear to go up in about fifteen minutes."

"What's the call?"

"Penthouse. New tenant. Building to suit. They've finished the framing, we just have to get in there today before the new flooring shows up."

"Cool."

Carlos climbed into the van and threw on some overalls, spattered in paint. He grabbed a hat, and the next thing he knew, he was "invisible." After the promised fifteen minutes, during which he learned all about the various perils his colleagues had undergone to get from Mexico - or farther south - to San Francisco, they were all allowed to load up their carts and head up to the twenty-third floor. They were accompanied by the police officer, who proceeded them out of the elevator.

As they entered the lobby, a contingent of policemen and a couple of detectives – Carlos didn't recognize them – were waiting to head down. "No point in hanging around here anymore," said one of them. "It's not like anyone did this from inside the building."

"Besides," said another as they filed into the elevator, "it's not like a crime was committed. At least not a crime in any traditional sense…" And the elevator doors closed, cutting off the rest of the conversation.

After the initial taking in of the spectacular view, and of the strange faceless creatures outside the windows now looking in – with more than a few whistles of disbelief and every man crossing himself - the crew got to work. Carlos worked smoothly alongside them, causing no suspicion whatsoever. His dad, after all, had been a day laborer in Modesto, and Carlos had spent some time in the trenches himself to help his family make ends meet. The straight A's he had gotten in high school, and the AP classes, were all that made the difference between his building tract homes in 100 degree heat and a scholarship to Columbia. He had made his immigrant parents proud.

Even though he was gay.

Coming out had been hard, but, well, his mother loved him regardless, and his father, over time, grew less and less conflicted. Carlos was grateful that he had two sisters who were even now carrying on the family genes, if not the name. That helped. At least he could now go home at Thanksgiving again.

A break was called. Carlos went, ostensibly, in search of the restroom. He found, instead, the door labeled "Roof Access" with a "Police Line – Do Not Cross" tape plastered across it. To the devious, the spoils, thought Carlos as he tested the handle of the door. It gave.

Someone forgot to lock up, he thought. And I can't read English, he smiled as he gently removed the tape.

But it wasn't as easy as all that. The door opened onto a stairwell, going up several flights. The "mechanical" floor of the building between the penthouse and the roof took up a whole story, with a door off of a landing. Carlos continued up to the top, encountering another door at the end. It was locked. Carlos had picked a few locks in his day, but he had nothing on him with which to work. He turned back down the stairs, resigned to being so close, but not close enough, when it occurred to him to try the door to the mechanical floor. He reached out to turn the knob when he stopped himself.

He got down on his knees and looked at the knob carefully. It had been nagging at the back of his mind that doors opened too easily in this building. He had to angle himself just so, but there, on the knob, was a faint thumb-print. Carlos sat down on his haunches and thought for a moment. He looked at the dust on his pants from all of the drywall work and got an inspiration. He rubbed his knees with his hands, took his hands and clapped them next to the door knob and let the dust settle on the knob. He then gently blew the dust away, revealing a perfect print. He pulled out his iPhone and took a photo of the print, hoping the resolution of the camera would be good enough. It had served him well enough in the past.

He then debated touching the knob. Pulling a rag from his pants he covered his thumb and forefinger and gently turned the knob, twisting himself so that he didn't smudge the print. He would have felt bad if he had destroyed some evidence. At least a little.

The knob turned.

Carlos stepped through and gently shut the door behind him. The whole floor vibrated under him. The room was filled with banks of machinery for ventilating, heating and cooling the enormous building, thrumming away relentlessly. Carlos had the sensation that he was standing within the lungs of a giant and felt distinctly ill at ease. He turned to look for the light switch and then realized that there was enough stray light coming from somewhere that he could make his way into the large room. Some of the light came from indicator panels on the machines, but there was light coming from above. He scanned the ceiling and saw the hatch – slightly ajar - with a ship's ladder coming down. There was more than one way to get to the roof.

This is how he found himself standing on the top of the building when Maddy called. He had immediately spotted the window washing apparatus, pulled in from the edge of the parapet that rimmed the building. Hanging off the scaffold was a safety harness, with a safety cable attached. As he headed over to the scaffold, he heard the chopping of helicopter blades. Crap. At what point would Channel 5 have enough footage? He slid under the scaffold just as the copter crested the parapet, managing to duck out of sight in the one place on the whole roof that offered cover. He lay under the scaffold until he heard the helicopter move away, heading back towards SFO to the south.

I really shouldn't be up here, he thought to himself. He had reached the point where his nerves were just starting to fail him. But in for a penny, in for a pound. He figured that if he was caught up there, it would at least be a good story, and he might even get some sort of bonus point cred amongst his colleagues for managing to get where no one else in the press had gotten. Carlos steeled himself and went for a peek over the edge of the parapet. He had never been great with heights – after all, how many buildings over two stories were there in Modesto? – and this challenged his intestinal fortitude.

He peered over the edge, grateful for the harness – and the safety cable. The goddesses were tall, almost twelve feet - the height of the penthouse floor - so he only had to look down about ten feet to see the tops of their heads. But he was flummoxed. How had they moved? He squinted down to see if he could make out the bases of the statues. They were just obscured enough by the flowing robes of the creatures' strange raiment that Carlos couldn't be sure of what he was seeing. It was as he braced himself to lean as far as he dared that he felt it with the tips of his fingers. The slight indentation in the top of the parapet. He removed his fingers and saw the slight crease in the metal sheeting that covered the parapet top. It lined up with the side of the goddess below him. Carlos slid his safety cable over to the spot and it became apparent that significant pressure had been applied onto a single location. A rag or leather strap must have been used as a cushion, because there was no paint removed.

Carlos worked his way around the rooftop, finding a similar indentation next to each goddess.

Upon completing his inspection he scratched his head and weighed his options.

There was nothing left to do but suck it up.

XIV

Jimmy flashed his badge at the guard at the gate and they were waved through. It had been an interesting drive for Maddy as they worked their way into Hunter's Point. They had taken the freeway down to the Candlestick exit – the Monster Park exit, but no one called it that – and then followed the Bay around to the east and north. Passing the hulking football stadium, Maddy had been impressed by its age. It had not worn well – after fifty years of being buffeted by the winds off the Bay the concrete was pitted and rust stains streaked the walls. It was in desperate need of repair, but no one would spend any money on fixing it up. There had always been some private scheme by the billionaire owners of the football team to get the public to pay for renovations, or even a new stadium, but the people of San Francisco were wary of such "initiatives" and ritually voted them down.

To call Hunter's Point a depressed area would be a gross understatement, thought Maddy, who had never been to this part of the City. She felt that this is what it must have been like behind the Iron Curtain when there was one. It was as if they had gone back in time and that all of the color had been leached out of everything, leaving behind only grayness. What had been a naval shipyard of tremendous activity during the Second World War was now left derelict. It was a depressing place.

"We're here," chirped Jimmy, as they pulled into a parking space in a relatively empty parking lot next to what looked like an old warehouse. "Building 606. Are you ready?"

"Dude, there's nothing you could throw at me now, after all I've seen in the last eight hours, that could faze me," said Maddy, trying to be brave, but fearing that there could, possibly, be something left that could be thrown at her that would kick her ass. It occurred to her at that moment how hungry she was, having barfed up her breakfast back at the Russian church.

They entered the extremely non-descript building, itself as gray as the rest of Hunter's Point, and it was as if Maddy had passed through into a completely different dimension. The interior of the building was gleaming and sleek, completely belying its exterior. Glass walls, high-gloss floors, banks of computer monitors, European minimalist fluorescent lighting.

"Whoa," said Maddy. "What is this place?"

"This is our new forensics lab. You wouldn't think, would you?"

"Talk about Adaptive Reuse," said Maddy with admiration as they walked down a long corridor.

"We got the building cheap. And it's strangely secure. No one would know that our most high-tech facility was buried inside this old military building. It's quiet out here, other than the nightly gunshots from the 'hood across the way. And an amazing view from the roof-deck. Let's see if we can find Jose."

Jimmy swiped a card through a reader, which chirped its acceptance, and a set of massive glass doors slid open. Jimmy and Maddy passed through, and entered into the main body of the facility – an enormous open space with the ceiling forty feet up. A grid of linear fluorescent fixtures were suspended overhead, causing Maddy to feel as if she were entering an Audi commercial. On the periphery of the space, workstations lined the walls, each with the largest monitors Maddy had ever seen. At one workstation a big man with dark brown skin and large earlobe rings, wearing a San Francisco Goliaths baseball cap backwards, was staring intently at his monitor. As Jimmy approached, the man called over his shoulder.

"Dude, it's a good thing I love my job – 'cause I'm going to be here a long time puzzling over all of last night's shit."

"It was a full night," said Jimmy, making a face.

I'll say, thought Maddy. Three of the weirdest crimes she had ever heard of happening in the space of several hours.

"Jose, this is Maddy Stevenson. She's a friend."

"*The* Maddy Stevenson?" Jose rose up out of his chair, towering over Maddy. He looked at her with a certain admiration, then took her hand in his big paw. "It's a pleasure," he said. He then narrowed his eyes. "Although I'm not sure I can forgive what you did to my team." Thank God he smiled afterwards – Maddy was relieved that he wasn't too pissed that she had exposed the illegal steroid use of San Francisco's star baseball player last fall, just before the playoffs. She winced at the memory of being throttled by Benny Cashman in the process. Investigative journalism could be a painful line of work.

"Sorry about that," she said, trying to sound sincere. "Just happened to be in the wrong place at the wrong time. Couldn't help it. I'm a Goliaths fan, too."

"That's alright, then," said Jose.

"So what have we got?" asked Jimmy. "Cryptic email you sent me."

"We got some cryptic shit," said Jose. "Literally."

He gestured at his monitor. The screen was filled with zeros and ones, black numerals on a white background.

"Is it some kind of code?" asked Jimmy, furrowing his brow.

"It looks like binary. But what it means is anyone's guess."

"Where did this come from? The thumb-drive?"

"Yeah. Both thumb-drives had this stuff on them – nothing else. Different pages, but the same sort of zero-one-zero-one thing on each page."

"Page? This isn't code?" Maddy couldn't help herself. She wasn't good at the fly-on-the-wall thing.

"It's a pdf. There are a half-dozen pdfs on each drive. Each a page of what looks like a code, but could just as easily be a Word document. It's not anything we can just drop into a machine and have it crunch."

"Huh," grunted Jimmy. "So we would have to manually input this into some binary device to see what happened?"

"Assuming we wanted to take the time. Assuming it *is* code."

"And not some weird prank," said Maddy.

"Oh, it's a weird prank, alright," replied Jimmy. Maddy reflected that it couldn't be anything else, after all.

"What else have you found out?"

"The head, well, we think we know how the guy died."

"Having his head cut off wasn't enough?" Maddy couldn't help herself, and pretended to gag.

"Nope. He was dead before his head was cut off."

"How did he die, then?" asked Jimmy.

"Come with me. Let's go downstairs," replied Jose. He motioned for Jimmy and Maddy to follow him.

Oh, God, thought Maddy. I really don't want to see that head again.

As they left the workstation, Maddy looked back at the screen. There was something about the sequence of numbers... she shook her head. This was a job for a cryptologist, or a symbologist. Where was Robert Langdon when you needed him?

They took a large elevator down to the basement. It occurred to Maddy that the elevator was large enough for several gurneys. It then occurred to her that she was in a space that routinely hauled dead bodies up and down. No amount of cleaning solution could make her touch the walls. A shiver ran down her spine.

The doors of the elevator opened, and they entered the most clinical environment Maddy had ever seen. A luminous ceiling filled the space with a cool, shadowless light. It looked just like a hospital operating room with several stainless steel tables, except for the grisly sequence of cutting implements along one wall. Not normal operating tools – more along the lines of what one would find in a wood shop.

"Sometimes you just got to use the *big* tools," said Jose with a grin as he observed Maddy's reaction. She was also disconcerted by the bank of stainless steel doors along the opposite wall. Refrigerated lockers. Dead people.

"The Russian priest... is he?..."

"Yup. Locker 17. Want a peek?"

"Hell no. I mean, no thanks." Would this day never end? And then, what sort of dreams would she have when it did? "Is the head here, too?"

"Next room. We brought in an specialist for that one."

They went through the doors at the opposite end of the morgue and entered what looked to be a laboratory, with large computer monitors along one wall. The room hummed, large machines grinding away. Hunched over what looked to be the control console of the Starship Enterprise was a bald man. As Maddy and Jimmy approached, he turned.

He had no face.

There were a couple of pinholes for eyes, a couple of slots which might have been nostrils, and a strange hole/flap where a mouth might once have been. It was as if someone had taken an eraser to the man's head – any normal distinguishing characteristics had been dissolved and pasted over with scar tissue. The visage was horrible and shocking.

Maddy ran up and gave the man a hug.

"It's so good to see you!" she said. "I'm sorry I haven't been better about keeping in touch."

The Man Without a Face returned the hug, with claw-like hands patting her on the back. "It's okay," he said. "I know how busy you've been. I look for your byline every day in the paper."

"How have you been?" asked Maddy pulling back to take him in. "You look good!"

As much as a creature without any real facial features could smile, the man did. His voice rasped through the strange hole where his mouth should have been. There was something Darth Vader-ish about his breathing, but with a touch of the Elephant Man's gentleness to his voice.

"You're just being sweet. I've gained weight."

"It suits you," said Maddy with a smile. She reflected on her first encounter with The Man Without a Face – an encounter that scared the wits out of her at the time, and she recalled Carlos actually passing out when he first met him. A brilliant chemist on the faculty of UC Berkeley, The Man Without a Face had been an ally of the Masked Avenger, and had aided Maddy and Carlos in solving a series of murders in the Tenderloin the previous fall. An accident in his youth had robbed him of his face and several fingers, and his residence was the sub-basement of the Chemical Sciences building at Berkeley – a hidden dungeon chamber from which Maddy was surprised and glad to see him emerge.

"We turned to the best for help on this one," said Jose. "We couldn't figure out what the heck was going on."

"What the heck *is* going on?" asked Jimmy, rubbing his hand through his hair, more than a little bewildered.

"Polonium-210," replied The Man Without a Face.

"What?!!" Maddy and Jimmy reacted as one.

"Polonium-210. Radiation poisoning. The man whose head was in the tank died of Acute Radiation Syndrome. It's only been done a couple of times before - most notoriously in the case of Alexander Litvinenko, the former KGB operative who was murdered in London."

"How can you tell?" asked Maddy. She had a vague recollection of the incident from several years before. It had been rumored that Litvinenko had been murdered at the behest of the Russian President, Vladimir Putin, and that the FSB – the Russian Federal Security Service, the descendent of the KGB - was responsible.

The Man Without a Face turned towards the electron microscope over which he had been working. He tapped a few keys on the computer keyboard, and a large image of gray and black lumps appeared on a giant monitor. Maddy was glad there was nothing left in her tummy to barf up. "His brain tissue is crawling with it, although it would be hard to understand if you didn't know what you were looking at." Jose rolled his eyes. "It was a massive dose. Probably died within half an hour. Extremely painfully, of course."

"Um, that doesn't sound like an easy poison to get. Not quite like arsenic or anything."

"You would be right about that. It was quite the signature of the FSB."

"So he was killed by the FSB? What would a Russian spy agency have to do with a missing killer whale?" Maddy needed to sit down.

Jimmy shook his head in wonder. "As clues go, this would be on the huge side... And the head itself – any idea of how it was... detached?"

"That's an easy one." Again Jose rolled his eyes. Jose was good and all, but he was being schooled by a super-genius.

"An easy one," Maddy repeated and nodded her head as if she understood, of course.

"Industrial laser." There was a pause. There is only so much weirdness that one can take in any given day, and Maddy and Jimmy had reached their limit. And it wasn't even noon.

"No, Mister Bond, I expect you to die," quipped Jimmy under his breath. The image of James Bond on the steel table about to be cut in half by Goldfinger's industrial laser flashed across his mind.

The Man Without a Face made a noise that Maddy had by then learned was his version of a laugh. "They've gotten smaller since then. With the right connections, one might get one's hands on a laser of considerable power that could be wielded like a gun." He tapped the keyboard again and a new image evolved on the screen.

At least it's not the real thing, thought Maddy with a grimace.

It was a close up of the dead man's neck. "You can see the cauterization caused by the intense heat. You may have noticed that there wasn't any blood in the tank."

Right, we noticed that, thought Maddy. She hadn't even thought about it. Jimmy rubbed his chin, thoughtfully. When he spoke, it was the voice of a man just hanging on by his fingernails.

"So we have a dead man, killed by as exotic a method as one can think of..."

"Except, maybe, blowfish toxin..." interrupted Maddy, who then regretted it.

"...whose head was cut off by a laser...'

"Right," said The Man Without a Face, nodding sagely.

"...Who had a thumb-drive placed under his tongue with binary code on it..."

"Yes, but only *maybe* on the code," chimed in Jose.

"...Who should have been a killer whale floating in a contemporary art piece worth millions of dollars."

Everyone looked at their shoes.

Jimmy turned to Maddy. "If you can turn this into any kind of cogent story that anyone could possibly understand, then knock yourself out. No comment from the SFPD."

At that moment, Jimmy's BlackBerry vibrated. He looked at the screen and then looked up to the heavens.

"What?" asked Maddy.

"Carlos has been arrested...

"Again."

XV

It was a late lunch – later than they had planned – but it worked out okay because the crowd had thinned somewhat at House of Nanking and they could finally sit down and talk without it being too noisy. Maddy had been about to pass out – literally – she had only had that muffin at eight o'clock, which had left her by nine. Carlos made some sort of crack about how being arrested always gave him an appetite, and Jimmy just smiled that smile he got when he really just wanted a stiff drink, and felt like the only adult in the room.

After the Kung Pao Shrimp, the Mu Shu Pork, Crab Wontons and Hot and Sour Soup were pushed out of the way, everyone pulled out their notepads.

"Why is it stuff like this always comes in threes?" mused Jimmy.

"Threes? Is it? Let's add it up," said Maddy. She felt like the recorder-secretary for the session. She had always been a good note-taker – a strength in high school and college. "Let's start with the whale, what do we know so far?"

"Killer whale missing, severed head in its place with massive radiation poisoning – suspected involvement by the Russian state security agency. Thumb-drive in its mouth containing some sort of code."

"Jesus," exhaled Carlos, who was just now grasping the enormity of what Maddy and Jimmy had uncovered with the help of The Man Without a Face. "That's a shitload of weird."

"The current theory is that the whole tank was replaced, not just the whale with the head," replied Maddy, reading from her notes. "Most likely suspect in aiding this endeavor is the assistant to the artist, Richard York, currently on a plane back to London."

"But how do we find out who could be behind this, and to what end?" asked Jimmy.

"We talked about how the tank could have been swapped," said Carlos. "It would have to have been while it was en route from New York to here. It would have to have been while the truck was stopped overnight while the driver was resting."

"But the lock, the code, the whole thing – how do you remove a tank that big from a refrigerated truck without anyone noticing?" asked Jimmy.

"Wait a second!" Maddy gasped. "Maybe we have to take one step further back."

"How do you mean?" asked Jimmy.

"Maybe it wasn't just the tank that was swapped, but the entire refrigerated container?" Maddy went on. "That would be profoundly simple. Just pull up a second truck, unhitch one and hitch up the other. Who would really notice?"

"I'm not sure I would use the expression 'profoundly simple,'" replied Jimmy. "This would involve a duplicate refrigerated container with duplicate tare and ID numbers. Where do you get such a thing?"

"I guess from the same place you got the first, and patching on the new numbers. Has anyone contacted the trucking company to see if anyone arranged for a similar shipment on, or about, the same day?"

Jimmy made a face. "No, but we will."

"And when you interviewed the driver, did you ask him where he stopped?"

"We're smart enough to do that," said Jimmy, more than a little irritated. He pulled out his notes.

"He stopped for overnights only twice."

"How do those guys do that?" wondered Maddy. "That's a lot of driving in each leg."

"Drugs," said Jimmy and Carlos in unison.

"Where did he stop?"

"Just outside of Des Moines, and again at a truck stop outside of Denver."

Maddy chewed on the end of her pen. "Those places must have some sort of video monitoring – I mean, who doesn't?"

"We can ask. Maybe something will show up." Jimmy's to-do list was starting to stack up.

"And the lock?" asked Carlos.

"We're obviously dealing with someone with a level of technical sophistication and monetary resources that something as simple as a digital lock would be a snap," replied Jimmy.

"Well, that narrows the field a little, I suppose," said Maddy brightly. "Triangulation will get them every time – we're now looking for someone really wealthy, with access to high-tech gear and a really smart crew, who likes art."

Everyone looked up towards the ceiling as they tried to think of anyone matching that description. They all shook their heads. Back to their notes.

"Okay, what about the thumb-drives? And there are two of them." said Maddy.

"Yes, the second you found at the church."

"Linking, obviously, the two events to each other."

"What would the theft of a multi-million dollar contemporary work of art and a priceless Russian icon have to do with each other?" asked Carlos, more to himself than the others. "They are both extremely valuable, both involve murder…"

"They're both art," said Maddy. "I mean, let's not overlook the obvious…"

"By Russian artists." Everyone looked at Carlos.

"Well, the icon is by this apparently famous medieval painter..." said Maddy, a little embarrassed that she couldn't pronounce his name.

"Andrey Rublyev," said Carlos, nodding. "And Donovan Hirsch was born in Russia, but emigrated to the UK when he was a small boy."

"How do you know that?" asked Maddy in wonder.

"They let me keep my phone while I was hanging out at the station waiting for Jimmy to sign me out. I just did some basic research online."

"Who's better than you?" said Maddy with a smile. Jimmy was still frowning, though.

"So motive?" he asked.

"Well, it seems that the 'message' theory is still in play. I mean, why would anyone leave behind the clues that they have unless they wanted someone to know who was behind this?"

"Or that we're being taunted by someone who thinks we'll never figure it out," sighed Jimmy. "No one ever caught the Zodiac Killer, and he sent letters to the police and the press."

"Sounds like work for a profiler," said Carlos. "So this icon, worth millions since it's the only one like it outside of Russia, why was it so unsecured?"

"You'd be surprised by how unsecured some of the greatest art in the world is," said Jimmy. "Just the other day a guy walked in off the street in Paris and stole five paintings from the Museum of Modern Art. Just took them off the wall in broad daylight and vanished with over one hundred million dollars worth of art."

"Holy crap!" said Maddy. "So no 'Thomas Crown Affair'?" She was remembering the popular caper movie in which a famous Monet painting was stolen for the fun of it from the Metropolitan Museum of

Art. "No super sophisticated security systems foiled by some super smart, but bored billionaire. Just balls."

Jimmy and Carlos looked at her with their mouths open.

"You just totally profiled our killer," said Jimmy after he recovered himself. "Thomas Crown. With maybe a sadistic streak."

"No maybe," said Maddy. "I saw that crime scene. And severed heads. Whoever is behind the whale and the icon is one sick puppy. But a bored, super smart billionaire sounds about right."

"But he would still need a crew," mused Jimmy. "Wait, you know in the movie – the remake with Pierce Brosnan – he used an eastern European gang to create the diversion… I have an idea."

"What's that?"

"The Pink Panthers."

It was now Maddy's turn to look at him with her mouth open. "The Pink Panthers? I'm all for filmic references, but I think we're maxing out here."

"No, seriously. There's a loose affiliation of jewel thieves in eastern Europe that have been dubbed the Pink Panthers by Interpol. They work all over the world – London, Paris, Tokyo, Dubai, you name it – displaying a total, brazen disregard for danger and the law. They've moved billions of dollars in jewels and art in the last few years, in some of the most audacious crimes on record. Most of them are poor, disenfranchised and disaffected young men recruited out of Bosnia and Albania, but there are cells in every major city in Europe. And the St. Petersburg cell is considered the most ruthless, and the most sophisticated."

"Who do they work for?" asked Maddy, fascinated.

"Anyone who's willing to pay their price. They're completely mercenary. They're not interested in the loot, just the crap that the money they receive for it can buy and the adrenaline rush they get from the jobs. They're a hard-drinking, fast-car driving, nightclubbing crowd."

"Where do I sign up?" asked Carlos.

Jimmy tried not to laugh at the thought of Carlos hanging with brutal thieves and killers, and went on. "The most intriguing aspect of their organization is that no one has been able to determine who runs it. There are stories and rumors, but nothing concrete. There's an entire Interpol task force dedicated to catching these guys and they've never been able to figure out who makes their deals and who sets up the hits. And the level of sophistication of the jobs is pretty breathtaking – well beyond the capacity of the poor assholes who do most of the grunt work."

Maddy reviewed her notes. "Bored billionaire with Russian underworld connections, interested in art, with a sick sense of humor." She looked up with a smile. "Now we're getting somewhere!"

Jimmy arched an eyebrow. "So that leaves 580 California and the Goddesses. Carlos – what do you have to say for yourself? Other than the obvious that you did one of the stupidest, craziest, most uncool things I've ever heard of."

"Thanks, boss," said Carlos with a grimace. "All in search of the truth. I mean, you would have done the same."

"Hardly. I'm not good at those kinds of heights. I mean, twenty-something floors above the street on a window-washing platform."

"Jesus, Carlos," whispered Maddy.

"Hey, I had my safety harness on!"

"So what did you find?" prodded Jimmy.

"Well, you know the Goddesses, they're made

out of fiberglass."

"Really? They look like metal statues."

"Just painted to look like that. They're resin. Epoxy. They're hollow, and really light."

"So not living beings that move under supernatural power?" asked Maddy, a little disappointed that there might not be ghosts involved.

"No. You could see the place where each one was detached from its base and then re... reglued, I guess you would say."

"How were they detached?" asked Jimmy, impressed in spite of himself.

"Really clean cut, sort of like a hot knife or..."

"...an industrial laser," said Maddy and Jimmy in unison.

"You owe me a Coke," said Jimmy.

"You didn't find a thumb drive, did you?" asked Maddy.

"No, but I did find this," replied Carlos pulling out his handkerchief. He unrolled it and there was the butt of a cigarette.

"Um, that's the butt of a cigarette," said Maddy. She wrinkled her nose.

"Not something you expect to find 250 feet above the street on a ledge," replied Carlos proudly. He had, after all, worked really hard for that cigarette butt.

"Something else for the Man Without a Face to look at under his electron microscope. Perhaps we can determine where it came from." Jimmy gathered up the new evidence.

"You can do that?" asked Carlos.

"Totally!" said Maddy, excited by this. "You know Sherlock Holmes could identify over fifty different types of tobacco. Solved several cases that way."

Both men looked at her, then shook their heads. She was irrepressible.

"We also have this," said Carlos, holding out his iPhone and displaying the photograph of the thumbprint. Jimmy could not arch his eyebrow high enough to show his surprise, admiration and displeasure all at once.

"What is it with you guys and tampering with evidence?" he said, taking the iPhone from Carlos.

"Look, if I hadn't found it, it might not have been found," said Carlos, doing his best Clint Eastwood squint in an effort to intimidate Jimmy. It didn't work.

"I... thanks. Still working on not sounding like my dad," exhaled Jimmy. "This is a huge clue. This should go to Interpol, Pink Panther Task Force. Between this, the cigarette, and the modus operandi that we've established so far, we might have a chance of figuring out who did this."

"And who's behind it," said Maddy. "I sort of feel like Rene Russo, all of a sudden." Jimmy couldn't help letting out a low growl. He got poked for his efforts.

"So it looks like we all have our work cut out for us," said Jimmy closing his notebook, reverting back to full professionalism.

"I like the title, The Whale and the Icon," said Carlos. "Working title for the series of articles…"

"Well, get your shit correct before you publish anything," admonished Jimmy. "I mean, there are miles to go still – nothing but theories, very little in the way of facts."

Just then Jimmy's BlackBerry buzzed. He looked down and his brows furrowed in concentration, then wonder.

"It looks like Richard York never made it to London."

"How do you know that? His flight shouldn't have landed yet," said Maddy looking at her watch.

"His flight was diverted to Denver. Seems like

there was a medical emergency."

"What kind of medical emergency?" asked Maddy, alarmed.

"He died. Massive heart attack."

A beat. "Or so it would appear," said Maddy her eyes growing wide.

"Looks like whoever is sending the messages is now cleaning up after himself," said Carlos.

They all looked at each other, Jimmy threw down enough cash to cover the bill and a tip, and they bolted from the House of Nanking.

XVI

"London."

A pause.

"St. Petersburg."

Carey Portman had a way of making you feel like a complete idiot. She had this way of just looking over the top of her glasses at you, then looking back down at whatever piece of paper was on her desk, allowing you just long enough to get tired of shifting your feet in discomfort. Both Maddy and Carlos shifted their feet.

"Last I looked we were still neck deep in a recession with less than zero in the way of discretionary funds. This had better be good." Carey was the task-master for both Maddy and Carlos and was, appearances usually to the contrary, their biggest supporter. But she also had this Dame Judy Dench thing that was all about no-nonsense, don't fuck this up. Asking her permission to take what each young reporter felt was the next logical step in their investigation took a lot of courage. There was a story that Carey actually ate an intern once, after ripping his spine out. No one really believed it, but still. Maddy and Carlos had barely lived to tell the tale when *they* were interns.

That which doesn't kill us, makes us stronger, Maddy had reflected to herself at the time.

So they went through it by the numbers. Even Carey, a senior correspondent for the San Francisco Clarion who had seen her share of weird in the day – especially from Maddy and Carlos - had to pause periodically. It was a lot to absorb. When the young reporters finally finished their tale, she allowed them to sit down, and she rubbed the bridge of her nose.

"So London."

"It's a huge part of the story. Now that Donovan Hirsch's assistant has been murdered..."

"He died of a heart attack. Did anyone say he had been murdered?"

"No, well, not really, it's just... don't you think it's more than a little suspicious?"

"Well, duh, yes I do. That doesn't mean I'm going to go around saying that it's so. Facts, people. Facts. We're not the Sun or the National Enquirer. Or Strange Tales, either."

"But we might find out who contacted Richard York..."

"You're assuming that he was involved in any way with the disappearance of the killer whale. So far I haven't heard any proof."

"Yes, well..." Maddy felt at a loss for a second. There was always this part in any investigation where there was a lot of circumstantial evidence, when one had to rely on instinct to sift through it all and find a direction towards the hard facts. "I'm following my instincts on this one, Carey. You're right. Nothing concrete yet, just a lot of disparate threads that need to be pulled together."

"Now you're making sense. Instinct is good. Alright, you get a hall pass." Carey could do this, too. Just suddenly make that hard turn in a direction you weren't expecting. She pulled out a form and handed it to Maddy. "Just fill this in and take it to Madge. She'll set you up. But you get only three days on site, then you have to come home – unless I authorize you to stay on. By the way, you might find this interesting..." Carey pulled a copy of ArtForum magazine out of her bag and handed it to Maddy. On the cover was a man with a bald head, black clothes, black-rimmed glasses and a whole lot of attitude. Elvis Costello with no hair.

Donovan Hirsch.

"Yes, ma'am!" said Maddy. She started to flip through the magazine in search of the cover article. She had a lot to learn about the art world in a short amount of time. Something caught her eye.

"Holy Crap! I mean, Cow!" Maddy caught herself. Inside the magazine was an ad for Christie's London. An impressive private collection of late 19th Century Russian painters was coming up for auction. The next evening. Repin, Vrubel, Serebryakova. "If I were really following my instincts, I would say that our working profile of our criminal mastermind would have him – it's got to be a him…" she frowned, not sure why it had to be a him, "… he would be at this auction."

"Then we need to figure out how to get you in. I'll make some calls. Robert should be able to get you a seat." Robert Portman, Carey's husband, was a prominent lawyer in the City, and a collector of some note in his own right. Maddy had once been invited to a cocktail party at the Portmans' home in Pacific Heights and was impressed by their collection of abstract impressionists. Robert Portman was particularly interested in Diebenkorn and Rothko.

"Now you." Carey looked at Carlos and slowly took off her glasses, setting them precisely in front of her on her desk as she composed her thoughts. "Are you out of your fucking *mind*?" Both Maddy and Carlos winced. "I mean it's one thing to be hanging off the side of a building twenty-three floors up to get a story… nice work, by the way… but a whole different kettle of fish to be hunting down Russian Mafia types in St. Petersburg. Not. Going. To Happen. You would need to be twenty years older, about a hundred pounds bigger and a whole lot less gay." Only Carey could get away with saying something that blunt and politically incorrect. "And, of course, speak fluent Russian."

Carlos gathered himself. "But everything points to the Russian connection – the Panthers, the art... And I wouldn't need to speak Russian. They all speak English, anyway – it would be a prerequisite for the job, working internationally... don't you think?" Chilly glare. "And the gay thing, well, that could play to my advantage. It removes the whole testosterone bullshit. I could be considered relatively harmless. I'm not scared." He was scared, actually, but it would be an amazing adventure.

"Request denied," said Carey. She started to put on her glasses.

"I've got some vacation time..." said Carlos. "And a mess of frequent flier miles from going back and forth to Columbia..."

Carey had to admire this. A veteran of two Gulf wars and Afghanistan, as well as being on the ground in Berlin when the wall came down, she had placed herself in more harm's way than anyone had a right to in pursuit of a good story. No guts, no glory. Carlos was showing guts.

"What you do with your own time is up to you..." she sighed. "All right." She pulled out another form. "But if you get killed, don't think I won't fly over there myself and kill you again. And it will hurt more when *I* do it." Carlos grabbed the form as if he had better act quickly before Carey changed her mind.

"Thank you, Carey."

"Now don't disappoint me. Either of you. Daily reports. And *Facts*." She placed her glasses back on her nose and returned her attention to some papers on her desk. After a pause she looked over the top of her glasses. "Well? What are you two doing sitting on your asses? Go, go, go!" She waved them off.

They ran.

XVII

Jimmy was late to his meeting with Thomas Bradshaw. It was just as well. Bradshaw was one of those people who ran at least half an hour behind. Jimmy had had a lot of phone calls to make and a few emails to send. Starting with a series of calls to the Denver police. It took more than a little negotiation to get them to agree to sharing information about the incident on the plane. What was it about policemen and their strong sense of territoriality? Sheesh, thought Jimmy. We should all just get along. He also asked if it was possible for one of Denver's Finest to go out to the Pilot Travel Center off of I-70 to obtain any security videos for the period twenty-four hours prior to Sunday night.

Was it only Monday afternoon? Not even twenty-four hours since this all started?

They don't make days any longer than this, he thought as he cooled his heels in the reception area of the executive office suite on the fourth floor of the museum. He had also sent an email to Interpol in France, requesting information on the Pink Panther cell in St. Petersburg, along with the thumbprint. At 2:30 in the afternoon in San Francisco, it had been 11:30 at night in Lyon, where Interpol was headquartered. Jimmy had been more than a little surprised to get a phone call almost immediately after hitting "send."

"You're working late," he laughed into the phone.

"My friend, we have to keep the same hours as the enemy," sighed Francois LeNotre on the other end of the line. "Those bastards don't ever sleep, and between you and me, I'm super-fucking tired." Jimmy and Francois were friends of a sort. They had met during a conference in New York on international terrorism and landmark targets – of which San Francisco and Paris were chock-full, for better or worse - and had bonded over single malt scotch, of which both were very fond, and with the requisite tests of the other's knowledge and taste. They had stayed in touch over the years, with Francois threatening to come out to see San Francisco every year, and annually failing to do so.

"Sorry about those five paintings…"

"Shit. We all look like assholes. Worse. Thing. Ever. Everyone is running around like the proverbial chickens with their balls cut off…"

"That's heads cut off…"

"Balls, heads, whatever. Amounts to about the same thing." A throaty chuckle. "You staying out of trouble?"

Jimmy could only laugh. "I'm in as much trouble as the next guy."

"So what's with you and the Panthers? I don't know of any action lately in San Francisco…"

"That's just it. We've had a few bizarre incidents, and the theft of a Donovan Hirsch - which has not yet been reported - all within a twenty-four hour period. The MO is brazen enough to potentially be Panther work. And there seems to be some FSB angle as well."

"Assholes! Those guys…" Jimmy could hear Francois exhaling his cigarette smoke through the phone. "I don't know who's more ruthless, the Panthers or the spooks. To tell you the truth, they all amount to the same thing. Not much difference between them, and for all we know, the Panthers work for the FSB. Could well be a front, in fact."

"No shit."

"Shit." There is something about the way the French say it that makes it sound particularly icky. "To say that the Russian government turns a blind eye towards their activities would be an understatement. It's not a bad way to launder foreign currency, and if you want to keep your mistress in furs, then these would be the cats to keep you current."

"So who's your man in St. Pete's?"

"Sergei Potemkin. He's good. At least he's still alive."

"How deep can he get?"

"He knows people who know people. Are you sending anyone over?"

Jimmy hesitated. No one from the SFPD or the FBI or Homeland Security was coming over, that was for sure. Just Carlos. Jesus.

"Look, I need a favor, okay?"

*   *   *

There were two very large men sitting in the reception area across from Jimmy. Very. Large. Men. They had excellent suits, however. Jimmy nodded to himself appreciatively. He had good taste, dressed well, and knew a Wilkes Bashford when he saw one. These guys were definitely Ermenegildo Zegna, but with bulges under their arms. They had Bluetooth headsets on, and were not reading any art magazines on the coffee table.

Inside, in the boardroom, Jimmy could hear the quiet purr of discreet conversation. Then shouting. It didn't sound pretty or nice. In the next instant, the door flew open and a tall, crisp-looking man exited the room. He had a military bearing, but wore the nicest suit Jimmy had ever seen on anyone but the President. This was beyond anything San Francisco had to offer. This was Jermyn Street bespoke. The two large men snapped to attention as the new man stormed through the reception area, giving Jimmy barely a glance. They followed, with a tight, quick sweep of the room with their eyes. Jimmy kept his hands where everyone could see them.

Those were the best dressed professionals I have ever seen, thought Jimmy. He exhaled and shook the kinks out. Thomas Bradshaw stood at the door of the conference room, with a sour look on his face. His assistant slid over to him, handed him Jimmy's card, and Thomas Bradshaw took a moment. Then professionalism took over.

"Welcome, Detective. I'm sorry to keep you waiting. Any news for me?"

"It depends on what you're willing to hear. Nothing much in the way of developments yet." Jimmy lied. But not by that much – he had little proof of anything at this point, just a whole lot of wild speculation.

Thomas Bradshaw ushered Jimmy into his office and shut the door. It was as spare a room as one could imagine. No desk, just three Wassilly chairs, two facing one. No carpet on the polished black stone floor, no art on the white walls. A nice view out the window of Yerba Buena park in the late afternoon sun, but nothing else. Minimalism taken to within one degree of the logical extreme. We could be sitting on the floor, mused Jimmy as he looked around. Maybe he hasn't moved in yet.

"Please have a seat." Thomas Bradshaw indicated one of the two chairs side-by-side. In the chair opposite rested an iPad. Thomas Bradshaw picked it up and set it on the floor next to him and settled in, the tight leather straps of the chair creaking slightly as he did so. "Don't really need a desk these days, not with this thing." He waved his hand, indicating the empty room. "One sometimes needs, though, a place for quiet contemplation."

"I would have thought you might have a favorite piece on the wall, or a photo or two," offered Jimmy by way of a reply.

"Between you and me, the contemporary art world is so fucking loud, if you'll pardon the expression, that I find I need a refuge from all of the over-stimulated, super-hyped, event-oriented work that pervades our industry. I need visual silence after all the noise."

"But you're putting on a show of that very kind of work, curated by yourself."

"If you don't have ironic detachment in this business, you won't get very far," replied Thomas Bradshaw with a sigh. "Truth of the matter is, we've moved so far into a sort of new Mannerism, that no one I know really believes in their own work. It's all so cross-referential in so many layers that no one can tell what's art anymore. They know they're about commerce and manipulating the marketplace, but any sort of artistic mission? Hardly. Thank you Andy Warhol."

This was a little over Jimmy's head. "So you're saying the Donovan Hirsch piece, the killer whale in the tank, is just a piece of clever marketing? That it's really just about creating a sensation, without any substance?"

Thomas Bradshaw shrugged and said, "Exactly. But then, once you've created the sensation, the piece evolves into a new perception. It becomes an icon. It becomes a lightning rod. And somewhere along the line, it becomes art."

"Without anyone originally intending it to be so."

"Precisely. Which is why it can be so exhausting doing what I do. There's only so much bullshit that one can process in any given day. And now this."

Bradshaw passed his hand over his close-cropped, balding head.

"So what is your plan?"

"Take a page out of the contemporary art playbook. Leave the tank in the gallery empty, with the Police Line Do Not Cross tape around it. Pure sensation. Almost better than having the damn whale in the tank."

Jimmy had to admire it.

"So, press releases? We've been holding back letting the press have anything until we know more." Again, Jimmy was fibbing, Maddy was going to press the "submit" button before she left for the airport.

"We're releasing one in just a few minutes. What else can we do? The show opens in three days. If this tanks – pardon the unintended pun – you certainly can't be unaware of the precariousness of almost any arts organization in this economic climate. We would be in a hole that would be almost impossible to climb out of."

"So it would almost be to your advantage that you've had this sensational incident?"

"I didn't say that," replied Thomas Bradshaw quickly. "Look, we still have a mission here at SFMOCA, and we still have something of a heart."

"Glad to hear it," said Jimmy, dryly. "Listen, there are a few things about which we need some clarification.'

"Of course. Completely at your disposal." Thomas Bradshaw tried to look relaxed.

"The Hirsch. Whose property is it?"

"It's funny that you ask that."

"Why?"

"Well, because the provenance has been clouded somewhat. It was the property of a private collector – you've heard of Charles Saatchi..." Jimmy nodded. Saatchi was arguably the most famous and influential patron of cutting edge contemporary art in the world. "Well, he put it up for sale, and we agreed to purchase it, using an anonymous gift provided to the museum specifically for this acquisition. The donor, however, is now refusing to provide the gift, placing our capability to purchase the piece in doubt."

"I'm not sure I would blame him," said Jimmy. "I mean, assuming it's a him." Thomas Bradshaw had already given himself away when he didn't react to the use of the masculine pronoun. "After all, he has yet to see his piece in place. I suspect his confidence in the institution is somewhat shaken."

Thomas Bradshaw glanced up at Jimmy sharply. "You are remarkably quick on the uptake, Detective Wang. His confidence is quite shaken."

"That was him just now, wasn't it?"

"I'm not at liberty to say. It was an anonymous gift."

"I think we can dispense with the pretense of donor confidentiality," said Jimmy. "First, by your own admission, the gift is now in question, so there's little to protect. Second, a murder has been committed, which, by almost all rules of engagement, should remove any qualms you might have regarding confidentiality, or that I might have about demanding the information. Your donor might hold a significant piece of the puzzle."

Thomas Bradshaw sighed. "You're right." After a hesitation, "That was him."

"Quite the entourage he had with him. Those two cats had a 'shoot first, ask questions later' kind of vibe to them."

"I call them Frick and Frack. I'm not sure where he got them, but they're Russian, and they have no sense of humor at *all*." Thomas Bradshaw waved his hands theatrically.

From the training he had, Jimmy was quite confident that they were former military. Those guys had Special Ops written all over them.

"So their boss. Who is he?"

"Ivan Orkin."

Jimmy searched his mental database. There was something lurking in the back of his brain, but he couldn't access it. A few hours of sleep would make all the difference. He shook his head.

"Can't place the name, although it sounds familiar."

"Do you follow sports?"

"I do. College football, mostly. Cal man."

Thomas Bradshaw was impressed. He knew UC Berkeley to be one of the great universities in the world. Half of his donors came from there. The other half were Stanford grads. "The San Jose Orcas. He just bought them."

The penny dropped. That's where Jimmy had heard the name before. But there had been very little biographical detail in the news about the new owner of the team.

"What do you know about him?" asked Jimmy. "I mean, he sort of appeared out of nowhere."

"Most of the truly wealthy people in the world are unknown to most of us. How many billionaires could you name?"

Jimmy could think of about five. Maybe ten.

"There are a couple thousand. More than a few living within fifty miles of us – I should know. I'm on my knees to them on a daily basis. And most of them got that way by doing the kind of unglamorous work that doesn't garner headlines. Think about it – if you could have one percent of the sales of all of the staples or thumbtacks in the world…"

"I would be an extremely wealthy man," finished Jimmy. "So what's our guy do?"

"He's quite well diversified. Microchips, heavy industrials, scrap metal. He's just started to flex his muscles in the art world. He could do some damage with the money he's got."

"He looked, I don't know, military himself."

"Russian Army colonel. Bit of a bruiser."

It was all coming together for Jimmy, now. Billionaire. Bored. Ruthless. This was turning out to be much easier than he thought it would be.

"Where could I find him?"

"He's moving into new offices downtown."

"Really?" Jimmy was poised to jot down the address in his notebook.

"Yes. His firm has just leased the top two floors of 580 California."

Jimmy's pen remained poised above his notebook.

Scratch that about being easy, he thought as he slowly put his notebook away.

Crap.

XVIII

They said their goodbyes at the point of divergence at Heathrow where you either go through Customs, or you stay in the secure area of the international terminal. Maddy was to head down to Baggage Reclaim, Carlos heading over to the International Departures Lounge to await the announcement of his gate assignment to continue on to St. Petersburg. The flight from San Francisco had been relatively uneventful – Maddy fell asleep almost as soon as she sat down, while Carlos caught up on all of the movies he had missed in the last six months. Maddy was so tired that she slept through the dinner service, but Carlos watched out for her and saved her dinner. Six hours into the ten hour flight, Maddy finally awoke and wolfed down her food.

"Good thing I've got my seatbelt fastened," said Carlos as Maddy finished off her chocolate cake. "Otherwise I would have gotten sucked in. Hey - did you know you snore?"

"I do not!" From almost the first day they worked together there was something of an immature sibling relationship between the two young reporters. Maddy stuck out her tongue at Carlos who poked her back. "Hey, shut *up*," she continued with a giggle. "Try to behave like you belong in Business Class, you big dork."

They were saved by the flight attendant who came to gather up Maddy's tray. After they settled down, Maddy flipped open her laptop. She had downloaded over fifty articles and Wikipedia entries regarding Donovan Hirsch, Russian art and Christie's auction house while they had waited in the departure lounge at SFO. Now she needed to do some cramming before she hit the ground in London. Carlos returned to his movie. There looked to be some spectacular car chase through the streets of some eastern European city. Must be one of the Bourne movies, or the most recent James Bond – neither of which Maddy had seen. The action was pretty intense, and made Maddy's head hurt.

"Don't you have to do some research?" Maddy asked. Carlos didn't hear her because of the headphones. She poked him, and then mouthed "Research" and pointed at her laptop.

"Nah," he said, pulling his headphones off one ear. "This one's going to be done by feel. I'm just going to have to be sharp when I get there." Maddy raised one eyebrow – a trick she picked up from Jimmy. "Seriously. When you're going in as clueless as I am, you might as well roll with it."

There was something to what he was saying. Jimmy had arranged for Carlos to meet an Interpol agent in St. Petersburg who would get Carlos oriented and potentially connected. There was only so much research one could do regarding shadowy underworld organizations that trafficked in stolen art. And Carlos was one of those people who would rather be lucky than good.

Maddy left Carlos alone, and stared out the window before diving in on her research material. She smiled inwardly at how different she and Carlos were. She was one of those people who couldn't bear to be unprepared for a test, and spent a lot of her time at Stanford hunkered down in the library. It was only through her passion for musical theatre that she made any social connections at all, acting in musicals put on by the various campus theatre groups. Otherwise, she was, by and large, a big geek. She envied the easy intellectual prowess that Carlos displayed. She was smart enough, but she got where she was by putting in the extra effort. She couldn't figure out, though, where she got that gene, because her mother was hopelessly lazy and self-involved, and her father, who did work hard, wasn't ever around enough to be much of a role model or influence. She ascribed her dedication to having a few good teachers when she was little who rewarded her enthusiasm and encouraged her to push beyond her talent. A good swim coach in high school further developed her work ethic. Now, she just knew that if she was ever going to keep up with the Carey Portmans of the world, she was still going to have the burn the midnight oil.

The sun was just beginning to cut a sliver of burnt orange on the horizon as they were passing over Iceland. It was still dark enough outside that she could see her reflection layered on top of the cobalt blue sky and the ice flows below. She thought she looked tired, and much older than her twenty-four years. I'm going to need a disco nap when I get to the hotel, she thought. And a hot shower. She sighed and turned her attention back to the glowing screen of her laptop.

*   *   *

"Please, Carlos, don't get shot!" Maddy wailed melodramatically, and then realized that all of the airline personnel around them were giving them odd looks. She gave Carlos an enormous hug. At 5'-2", Maddy was petite, but Carlos had that slender frame that made him feel like her kid sister in her arms.

"I couldn't possibly be worth the trouble," he grinned. "I'll be fine. You're the one swimming with sharks – all those art world types. I bet there's more danger in the Grand Room at Christie's than in any nightclub in St. Petersburg."

"At least they don't carry guns," said Maddy with a grimace.

"Be careful, all the same." Carlos gave her a squeeze on the shoulder. "See you in a few. Write when you can."

"Will do. 'Bye!" Maddy gave him one last wave, then headed down to Passport Control and waited in as long a line as she could remember. Longer than any line at Disneyland.

"Business or pleasure," said the man in the turban when she got to the counter. He had a full beard and long mustache pulled tight along the side of his face. He swiped her passport and tapped some keys on his keyboard. He had a cockney accent, which Maddy found disconcerting.

"Business, sir."

The man looked at her for a second over his glasses, which softened his otherwise intimidating appearance. As much as Maddy thought she looked older than her years, the rest of the world saw a spunky little blonde girl, who could easily pass for a teenager. After a beat, he handed Maddy her passport. "Stay out of trouble," he said with a mischievous grin.

Maddy smiled - fighting the impulse to curtsy - and headed off towards Baggage Reclaim and then Customs. Nothing to Declare, and she was through the doors to the Meeting Point. There, holding a placard with her name on it, was a young, very tall, very black man.

"Hi, I'm Maddy Stevenson," said Maddy. "Are you waiting for me?"

"Miss Stevenson, I am here to take you to your hotel," replied the man with a thick but melodious accent. "My name is James." His teeth were spectacularly white. It wasn't until he juggled the placard and tucked it under his arm to grab the handle of her roller bag that Maddy realized he was missing a hand. Maddy tried to help him, but James wouldn't think of it, and he moved as if there was nothing at all the matter. Maddy shook her head in wonder. She was from one of the most cosmopolitan cities in the world, but she was already encountering more cultures and characters per minute than ever before in her life. James took her bag and led her to the limousine.

This part I could get used to, thought Maddy as she nestled into the voluminous back seat of the car. Traveling in style.

As the limo wended its way through the Heathrow traffic and onto the M4 towards London, James chatted away with enthusiasm. Despite her fatigue, and the leaden sky, Maddy was charmed, and found some perk.

"Where are you from, Miss Stevenson?"

"I just flew in from San Francisco."

"Most beautiful city in the world," replied James with full conviction.

"You've been?" asked Maddy, a little incredulously.

"No, of course not. But I've seen photographs. Golden Gate Bridge. Tales of the City on TV. Wonderful! And everyone I've ever met from there is beautiful. I can tell you're from there."

Maddy blushed at the compliment. She was about to tell him she was really from Orange County, but then changed her mind. She was enjoying now being from the more sophisticated urban environment. It certainly sounded more worldly than Newport Beach.

"You are here for work?"

"Yes. I'm a reporter... a journalist. I'm working

on a story for my paper back home."

"Must be a good story to fly to London."

"I think so. I hope so." She prayed so. "Where are you from, James?"

"Me? From Sierra Leone. Small village near the coast."

Maddy suddenly had an inner moment of horror. She remembered reading about the young boys whose hands had been chopped off by rebel fighters during Sierra Leone's devastating civil war as a form of retribution and institutionalized terrorism. Her heart broke for the young man, and for the things he must have lived through. She tried to recover.

"Do you like living in London?"

"It is cold and rains too much, but it is okay. Safer than where I come from." Maddy shuddered. "I live with my big sister and her family. Do you have family?"

"A little sister."

"Is she also beautiful?"

"Well, I... I mean, she's the beautiful one in the family... I'm not... I mean..." Maddy was flustered a bit. Her little sister, Austin, wasn't so little any more - now a senior in high school. And a complete handful for her parents. She was a tonic for Maddy, who was reminded every time she saw her sister how self-involved and disconnected teenage girls could be. Austin was smart, and could be anything she wanted to be, but she was too concerned about the latest fashions, her hair and her bitchy friends to concentrate on much else. Maddy sighed at the thought of it.

There but for the grace of God...

James chatted on, especially interested in the upcoming World Cup to be played in South Africa. Maddy began to tune out a bit, mesmerized by the city evolving outside her rain-spattered window.

London had one of the most distinctive skylines in the world – an incoherent jumble of medieval and modern architecture living side by side in a certain compelling dissonance. As they worked their way from the South Bank into the heart of the city, she wondered at the civic energy that could embrace the juxtaposition of a building as graceful, understated and elegantly proportioned as Christopher Wren's St. Paul's Cathedral with the chutzpah of Sir Norman Foster's "Gherkin." She was excited to be there.

James pulled the limo up to the front of the Dorchester Hotel. For all of Carey's fuss about budgetary constraints, Maddy appreciated that Carey also knew how to treat her people right. A five star hotel at the edge of Mayfair. As it was, Maddy was working somewhat undercover – it was not to her advantage to be known to be a journalist at the auction that evening. She was meant to be one of the jet set art cognoscenti, so a five-star hotel was part of the role.

She tried to tip James, but he wouldn't hear of it – it was all taken care of he said. But he offered her his card, and told her that if she needed a ride anywhere to give him a call. He flashed his beautiful smile, climbed back into the car and pulled away.

By the time Maddy got to her room, all she could think about was taking that nap. It was now three in the afternoon. The auction was at eight, with the preview session starting at seven. As she crawled onto the bed, feeling more and more like a sack of potatoes as she did so, she figured on two hours of sleep, a shower, a room-service snack with tons of coffee, allowing just enough time to climb into her "costume." She managed a quick text to Jimmy, letting him know she had arrived safely, set the alarm on her phone, and then promptly passed out.

XIX

Jimmy had just finished shaving when his BlackBerry buzzed on the counter next to him. He wiped of the shaving cream and smiled as he saw "Safe in London... going to bed... luv u!" He felt like a million bucks. After his interview with Thomas Bradshaw he had gone back to the office, filed an insane number of reports, made some travel arrangements, and then walked up and over Telegraph Hill down to the Fog City Diner for a late dinner. He sat at the bar and watched the Orca game on the bar TV while he worked his way through some small plates and a couple glasses of Rioja. Gareth, his favorite bartender, had some serious money on the game and figured the Orcas to lose by at least 12. Gareth was uncanny with his bets, and Jimmy had to smile as the Orcas' final shot clanked off the rim, causing them to lose by 13.

"How much money did you win on this one?" he asked Gareth.

"Cleared five hundred," said Gareth, with the poker face he always maintained. Jimmy whistled. "Those guys suck, you know? I've never seen them beat the spread. Not once."

"New owner, though. Could be some changes in the off-season." Jimmy tried to sound knowledgeable.

"I don't care, really," said Gareth. "Doesn't matter to me if they win or lose, just as long as they do what I think they're going to do. Right now that's lose, and it's money in the bank to me." He started wiping down the liquor bottles. Jimmy realized that it was closing time, and he was the last person in the place. He settled up – Gareth insisted the drinks were on the house - and said goodnight.

He then worked his way up the Filbert Steps to his apartment, which was perched on the edge of the hill, unlocked the door and took a deep breath. He undid his tie and poured himself a neat Caol Isla. As he sipped the single malt, he debated whether or not this was his favorite. He felt like sending an email to Francois to make him jealous, but thought better of it. Instead he opened the sliding glass door that let onto his balcony, and went out into the cool San Francisco night. It was a rare clear evening, and the lights ringing the Bay shimmered on the water. He wished he could talk to Maddy, but she was still on the plane. He sighed, finished off his whisky, blew a kiss to the East, and went to bed. After a forty-hour work day, he fell asleep before his head hit the pillow.

Nothing like a straight eight, a shower and a shave, he thought to himself as he adjusted his tie the next morning.

And a sweet text from his girlfriend. He tapped a quick response, letting her know that he was missing her, and just starting his day. It was going to be another full one - a quick round-trip to Denver the main part of his agenda. He felt he needed more facts under his belt before he paid a visit to Mr. Orkin, and there were more than a few to be gathered in the Mile High City.

Five hours later he was in the morgue with Detective David Rogers of the DPD, and Ernest Holloway from the British Consulate.

"That can't be him," said Jimmy, as the sheet was pulled away, revealing a bald man lying on the stainless steel shelf of the refrigerated locker. "He had hair the last time I saw him."

"It fell out," said the forensic pathologist.

"What would cause that to happen?" asked Jimmy, already suspicious of the answer.

"Mammoth radiation poisoning," replied the pathologist.

"Don't tell me. Polonium-210."

Everyone in the room looked very impressed. "How did you guess that?" asked Detective Rogers.

"Not a guess. We've got a decapitated head that turned up in San Francisco just riddled with the stuff. We suspect Mr. York was involved in the heist of a valuable piece of contemporary art, and the perpetrator - or perpetrators - look to be trying to remove some of the links in their chain. It sucks being a link, sometimes." The men all looked at the body. There was a collective sigh.

"How was it administered?" Jimmy asked finally.

"There's a small puncture wound in his right shoulder," replied the pathologist. "Looks to have been injected as he slept."

"Window seat?"

"Yeah – oh, right. That would make sense."

"So who was sitting next to him on the flight?"

"We're still trying to work that out."

"How so?"

"There was no one sitting next to him when he was discovered. The passenger in that seat must have repositioned himself in coach, probably after a trip to the restroom. By the time we figured out that we weren't looking at natural causes, all the passengers had disembarked and been re-routed. Passenger 2B had effectively vanished."

"What was the name of the passenger that was booked in that seat?"

"John Smith."

"No shit."

"Yeah," sighed Detective Rogers. "As false a passport as you could hope to find."

"But we at least have a photo of the guy from when he checked in and had the passport scanned?"

"We do. Handsome devil." Rogers passed over a printout.

"Looks like he should be a movie star, or lead vocalist of some band," said Jimmy. "He looks familiar…" he shook his head. Couldn't place it. "So our next move?"

"We've got this image posted at the airport, should he attempt to fly out under a different name." Detective Rogers made a face. "Although that horse has pretty well left the barn, if you ask me. I'm sure he took off already, before we could react. He could be anywhere, and look just different enough."

"He was on a flight to London. Perhaps he intended to get there eventually." Jimmy rubbed his chin. "Have you checked the private airfields?"

"Why would we do that?" asked Detective Rogers.

"A hunch. We're building a profile, and we're thinking that whoever is behind all of this - assuming there's an 'all' that makes sense - has significant resources. I mean, how hard would it be to get off at DIA, take a cab - or better yet a limo – to your private jet waiting for you at a private airfield and continue on to your desired destination?"

"How would he know that the plane would divert to Denver?"

"He wouldn't. But within the continental US there would be only a few hours delay while his jet caught up with him, wherever he was. All it takes is a text upon landing in Denver, and by the time he got to a private field in, say, Golden, the plane would be waiting."

"Okay, we'll move on that. Any other thoughts about what we're looking for?"

"Well, what sort of private plane can do

intercontinental travel? Assuming, of course, that he wants to continue on to a destination like London."

"A Gulfstream V," replied Ernest Holloway, who had so far been following all of this quietly.

"A Gulfstream V," repeated Jimmy. "How many of those are out there? Only supercats like Larry Ellison get Gulfstream Vs." He smiled inwardly. It was coming together.

"So we hit the two or three private fields within a two hour radius of Denver, and check flight plans for a Gulfstream V." Detective Rogers shrugged. "That will take some time, but it should triangulate pretty well."

"Great," said Jimmy. "Now for the security videos from the Pilot truck stop. Anyone hungry, though?" The pathologist placed the sheet back over Richard York's face, and slid the shelf back into the locker. No one else was hungry.

Huh.

*   *   *

Jimmy picked up a sandwich at a deli down the street and climbed into a cubicle at the Denver Police Central Headquarters on Cherokee. They told him it was the "Guest Suite," but Jimmy suspected he was just sitting at someone's old desk who had been a victim of the budget cuts that plagued every police department across the country. He slid one of a stack of DVDs into the computer and started scanning. The Pilot Travel Center had a pretty solid security video system, with several dozen cameras covering the property. Jimmy sighed thinking about it. That much more stuff to review. The officer who had requisitioned the video had been canny enough to draw up a map of the camera placements, so Jimmy could tell which camera was looking at what. He wished, however, that someone on his end had been canny enough to get the truck driver to tell them where he parked. It hadn't seemed important at the time. Shoot. Now he had over 160 hours of video to comb through – thank God, at least, for high speed scanning. He decided to start with the central lot, putting in the DVD that clocked from midnight to eight in the morning on Sunday. He wasn't all that sure what he was looking for. To save memory, the system recorded at half second intervals, so the images were inherently herky-jerky. At fast forward, it was a little like watching Koyaaniskatsi – trucks streaming in and out at a tremendous rate, and slotting themselves into and out of the parking lot like manic pieces of a game of Tetris. Jimmy couldn't help feel impressed at the volume of traffic. He suddenly became conscious of how much stuff traveled by truck, and what the carbon footprint of everything he consumed must be. He took a vow to try to buy more locally produced food – if nothing else.

He knew he couldn't concentrate on every frame. He sat back and ate his sandwich while the images washed over him – his eyes focusing on the middle distance. He hoped that something would suddenly not feel right – a burp in the flow.

The first few videos rolled through without any incident that Jimmy could discern. He had shifted to a back lot – it was set up for the truckers who were sleeping over and had a little more isolation from the fuel center and restaurant. It was now about three in the afternoon and Jimmy was growing sleepy. He longed for a Caffe Greco espresso, but that was a thousand miles away. His eyelids were fluttering, and he fantasized about climbing under the desk and taking a nap. Just as he was feeling his head drop onto his chest, he snapped up. Rewind that. He streamed backwards for a minute, then forward again at normal speed.

The date/time stamp showed it to be 3:31 AM. A truck pulled up in the background, but it didn't pull into one of the designated spaces. It idled there for a few minutes, then two men in what looked like black fatigues jumped out of the cab and approached one of the parked trucks. What had caught Jimmy's eye as he was starting to drift off was a flash of light on the screen. He watched in fascination, suddenly quite alert, as one of the men pulled out what must have been a digital camera and took several shots. The man then climbed up to the cab of the parked truck, fussed at the lock for a few seconds and then climbed in. The other man had disappeared into the gap between the cab and the trailer. After a few minutes, the cab pulled forward, leaving the trailer disengaged and standing on its stanchions. The cab then circled around pulling up behind the idling truck. The driver climbed out and the routine was repeated with the idling truck's trailer. After about fifteen minutes the switch was complete – including the careful maneuvering of the new trailer into the exact position of the old – with the man guiding the truck referencing the glowing screen on his camera from time to time.

It was a very smooth switch. Jimmy had to admire the simplicity and the daring of it. The poor truck driver who showed up at SFMOCA would have had to have been operating at peak mental clarity to spot anything amiss. After the hijacked trailer was pulled away, with the driver flicking the butt of a cigarette casually out the window of the cab, Jimmy fast-forwarded to dawn. Again, a very Koyaanisqatsi-esque time-lapse effect of the sun rising, with the trucks and their trailers beginning to glow, then their shadows shortening on the ground as the sun climbed higher in the sky. Sure enough, a man shuffled towards the truck with what looked like a venti Starbucks in his hand. Jimmy felt his pain. He knew that the poor bastard wasn't going to be functioning fully until all of that coffee had entered his bloodstream. The truck fired up, a little belch of exhaust out of its stacks, and it pulled away with the driver none the wiser.

Jimmy shook his head. That Carlos. Nailed that one.

He was about to text Maddy and Carlos with the news when he had a revelation. The butt of the cigarette. He picked up the phone on the desk and dialed Dave Rogers' extension.

"How do you feel about going on a road trip?"

XX

Carlos woke from his nap completely disoriented. He had no idea what time of day it was anymore. The glancing light through the window of the Airbus could be sunrise or sunset for all he could tell in the moment. After a few minutes, the fog in his head began to clear and he realized that it must be sunset – the light was gleaming gold from behind him, and he should be moving eastward. His body ached from sitting so long. This was the rare moment when he wished he had more meat on his butt. He struggled out of his seat and went for a walk to the back of the plane. He hoped to score a cup of coffee from the flight attendants so that he could function at all when he landed. After chatting up a tall, blonde stewardess who looked like a supermodel – actually, they were all tall and blonde and looked like supermodels – he remained standing at the bulkhead while he sipped his coffee. He looked out the little window at the ground below him. It was early April, but everything was still blanketed in white. He glanced over at the flight map that was running on the overhead screen and realized how close to the Arctic Circle he was.

Brrr, he thought. He had been cold before – four years at Columbia, during one of which he experienced the Storm of the Century, when the entire East Coast was shut down for a week with snow – but this was going to be a whole new kind of cold. He was grateful that he hadn't put his heavy winter gear into deep storage – he had had only fifteen minutes at home to throw his stuff together in a mad dash to the airport. Robert had been impressed that his boyfriend could suddenly jump on a plane to St. Petersburg on assignment – it was extremely glamorous, and added a sense of mystery and excitement to their relationship. At least Robert had still been home when Carlos ran in and out. He had been getting ready for his evening shift at the restaurant, and had just climbed out of the shower. Carlos' heart jumped when he saw his beautiful lover still wet, with only a towel around his waist.

"How long will you be gone?" asked Robert, with just a little trepidation.

"No more than a week. I'll text you every hour on the hour…"

"Don't be so silly. Just text me when you can." There was a hesitation – theirs was still a young relationship, and this was going to be the longest they had been apart from each other. "I love you, Sweetie. Come home safe."

After a bittersweet smile, Carlos gave Robert a giant smooch and a deep, wet embrace before running back to Maddy's waiting car with his London Fog and wool scarf thrown over his arm.

* * *

Back in his seat, Carlos dinked around on his iPad. Something was troubling him. Maddy and Jimmy had told him about the thumb-drives and their contents – pdf'ed pages of binary code – and Jimmy had learned over time that Carlos had an intuitive grasp of puzzles and complex visual problems. Jimmy felt he had little to lose in providing Carlos with a copy of the pdfs – perhaps Carlos could see something that no one else would. Carlos wasn't so sure about that. The stuff was pretty dense and there were no patterns that he could discern. He had already spent the better part of his battery looking at them, trying to squeeze out any kind of sense. But he now had some coffee in him and was feeling as alert as he had in twenty-four hours. He opened each page again one by one, and scanned them one more time. Nothing. He sighed. He hit the key that placed all twenty-four pages open, evenly displayed on his tiny desk-top, and looked out the window to catch the last rays of the sun. After the golden streak disappeared into a deep violet twilight, he turned his attention back to the little screen that rested in his lap.

Holy shit.

It wasn't configured properly, but the accidental layout of the pdfs was most of the way there – just two out of place. It was only when the twenty-four pages were viewed together, from a great distance – or on a small screen in this case – did they make any sense at all. But even with two pages misaligned, the image was clear. It wasn't code at all.

It was a portrait. In black and white. The sequences of zeros and ones providing the gray-scales and shadows that defined the face.

Carlos was about to pop. He was still 30,000 feet above the ground, and had no way to let Jimmy and Maddy know. All he could do was write the email, and hope that the airport in St. Petersburg had wi-fi when he landed.

*   *   *

It was nine o'clock at night when he disembarked from the plane. He had always been impressed with how cold and moist San Francisco was. San Francisco had nothing on St. Petersburg. In the brief instant when Carlos passed from the plane onto the jetway, the gap between the two let in a blast of ice cold mist that cut him to his very marrow.

He was grateful for his Timberlands. Good boots and wool socks were going to save his butt in this place.

Contrary to any preconceived notions about post-Soviet decay and Russian wariness of international terrorism, he moved briskly through Passport Control and Customs. He remained impressed at how beautiful all of the women were – talk about "bone structure," he thought. His Passport Control officer, whose name badge said Yelena, scanned his passport and then turned ice-blue eyes on him from under white-blonde bangs. She confirmed that Carlos was, indeed, only five-foot six. She gave a bit of a smirk, as if to imply that he might be too small and she would have to throw him back, but she stamped and returned his passport and waved him on through.

After passing through Customs, Carlos turned on his iPad, having been under strict instruction while in line not to use it in the secure area. He did a quick calculation and realized that Maddy would be heading to the auction, but he hoped she would get the message before too much longer – it was an amazing clue, and convinced Carlos that the perpetrator of the series of bizarre crimes was not above having some fun at the expense of the police. Very Zodiac, with a touch of John Dickson Carr. Sure enough, St. Petersburg was wide open enough of a town that there was no problem getting reception. He was, after all, standing next to a giant backlit ad for the iPad. What he found funny was that it was mostly in English. He couldn't get over the word iPad in giant Roman letters – he had expected everything to be in Cyrillic. He then looked around and saw that every ad and logo was in English – Nokia, Samsung, British Petroleum. He shook his head remembering Carey Portman's insistence that he speak fluent Russian. He would be just fine. He pressed "Send" and then stood for a moment in the middle of the reception area, not sure what to do next. A tall, skinny man with closely cropped dark hair and a five o'clock shadow approached him with a large, wolfish smile and his hand extended. Carlos hesitated.

"Carlos Rodriguez, I presume," said the man with something of a British accent.

"Yes... how did you know?"

"We don't get many Mexicans here. You stand out." Carlos blushed, but put out his hand. "My name is Sergei Potemkin," said the man as he took Carlos' hand. He pronounced it Potyomkeen. "Your friend, Detective James Wang, asked my friend, Francois LeNotre, to have me look after you. I'll see what I can do to keep you from getting killed."

XXI

"Ms. Stevenson, your ride is here."

Maddy's brain was swimming through molasses. "I... what? What time is it?"

"It's 6:45, ma'am," replied the hotel receptionist over the phone.

Maddy's eyes grew wide. What happened to her cell phone? What ride? How in God's name am I going to get ready in time?

"I'll be down in five minutes, thank you," she said, trying not to sound like she had just awakened from the deepest sleep she could remember having. It still took her a couple of minutes just looking around her room to put the pieces together. London. Christie's. Auction at eight with preview beginning at seven. Crap. I've got, like, three minutes to look like an international jet-setting art maven. Just enough time, really, to wash the drool off her chin, brush her hair and slip into her dress. She was grateful that she kept her hair short – just a few strokes of the brush and maybe some gel to give her some edge – and that she had a French room-mate at home who kept an assortment of sophisticated little black dresses. Angelique was six inches taller, but wore her dresses short. This left Maddy with enough hemline to not feel like a complete vamp. Some lipstick, heels and her mother's cast-off fur jacket, and she had to admit, as she took one last look in her mirror, that she looked... hot. In spite of herself.

Now what's up with my phone? It was dead in the water... what a doof! It was an older vintage – she had been about to replace it. It was also plugged into an adaptor that was old enough not to recognize the different current. 240 volts instead of 120. Her phone wasn't quite smoking, but it sure as heck wasn't going to work any more.

Dammit! Some experienced, super-sophisticated international investigative journalist she was turning out to be.

She flipped open her laptop to establish some sort of sense of communication with the outside world and was relieved when it downloaded the fifty-plus emails. No time to go through them all – she just wanted to hear from Jimmy. Just a sweet email saying he missed her. She smiled to herself that life wasn't so bad having such a boyfriend – in spite of their differences, or the stress they each caused the other. She just didn't have the time right now to reply. She would buy herself an international calling card and call him when she got back to the hotel later. Go Old School.

Nothing from Carlos – he would be landing right about now anyway...

She was just closing the door to her room when her laptop gave the little ping announcing the arrival of a new email.

I'll get it later, she said to herself as she ran to the elevator.

*   *   *

"James! What are you doing here?"

"You said you were going to Christie's this evening, miss. I am here to take you."

"Did I say that? I guess I did. To be honest, you saved my evening – if you hadn't shown up, I would have slept until tomorrow."

"I am lucky for you, yes?" He flashed his spectacular smile.

"Yes. Thank you."

James led her to the waiting town car, and held the back door open for her. She settled into the back seat and snuggled into her fur coat. It was cold. She thought about poor Carlos and shivered. James climbed into the driver's seat and Maddy couldn't help herself.

"Indulge me for a moment," she said. Putting on her best Auntie Mame she went on: "Christie's, James." She giggled as her driver looked perplexed. "I've always wanted to say that, that's all. Thanks for putting up with me!" She settled back into her seat and they pulled into the London traffic.

It really was just a few blocks – she could have walked. But it looked really good for her to be pulling up in a limousine, James opening the door for her.

"I'll be just down the street, miss, whenever you need me."

"Oh, James, don't wait up for me – I don't know how long this will go, or what will happen afterwards."

"No worries, miss. I'll be here just in case."

"Thank you." She gave him her sweetest smile.

He tugged his forelock in the way of liverymen of old. How charming was he? thought Maddy as she went up the steps and into the lobby of the venerable auction house. She signed in and left her coat at the coat check. She picked up the catalogue and began to work her way through the lots, pen in hand. She circled the paintings she thought would be of interest to her collector. The one that looked to be most interesting was a piece by Serebryakova, a famous female Russian Impressionist – it was certainly the most expensive at an initial bid price of two hundred and fifty thousand pounds. Maddy did some quick math – about four hundred and fifty thousand dollars. She whistled to herself. That was the starting price. It would be an exciting evening.

"Maddy? Maddy Stevenson, is that you?"

Maddy was startled. She had certainly not expected to meet anyone she knew at this event. She turned towards the voice and her eyes grew wide with wonder.

"Sasha! Oh. My. God! Is that you?"

"It's only been four years. Have I changed that much? I almost didn't recognize you, though... your hair is much shorter. I like it."

"You... you look great!" stuttered Maddy, taking in the young man. He did look great. He had been one of those sleepy cute boys in school – geeky and quiet. Now at, what, twenty-six or twenty-seven he had shed the geeky. He was gorgeous. Tall, dark and handsome, with a little bit of edge - Sasha Borodin now looked like a movie star. He had the perfectly calculated amount of stubble to indicate that he wasn't poorly groomed and just enough spike in his hair to provide some tension to his otherwise spectacularly impeccable suit. Who did he remind her of? Ethan Hawke? Colin Farrell? In any event, Maddy found herself a little weak in the knees as he took her hand and looked into her eyes.

He used to wear glasses, thought Maddy. She had never really noticed his eyes back when they were at Stanford together. They had both been members of Ram's Head, the amateur campus theatrical group. Maddy had played Sarah Brown in the Ram's Head production of *Guys and Dolls* her sophomore year. Sasha, a senior, had been one of the show's producers. He wasn't one to be on stage – he preferred to quietly pull the strings. Maddy had been intrigued by the dark and somewhat mysterious Sasha, but she had already started dating another boy, Justin, so she kept her distance. Once Sasha had left Stanford and gone into business with a fellow computer-science student to create a small internet start-up, Maddy could only periodically shake her head at the paths not taken. Sasha and his partner had developed an algorithm that out-algorithmed Google's, and had created a sensation in Silicon Valley – just a year out of school. Their Initial Public Offering last year had made the two partners billionaires overnight, and their search engine, Infinity, with its catch-phrase "To Infinity and Beyond," was poised to become fully stitched into the fabric of everyone's consciousness. The two internet entrepreneurs had even graced the cover of the most recent issue of Wired Magazine, looking for all the world like rock stars. Maddy wondered for a split second what life could have been like for her as a billionaire's wife, then shook herself back to the real world. Things happen for a reason, she reminded herself.

Still. The money and fame had wrought changes in Sasha. He projected now a confidence he didn't have in school, and that made him appear bigger, taller and stronger than he had before. And the glasses were gone. Where his eyes really that color? They were striking. A pale green.

"May I get you a drink?" he offered. "Champagne?"

"Oh, yes. Thanks, that would be lovely!" Actually, it was a Really Bad Idea, she thought as Sasha slipped over to the bar. She enjoyed a glass of wine now and then, but champagne had always done funny things to her. And the evening was just getting started.

But how much fun was this? she thought as Sasha returned. Hanging with the rich and beautiful at an art auction in London. People *dream* of doing this.

"To meeting friends in strange places.

Nazdarovya." He was smooth. Made eye contact when they clinked glasses.

"Cheers," replied Maddy suppressing a giggle.

"So what brings you to London? You buying?"

"Oh, no! I mean, no, not in the market today," replied Maddy, a little flustered. Got to work on playing the part. "Actually I'm doing research for a book," Maddy fibbed, but said it in a way that made it sound like it was meant to be a secret. "A book on the inner workings of the art world."

"It sounds fascinating." He leaned in conspiratorially. "Although be careful – it's a dark and dangerous place, the art world."

"How do you mean?"

He shrugged. "Just that with so much money, and so much passion – reputations at stake and careers on the line all the time – you can imagine that things can get... fraught."

Don't I know it, thought Maddy. At least three people dead that she knew of at last count.

"Well, I'm just getting started on my research. Thought I'd observe the transactional nature of the game first."

"You are in for a treat, then. You like theatre? This is the best theatre there is. You can see more personalities revealed at an auction than anywhere else. People can get swept up and carried away. It can be quite intoxicating."

"And you?" asked Maddy over her champagne glass – it was good champagne and she was enjoying it. "What brings you to London?"

"Just taking a break. It's nice to be out of the Bay Area for a few days. The air can get a little thick on the Peninsula sometimes." Sasha was referring to the stretch of land that ran from San Francisco to San Jose, and which was the navel of the internet

DUANEreade
YOUR CITY. YOUR DRUGSTORE.

#14524 1627 BROADWAY
NEW YORK, NY 10019
212-586-0374

212   0319   0002   06/20/2013 1:43 PM

```
NIVEA MEN SENS SHAVE GEL    A   7OZ   3.99
  07214081740
SWISSPERS SUPREME 80C ROUNDS A      2.99
  04834100014                  5.40Z
W(NICE) ASSORTED LICORICE   A       1.69
  04902259894                  8OZ
    STRAWBERRY TWISTS       A       1.29
                                 2.75OZ
```

RESTRICTIONS APPLY, SEE PROGRAM RULES FOR DETAILS. PLEASE GO TO DUANEREADE.COM/BALANCE.

RFN# 1452-4020-3192-1306-2003

****

balance

POINT BALANCE 170

BALANCE REWARDS ACCT # *********9617

****

FLEX REWARDS IS NOW BALANCE REWARDS!
GET SALE PRICING WHEN YOU USE YOUR
CARD. EARN POINTS IN STORE ON SELECTED
ITEMS. REDEEM STARTING AT 5,000
POINTS. FOR MORE INFORMATION, PLEASE
GO TO DUANEREADE.COM/BALANCE.

How are we doing?
Enter our monthly sweepstakes for
$3,000 cash

Visit
WWW.DRECARES.COM
****
or call toll free
1-800-821-9096
within 72 hours to take a short
survey about this Duane Reade visit

SURVEY# 020-319

universe. Burlingame, San Mateo, Menlo Park, Palo Alto, Sunnyvale – the Silicon Valley.

"I can imagine – especially after the spread in Wired."

"I wish I hadn't done it – I prefer a certain... anonymity." He said this in a curious way.

"And the auction? Just taking in some 'theatre,' or are you in the market?"

"Oh, I'm interested in a couple of pieces..."

"Really? I wouldn't have pegged you for this sort of thing."

"It's funny, but I like old things."

"It *is* funny. I imagine you in a gleaming office building surrounded by all of the latest technology... white rooms, clean lines."

"I am. It's true. That's why I sometimes like to be around things that have some... depth and patina to them." He took her arm. "Come on – we should be examining the lots while we can. And it's always better to do so with some champagne. Your glass is empty..."

"Oh, I'm good for now..."

"Then we'll share some over dinner after." He said this in such a way that Maddy could only smile at the confidence.

"O... Okay. Sure." She made the motion of tucking a stray hair behind her ear before remembering that her hair was cut short and already perfect. It was a vestigial impulse. It was the flirt instinct. She found herself blushing, then collected herself and took his arm.

Hang on to your hat, girl, she thought. Hang on to your hat.

XXII

"This so gross."

Dave Rogers made a face as he surveyed the parking lot. "I mean, doesn't it just make you sick how many people still smoke these days?"

Jimmy had to admit he was impressed. There were a lot of cigarette butts out there. He imagined all of those cigarette butts eventually working their way into the ocean to form Sargasso Seas of square miles of cigarette butts. The thought made him sad.

"So maybe this was a bad idea," he said.

Dave Rogers wandered over from the far corner of the parking lot where he had been surveying the scene. Jimmy was scrutinizing a map he had made based on the security video. He had laid out the parking lot and had circled with chalk the end of the white stripe of the parking stall in which the transport truck had parked, and where the suspect had dropped his cigarette so nonchalantly.

"I don't know. Gets me out of the office, at any rate," replied Dave Rogers. "Turned into a nice day." It had. The late afternoon sun was causing the Rockies to glow a pale amber. Early April and there was still plenty of snow on the peaks surrounding the Pilot truck stop to catch the glancing light. It was cold, though, and Jimmy was wishing he was wearing more than his suit jacket. He was also starting to feel light headed – the altitude starting to affect him.

"Here's the drop zone. Only about thirty butts here." He sighed. He snapped on the rubber gloves and started to gather them up and lay them out on the back side of the map – a clean white surface. He then stood back, surveyed his handiwork and pulled out his cell phone. "Jose? Any word on the cigarette butt that Carlos found?"

"Your timing is impeccable, man. Our friend from Berkeley just handed me the analysis. He's a trip, you know? Best damn chemical analyst I've ever seen…"

"Yeah, he's the Man, alright. So what's the make and model number?"

"Well, it's pretty fucked up. There's a Marlboro imprint on the filter, but it's not a Marlboro. It's faux Marlboro."

"How's that?"

"The tobacco is certainly not from anywhere in the US. It's actually, as gross as it sounds, made up from the leavings of partially used cigarettes with tobacco from somewhere like Turkey or the Caucasus. Apparently, there's quite the black market in American cigarettes in Eastern Europe, and someone has figured out a way to pass off fag's ends, reconstituted, as the real deal."

"So who would smoke such a thing?" Jimmy couldn't imagine.

"One tough motherfucker," said Jose. "Actually, the most likely candidate would be someone who was part of the trade, a smuggler perhaps, who had acquired the taste."

"But that would certainly point to an Eastern European."

"It would."

"Any DNA?"

"Yes, we've got a sample. If you can find a twin, then we're getting somewhere."

"Okay." He sighed. "I'm going in." He hung up the phone and went over to his backpack. He pulled out a magnifying glass and went and knelt down by the cigarette butts.

"Woah. Sherlock Holmes!" exclaimed Dave Rogers in some dismay.

"Sometimes Old School is the best school, you know?" said Jimmy over his shoulder. He slowly sorted through the cigarettes, pushing the failing candidates out of the way. There were three Marlboros left. One had lipstick on it. Jimmy was momentarily impressed that there were women truck drivers who still took the time to put on lipstick, then he realized that the more likely scenario was a little less savory. Truck driving could be a lonely gig, and certain needs could be satisfied even in a place like this. Actually, very much in a place like this.

Police work can be pretty lonely, too, he thought. In that moment he really missed Maddy. He wondered how she was doing on her end of the investigation.

XXIII

Maddy had never had so much fun in her life. She had seen more drama in the previous two hours than she had on any Broadway stage. And there was something about sitting with Sasha that was empowering and validating. She kept glancing over at him as he took notes on who was paying how much for each lot. He was one cool customer, she thought, and he looked like he was very comfortable in his surroundings.

How sexy was that?

Maddy was still capable of staying on task herself, and took her own notes. But there was nothing that she could discern in the way of a pattern in the bidding that might indicate a ruthless killer in their midst.

"Lot 157. One painting by Zinaida Serebryakova, a nude blonde woman reading a book. Painted in 1910, in gilt frame. The reserve price is 250,000 Pounds..."

"Buy this for me," whispered Sasha, his lips just brushing Maddy's ear.

"What?!"

"You've seen how it's done. Buy it."

Maddy suddenly broke into a sweat. "Do I have a limit?"

"No. Now on your marks, get set..."

"Do I hear 260?"

Maddy was so flustered she thought she might pass out. An old woman in heavy sunglasses raised a gloved finger.

"260." The auctioneer gestured towards the old woman. "Do I hear 270?"

He spoke so quickly that Maddy felt that she had to stomp on her mental accelerator to catch up. She raised her program trying as hard as possible to look casual. She didn't succeed. Her hand was shaking violently.

"270 to the young woman in the center." The auctioneer pointed at her. Maddy felt like a spot light had been turned onto her and could feel the entire room take her in. But only for a second. The bidding rocketed along while she recovered from the momentary hit of adrenalin. Two other bidders entered the fray - this being the prize lot of the evening - and before she knew it the price had risen to over 300,000 Pounds.

"320."

Maddy raised her program again. She glanced at Sasha, who was smiling an enigmatic smile. He winked at her in encouragement.

One of the bidders fell to the wayside. It was a little like watching a car wipe out at the Indy 500, the other cars just driving on by. But the old woman was hanging tough, as was a bored looking bald man dressed entirely in black sitting off to the side. He looked vaguely familiar, but Maddy realized that she had no time to try to figure out how. A fourth bidder was working it over the phone, a Christie's employee managing the call from a bank of phones near the back of the room.

"350. Do I hear 360?" It was Maddy's turn, and she went for it. Her heart was pounding. She barely had time to calculate that she was throwing around the better part of $700,000. The old woman sat motionless, only a slight tightening of the jaw indicating that she had thrown in the towel. The bald man in black was still taking the ride, however. When the bidding hit 400,000 Pounds, the bidder on the phone also checked out, the Christie's broker making a slight gesture and hanging up the phone. Now the bald man in black took Maddy in for a moment. After a beat, he acknowledged the next raise in price. The painting was now at 420,000 Pounds.

Holy Crap, thought Maddy. She glanced again at Sasha who chose to be inscrutable in that moment. He's letting me make the call, she thought. Jesus. Her heart in her mouth, she again raised her program. She and the bald man in black went back and forth for several raises, the price finally hitting 500,000 Pounds. The ball in his court, the bald man in black pursed his lips, then bowed his head in Maddy's direction, admitting defeat. The gavel went down.

"Sold, for 500,000 Pounds to the young woman in the center." Maddy couldn't help pumping her fist, never mind how uncool that was. "Now, Lot 158..."

But half the people in the room were slipping out, the main event over. A record price for a Russian Impressionist. And Maddy had bought it. She was shaking all over. No ride at Disneyland, Knott's Berry Farm or Six Flags Magic Mountain could touch the ride she had just taken.

Best. Date. Ever.

"Now we celebrate," said Sasha with the grin of the cat who just ate the canary. He offered Maddy his arm.

She took it.

XXIV

St. Petersburg took Carlos completely by surprise. On the way in from Pulkovo airport he and Sergei passed more bombed out buildings and shacks than anywhere Carlos had ever seen outside of Tijuana. But there was a weird, Doctor Zhivago-esque quality to all of it. Blanketed in freshly fallen snow and screened by birch trees, the buildings became romantic - the patina of age, the peeling plaster causing them to become evocative, rather than depressing. As they swerved their way deeper into the city center in Sergei's old Volvo – 'swerve' putting Sergei's driving style in the nicest possible way – Carlos grew more and more enraptured by the 18th Century buildings with their faded yellow, pink and green facades. Sergei wove his way onto the Admiralteskaya Nabarezhnaya, and suddenly the Saints Peter and Paul Fortress appeared dramatically lit across the ice-bound Neva River. It took Carlos' breath away.

"Beautiful, yes?" asked Sergei casually, after flipping off the driver of a black Mercedes that he had nearly side-swiped.

"It's gorgeous," replied Carlos. "It's like a fairy tale. A faded fairy tale, with frayed edges, but not without its magic."

"More than a few people were tortured to death in that fortress. The son of Peter the Great among them. By his own father." Sergei shrugged. "Russians families... It can be tough."

Carlos gazed at the golden spire of the fortress that thrust its way into the dark and cloudy sky like a stiletto blade, and felt a creeping dread in the pit of his stomach. He sighed, then pointed at the white expanse between them and the other embankment. "Is the river still frozen?"

"It's been especially cold this year. By now the ice is usually breaking up, but not this year. People still occasionally walk across - they're usually drunk, or missed the last bus and are desperate to get home." Sergei took one last drag on his cigarette and flipped it out into the cold night air. "I wouldn't do it. The last thing you would want is to have that ice crack under you – instant death. Your heart and lungs would crumple before you knew what happened."

Carlos just stared at the frozen river and its formidable fortress and shuddered at the thought of it. But before he could ruminate further on icy cold ways of dying, they careened onto Nevsky Prospekt, Sergei cutting off an old man in an old Volga as they did so. Suddenly, the bright lights and the throng of late night shoppers and revelers made Carlos shift mental gears. The street was the Champs Elysee, 5th Avenue, and Rodeo Drive of St. Petersburg, packed with boutiques and flagship stores for all of the latest and most fashionable brands of clothing and electronics: Apple, Gucci, Chanel, Prada, Sony. With the exception of the faded facades of the ancient buildings, Carlos could have been in Union Square back home.

"Wow... it looks like the economy is booming here," he remarked. He was wrestling with the disconnect between the bombed out buildings throughout the city and the glamour that surrounded him.

"I can't afford to shop along here," said Sergei, lighting another cigarette with both hands while steering with his knees. Carlos couldn't look.

"Who does?"

"Let's just say there are two different economies in Russia. The economy of the normal people, and the economy of the underworld. Yes, of course, there are hard-working businessmen and women who have risen to a certain… how you say? Affluence. But this kind of money…" Sergei exhaled his smoke ferociously through his nostrils causing him to look more than a little like a dragon, "let's just say that there is a culture in Russia of getting where one wants to go by taking the path of least resistance."

"Corruption."

"Corruption would somehow imply that this is hidden. It is how things get done. Everyone understands this. It is out in the open. No one really cares. And this… darker source of affluence needs its release. Russians like their toys. Here we are."

'Here' was the Evropaskaya Hotel, or the Grand Hotel Europe. Carlos could only shake his head. That Carey. At least, if he didn't live to tell the tale, he would go out in style.

"Are you hungry?" asked Sergei.

"Very. It's been hours since that 'snack' on the plane. But it's eleven o'clock."

"Prime time. Get yourself checked in, freshen up, and we'll get a bite and I can give you the lay of the land. I'll meet you in the bar downstairs."

"Sounds great. How can I thank you?"

"You're picking up the check. Oh, even though the exchange rate sucks at the hotel, get cash at reception. You don't want to be using your credit card anywhere else. Trust me."

"How much should I get?"

"How much can you afford to lose?" Sergei gave Carlos a knowing look. Carlos looked back at Sergei and all of the tiredness and tension came out in a laugh.

"Cool," he said climbing out of the car so Sergei could park it – he certainly wasn't going to hand it to any valet. "Give me half an hour."

It was a little longer than that. It had been over thirty-six hours since Carlos had taken a shower – an eternity for a boy who prided himself on his impeccable grooming – and he had worked as a day laborer, hung off the side of a twenty-three story skyscraper, spent an hour in jail and had been traveling for the better part of twenty-four hours in the meantime. It was the Best. Shower. Ever. As he got out and toweled himself off, he looked at the fluffy terry cloth bathrobe and had that moment: he was both really energized and jazzed to be on the ground in St. Petersburg, but a bathrobe, room service and those super soft sheets sounded really spectacular. He fought the momentary jet-lag induced lethargy. If you've got an ounce of energy, better work it, he thought with a sigh. I get one chance at this.

He threw on his most expensive jeans with the best rips in them, his best pair of shoes with some thermal socks to buffer him from the frozen streets, a crisp new shirt and a sport coat. He accessorized with a silk scarf and threw his overcoat over his arm. He scanned his iPad for any messages from Maddy, but there was nothing. I hope she's alright, he thought as he pulled the door to his room shut. She's probably identified the perp and is bringing home the bacon as I stand here. Carlos smiled to himself.

Downstairs, Carlos entered the dark and smoke-filled lounge. In the shadows of the room lurked heavy-set men in expensive suits and beautiful women in very short skirts. There was an animal energy combined with a lassitude that Carlos found intimidating. It was as if he had walked into a Serengeti watering hole. Lions and lionesses lounging around, both lazy and wary at the same time. The women were purring into their cell phones, the men indolently tapping away at the latest apps on their iPhones. At the bar, Sergei was sitting with a shot glass and a bottle of Russki Standart.

"Here, pull up a chair and have a drink," he said. His eyes looked a little out of focus.

"Um, how much was in that bottle when you started?" asked Carlos a little unnerved.

"The seal was unbroken. Only way to buy your vodka." Half the bottle was gone. A shot was poured for Carlos with Sergei filling up his own. "Nazdarovya," said Sergei.

"Naz... naz..."

"Nazdarovya. It means 'to your health.'"

"Nazdarovya," replied Carlos. "Are you.. is it... okay for you to be pounding it like this while we're working?"

Sergei looked at Carlos as if he had two heads. "This? This is nothing. Just wait until we step outside. Besides, I'm not a cop. I'm not on 'duty,' as it were."

"I thought, you know, Interpol and all..."

"Could you say that any louder?" Sergei looked around the room. The lions and lionesses seemed completely disinterested. Perhaps a flick of an eyelid or a slight pause in a conversation, but if they gave a damn, they didn't show it. "Bozhe moi." He sighed. "It's not as if anyone can't tell, or doesn't know, but we like to keep things a little more nuanced. Okay?"

"Okay. Sorry."

Sergei spoke in an undertone. "Interpol confuses a lot of people. It sounds like we're police, but we're not. We're just the Keepers of Information. We track the movements of criminals all over the world, but we rely on the local jurisdictions to do any arresting. No guns for us."

"So what do you do here?" Carlos normally liked some cranberry juice in his vodka – he was particularly partial to Cosmopolitans - but felt that ordering one here would be like ordering Chardonnay in an Irish pub. Suck it up and sip the vodka straight. When in Rome…

"Are you sipping that?" asked Sergei jabbing a finger at Carlos gingerly tasting the vodka. "Just drink it. Don't fuss. Bozhe moi. Anyway… what do I do here? I get to file hundreds of reports a week and watch the stack of paper on my desk get higher and higher. And not much comes of it, to be honest. It seems that the local economy thrives on the very people that Interpol keeps tabs on. You're from San Francisco. How often does Larry Ellison or Mark Zuckerberg get arrested?"

"Um, never."

"Exactly."

"Well, not really. They're not criminals."

Sergei snorted. "Tell me honestly that anyone who's worth a few billion isn't a criminal. It's all a question of cost/benefit. They're just more valuable greasing the wheels of your economy than where they most likely belong, which would be in jail. Same thing here. Just more so." He filled both his and Carlos' glasses.

Whew, thought Carlos. This stuff is kicking my ass. He shook it off.

"That's more than a little cynical," he said, bracing himself for the next hit.

"I'm Russian," replied Sergei with his now characteristic shrug. "What do you want?"

"Your English is excellent, by the way." Carlos shivered as the shot went down. "You have something of an English accent. Been to London?"

"No. Just went to a special school when I was a boy. English school. Here in Lenin... I mean, St. Petersburg. It was Leningrad when I was in school – I have dated myself, for sure. The school was for children whose parents wanted them to be diplomats, translators. Our teachers were trained to speak the Queen's English, so were we."

"So instead of diplomacy, you chase criminals." Carlos gestured for the check to a dark-haired, heavily made-up beauty from somewhere east of the Urals who was busy with a cocktail shaker. She barely nodded in acknowledgement. Girls are super-tough here, he thought.

"Don't think it doesn't take diplomacy to negotiate this world." Sergei drained the last of the bottle, slugged his shot and pushed back from the bar. "Now that we've warmed up a bit, let's go get some dinner. I think you'll be amused by the clientele of the place I have in mind."

"Where are we going?" asked Carlos whose eyebrows raised slightly in astonishment at the bill. This was going to be an expensive date.

"A den of thieves. Otherwise known as the best restaurant in town."

XXV

The flight home was long. Something about flying against the jet stream. Always made the flight west take an hour longer than the flight east. And it was hard to be without communication for three hours, especially with so much going on, and it now going on twelve hours since he last heard from Maddy. But it gave Jimmy some much needed thinking time, even though much of his thoughts centered on his concern for his girlfriend.

Girlfriend. He stared out the window and sighed. The word girlfriend seemed so... sophomoric. One had girlfriends in high school, maybe in college. At thirty, he felt too old for the idea, wishing there was some more mature term for the woman for whom he cared so deeply. But she's still pretty young, he reminded himself. Twenty-four. Not long out of college. She's got a lot of life ahead of her...

How did I get here?

It was as classic a case of opposites attracting as one could hope to find. A little over the top, actually. She was light and sun and enthusiasm and spunk and little – no 'compact' was the right word - and ... well, white. He was tall, dark, and despite his outward bonhomie, prone to self-doubt and world-weariness, and well... Chinese. It was a very unlikely match, but it made sense to both of them when they were together. They fit. They 'smelled right.' The way each of their brains worked complemented the other. They found common ground in their strong desire to uncover the truth, to solve the mystery, to achieve some kind of justice and to defend those who needed defending. It was good.

So why did he feel this strange pit in the bottom of his stomach? Was it that they were farther and longer apart than they had been in the six months since they first met? Was it that the reality of their careers meant that they would always be passing each other like the proverbial 'ships in the night?'

Was it that they were still learning to trust each other?

Trust. It had come hard when they first met. They each knew instinctively that they would never do anything consciously to hurt the other, but they had often been at odds as to the best way to get to a desired shared result. The previous fall, as Maddy had discovered and supported the homeless, violent and delusional vigilante, the Masked Avenger, Jimmy had been trying to remove him from the streets. She continuously stood in his way. Their relationship had been tested right from the beginning, but they survived the initial tests, finding compromise and give-and-take the way to survive as a couple. Once initial headstrong tendencies were overcome, they found they could talk to each other, work things out. But it could still be hard.

Complicated. That's what it was. And life couldn't be more complicated right now. A part of him wished that he was flying home to a quiet, uncomplicated woman who would be waiting for him at the door. Who would massage away the cares, listen to his troubles, hold him while he slept. Instead… well, instead he was going home to an empty apartment carrying with him a real anxiety about Maddy. He was tired, and the anxiety and emptiness made him sad.

He was self-aware enough to realize he was spiraling into depression, and turned his mind to his notes to pull him out. The email from Carlos was sensational – a huge break in the investigation. The image was fuzzy and pixilated, but it was definitely a portrait. It reminded Jimmy of the famous, iconic portrait of Che Guevara, with his messianic gaze. The pixilated face looked up in the same way, and wore the same beard. Who was this guy? He looked so familiar… Jimmy then looked through the other items in his folder. The Marlboros in their plastic bag, the thumb-print image, the photos of the severed head, the photos of Richard York, the image of the Annunciation by Andrey Rublyev that had been provided to him by the church, the photos of the Corporate Goddesses with their backs turned away from the world, the brochure from the Museum of Contemporary Art with the killer whale as the central image. Whew. It was hard to believe that there was a unifying theme to all of this. The Sam Spade voiceover in his head thought, Whoever put this story together was out of their mind…

The last document in the folder was the passport photo for John Smith. Jimmy stared at the image long enough for it to be burned into his retinas. He then closed his eyes and leaned back in his seat, the afterimage of the photo glowing in negative on the backs of his eyelids. There was something about the fuzzy, graphic quality of the burned-in image that jolted him with recognition. He jumped up so quickly he almost knocked his glass of white wine all over the opened folder on his tray table.

He pawed his way back to the printout of the pixilated portrait. He set it next to the image of John Smith. One had a beard, the other didn't. But there was something about the cheekbones and the look in the eye. It had to be.

*   *   *

Building 606 was on the way home from the airport. It was getting late – even with buying back the hour coming from Denver it was nine o'clock. People should be gone, but he figured it was worth a shot. As Jimmy entered the large, open work area, the Linkin Park thundering through the space indicated that Jose was still at it. Jimmy walked up behind the large man and clapped him on the shoulder.

"Jesus. You gave me a fright," said Jose. It was weird that a 6'-4", 260 lb. Hispanic man with tattoos on the back of his neck would be afraid of anything. Jimmy couldn't help laughing. As Jose finished massaging his heart, "What's up with you? Another long day?"

"Just keeping up with the Joneses," replied Jimmy gesturing at Jose's overcrowded desk with one hand. With the other he held up the six pack of Negra Modelo. "Can I buy some of your time to do some photo manipulation?"

"Bring it, Detective!" It was profoundly against official policy for anyone to be drinking on the job, especially in the lab. But both men knew that understaffed and underpaid as they were, there had to be some sort of motivating agent to keep them going. "What have we got?"

Jimmy pulled out a thumb-drive with the file of the John Smith photo on it. He then showed Jose the image that Carlos had sent him. Jose could only whistle and shake his head.

"That's fucked up, man," he said with some admiration. "How'd anyone figure that out?"

"Luck, mostly."

"Good detective work usually involves more of that than any of us would care to admit to the public," replied Jose. "Let's clean this up." The image Carlos had emailed was simply a print screen of the jumble of pdfs. In less than a minute Jose had organized the images properly. Then with a few keystrokes in PhotoShop he pulled the image out of its binary code, pixilated state and created an image that looked almost like a photograph.

"Cool," said Jimmy. This was sort of fun, watching Jose do the voodoo that he did so well. It was even better with a cold beer in his hand. "Now open this other file. Can you manipulate this photo so that it has the same graphic quality as the first one?"

"No problemo." A few keystrokes later, the passport photo looked as if it was shot by the same camera as the first image.

"Can you add a beard?"

"Can I add a beard..." Jose gave Jimmy a half-lidded look. "Why don't you give me something *hard* to do?" The paintbrush tool was applied to the passport image. Within thirty seconds, the same man looked out at them from the monitor with two different poses.

"That's him," said Jimmy.

"Um, why are we dinking around?" asked Jose.

"What do you mean, dinking around?" asked Jimmy. This was a huge breakthrough.

"Watch." Jose opened a new software. He clicked on the first image. The screen was suddenly filled with dots all over the face with lines connecting the dots. Numbers were scrolling at high speed next to each dot until after a minute a map was formed over the face. The face now looked as if it were formed of crystal.

"Woah. What did you do?"

"Beta version of a new facial recognition software. Better than fingerprints. Every face has thousands of metrics – distance between pupils, distance between nostrils, distance between earlobes, etc. No two faces have the same pattern of metrics.

The computer scans each of these thousands of points and calculates the distances in seconds, creating a face print that's unique to the individual. Now let's see what happens when we apply this to the other image."

In less than thirty seconds, the second image was calculated.

"Ding, ding, ding!" Jose mimicked a slot machine. "And we have a match."

Jimmy sat back in his chair in wonder. It wasn't the first time he was struck by the level of forensic sophistication he could muster in pursuit of the truth. His poor dad didn't have anything like this kind of firepower. But then his criminals didn't have the same kind of firepower they did now, either. Back in the day, Dirty Harry was a force to be recognized with with his .357 Magnum, intimidating and overpowering criminals with brute force. Nowadays, brute force didn't stand a chance against all of the tools at the underworld's disposal. Small arms and small time crooks didn't even enter the equation anymore. It was now about armies of well-equipped "soldiers," dizzyingly rapid international internet transactions, levels of corruption layers deep and high, and a ruthlessness that would leave Genghis Khan impressed. Colombian and Peruvian drug cartels even had submarines for Christ's sake. Now he was looking at the portrait of someone with access to radioactive chemicals who had the ability to vanish at will to anywhere in the world.

He was glad that he had Jose and The Man Without a Face on his side.

"A complete match?" Jimmy had to ask.

"Well, now that you ask, it's only about 98 percent sure. Close enough for government work."

"Now we have to figure out who this guy is," said Jimmy with a sigh. "I don't suppose we have this 'faceprint' lining up with anyone in the database?"

"Let's give it a try," said Jose. He accessed the Homeland Security database and input the file with the facial metrics. After a couple of minutes, during which Jimmy watched as a million faces flew by, the response came:

No matches found.

XXVI

He had sent his bodyguards home. Dmitri and Vassily, well, as good as they were at their jobs, there was a certain lack of... depth to them. He needed time to think and to breathe, and their hanging around had gotten on his nerves. Standing in the middle of his unfinished office suite, Ivan Orkin stared out at the lights of his adopted new city, hands thrust into his pockets, jaw clenched.

This is not how it was supposed to be.

He turned slowly taking in the panorama, then taking in, individually, each of the Goddesses. Each was distinct. Each writhed and mocked and condemned in her own way. All were looking at him now. His first instinct was only human - to shrink from their grim, relentless, faceless accusation. To run from the fingers pointed at him, the eyes he knew were there deep within the folds of their cowls – each digging deep into his soul and challenging everything he believed. But he didn't get to where he was now by turning tail, by hiding from a fight. Summoning his inner strength, flexing his spine of steel, he approached the first wraith-like figure, who towered above him, uplit from behind.

"Fuck. You."

It wasn't a shout, it wasn't a war-cry. It was spoken quietly but clearly with an intensity that cut like a saber. For a moment, he imagined the demon in front of him shivered, maybe even recoiling slightly. He then turned and walked to the next Goddess. He didn't even have to say the words. His eyes burned back at her and she too seemed to dip her head like a dog recognizing its master. After confronting each Goddess, Ivan Orkin returned to the middle of the penthouse suite and planted his feet at the center. He now owned his world again. He now reveled in his regained strength.

And he knew he was now going to have to have a word with his son.

XXVII

As they settled into their seats - the Maitre d' adjusting Maddy's seat behind her - a rich, silky baritone with a hint of a cockney accent floated towards them. Maddy turned and saw the man from the auction – the bald man with thick black glasses who had bid against her for the Serabryakova. As he approached, and without the heat of bidding fogging her brain, Maddy recognized him and almost passed out.

Donovan Hirsch.

"Please allow me to make your acquaintance," he said, extending his hand to Maddy. Sasha stood up.

"Donovan, this is Maddy Stevenson, an old friend."

"An honor, Mr. Hirsch." Maddy thought fleetingly that this was the most famous person with whom she had ever shaken hands.

"The honor is mine, Ms. Stevenson," replied Donovan Hirsch. "Sasha, a pleasure as always. I expected to find you here."

'Here' was the top floor of the OXO Tower with its commanding view of the Thames and the City of London. The restaurant was purring away with the elite and beautiful of London society sipping champagne and artisanal gin martinis. Sasha had organized a table by the window, and Maddy's breath had been taken away by the lights of the city. The drizzle of the afternoon had abated, leaving dark clouds underlit by the warm glow of the floodlights that illuminated St. Paul's Cathedral. Maddy had fallen in love and wished she could move to London, which, she had to admit, for a girl from San Francisco was saying something. Yes, that was it, she could be a London correspondent... or pretend she was Scarlett Johansson in a Woody Allen movie....

"Fun wasn't it?" asked Sasha.

"You're an arsehole," said Donovan Hirsch with a grin. Maddy was a little uncertain as to whether or not he meant it. Sasha gave a sheepish smile.

"It's just a painting. You could paint one just as good. Have a seat – join us."

"I haven't painted a thing in years. No money in it." Donovan Hirsch winked at Maddy. "Now some crazy stunt like a dead whale in a box with a catchy title, that'll pay the bills." He took in the two young people and he winked again. "You kids look like you need some time alone. Just paying my respects to the lady who kicked my arse at the auction. I've got to be shuffling off."

"Mr. Hirsch," said Maddy, finding her voice. "I'm doing research on the contemporary art world for a book I'm writing." She thought fast and furiously. "I am hoping to observe a day in the life of a world famous artist – how he creates, how he manages his work and career, things like that."

"And you're looking for me to hook you up with someone famous for you to observe," replied Donovan Hirsch. "Let me think." He screwed his finger into his cheek and pretended to look thoughtful. The pretense over, "How about I send a car round for you tomorrow morning. You can come out to my studio and watch the sausage get made."

"I don't think I've ever received a better offer!" Maddy blurted. She blushed as Sasha coughed theatrically and rolled his eyes. She put her hand on his arm to acknowledge his efforts, and to reassure him of her gratitude for an amazing evening so far. "I should love to. Thank you! I'm at the Dorchester. What time should I expect you?"

"We're early risers, you know. How about noon?"

"That's perfect."

"See you then. Dress warm." Donovan Hirsch bowed slightly, and with a last wink, headed towards the door.

"Holy moley," said Maddy breathlessly as she returned to her seat. "I must be dreaming. Either that or I'm just about to run out of good luck."

"Good luck?" Sasha again had that enigmatic smile. *What is he thinking?*

"I've been told that being in the right place at the right time is ninety percent of good detecting…"

"Good detecting?"

Crap.

"I mean good reporting… it amounts to the same thing, I've found."

A flicker of… something… passed across Sasha's face. It was as if his eyes momentarily changed color – a shift to black. Then back again, and the winning smile returned.

"I hope you're hungry, because I'm famished. I could eat anything on the menu. In fact, why don't you order for me – I'll be right back." He motioned to the waiter. "Whatever she wants." Sasha rose and before departing the table leaned in for a kiss. After only the slightest hesitation, it was returned. He smiled and moved across the room and out of sight.

The waiter signaled that he would be right with Maddy. This gave her a moment for her heart to sink deep into her stomach. The light glancing off the white table cloth lit her face softly from below. It was enough for her to be able to see her reflection in the window, a spectral image floating over the City of London. Who was this woman looking back at her? Less than a year before she was a moony, goofy college student from a sheltered, guard-gated community in Newport Beach, California. Now she was a globe-trotting, crime-fighting, investigative journalist... who was also one foot onto the slippery slope of her first affair. She had never felt the range of emotions she was feeling in this instant. A week ago, if anyone had asked – no, even yesterday – she would have told them that she was in love with Jimmy. Now she felt so unbalanced, so disoriented, that she didn't even know who she was anymore. The woman floating over London looked at her with a challenging expression on her face, as if to ask, What the fuck are you doing, girl? To which Maddy could only reply, I don't know... living a full life? I get only one shot at this, right?

Her reverie was broken by the appearance of the waiter. She had hardly glanced at the menu, and by then all hunger had vanished - her stomach so full of butterflies.

"Um, do you have a tasting menu, or may we have the chef's choice?" She had decided to completely abrogate any decision-making at this point – she felt that she was doing terribly making choices right now, and felt it more than likely that it would continue this way for a while.

"Yes, ma'am. We have many people simply place themselves in the chef's hands. He has good taste, if I may say so."

"Then two chef's choices, please. And please, could you pair us up with a couple glasses of wine for each dish? That way I don't have to take any responsibility..."

"For what? Feeling pressure?" Sasha had returned.

"Well, I'm feeling indecisive, but I don't want you to suffer as I struggle."

"Trust me, I won't suffer. We'll be fine. Sounds

like a great plan. This way we just take it as it comes, and turn our attention to more interesting things." The way he said that made Maddy feel that somersault in her stomach again. Sasha dismissed the waiter with a nod, and he looked straight at Maddy. With that gaze of his pale green eyes, Maddy knew she was in deep, deep trouble.

XXIX

When Carlos stood up from the bar at the Evropaskaya, he thought he would simply pitch over. Three shots of vodka and he was flying. But as soon as he stepped outside and felt the five-degree night air with the minus-twenty wind-chill off the canal slap him in the face, he felt as clear headed as he ever had.

"Damn. That's amazing," he said, half to himself.

"What's amazing?" asked Sergei, inhaling his umpteenth cigarette.

"That I can function at all. You're right, the cold totally counteracts the alcohol."

"Or so it seems. Don't get too cocky. I can tell you're not hardened like the rest of us."

Couldn't get much more hardened than Sergei, thought Carlos. He had figured out that Sergei was about forty, but looked more like mid-fifties. I'm glad I quit smoking. And I'm going to cut back on the drinking. For sure.

"So are we walking?"

"Sure. It will only take about fifteen minutes. And parking is a bitch. Besides, the legal blood alcohol limit is zero, so better to play it safe."

"Zero? You mean zero-point-something?"

"Nyet. Zero. Thank you, Comrade Gorbachev."

The two men worked their way off Nevsky Prospekt and along the Griboedov canal. The city has often been called the Venice of the North, but Sergei explained that it bore a stronger resemblance to Amsterdam in layout – a series of concentric half-circles of canals cutting the city into rings. This was most likely due to the city's founder, Peter the Great, having a great affinity for the Dutch capitol, and things western.

"So Peter the Great. Sounds like a pretty tough guy," said Carlos, by way of making conversation.

"Super-tough. But a great man. Brought Russia out of the middle ages. Beat the Swedes. Built this city. A giant."

"A giant?"

"Both figuratively and literally. He was huge. Was over two meters tall. This at a time when most people were about a meter and a half. Literally towered over his people. Scared the shit out of everyone."

"So who's the man in St. Petersburg now? Who runs the show?"

Sergei shrugged. "It's not known for sure. There are several operators who look like they're the top guys – we'll probably see at least one of them tonight – but they're not smart enough to be criminal kingpins or sophisticated enough to organize the level of international logistics that the Pink Panthers are known for. They're certainly ruthless and daring enough, but they lack a certain... vision. It is our assessment that there is someone, maybe two layers beyond what we can see, who pulls the strings. It puzzles us still, and we can't seem to make any headway in finding out who it is."

"So we're going into the lion's den. Full frontal assault?"

"Nyet. We're just going for a nice dinner. Look, they know who I am, and yet I am tolerated because I am, in essence, ineffectual. They might give me a hard time, but it's really not worth their energy. We'll stay out of their way."

After as cold a walk as Carlos could remember along the frozen canal, they finally arrived at their destination, Krasnaya Ploshad – Red Square. It didn't have a name over the door, just a glowing red square as its logo, mounted in a concrete plinth. Carlos had checked it out at zagat.com as they approached, and it came up with a spectacular score. Somewhat depressingly, it also came up with a spectacular price tag. Carlos was grateful that he was young enough and fastidious enough paying off his student loans that his credit score was high enough that American Express had allowed him to cash advance as much as he did back at the hotel. He hoped Carey would understand. But it really was a nice place, thought Carlos as they climbed up the steps of the elegant 18th Century building. And the clientele had to be crazy rich. Parked in front were more Mercedes, BMWs and Audis than Carlos had ever seen anywhere – even at a dealership. The valets must really love their jobs, he thought. But the scene-stealer was the lemon-yellow Lamborghini parked at a rakish, fuck-you angle. Nothing like a car worth a quarter of a million to set the record straight on the failure of Communism.

Whew. Time to cowboy up.

After being given a thorough going-over by two of the largest bouncers Carlos had ever seen - with Carlos receiving extra scrutiny before passing "face control" - the two men were ushered through large wooden doors. In the foyer they passed through a metal detector, with one last pat-down for good measure.

"At least there are no guns in here," said Carlos under his breath.

"Guns are for pussies," replied Sergei out of the side of his mouth. "These guys don't need guns."

Carlos did not find this comforting.

They approached the reception desk. A

spectacularly beautiful woman with waist long white-blonde hair greeted them. 'Greeted' being generous. Like all the other women Carlos had encountered so far in St. Petersburg, she managed to curb her enthusiasm to a chilling degree. She simply raised her eyes from the desk and acknowledged their presence with a slight shift of an eyebrow. But much to Carlos' surprise, without saying a word, she picked up two menus and led the men to a table with a commanding view of the whole restaurant, which was resplendent in crimson drapes and crystal chandeliers. The air was thick with cigarette smoke, adding to the illusion of having entered a distant era and an exotic locale. After the hostess situated them, and after she turned on her extremely high heel and slid away in her extremely form-fitting dress, Carlos leaned over to Sergei.

"I have to ask. How the F did we manage to get in here?"

Sergei shrugged and gestured towards the departing hostess. "My girlfriend."

"Your...? She...?" Carlos was speechless. Sergei was a tall, skinny wreck of a middle-aged man with teeth that could be generously called terrible.

Sergei could not look more nonchalant. "It comes in handy. She's able to help me keep track of who's in town."

Carlos looked at Sergei in a new light. Damn, he thought. What it must take to keep a girl like that happy. It must be his sense of humor. As if reading his thoughts, Sergei said simply, "She's a nice girl from a small town, but like many silly girls with big dreams, she became a runaway. She was busted for prostitution at the age of fourteen and was looking at prison time, which, to be honest, in this country is pretty close to a death sentence, what with the heroin and the AIDs that she would no doubt contract. Her father and I were in the army together, and he asked me for a favor. I helped her get back on track." Sergei exhaled his cigarette smoke and leaned back into the banquette. "She's grateful, that's all."

Carlos could only shake his head in wonder.

"Actually, that's not true. She's a ball-buster. Almost not worth the trouble. After what I spend on her clothes, I've got nothing left." The Russian sigh. "Nothing comes easy, my friend."

"So what have we got?" asked Carlos, surveying the room. "I feel like I need a program so I know all the players."

"Don't stare too much. The only thing that keeps us alive is our appearance of indifference. I use the mirrors."

There were three large mirrors framed by red curtains on the far wall. The mirrors were splotchy with age, making the room look even more elegant – in a dissipated and dilapidated way.

"Okay," continued Sergei, looking at his menu, and not at Carlos or the mirrors. "Clock your position."

Carlos could see himself and Sergei in the center mirror.

"Alright, in the left-hand mirror, in the booth on the left, is Boris Treplev. We call him Uncle Bob. Something of an elder statesman of the underworld. Ruthless as anything - that's how he's managed to live to be sixty – but has something of a sense of honor. He made his money in the 80's working the heroin trade out of Afghanistan. Now he's diversified, with nothing but 'legitimate' businesses."

Carlos took in, as discreetly as possible, a heavy-set, but well-dressed gentleman with silver hair. He bore a passing resemblance to Boris Yeltsin, which was a little disconcerting, especially since he was surrounded in his booth by four beautiful young women a fraction of his age.

"It's good to be the King," said Sergei with a smirk.

"Must be," said Carlos, doing his best not to stare. "I heard the quotation marks around 'legitimate.' Not really?"

"He now finances internet start-ups, which is code for running questionable websites which flirt with identity theft."

"That's not illegal?"

"He's got just enough layers between him and his companies to be just beyond our reach. The internet is a remarkable safe haven. Now, in the far right mirror, that's Stefan Chebutykin."

Carlos, who had adopted Sergei's trick of pretending to read the menu - which was useless anyway because it was all in Russian – glanced up to observe a dark-haired man with rugged good looks who was reading the Wall Street Journal and sipping a martini. Sort of a Humphrey Bogart type. He was in an impeccable silver suit, and, as Carlos watched, an elegant but somewhat desperate-looking woman in a red dress approached him. Chebutykin looked up at her over his martini with somewhat sad eyes. He made no gesture for her to join him. She started to sit down, but Chebutykin only raised his hand towards the reception desk and one of the enormous bouncers came up briskly and took the woman by the arm. She struggled to free herself, with no small amount of cursing in Russian, but the bouncer was implacable and relentless. After the brief commotion, Chebutykin returned to his newspaper and resumed sipping his martini.

"What's his story?"

"He owns the place. That was his ex-wife."

"Oh. That was like a scene out of *Casablanca*."

"You're more right than you know. Rick's was a refuge for those who were trying to get somewhere else, or hide from where they came from. Chebutykin, like Rick in a way, is also a trafficker in human misery. The restaurant is his way to launder his money. He's at the front end of a white slave trade. Girls from the provinces suddenly disappear from their small, miserable lives in their small miserable little towns, and reappear in places like Bahrain and Dubai – as slaves or prostitutes. He constructed the trade networks and transportation systems, and he negotiates the fees. He has a small army of 'recruiters' – mostly young men who trade in their girlfriends for cash."

Carlos was aghast. "That's horrible. And he's not behind bars because…"

"Such a trade relies heavily on the complicity of local authorities. Again, our job is to file the paperwork, but we don't mete out justice. That would be up to someone here in Putin's Russia to do – and you won't find many policemen brave enough to take on the task."

A waiter appeared.

"I'm suddenly not all that hungry," said Carlos with a sour face.

"Come on, the food is really good here."

"I have no idea what's on the menu…"

Sergei turned to the waiter and spoke quickly in Russian, with a couple of gestures towards Carlos. The waiter said a few words in reply and then took Sergei's menu. He reached out for Carlos' menu, and Carlos, after a moment's hesitation, gave it to him.

"What did you get me?"

"Some smoked salmon, and herring with potatoes to start, followed by some medallions of venison."

Carlos's appetite returned. "That… that almost sounds good. It's a good thing I'm not a vegetarian."

Sergei arched an eyebrow as if that was inconceivable. "And some vodka. Nothing like smoked salmon and vodka. It all comes together then."

"We haven't had enough?"

Sergei looked at his watch and then did a mental calculation. "No, not yet."

"Anyone else of note in the room?"

"The main attraction. In the corner booth – you can see it in the right mirror."

It was a large booth with a group of young men lounging languorously. They all wore expensive jeans and even more expensive shirts untucked with several buttons open. More than a little bling as well, thought Carlos. At the center of the group was a young man who looked vaguely familiar to Carlos. He had a spike of dark hair and a wispy dark beard. He looked to be in his early twenties – the youngest of the group – but it was obvious from the body language of the other men that he was the leader. He sat quietly while the others chatted away, unsmiling as his colleagues laughed. Every once in a while someone would touch him on the arm and he would lean in to listen, but he seemed disengaged. It was as classic a scene of a star player and his entourage as Carlos could imagine.

"Konstantin Ranevsky. A Panther."

"A Pink Panther?"

"They call themselves the Red Brigade. None of them refer to themselves as Pink Panthers - I mean how gay is that?" Carlos smiled inwardly. "That's the name that the various crime fighting authorities gave them. But yes, he's the leader of the St. Petersburg cell. Word is he and his crew were behind massive jewelry heists in Tokyo and Abu Dhabi. They both involved smash and grab in broad daylight, strange costumes, fast cars and forged passports."

"Don't tell me. He owns that Lamborghini out front." Sergei nodded. "He looks barely out of high school." And he's kind of cute, too, thought Carlos. A little bit of rough...

"Kids, these days," said Sergei with a shrug. "There are rumors that he achieved his place of prominence through family connections."

"How so?"

"That the person behind the network of cells - all seeming to operate independently on a superficial level, but with a level of logistical acumen that would require a central organizing intelligence - that that person is somehow related to Ranevsky."

"And no one knows who that is?"

"No. All we ever hear are whisperings. An occasional reference from someone low on the food chain. A ripple through the cells of Kresty Prison."

"And what are the whisperings?"

"Pikovaya Dama. The Queen of Spades."

It was as if, with those words spoken, a cold wind blew through the restaurant. Candles flickered for a moment, conversation stopped. Carlos found himself shivering.

"That sounds sort of creepy," he whispered, grateful that the waiter had arrived with another bottle of Russki Standart and two shot glasses.

Sergei nodded. "Nazdarovya," he said.

"To the Queen of Spades, whoever and wherever she is," replied Carlos, who felt very much as if he needed that drink, after all.

XXX

"How are you? I've been... I've been worried about you. Everything okay? Wait. It's like six in the morning over there."

"I'm... I'm fine. Everything's okay. I met an old friend, and well, we... we went dancing."

There was a pause. Maddy could hear the arch of Jimmy's eyebrow.

"Dancing."

"At this amazing club. Super-exclusive. Prince William was there. So was Gwyneth Paltrow. Crazy. Really exciting."

"That's some club. You get in on your looks?" There was an attempt at humor.

"Um, well, Sasha, he knows people."

"Sasha." The humor drained out of his voice.

"Yeah, Sasha Borodin. We knew each other at Stanford. He's, like, super-rich and famous now. Infinity search engine. He was at the auction."

"The auction..."

"Are you going to repeat everything I say?" Was that a tone of annoyance?

"Sorry – just slow on the uptake after a really long day. I almost didn't answer the phone – the number wasn't anything I recognized..."

"Oh. I totally spaced and fried my phone. Aargh. I'm calling from the hotel with a calling card."

"Oh. That explains... I've been trying to reach you. Have you checked your email recently?"

"No, I just got in and wanted to call you right away..."

"Just got in..."

"Stop it, okay?" Now the tone was less annoyed, more defensive. After years of training and conducting interrogations, Jimmy could tell a voice under stress. He was sensitive enough to Maddy's moods, which were rarely dark, to know that she was holding something back - and in the rare instances that she did so, it wasn't good.

"I... I guess I was just really worried. I guess I shouldn't have been. It sounds as if you're doing fine. More fun than a girl should have, I'm sure. Listen, I've got to go. We've had a breakthrough, and I've got a lot of following up to do. But you should probably get some sleep – I'm sure you're exhausted. Why don't you call me later."

"But... I..."

Jimmy hung up.

He sat on the hood of his car. He had just left the lab, and was about to head back to his office to start the process of putting out the APB. At 9:30 the sky was cobalt in color with Venus glowing bright on the horizon. A cold April evening, but clear. He wondered what the weather was like in London at 6:30 in the morning. Suddenly, his shoulders slumped. He didn't know if he was angry, or scared, or just plain exhausted. He knew that something had shifted in his universe, but he was suddenly too tired to be able to make sense of it. He knew that he had blown it by running away in that moment, but he hadn't known what else to do.

Fuck it.

He got in his car and pointed it northward. He found that suddenly, solving the world's problems didn't matter all that much. At least not right now. Right now he just needed a drink. Maybe more than one.

Maybe a lot.

XXXI

Maddy stared at the phone for about five minutes listening to the dial tone, wavering between redialing and slamming the handset down onto the cradle.

What was that all about?

She laid back on her bed and stared at the ceiling. She knew exactly what that was all about, and a sense of shame crept over her. He had expressed concern for her, and all she could talk about was how much fun she was having and her brushes with celebrity. She replayed the conversation in her head and realized how shallow and self-involved she must have sounded. And how entranced she was with her rediscovered friend. No wonder he was having trouble with the conversation. She didn't even get a chance to ask how he was. Well, she had the chance, but she never took it. It... it hadn't occurred to her in the moment. Why was that? Perhaps she had wanted to believe that she was secure in their relationship - even after the night she had - and she was disturbed that he was obviously less than secure – even threatened. But did he have to hang up on her? He didn't really hang up, but, well, he did.

She got cross for a second. It's not like anything happened. Nothing *happened*. Well, there *was* some pretty sexy dancing, and the kiss goodnight was excellent and not without the implied offer to go back to his place – which was declined, of course, without actually having to say anything - but it was only a kiss...

Who was she kidding? She had handled it all like a first-class schmuck. She rolled over and buried her face in her pillow. She started to cry. What was going on? After a moment of self-reflection she knew that what was going on was that she enjoyed the attention she was receiving from this handsome and exciting man, and it was addicting, and the world that she found herself navigating was intoxicating. A part of her knew it was only a dream, but in this dream she was having the time of her life.

* * *

The phone rang and Maddy once again found herself startled out of a deep sleep, a damp spot on her pillow and drool on her cheek. Goddammit! I am never going to get over this jet-lag, she cursed as she grabbed for the phone.

"Miss Stevenson, your car is waiting for you," said the receptionist.

"Please tell them I'll need about fifteen minutes. I'm so sorry. I'll be down as quick as I can."

"Yes, ma'am. Would you like some coffee sent to your room?"

"If you can get it here in ten minutes that would save my life."

"Not a problem."

"If I'm in the shower, please just ask them to leave it outside the door. Thanks!"

Shower. Maddy did some terrible math and realized that she hadn't taken a shower since the one she shared with Jimmy over thirty-six hours before. Between a trans-Atlantic plane flight and partying until dawn, she stank to high heaven. No way was she interviewing a world famous contemporary art figure in this condition.

I've got to go through my email, she thought, as

she waited for the shower to come up to temperature. Jimmy talked about a breakthrough. She flipped open her laptop, and scanned through her inbox. There were three from Jimmy and two from Carlos. She started with Carlos. She was too apprehensive to open the ones from Jimmy just yet. The first one had no text, just an attachment. It was a slightly garbled black and white portrait... Boy did that face look familiar... huh. The second one was a simple text:

The Queen of Spades.

Maddy shivered. Jesus. Just when this investigation couldn't get any more weird, it does. I hope he's all right. I really need a cell phone right now. Perhaps I can get one later today...

Maddy then opened the first email from Jimmy. It had his itinerary to and from Denver, just in case. The second must have been sent from the airport at Denver before he flew home. It broke down the developments so far: the cause of death of Richard York, the search for the Gulfstream V, the confirmation of the switch of the truck trailer, the cigarette analysis.

And the passport photo of John Smith.

Maddy stared at the photo. Steam was working its way out of the bathroom and into her suite.

It's not possible.

She then opened the third email. It contained the two images doctored by Jose. Maddy felt faint.

It really couldn't be.

The knock on her door woke her from her awful reverie. She wrapped her bathrobe tightly around her and accepted the tray with hot coffee from the room service boy. After signing it to her room, she poured herself a cup and returned to her computer. The coffee started to peel away the cobwebs still covering her consciousness.

With her stomach still struggling to swallow her heart, Maddy went to the Wired Magazine website. There, gracing the cover was Sasha, clean-shaven. She placed the image next to the passport photo and the image built from the binary code.

Could it be the same man? There was something off about the pixilated image that didn't quite jive with the passport photo that didn't quite jive with the cover photo of Sasha. There was something about the eyes. They could be the same in the passport photo and the cover photo, but the eyes of the man in the passport photo had a hardness to them that Sasha's didn't have. Of course there's always airbrushing, thought Maddy ruefully. And the eyes of the Che Guevara image were black with intensity – again there could be some sort of photomanipulation. But, if she had to articulate it, there was also a quality of madness to them.

On one hand if it was Sasha in all three images, that meant she was spectacularly close to solving a crazy mystery. On the other hand, if it *was* Sasha in all three images, she had just kissed a murderer.

*   *   *

I'm going to lose too much weight at this rate, Maddy thought, as she flushed the toilet after barfing. Again. The thought that she had been even remotely intimate with the person behind the murder of that priest and the head in the tank caused her to be sick to her stomach. But the longer she stood under the streaming hot water in her shower, the more she was convinced it couldn't be true. She simply wouldn't allow it to be true. Someone was doing a double, if not triple blind. She just had to work her way through the maze.

And she had agreed to meet Sasha for a West End

show and another late dinner. It would totally suck, she thought, to turn that down because her new friend had orchestrated the theft of several works of art with a level of ultra-violence that had the San Francisco Police Department still struggling to comprehend it.

The SFPD. She really needed to talk with Jimmy, but there was no time right now. Maybe it was just as well. Too much at stake, and, maybe, not enough facts yet on the table. Both Jimmy and Carey had demanded facts. Right now, they were still in very short supply. And, of course, she still wasn't sure what to say about Sasha.

She drank her coffee in the shower, using up way too much time just standing there with the water streaming over her. She began to feel more human, though. She eventually found the will to climb out of the shower and towel off. Again grateful for her short hair - which she left damp and chicly disheveled - she threw on some jeans, boots and a very thick wool sweater. No time for make-up, which, she thought wistfully was too bad – those dark bags under her eyes were getting darker and baggier all the time. With any luck at all, she could wrap up with Donovan Hirsch with enough time to grab a disco nap and still finally spend some real time on her appearance before her date – something she hadn't done in over two days. She grabbed her winter coat and scarf and ran down the stairs, that being faster than the old elevators.

Downstairs her driver was waiting. A young man with shaggy hair, scruffy beard, a paint-spattered white jumpsuit and army boots in an oversized trench coat was leaning against a shiny new Range Rover smoking a cigarette. He looked like a young Pete Townsend. He seemed impervious to the cold – Maddy was grateful for her thick sweater and was already worried that her hair might freeze, but he seemed nonchalant about the thirty-degree weather.

"'Allo. I'm Roger," he said, flicking the butt of his cigarette into the gutter, and proffering his hand. "You must be Maddy. I'm Mr. Hirsch's assistant. One of them, anyway."

"I'm so sorry to keep you waiting. Really late night last night, and I'm still pretty jet-lagged."

"No worries. Climb on in." He opened the passenger door for her. It was odd, getting into the wrong side of the car. Thank goodness I'm not driving, she thought. I'd be in a wreck within the first block.

"Lucky day for you," said Roger as they pulled into traffic. "You get to sit in on some serious stuff. The director of LA MOCA and his technical staff are here to work out the details of the boss's retrospective they're planning at the Geffen. They're all here to figure out how to get the new piece into the building."

"What's the new piece?"

"Fucking enormous tank with a white sperm whale in it."

"Um, like Moby Dick?"

"Yeah, but with a twist."

"You're not cutting it in half or anything like that, are you?" Maddy was quite sure she didn't want to see that, no matter how, um, cutting edge it might be.

"No, that's been done. We're tattooing it. Like a Maori warrior. It's really cool."

"How are you doing that?" Maddy couldn't imagine it.

"It's super hard and time consuming. We can only work on it for a few hours at a time before we have to submerge it in the formaldehyde solution."

"Where did you get the whale?"

They were now heading towards the east of

London, leaving the central part of the city behind them and moving into the industrial docklands. "We worked with a Japanese whaling company. It was pretty involved. The logistics of transporting it were pretty crazy. And the legal issues where not for the faint of heart, what with most countries ostracizing the Japanese for their defiance of international calls for them to stop their whaling."

"It sounds so politically incorrect, on so many fronts."

"That's what makes it cool. It's so offensive that it becomes great."

"It sounds a bit like Mr. Hirsch is still working the same themes."

"He's still on the edge."

"You like working for him? Where'd you come from to get a job as his assistant?"

"I was a small-time street artist. Never made it past my first year in art school. Fell in with a group that was trying to change the world through random acts of art on street corners – you know, agitprop, satirical graffiti. Didn't get very far with that group, but somehow got hooked up with Banksy's team."

"Woah. Banksy? Does he exist? I always thought he was a fabrication."

"All the greats are fabrications to some extent. But he exists – I've signed away my life not to reveal who he really is. But it was pretty intense working with him. Always a half-step from going to jail. When I heard that there was an opening with Hirsch, I went for it. It's a pretty good gig, and much more legit. I realized that I don't have all that much to say myself, as an artist – born to be an assistant, I guess, to someone who does."

"Or at least someone who has learned how to work the system to make a fortune, regardless of whether or not he has anything to say."

Roger shrugged. They were driving along a potholed road, large industrial buildings towering around them. Maddy changed the subject.

"So you worked with Richard York?"

"Worked? Um... still do. Why, has anything happened to him?"

Maddy realized with horror that it had only been a day and a half since Richard York had died mysteriously on the flight back from San Francisco. Since the police were still holding information pending notification of next of kin, Roger wouldn't have heard. She felt so stupid. Still a lot to learn in the investigative journalism game.

"Oh, um... shoot. I didn't realize you didn't know. Richard had a heart attack on the airplane. He died before they could get the plane diverted to Denver. I'm so sorry to be the one to break it to you."

Roger was visibly shaken. It was lucky that they arrived at their destination at that moment. He turned off the ignition as they parked in a gravel lot next to an enormous building and wiped his eyes, which had begun to tear up.

"He was a good guy. He had talent, not like the rest of us. Shit. A heart attack... he was like, thirty. That doesn't make sense."

"It doesn't, no." Maddy was sure she shouldn't be saying much more about this. Especially now that she noticed the police car in the lot next to the assortment of Range Rovers. Roger pulled himself together and they got out of the car.

"Here's the factory. Looks like we've got more company than just the museum people. I suppose this must be the cops giving Donovan the news."

They entered through a small metal door within a gigantic rolling door. Maddy was overwhelmed by the scale of the building from the inside, and surprised by the clinical neatness of the place. The main floor of the building was as large as a football field, and a huge gantry spanned the structure from wall to wall. Banks of metal halide floodlights filled the space with an intensity of light reminiscent of an operating room.

"The offices are upstairs. Shall we go up?"

They ascended a spiral staircase that arrived at a landing which overlooked the main floor. Maddy paused to take in the operation, which was breathtaking in its scope. At the center of the floor was an enormous glass tank. Inside the tank was the largest mammal she had ever seen, stretching for over fifty feet. The whale was almost luminous in its whiteness. It was resting in a giant cradle that was attached to a sequence of chains that arrived at a central hook off the gantry above. Surrounding the tank were dozens of rolling work tables covered with a panoply of jars of ink and brushes. Assistants in white lab coats and overalls were moving slowly and deliberately around the tables, preparing their tools and studying diagrams. In a far corner of the space was a shielded area from which sparks of light intermittently erupted. A welding station. In the opposite corner stood a series of machining tools, with racks of steel rods and beams up against the walls. There was a thrum to the place that made Maddy wonder how much money the whole operation took to run. To Maddy's eyes it was reminiscent of scenes from James Bond movies – the giant lairs of the evil geniuses that hoped to take over the world: the launching pad under the volcano, the nuclear reactor of Doctor No.

"It's amazing," said Maddy, her voice a whisper of awe. She turned to Roger. "What part do you do?"

"I'm the graphic designer. I created the tattoo pattern. Come into the studio – I'll show you how it's done."

They entered a large open room with a series of computer work stations along one wall. Two other assistants were working at their machines. Both were working with three dimensional visualization and drafting software. Large objects were being drawn and rotated on the screens.

"This seems more like a factory than an art studio," said Maddy.

"More than you know," agreed Roger. He gestured towards his compatriots. "This is Mia, and that rascal over there is Nigel." A pretty Asian girl looked up from her screen and took off her headphones. The young Indian man gave a sad wave.

"Oh, Roger," said Mia, her voice a little hoarse. "Did you hear about Richard?"

"Just now. It's horrible." They hugged for a long moment. Mia wiped away a tear. Nigel just looked miserable and continued to click away with his mouse. "Guys, this is Maddy. She's here to interview Donovan for a book."

"Good luck with that," said Mia, shaking Maddy's hand. "He's been a terror all morning. Having the police here hasn't helped. He's in there with them now." She gestured towards a set of double doors.

"Well, while we wait, let me show you what we do up here. Mia, what are you working on?"

Mia went back over to her computer and brought up what looked like the plan of a building on her screen. "This is the floor plan of the Geffen in Los Angeles. We're moving pieces around to see what works best, and where they're going to have to remove or add walls." She moved her mouse around and the plan was rotated into an orthographic view. As she moved the mouse, the view into the building adjusted. She could virtually move through the space, and it was as if Maddy were within the building walking around. "This saves us a lot of time during installation."

"I'll bet," said Maddy, impressed.

"This also helps us as the retrospective moves on to the Guggenheim Bilbao." She opened another file and a new floor plan was superimposed onto the first. It became clear that adjustments would have to be made from one place to the next.

"And what is Nigel working on?" asked Maddy.

"He's drafting the construction drawings for a new piece. It's a wall of 55-gallon drums containing shit. It's twenty-four feet high and sixty feet long."

"Wait. Did you say... *shit*?"

"Human excrement. Yes."

The drawing showed a tall wall of drums, each with a dollar sign graphic stenciled on it in a parody of the biohazard symbol.

"What's it called?"

"'Capitalism at Work.'"

"Profound," said Maddy with a shudder. "And it has to be the real thing inside the drums?"

"Sure. Otherwise it's not art," replied Roger without any hint of irony.

"Of course. And where do you get all the, um... human excrement?"

"We've been working on that for months. If you need to use the loo, you, too, can be part of the exhibit."

Maddy found herself thinking that she would simply have to hold it until she got back to the hotel. She was not interested in making 'art' that day. "Cool," was all she could say.

"And this is my station," said Roger as he guided her over to his computer. He tapped it awake, and with a few keystrokes brought an image of the Sperm Whale onto his monitor. "This is the whale when we got it, and this," he made a few clicks with his mouse, "is what it will look like finished."

It was awesome in its ridiculousness. But the graphic was beautifully done.

"We flatten the graphic, break it down into its constituent parts in a grid pattern and plot each piece of the grid onto large sheets of translucent plastic. We then use the plastic sheets with perforating rollers as stencils for the tattoo artists."

"So what part does Mr. Hirsch play in all of this?"

"He provides the overarching artistic vision. And he gets the commissions. And he writes the checks," replied Roger with his now characteristic shrug.

"Just like any corporate CEO," said Maddy. "Where did Richard York work?"

"Over here." Roger took Madddy over to a separate work station, away from the others, that had a few dirty windows to look out from. It looked a little like a supervisor's desk in the corner office. "Seniority had its privileges. He got some daylight."

"How long did he work with Mr. Hirsch?"

"Better part of ten years, I think. He started with Donovan right out of school."

"The killer whale – when was that done?"

"Ninety-two. About twenty years ago. Why?"

"I was just looking forward to it coming to San Francisco. It's what Richard was working on, wasn't it?"

"Yeah, it was meant to be more of a perk, really, that trip – a few days all-expenses-paid in San Francisco. There wasn't meant to be much work involved."

"So if the piece was originally designed and constructed in 1992, that was before any of the software you use now was around."

"Yeah, that's true."

"So where would the original specifications for

the tank be? Would they be hand drawn?"

"They would be. They would most likely be in here." Roger led Maddy to a tall cabinet with wide drawers – a flat file. "See, here's the drawer." 'Whale – 1992' was on the label in a neat but faded draftsman's hand. Roger pulled open the drawer. It was empty. "Woah. That would be a breach. Even the drafting is worth a lot of money. It must be here somewhere…"

"May I use his computer to go online for a second? I never got a chance to check my email this morning… I mean, while you look for the whale drawings…"

Roger was profoundly distracted by the revelation of the missing drafting. He nodded and then started looking in each drawer systematically. Maddy sat down at Richard York's desk and tapped the computer awake. She quickly opened Richard York's email and scanned for a folder that might give some sort of clue to his movements. Nothing leapt out. She thought for a second. It would take several weeks to assemble the materials and construct the tank, so she scanned outgoing mail for the period of two weeks to a month prior. Like many people, Richard York had not cleaned out or organized his Sent mail in a while. There were still emails from that period sitting in the Sent folder. Maddy scanned for those that had attachments. After clicking through a dozen emails, she found one with a large pdf attached. She clicked on the attachment and after a tense moment while the computer opened the large file – and Roger continued banging around - she was rewarded with computer drafted drawings of the large tank. Richard York must have re-drafted the original drawings and then emailed them to… the address made Maddy jump.

sborodin@internationalx.rus

XXXII

Jimmy stumbled up the Filbert Steps.

This was a bad idea, he thought as he finally sat down about half way up. His head was swimming. It might have been from exhaustion – it had, after all been another sixteen hour work day, after the forty hour day he had the two days before. It might have been from the increasing fog of depression that was building around him. But it was most likely from the three martinis he drank at the Fog City while he picked at his crab cakes and Caesar salad.

And the four shots of Lagavulin he had at the dive bar around the corner after Gareth told him to go home.

Dumb ass. He was mad at himself for feeling so sorry for himself. So what if the other guy's a billionaire? So what if he's young, good looking and on the cover of Wired Magazine. I could still take him...

Wait. What was that again?

The lights of the Bay stopped swirling around him. The cool night air was starting to work its magic. His head began to clear and he had the sudden impression that he was on the verge of a breakthrough. On the cover of a magazine...

He pulled out his BlackBerry and went to Wired.com. On the home page was no one other than Sasha Borodin, boy wonder, looking for all the world like King of the Fucking Universe. And for all the world like the guy on the thumb-drive, and the guy in the passport photo. Jesus.

Jimmy's heart began to flip. He pounded away at his little keyboard.

Get out of there.

Now.

XXXIII

It was an outstanding dinner, Carlos had to admit. And he began to find Sergei much more charming than he had first figured him for. He might really have a way with the ladies after all, thought Carlos as Sergei regaled him with stories of his exploits in Afghanistan back in the early Eighties, and darkly humorous anecdotes about the local underworld figures around them. The only one who escaped Sergei's dry wit was Konstantin Ranevsky. Carlos pointed this out.

"Because there is so little to tell. Either he's the smartest one of the bunch, or he's very carefully protected by someone who's extremely powerful. We can pin nothing on him, as much as we speculate. We're just looking for anything we can find, or for him to trip up somewhere where the local authorities might be more... interested."

"Can you tail him? Follow him out of the country?"

"With what manpower? I mean, you're looking at it. Well, that's not strictly true, we've got a dozen people in our office here, but, as you can see, there's a lot to keep track of, and what with budget cuts..."

"But wouldn't the insurance companies rather kick in a few million to keep you guys funded than several hundred million to meet their obligations?"

"You would think so, but insurance companies are weird. If they really want someone or something, they prefer to work with independent contractors rather than pan-governmental agencies. And they never settle for the insured amount." A deep Russian Sigh. "The world is complicated."

The two men stared at their mostly finished bottle of vodka. Carlos was once again feeling no pain. Sergei leaned back into their booth and lit another cigarette.

"So what more can I do for you? I'm not sure I understand your interest in these creeps. Francois was vague as to what you were really looking for."

"I'm looking for the people who committed three different crimes in one night in San Francisco. There are bizarre signatures that point to a Russian connection, and point to a unifying element behind them." Carlos then regaled Sergei with the sequence of events of the previous Sunday night/Monday morning. Sergei pursed his lips then gestured to the waiter. After placing a quick order in Russian, he turned to Carlos.

"You know Sherlock Holmes?"

"Of course. My coworker and I joke about him all the time."

"You know how he makes reference often to a 'three pipe problem'?"

"Um, I think so…" Carlos liked Sherlock Holmes and all, but wouldn't ever consider himself an aficionado like Maddy.

"This is a three whisky problem."

Oh, Jeez, thought Carlos. It's amazing this guy is still alive.

"Seriously," continued Sergei, only just aware that Carlos didn't get the joke, "it's obvious that there are so many points of similarity. To my mind, however, it seems like there are just as many points of difference. As much as there are indications that the same person or group of persons were behind the crimes, it seems to me that there are distinct differences between the styles of the crimes."

"How so?" Carlos grew more alert. Two whiskys arrived. "You know, I really don't..."

"It's good. American Bourbon. You'll like it. Not like Scotch." Carlos sniffed it. It smelled like caramel. He took a sip. Not bad – and then the burn at the top of his chest... whew. Sergei went on. "You've got three events: the theft of the killer whale, with a head substituted. There's a level of sophistication to this crime, involving much in the way of logistical acumen. And a ruthlessness, certainly, but with a certain... élan. The second event, the shifting of the statues, the... Goddesses you call them? This shows a dark sense of humor, and shares the same outré quality as the first, but there is nothing so violent. All things considered, it's not a complicated affair, just daring. The third event, the theft of the Rublyev and the murder of the priest, is brutal and unsophisticated in its execution. But it still took some knowledge, advanced planning and sophisticated taste."

"So what are you saying?"

"I'm saying that it's as if one person had a single vision for all three crimes, but then had different people carry them out, each in their own... idiom. And whoever planned this, it seems they knew the individual personality of each actor."

Carlos's eyes got wide. Sergei had nailed it. He felt Sergei's hypothesis to be true. It would explain so much. He then had an inspiration. He pulled out his phone.

"Okay, check this out. Here's the passport photo of a suspect in all of this. He was on the same plane as the assistant to the artist behind the killer whale. The assistant died mysteriously – in the same manner as whoever it was whose head ended up in the tank." He showed it to Sergei. Sergei looked at the photo, raised an eyebrow, blew smoke out of the side of his mouth and gestured at the mirror. Carlos looked into the mirror and the pieces fell into place. The passport photo was of Konstantin Ranevsky.

Shit.

No doubt about it. It was just that the photo showed a clean cut young man, with his hair neat and wearing a tie. Ranevsky, in his natural element, was scruffy, with disheveled hair. But the eyes were the same. Pale green.

"But wait, there's more." Carlos showed Sergei the image that was generated by the pixilated, binary code. After a moment's hesitation, and a look again at the mirror into the corner booth, Sergei shook his head.

"Not the same guy."

"Could have fooled me."

"Perhaps that was the intention, although whoever was behind the images was taking a chance – not every police department has the intuition to discover the meaning behind this. This all could have gone unnoticed."

"We found it completely by chance, to be honest," said Carlos, downplaying his role in the discovery.

"Then whoever did this is a gambler, wouldn't you think?"

Carlos, who often enjoyed being the smartest guy in the room, was really impressed by Sergei. Or maybe it was just the bottle of vodka and the glass of whisky that he had consumed in the last hour and a half. "So not the same guy?" he asked.

"No. Look at the eyes. There's an intensity that our boy in the corner doesn't have, not that he isn't intense. I think 'madness' is a better word. The look is familiar to me... wait... wait..." Sergei shook his head. Then he started up. "Google something for me. Repin..."

"How do you spell that?"

"R-E-P-I-N. And in the search type also 'Ivan the Terrible'."

Carlos did so. The Google image popped up. It was a horrific scene that opened up on his little screen.

"The original painting is life size."

"Jesus." The small version was chilling enough. "What has just happened?" Carlos was staring at a man with wild, insane eyes, clutching desperately and despairingly at a younger man with blood flowing from a horrible wound on his head.

"Ivan the Terrible. That's him holding his son, whom he has just murdered in a fit of madness."

"You weren't kidding about Russian families. Whew..." said Carlos shaking his head. "But you're right about the eyes. The guy in the image has the same look in his eyes. Jesus," he said again and shivered.

At that moment, out of the corner of their eyes, they became aware of a stirring in the corner booth. Ranevsky was climbing out. Carlos thought for a second that he was leaving, but his entourage remained lounging around.

"He's going to take a leak," said Carlos in a whisper.

"So?"

"I do some of my best work in men's rooms," said Carlos with a wink. This wasn't true – Carlos wasn't the promiscuous type - but he enjoyed the look of surprise on Sergei's face. "I'll be back." Carlos hesitated for a second, then pulled out most of the cash in his wallet and handed it to Sergei. "Or maybe not. Just in case I take a detour. Just be sure to get the receipt, okay?"

Sergei palmed something into Carlos's hand as they made the exchange. "Just in case you take a detour." He squeezed Carlos's hand so that the small object poked hard into his palm. "Shove it up your ass."

"What?!" And here Carlos thought they had been getting along so well.

"Or you could swallow it. Whichever you prefer. Just do it, okay?"

Carlos figured it out, blew Sergei a kiss and headed towards the men's room. Sergei just nonchalantly turned his head and gestured to the waiter for two more whiskys.

XXXIV

The doors to the conference room flew open, causing Maddy to jump. She closed out of everything on Richard York's computer as quickly as possible, and stood up at attention. Donovan Hirsch burst into the studio, highly agitated. He was followed by two men in trench coats, one of whom was tucking a notepad into his coat pocket. The interview was obviously over.

"Next time you make such a suggestion, make it to my legal counsel. Please leave," said Hirsch brusquely. "I don't have time for this – I have another meeting in five minutes."

"We'll be back, I'm afraid, sir," said the man with the notepad. "There are still a few questions…"

"Just get the fuck out! And bring a warrant with you, next time."

Maddy was impressed how cowed the two men were by Donovan Hirsch. They scooted out of the studio and she could hear their footsteps clanging down the metal staircase.

"What the fuck do you want?" He was looking right at Maddy. Jesus, he was ferocious. "Oh. Right." Complete shift of gears. "Glad you could stop by. Would you like something to drink? Some tea, coffee? Gin?"

"Uh, um, a cup of tea would be nice?" Maddy was almost wincing in fear.

"Mia…"

Mia was right on it – didn't have to ask twice. Whew. He's got them all really well trained, thought

Maddy.

"Sorry about all that. They were so clumsy right now. Pigs." Donovan Hirsch was just old enough to be of the generation that still called the police pigs. "How are you today? Did Roger show you around?"

"I just got a glimpse of the... the studio." It was odd calling such an enormous operation a 'studio.' "The sperm whale – what a fascinating idea."

"Nah, it'll just piss a whole bunch of people off. Nothing to it, really. Come on, let's see how they're getting on." Donovan Hirsch flashed a wicked smile and took Maddy by the arm. Mia came up and gave Maddy a glass with tea in it, supported by a metal holder with a handle.

"I've never had tea served this way," Maddy said.

"It's the right way to serve tea – Russian. Strong, with plenty of sugar in it."

Maddy sipped the tea and was surprised at the sweetness. It felt good, especially as they passed back out onto the balcony into the unheated main space.

"I understand you are of Russian heritage," said Maddy.

"A reasonably well-kept secret," replied Hirsch. "Dmitri Fyodorovich Herskovin at your service. Although I haven't been called that since I was a boy."

"How did you end up in England? You don't have much of an accent... or at least a Russian one."

"I came over young enough. Kids are natural mimics, so if you put them in a new environment when they're young enough, they'll pick it all up. I ended up in the East End, so I picked up a bit of a cockney, much to my parents' chagrin."

"When did you come over?"

"1961. My father was stationed in Berlin. KGB, to be honest – a bit of a scandal, really. But his heart was never in it, and he had wind of the Wall being built before almost anyone else knew of it. He was smart enough for us to be on the western side the day it went up. A fairly routine defection. He was just high enough up in the Bureau hierarchy to be valuable to MI6, so we ended up here. I was nine at the time.

"It was a pretty raw deal, though. After his debriefing, he was given a British passport, a few thousand pounds and shown the door. The arrogance of the British, assuming that simply being allowed to live in England – a 'free country' - was compensation enough for the pain of never seeing his homeland again, and uprooting his family. It was a hard go. Not many people in London were comfortable with Russians about in the Sixties. It was a struggle to get by. He had always been a pretty good mechanic, so he eventually found work for a fellow émigré fixing lorries. My mum worked as a charwoman. This after having been a member of the elite class within the Soviet Sphere of Influence."

"Is he still alive?"

"Yeah. I set him up in a nice place – up in Oxford. Spends most of his time in the garden or in the library. He likes the rhythm of a college town. My mum, she's no longer with us..."

"Oh, I'm sorry. So how did you end up where you are now?"

"I was a pretty good pure artist as a boy – could draw and paint with the best of them back then - and I ended up at the Royal Academy on scholarship. I came of age when irony started to mean something to the average person. The world was so profoundly fucked up then, and with my Russian dark sense of humor, I guess I saw things differently from many of my contemporaries. Made a sensation early on, and built on it from there."

Now 'Capitalism at Work' started to make sense, thought Maddy. Donovan Hirsch was just 'sticking it to the Man.' And making a killing in the process.

They had worked their way down to the main floor. A buzzer sounded and a large engine came to life. Maddy saw the chains on the harness around the whale go taut and an enormous shudder could be felt. Slowly, the whale rose out of the tank, leaving a remarkably small amount of liquid remaining. The room was suddenly filled with an overpowering stench of formaldehyde.

"You'll want to put on a mask," said Hirsch knowingly, and he handed one to Maddy. The whale was then surrounded by half a dozen rolling ladders with platforms, as if it were a jet plane that had arrived at an airstrip. Large sheets of plastic with graphic patterns were then pinned to the whale and the tattoo artists went to work.

"How has this project been funded?" asked Maddy, her voice sounding strange from within the mask.

"Commission from a private collector, who has graciously allowed for a single public viewing in Los Angeles prior to taking possession."

"Wow. This must be one very expensive undertaking."

"From start to final delivery, it's about three million in expenses. Add my percentage and you've got a six million pound piece of contemporary art."

Not bad, thought Maddy. Three million pounds in the bank for essentially waving his arms about. "So this private collector…"

"Client confidentiality prohibits me from revealing their name."

"Right." Maddy was feeling more at ease with Donovan Hirsch, so she broached the subject. "Do you have any theories regarding the disappearance of the killer whale?"

"Those arseholes had a theory that Richard had something to do with it. Why would he do such a thing?"

For the money, thought Maddy. It must be pretty depressing watching the modern equivalent of P. T. Barnum making all the money while you did all the work.

"Would there be any advantages to you, or the owner of the killer whale, for this to happen?"

Donovan Hirsch looked at Maddy darkly through the goggles of his mask. He gestured for her to return with him upstairs. Once they reached the confines of the conference room, and Donovan Hirsch had shut the doors, he took off his mask and Maddy did the same.

"I'm sorry to offend you – it seems that I did," she said. "It's just that so much of the appeal of your work is its provocative quality. This event would add a certain notoriety to the piece. Sort of like the theft of the Mona Lisa."

"You're much sweeter than those sons of bitches who were here just now, so I'll answer you. But they suggested something along the same lines." He sighed. "Yes, there might actually be some financial advantage to the owner of the piece, should it ever be recovered. Any time something ends up on the news, it increases interest, and naturally, the value of a piece. And I guess that having my name in the news so prominently attached to such an event also adds interest in my other work. It could be a boon, actually. Does that make me a suspect?"

Maddy smiled. "We prefer the expression 'Person of Interest'."

"We?"

"Reporters. I'm a reporter in my 'day job.' You would definitely be a person of interest. In a good way, I mean," she added with a winning smile. More flies with honey than with vinegar, girl, she reminded herself.

"Thank you. I guess." Donovan Hirsch looked doubtful.

"It's just the way the world works, of course. People want to know who stands most to gain from such a crime. We could try it on in a different way: Do you know anyone who might want to harm your reputation, or to damage your work in any way?"

"Do I have any enemies, you mean?" Donovan Hirsch ran his hand over his stubbly scalp. "Where do I start? You don't make an omelet without breaking a few eggs, right? I've made an awful lot of omelets. Comes with the Avant Garde territory."

At that moment, a gentle knock was heard on the door and Mia stuck her head into the room.

"They're here," she said.

"Right." Donovan Hirsch turned to Maddy. "You planning on sticking around for this? You're welcome to watch."

"Thank you, that's why I'm here," she replied. It's not really, she thought. I'm here to help catch a ruthless international killer. But there could be a good story in this, too – maybe a left column article when she got home. And for all she knew, she might be having dinner with a ruthless international killer later that evening.

So there was still hope.

XXXV

It hurts to be alive, thought Jimmy. Just his luck that he had been so out of it that he forgot to close the blinds when he got home. The morning sun smashed him in the face through his east-facing sliding glass doors. He could barely open his eyes, they were dry and scratchy, and the sharp sun cut into his brain when he tried.

Or was it the shag carpeting pressed up against his face?

If I *ever* have the great idea of drowning my sorrows again, I'll just shoot myself, instead. It would hurt so much less. And be a lot less expensive. He looked down at his suit, rumpled beyond any sort of domestic repair.

After peeling himself up off the floor, he went through the rituals of recovery. Four Advils, a brutally strong cup of coffee, and the longest shower ever. By the time he looked himself in the mirror after toweling off, he figured he had climbed half way back up the evolutionary ladder towards being human again. The eyes were still bloodshot, but that's what sunglasses were for.

There was still a sharp pang in his heart, though. Where was that girl? He hadn't heard from her since their abortive, awkward call nine hours before. No response to his email. She must be having too much fun, he thought ruefully. So much for professionalism.

His BlackBerry was full of other news, however. Jose had worked late, as had The Man Without a Face.

And Francois had responded to the question of the fingerprint.

*   *   *

"I don't see how it's possible," Jimmy said to Jose. They were back at Jose's workstation at Building 606. "I mean, how do you stay awake all night doing this stuff?"

"If I said 'drugs' you wouldn't tell anybody would you?" replied Jose a little sheepishly.

Jimmy could only roll his eyes. "I didn't hear that, okay? Jeez, you kids."

They turned their attention to the results Jimmy held in his hand. "And I don't see how *this* is possible, either. How does the same guy be outside of Denver at 3:31 in the morning and be on top of 580 California at 4:00 in the morning? Smoking the same horrible cigarette? Isn't that physically impossible?" His head hurt so badly that he really just wanted to lie down on the floor and press his forehead against the polished concrete.

"It would be. But it wasn't the same morning. Denver at 3:31 in the morning was 3:31 Sunday morning, remember? 4:00 in the morning in San Francisco was *Monday* morning. Do you need to take a nap or something?"

"I would kill for a nap."

"You look really terrible. What's up with you?"

"Just couldn't sleep last night. Resorted to drink."

"Asians and alcohol, man. You guys should just give it a rest. Leave the drinking to big Mexican assholes like me."

"Next time, I'll call you and you can be my stunt double, okay? Now what have we got?"

"Well, the cigarettes are a match. At least, they came from the same batch of reconstituted tobacco, and the ink on the imprint is composed of the same vegetable dyes."

"So the same guy was in both places. That's cool. I think," said Jimmy.

"It would seem that way, but we've got an interesting deal with the DNA found on the two cigarettes. The match is close enough that even a few years ago we might have said it was the same. But it's not. It's off by a few percentage points. Close but no cigar." There was a pause. "I guess I just made a joke…" Jose rubbed his chin thoughtfully.

"So what does that tell us?"

"It tells us that the two smokers are related, but not the same guy," rasped a voice from behind them. The Man Without a Face was leaning against the main work table, looking – as much as one could tell without any facial features to speak of – really tired. "Most likely brothers – with this level of DNA matching, most likely fraternal twins."

"Shit. That would explain more than a few things."

"It doesn't explain how more than one person could put up with that horrible tobacco," said Jose with a grimace.

"Weirdly, it does. With so much of the same genetic material, they would have virtually identical taste buds. If one could hack it, the other could, too."

"Okay," said Jose, "but riddle me this, Batman. Do twins have the same fingerprints?"

"No, they don't. Their fingerprints at birth would be extremely similar – most of the metrics would be identical. But not all, and within a few years, distinguishing characteristics would begin to creep in through environmental factors. It really is true – no two fingerprints are the same."

"Then check this out." Jose brought up two fingerprints on his monitors. "What *is* physically impossible - and brace yourself for this - is that the same guy who left a fingerprint on the door to the rooftop at 580, by all accounts at sometime prior to 4:00 Monday morning, wielded the candlestick at approximately the same time at the Green Street Church. Now if you can explain that, I'll kiss your butt and call you Sherlock." Jose superimposed the fingerprints and found a perfect match.

"Wait. What?" Jimmy was starting to see double.

"Thumbprint found at the scene at the little Russian Church matches the thumbprint your friend Carlos found on the doorknob."

"Well, that's complicated..." Jimmy rubbed the bridge of his nose. "Now add this into the mix." Jimmy showed Jose the email from Francois. The thumbprint was, in fact, in the Interpol database. "Just no name attached to it - or rather, it was assigned a number. Was found at two different robberies that occurred the same day within hours of each other. One, a smash and grab at a high-end boutique in Abu Dhabi, the other at a Cartier in Paris. The one in Abu Dhabi was a little out of control - the man who was behind the counter had his face smashed into pieces through the case. The photos were pretty gruesome."

"Sounds like a similar MO to the church killing," said Jose. "Pretty psychotic."

"Millions in jewels taken both times."

"Where did the jewels end up, anyone know?" asked The Man Without a Face.

"Moscow - some of them, at any rate."

"So Pink Panthers it is, then," said Jose.

"So it would seem, Watson."

"But the same day? Again, that doesn't seem possible. No way someone could get from Paris to Abu Dhabi the same day - at least not in any conventional way..."

"Think private jet?"

"What's up with that?"

"Still waiting for the results of Detective Rogers' inquiries in the Denver area."

"And if you factor in a two hour time difference between Abu Dhabi and Paris," said The Man Without a Face, "what looks like two crimes committed within, say, four hours of each other is really two crimes committed six hours apart. A private jet could cover the ground in half the time."

"Shit. That's true," said Jimmy rubbing his face. "I'm having trouble with my days of the week right now, let alone hours. What day is it, anyway?"

"Wednesday," said Jose. "I think."

All three men looked doubtful. After a minute, Jimmy went over to a whiteboard that stood in the middle of the room. He drew three columns with the black marker. The first was labeled 'Killer Whale.' The second was labeled 'Icon.' The third was labeled 'Goddesses.' He then picked up a red marker.

"So we know that the same guy who was on the roof of 580 California on Monday morning was also the same guy who was at the church. Let's call this guy 'Mr. Red'."

"Cool, just like Reservoir Dogs." Jose's favorite movie.

"Right." Jimmy took a green marker. "Now we have a guy who was in Denver making the switch of the tank with the whale for the tank with the head. Mr. Green."

"Wait, why isn't he Mr. Red, too?"

"We just went through this. The guy in Denver's DNA on the cigarette isn't the same as the DNA found on the cigarette at 580. Doesn't mean that he wasn't in both - or all three - places, for all we know, and it actually looks like he was. All we know for certain is that Mr. Green and Mr. Green are the same guy. Whose face seems to be on the thumb drive found in the tank and at the church."

"Wait. Why isn't it Mr. Red's face on the thumb drive?"

"At this rate, I suppose it could be, but then we have to determine if the placement of the thumb drives was done by the perpetrator, or by someone trying to identify the perpator."

"Woah," said Jose. "Why would someone go to all this trouble? Unless..."

"Unless what?"

"Unless he was afraid of the perpetrator, but took these risks anyway, but with enough plausible deniability – and ingenuity – that the perpetrator wouldn't know for sure who did it."

"Thank you for making this case even more complicated," sighed Jimmy.

"Hey, just rolling with it, you know?" pleaded Jose.

Jimmy then pulled out the blue marker. "We now have Mr. Blue, who was on the plane to London and who poisoned Richard York. Who then got off in Denver and disappeared."

"Wait. Why isn't he Mr. Red or Mr. Green?" Poor Jose.

"Because we don't know which of them it was. For all we know it's someone in disguise, using the photo with the false passport."

"Well, he would be the same guy as the guy behind the tank trick. The Polonium-210. Nice trick, by the way, getting that onto a plane."

"It wouldn't be that hard if he was diabetic, or pretending to be..." said The Man Without a Face, rubbing his chin, looking at the white board. "All it takes to get a needle on board is for it to be labeled with a prescription label. Should be easy enough for someone who could get Polonium-210 in the first place."

"The Sixty-Four Thousand Dollar Question is: is he the same guy who's on the cover of Wired Magazine?" Jimmy pulled out a copy that he bought on his way into the lab.

All three men gathered around. Jose whistled.

"Jesus. If not, then our Silicon Valley billionaire has a serious doppleganger. Why hasn't he be brought in for questioning?

"Because he's in London, dancing at super exclusive night clubs," said Jimmy with a sour look on his face.

"How do you know that?" asked The Man Without a Face.

"I've got my sources. Let's just say Mr. Borodin is under surveillance."

"It's like a fucking Easter egg hunt," said Jose, scratching his head looking at the different colors on the white board. "This makes no sense, whatsoever."

"It starts to, when you do this…" Jimmy looked around for another color. There wasn't one, so he just grabbed the black marker. He drew circles around the Whale and the Goddesses and drew a line between them. "These two items touch the same man, Ivan Orkin. He was the donor for the purchase of the whale, and he is the new tenant in the penthouse suite at 580. Looks like someone was trying to jerk his chain, maybe."

"So how is the icon involved?"

"It's Russian, that's the only line we have for now."

"Unless it's also something that Orkin wanted, or knew about."

"Or," said The Man Without a Face, "the person behind these crimes just really wanted to add this into the bargain. It could be a red herring."

At that moment, Jimmy's phone buzzed. He picked it up.

"Hey Dave. Mind if I put you on speaker? I've got my forensics team here."

"No problem," came Detective Dave Rogers' tinny voice over the phone. "I've got some news for you. Your instincts were correct. We found a flight plan out of Colorado Springs for a Gulfstream V on its way to London Stanfield. Departed less than two hours after the plane from SFO to Heathrow landed at DIA. Registered to Infinity Corporation out of Sunnyvale."

There was a pause as it sunk in.

"Um, Dave, do you read Wired Magazine, by any chance?"

"No, but my boy does – he's a total gearhead. Why?"

"Well, you've heard of 'To Infinity and Beyond!' haven't you?"

"Who hasn't? Buzz Lightyear."

"Well, yes and no. Infinity, the new search engine. They must have made some deal with Disney and Pixar for the rights to use that catchphrase – now that I think of it, it would be interesting to know if Steve Jobs was on the board of Infinity before he died. Bet he was angling to give the boys at Google a run for their money."

"It's a jungle out there," quipped Jose under his breath.

"Anyway, the Founder and CEO of Infinity is a dead ringer for the guy in the passport photo. And the fact that a plane flying on our projected route is owned by Infinity makes me extremely interested in knowing more about him."

"Jeez. Nothing like a killer with means," said Dave Rogers. "If what you're saying is true, this would be as sensational a case as you could find."

And as sensational a news story as one could find, too, thought Jimmy. No wonder I haven't heard from Maddy. She's going to be the next Barbara Walters if it kills her.

And it just might.

XXXVI

"Dude. Are you scoping my dick?"

Ranevsky turned to look at Carlos. For a moment he couldn't help himself and his eyes did, indeed, rove southward. Carlos smiled.

"Just kidding, man. Totally yanking your chain." There was a second when Carlos thought that he might, in fact, die right there in that restroom. Then Ranevsky laughed. Both men zipped up their flies, flushed their urinals and headed towards the sink. Ranevsky had a bemused look on his face.

"Where you from? I haven't seen you before." His English was excellent. Only a hint of an accent. Carlos looked into Ranevsky's pale green eyes in the mirror and sighed inwardly. Ruggedly cute. And he had a feline smoothness and confidence in his movements, like a panther. A real panther, not just a pink one. But Carlos' gaydar was sweeping all sectors and there was no ping. Totally straight.

"From San Francisco."

"Ah."

"Ah, what?"

"Ah. That explains why you're so comfortable talking with strange men in restrooms. You are gay, yes?"

"Hey now. I wasn't hitting on you or anything..."

"It's cool." Ranevsky was making minute adjustments to the spikes in his hair. "So why are you here?"

"Working on a story for my paper back home." Carlos figured that the more of the truth he told, the more he might actually be believed.

"Which paper?" Ranevsky was interested. Huh.

"The Clarion..."

"The Clarion? That's a famous paper. What's your story?" Ranevsky turned to look at Carlos directly.

"Well, I'm still trying to pull it all together. I came with one idea in mind, then I heard something interesting, and I'm thinking of following that lead, instead."

"I love San Francisco. Most beautiful city in the world." A hesitation. Then, was it bragging? Or a confidence? "I was just there."

"Really? That's cool. Where do you stay when you're there? You seem to be something of a high roller, if you don't mind my saying..."

Another hesitation. "I've got some family there. It's a nice place. Lots of room. Out of the way a bit."

"Cool. I have to tell you, St. Petersburg is pretty beautiful, too, though. And this restaurant – nothing better in SF. I just had a killer venison."

"This place? It's okay. Too many crooks hanging out here, you know?" Ranevsky smiled at his inside joke. "So what did you hear that made you change your story?"

Carlos was now facing the moment that separates the men from the boys. He decided to man up.

"The Queen of Spades."

There it was again. It was as if the lights flickered and the wind blew through the room. Actually the wind *was* blowing through the room. The door had just been pushed open. It was one of Ranevsky's entourage. He spoke quickly in Russian. Something to the effect of Dude, what the fuck? Everything okay?

Ranevsky gestured for him to get out. The other

man looked at Carlos, then at Ranevsky with a bit of the You're not turning gay on me look, then departed. When Ranevsky turned his gaze back to Carlos, Carlos thought he saw Ranevsky's eyes turn color briefly. Almost black, then back to green. Very scary.

But Ranevsky smiled. "You want some dessert?"

"What?"

"The desserts here are too fussy, and I'm bored with this place. And my friends. Let's go get some ice cream. I'm buying."

XXXVII

Maddy crawled towards her bed. She was exhausted, and the jet lag was catching up with her once again. She realized ruefully that she had lived a pretty sheltered life until recently. She hadn't even ever left her own time zone. Her parents were not travelers – her father extremely reluctant to be more than a few hours' drive from his office, and her mother perfectly content to move through her tight little geography of yoga class, the nail salon, the Balboa Bay Club, Nordstrom and the white wine cooler in the fridge. The only reason Maddy had a passport at all was because she had hoped to spend a quarter abroad during her Junior year at the Stanford school in Madrid. She was thwarted, however, by her parents' panic when Al Qaeda-inspired terrorists blew up the Madrid subway, killing almost two hundred people and injuring a few thousand, a few weeks before she was to depart.

Now she was struggling for consciousness, her world completely day-for-night. She had also experienced a very stress-filled afternoon and was emotionally drained. The meeting between Donovan Hirsch and the team from LA MOCA was fraught. The director of the museum was pretty blunt – the whale was larger than originally anticipated, and the costs of the installation, let alone the transportation, had sky-rocketed. The technical director had come to the conclusion that the only way to get the piece into the museum was to take off the roof and lower the whale in by crane. It was an additional half-million dollar expense. Donovan Hirsch fulfilled his enfant terrible billing and blew a gasket causing the hair of everyone in the room to be blown back. Maddy found it remarkable that he could care so little about what anyone thought of him. He certainly gave no indication that he was aware of Maddy's presence in the room.

"What the fuck is this?" he stormed. "It's not like one goes and finds a white sperm whale of precise dimensions. It is what it is. Are you telling me that you still want to play a part on the world's great art stage and not be able to accommodate the great art that's being created? Pikers! Jesus! What the fuck do you come in here and expect me to do? Cut the fucker in half so it will fit in through your doors? It's been done! We're all over that."

No one breathed. Everyone looked to the museum director to crumble. But he took off his glasses and set them precisely in front of him on the conference room table.

"We'll put the tank in the plaza in front of the museum. It should fit. Ted?" Ted was the technical director. He looked at the plans of the building and pulled out a scale rule. Although the plaza wasn't on the drawing, the frontage of the museum was able to be measured, and it could more than accommodate the seventy foot tank. "Light the shit out of it at night. Put a canopy structure up over it. Whatever."

Donovan Hirsch looked at the director for a second. Suddenly, and almost as terrifyingly, he laughed out loud. "Fucking brilliant! Couldn't ask for a better marquee, or a bigger statement in LA. I like it. John," he stabbed a finger at the director, "you are one clever motherfucker. How would you like to come and work for me? Ha ha ha!"

After a scene like that, Maddy felt she might not be cut out for the high art world, after all. Once all of the issues were resolved, the crew from LA crept out, almost bowing and walking backwards as they did so. For a moment, Maddy was alone with Donovan Hirsch. Once again, he switched gears on a dime and became quiet, almost reflective.

"Takes a lot of energy to be me," he confided in a tired and soft voice, as he pulled a bottle of Bushmill's out of a cupboard and poured himself a large drink. "So many bureaucrats, so many small thinkers. I have to continually kick them all in the arse to get things done. If I hadn't staged that tantrum back there, nothing would have been done. A huge retrospective, millions of pounds worth of art, all being managed by buffoons." He sighed and settled into a chair. "What do you think of the contemporary art world now?"

"More than enough to write about. This is all as intense as any mystery or gothic horror story."

Donovan Hirsch swallowed his whisky and set the glass gently down on the table. "What's art without suffering?"

"I don't know… perhaps it's just beautiful? And wouldn't that be okay?"

Donovan Hirsch smiled. He got up and went to a cabinet at the end of the room. He removed a little key from his pocket and unlocked a drawer. He pulled out a small piece of thick paper. He set it in front of Maddy. It was a simple, but beautiful water color. A boat on the ocean, tossed by a storm.

"It's gorgeous," whispered Maddy. "Did you paint this?"

"Jesus, no. I could paint, but not like that. It's a Turner. A water color study for 'The Shipwreck of the Minotaur.' It's the most beautiful thing I own. But do you see all those specks in the water? On the full-size painting, those are men drowning. An artist takes such suffering, such drama, an act of destruction, and makes it beautiful. The dichotomy is what makes it art. The disconnect between the horror of the event, and the natural beauty surrounding it that caused it.

"Art takes pain."

Maddy nodded her head. The shift of subject was almost inevitable. "I'm sorry about your assistant," Maddy said softly. Donovan Hirsch looked into his glass and sighed.

"I still haven't come to grips with it. I will miss him terribly."

"Did the police tell you how he died?"

"They told me it was a heart attack. But that it was suspicious circumstances. They wouldn't reveal any more than that. Apparently, his body is still in Denver pending further investigation. Must be horrible for poor David."

"David?"

"His... partner. I can't imagine what he must be going through."

Maddy paused, then channeled her inner Barbara Walters. "Mr. Hirsch..."

"Donovan, please."

"Donovan... I have some inside knowledge of the case. I have," here she hesitated again, "... a friend who is working with the authorities in Denver. Have you ever heard of Polonium-210?"

Donovan Hirsch looked at her - confused for a moment, then recovering. "Why is that familiar? I seem to recall something about a former Russian spy who was..." He stopped. His eyes grew wide.

"Yes. You're right. Richard York was injected with Polonium-210. The only people who have any history of using this as a method of assassination are the FSB. Your father used to work for them, back when they were the KGB. Do you think the link is coincidental?"

For a man with such profound energy and self-confidence, Donovan Hirsch suddenly collapsed into himself, crumpling up in his chair.

"I don't know," he said. He looked at Maddy with real pain in his eyes. "I'm sorry, Miss Stevenson. I think I need to end our interview. Roger will drive you back. Good day."

He then poured himself another drink and stared mournfully at the Turner.

* * *

As Maddy's head hit the pillow, she looked at the clock. It was 4:00 in the afternoon. She could sleep for an hour and a half – half a sleep cycle – order some coffee from room service, take another shower and get herself truly beautiful by the time Sasha was to collect her for the theatre. She hadn't even turned her computer on, she was so tired. Just as blissful oblivion took hold, she was jolted out of it by the hotel phone next to her head.

"This is not how it's done, young lady. Twenty-four hours on the ground without any communication at all? You better have some serious-ass excuse for leaving me in the dark for this long while I'm footing your bill. Cough it up or come back home."

Carey Portman had a way of kicking your ass even 9,000 miles away.

"I'm so sorry, Carey. To say it's been a whirlwind would be an understatement. I'm not sure I've slept since I got here. At least more than an hour."

"You're not there to party, if that's what you're doing," said Carey. How did she know?

"To be honest, Carey, I've had to do some partying to get to the bottom of the case. Part of the role."

"This better be good."

It *was* pretty good, actually. Once Maddy had downloaded Carey about the investigation so far, including the Polonium-210 poisoning of Richard York, the art auction, the deciphering of the thumb-drives, the potential involvement of two new members of the Bay Area's elite, including one who had become a virtual rock star in the Silicon Valley, partying with Prince William and Gwyneth Paltrow, and Donovan Hirsch with his own demons and his own KGB connection, Carey was uncharacteristically silent for a moment. Maddy could imagine her taking off her glasses, setting them carefully on her desk, and she braced herself.

"You two are incredible. You couldn't make this shit up, so you must be telling the truth. If it makes you feel any better, I haven't heard from Carlos, either. He's my next call."

God help him, thought Maddy.

"So I need this written up, names, places, dates, background, the whole ball of wax… On. My. Desk. In the next hour. Got that?"

"Yes, Ma'am," stammered Maddy. As she hung up the phone, she despaired of ever getting any sleep. A shower would just have to do. She called down to room service for some coffee, opened her laptop and got to work.

XXXVIII

As Jimmy pulled his car up in front of the little house in Oakland, it occurred to him that it had been a while since he'd been across the Bay. He had an old friend that he suddenly realized he hadn't visited in too long who lived just up the street. He would stop by after this interview.

"Hello Mrs. Richards," he said, taking the hand of the robust, light-skinned black woman who answered the door. "How is Darryl doing?"

"Please call me Agnetha. As well as could be expected. Sleeping a lot. Doctors have him on some serious medication – mostly to keep him from doing something stupid, that pig-headed fool of a man." The way she said it made Jimmy smile. It was obvious that she loved her husband, in spite of everything. Her attitude towards Darryl Richards reminded him of his parents. What was it about older couples that made them so feisty? Perhaps as they got older they realized both how frustrating the other person could be with all of their habits and idiosyncracies, and yet how much they needed them. Love. Huh.

"Thank you for allowing me to see him. Is he awake now?"

"Yeah, he's in his den. Getting a taste of day-time television. Thank god for ESPN – he's not much for Oprah. There's golf being played somewhere in the world, twenty-four hours a day." Agnetha Richards led Jimmy down a small, dark corridor lined with photos of what seemed like a hundred children and grandchildren. Large family. Jimmy smiled again.

Agnetha Richards showed him into a darkened room. Darryl Richards was reclining in a big, old leather chair watching the television. He was in a bathrobe, and he was holding a remote like a small scepter.

"Brought someone to see you," said his wife. She turned to Jimmy. "Can I get you anything?"

"No, ma'am, I'm fine," he replied.

"Don't get him too riled up, okay? We're trying to keep him calm for a while. All this ghost-story stuff..."

"I saw what I saw, woman," said Darryl hoarsely. "Get on with you and let me talk with the man." Agnetha Richards rolled her eyes theatrically and left Jimmy alone with Darryl.

"I'm glad to see you're home and doing okay," said Jimmy.

Darryl Richards rubbed his heart gently. "Been through it before. Ain't much to it." Actually, it looked like there was a lot to it. Darryl looked pretty grim. Jimmy reminded himself to watch his cholesterol.

"You okay to talk for a few minutes?"

"Sure. What can I help you with?"

"Well, you just said 'you saw what you saw.' What was that?"

"Damn creature turned and stared right at me."

"One of the Goddesses?"

"None other. Evil things, they are."

"Can you tell me precisely when you saw this?"

"Well, I start my mid-shift rounds at 4:00. Go to the top floor and work my way down. It takes a few minutes to get to the top, and I was up there for a few minutes before I saw it move. So maybe around 4:10 in the morning."

Jimmy looked at his notes, and wrote the time down.

"Did you see anything else before or after?"

"Not much after. Pretty much blacked out after that. There was something… caught my eye just before. Not sure if it was just one of the damn pigeons flapping in front of the lights, but there was a flash…"

"A flash… can you describe it any more than that?"

"Just an intense light. Saw it out of the corner of my eye. Maybe that's what made me turn to see the damn thing move. Jesus. Scared the crap out of me."

"Talk to me about access to the building. And the roof in particular. How would anyone get up there?"

"Without us noticing? Almost impossible. We've got cameras at all the entrances, and we'd know if any of the elevators was going up or down at that hour."

"Could someone enter the building during the day and hide somewhere? And then access the roof after hours?"

Darryl thought about it. "Could do. We've always got workmen going up and down during the day. A lot recently with the new tenant, and all. Pretty hard to track all of 'em. I suppose that's possible."

Jimmy knew it was possible – Carlos had done it.

"But the access to the roof is locked – at least from the inside. And they would have to get off the roof, too," continued Darryl. "No way they could have done that without Miles noticing."

"Cameras on the roof?"

"Yeah, but they're all pointed down towards the street – one on each corner."

"So they have blind spots at the penthouse level."

"Yeah. You can't see the Goddesses from the roof cameras. I mean, who would need to?"

Jimmy wondered if there was anyone who might have seen anything from the adjacent buildings. Perhaps a cleaning crew in an office across the way.

"It was foggy out that night?"

"It was. Could barely see the next building. Could just glimpse the near side of the Bay Bridge, but it was less foggy towards the East. North and West, well, pretty much thick as pea soup."

Making it even harder for someone in another building to see anything. Twenty-three floors up, no one would be paying any attention. Especially at that hour.

How was it done, and why was that fingerprint on that door?

"Anything else about that night that was unusual?"

"Just that the door to the penthouse was unlocked. Really unusual. It was as if someone had simply forgotten to lock up earlier, but that isn't likely."

Jimmy stood up and handed Darryl his card. "Please call me if you think of anything else. It doesn't have to be important. Could be the smallest thing. It would help a lot." He turned to the television. Sure enough, someone was tapping in for a birdie.

"Some tournament in Dubai. They got nice weather over there. I like golf. Relaxes me. Wish I could get out more myself." Darryl sighed. "I guess it's going to be a while until I can shoot a round."

"You take care of yourself..." Jimmy turned to go. Darryl called to him.

"Hey. You know a Damian Johnson? SFPD?"

"Old friend of mine. He's saved my bacon more than once," Jimmy smiled.

"Give him my best. Went to school together. He took the easy beat, over in the City. Tell him from me, real men work Oakland."

"I will," said Jimmy with a laugh.

*   *   *

"Oh, Jimmy! So good to see you, sweetheart!"

There are those smiles that are almost electric in their ability to shine light onto others. Clarice Bryant had one of them. Jimmy just had to give her a hug.

But he had to be careful about it. Clarice was as tiny as Agnetha was big. She was a little, bird-like woman of ninety-two. It had taken her a while to open the door, and she relied on her walker to keep her steady, but the energy she radiated, and her clear, bright eyes gave the lie to her age. As she opened the door, a big gray cat squirted out, rubbing up against Jimmy's ankles.

"Hey, Robin," said Jimmy, scratching the cat behind her ears. "You've gotten big." Robin gave him a few more rubs, purring away like a diesel locomotive, then got distracted by a bird in the yard. Instinct took over, and Robin was off.

"The place looks great," said Jimmy with no small amount of admiration as he took in the house. He had met Clarice the previous fall while working on the case of the Masked Avenger, and at that time her little old Victorian home in West Oakland was dilapidated and worn. Clarice had the vision, however, to recruit a group of homeless people to help her fix the place up, and provide them room down the street at another Victorian that was also looking better for the attention.

"Those kids are alright," she said, waving her hand. "But truth be told, it wouldn't have come together without Abe."

"Really?" Abe was an old wreck of a homeless former dockworker. Last Jimmy looked.

"Man just needed something useful to do. He's got skills. Rebuilt that house almost from scratch down the street. Works wonders with a saw and a hammer. And this place, after he got done with the sanding and finishing and painting – looks amazing. Best part of it, he doesn't drink anymore. When he isn't working here, he's down at the Mission helping in the kitchen."

"Pay it forward," said Jimmy with a smile. "Ms. Bryant, you are the Saint of West Oakland. Help a few folks out and they help others. I can feel the ripples radiating out from here. How's Charelle?"

"That girl's doing alright, although there's only so much one can do. As long as she keeps her strength up, she'll make it. Trick is to get her to eat. She fusses so about her figure. She's down at the Barnes and Noble – she pretty much runs the place. They made her Assistant Manager just last week. Sharp as a tack, that one, and she takes pretty good care of me."

Jimmy just shook his head. Charelle was a transvestite, would-be trans-sexual, Filipino runaway from the Central Valley who had contracted HIV. Not much hope there, except for Clarice Bryant who took her in, gave her a home, gave her a goal and gave her the kind of respect that few people would give someone like Charelle. Jimmy knew that Clarice knew all about Charelle, and yet she made no judgments. In Clarice Bryant's world, judgments only got in the way.

"Can I get you a lemonade?"

Jimmy hesitated, thinking that this really was meant to be a drive-by. But something made him want to stay and sit with Clarice for a bit. "Sure. Your lemonade is the best I know."

Clarice just clucked at him and went into the kitchen. Jimmy had a moment to take in her front parlor. It gleamed with fresh paint and refinished wood. On the wall were photographs of two large men – one obviously her deceased husband, who had a solid, rugged, earnest quality about him. He wore a MUNI bus-driver's uniform. The other man was younger, not much more than a boy from his face, and yet unbelievably almost a foot taller than the older man. The young man was wearing a football uniform, circa 1980, and had an intensity about him that was unsettling. He was Clarice's grandson, also now deceased. She would have been all alone in the world, having outlived everyone in her family, but she had adopted a new family and looked good for it.

"Here you go," she said as she came back into the parlor. Jimmy knew better than to try to help her – she was determined to be the best hostess, dang it.

"So how's that girl of yours?"

"Oh... she's fine. She's in London doing some research for a story and she's... she's been having a good time, and I really haven't heard much because of the time difference and I've been working long hours on this series of cases and..."

Clarice Bryant just looked at him like he was some sorry son-of-a-bitch.

"Now how long you gonna keep up with that crap, young man?"

Jimmy winced. "Mrs. Bryant, we could use you over at Interrogation Room Number One. No one is ever going to get away with telling you anything but the truth."

"So tell it, Detective Wang. And don't be sugar-coating anything for me. Seen too much and lived too long to need much of that."

And it poured out of Jimmy. His fears, his frustrations, his hopes. His tiredness and his longing. He actually teared up a little bit, which was something he never did. Chinese-American boys just didn't do that.

"Truth is, Mrs. Bryant, in less than two days I've gone from being secure and content to being miserable and anxious. I don't know what I want anymore."

Clarice Bryant looked at him.

"You're, what? Thirty? You're a good man. A young man, but a good one. She's darling. But she's how old? Twenty-three?"

"Twenty-four. Her birthday's coming up."

"She's lovely, but she's still a girl. She has no clue what she wants right now. And that's as it should be. Take it from one who knows, no one has any clue what they want or who they are until they're at least thirty. You might just have a clue, she certainly doesn't. And that's the natural order of things."

Jimmy felt strangely as if he were suddenly at an audience with Yoda or the Dalai Lama.

"So what's my role in all of this? Why am I so freaked out by her interest in some rich boy?"

"Don't it always seem to go, you don't know what you've got 'til it's gone… You're upset because you've started to fully realize how important she is to you. You probably didn't know it until now. And you're afraid of losing her. The more you fear losing her, the more she's going to feel as if she needs to be lost. Being lost doesn't have to mean you don't know where you are. It just means that you're letting yourself *be* where you are."

"What if I told you he's a murder suspect?"

"Girls like boys who are dangerous. Almost always have and always will. You got a bit of danger on you, and I'm sure that serves you well in this relationship. She's still pretty smart. I don't see her doing anything too stupid, do you?"

"So I shouldn't do anything?" Jimmy sighed.

"I didn't say that. You should do what you do. Is she in danger?"

"I think so."

"Then what do you do when something you love is in danger?"

"Protect it, I guess. Although she always gets mad at me when I do that."

"She just wants to be tough and feel that she's capable, and she's trying to find some balance in this relationship – you are, after all, older and have more under your belt. But that doesn't mean that she doesn't want you to be anyone other than who you are. You got together because you had a knack for looking out for her. As much as girls like boys who are dangerous, they really, deep down, want a boy who'll protect them. So do what you do, and be who you are. It'll work out…

"Or it won't."

"That's reassuring Mrs. B!" said Jimmy with a laugh.

"She's in London?"

"At last communication."

"Is the case in London?"

"Don't know for sure, although it's pointing that way. Could also be in St. Petersburg."

"Don't tell me… that little thing Carlos. He's not in Russia, is he?"

"Yes. He is. Couldn't stop him from going."

"Those two. Well, Mr. Detective Man, you best get on a plane. Looks like you might need to protect both of them."

XXXIX

Carlos was flying.

Almost literally. It wasn't the vodka, it wasn't the whisky. It was the purr of the Lamborghini as it blew through the late-night boulevards of St. Petersburg.

Nicest. Ride. Ever.

And it had that smell. There's a "new car" smell. And then there's a "rich car" smell. It was wonderful. Carlos thought that maybe a life of crime might be worth it.

But they were driving fast. Too fast for the width of the streets. Carlos was a little worried about being pulled over. He remembered Sergei's admonishment that there was a zero tolerance policy towards drunk driving, and he knew that Konstantin Ranevsky had a blood alcohol level of more than 0.00. But there was a confidence in the way Ranevsky drove that caused Carlos to reflect that almost everyone in St. Petersburg – certainly the police – knew who was behind the wheel of that car, and that no one would make a move to stop him. It probably was a good thing that it was a banana-yellow Lamborghini. Stood out in a crowd.

"So where are we headed?" asked Carlos.

"Baskin-Robbins."

"Say what?" Carlos couldn't help himself.

"Good ice cream. I am particularly fond of the Cookie Dough."

"But it's like, two in the morning."

"I called ahead. They'll open up for us."

And it was true. A beaten-down, little old man was just turning on the lights as they pulled up. The fluorescents were still flickering to life as Carlos and Ranevsky pushed their way into the ice cream parlor. The way the old man took his position behind the counter, ready to serve, made Carlos realize how afraid he should be of Ranevsky. The fear in the old man's eyes was clearly visible.

"What'll you have?" asked Ranevsky, apparently oblivious to the discomfort he was causing.

"Um, the Cookie Dough sounds good," said Carlos.

"Okay. Here's the true test. What kind of cone?"

"I always liked the old fashioned one."

Ranevsky looked at him appraisingly, then smiled. "Horosho. Good. I knew you to be a man of character." He then placed his order with the old man, who nodded. After a couple of minutes, two Cookie Doughs on old-fashioned cones were presented. Carlos assumed that no money would exchange hands, but Ranevsky pulled out a hundred ruble note. "Keep the change, Fyodor Illyich. You can go home – we're going to hang for a bit. I'll lock up."

The relief on the old man's face was palpable. He could not get his apron off fast enough. The scene reminded Carlos of Clint Eastwood westerns, where the shop-keepers all ducked for cover prior to the big shoot-out. After Fyodor Illyich was out the door, Ranevsky settled into a chair in the corner – facing the door – and licked away at his ice-cream cone.

"Tell me about San Francisco. Where do you live?"

"I live in the Castro."

"Konyeshna – of course," said Ranevsky. "It's a nice neighborhood. You homosexuals take good care of your homes." Carlos wrestled with whether or not he should be offended. He decided that he wasn't.

"Yeah, I like it. Feels like where I belong, you know?"

"Were you always from San Francisco?"

"No. I grew up in the Central Valley of California. Went to Columbia in New York and ended up at the Clarion as an intern."

"You are smart, then. Columbia is a good school. Hard to get into, yes?"

"Yeah. I got good grades in high school, and colleges like to have a wide spectrum of students. I was able to parlay being a poor, first-generation Mexican-American from California into a scholarship."

"And homosexual."

"Um, well, I didn't put that on my application. What about you?"

"I am not gay." There was that flicker – really disconcerting – where the eyes went dark. Carlos recovered.

"I meant, where did you go to school?"

There was a pause. "I wasn't cut out for the university. Didn't do well in school. More of a... natural entrepreneur.   Streets were my school. Not like my brother. He was smart."

"Your brother..." Carlos went 'Yes!' inside. "Is he here in St. Petersburg?"

"The smart one? No. His life is very different."

The smart one? Wait. What does that mean? Carlos's brain was racing. All he could say was "Oh."

"Do you have a favorite restaurant in San Francisco?" asked Ranevsky by way of changing the subject.

"There are so many good places. I think that's one of the things I love about the City. You couldn't spit out the window without hitting an excellent restaurant. I like mixing it up, but my... partner" – Carlos felt all squishy inside suddenly, using that term for Robert – "he works at a really good seafood restaurant. He sets me up sometimes. Really, I like cooking, so I'm happiest at home. You could say that Whole Foods is my favorite place. That and the Farmers' Market at the Ferry Building on Saturday."

"I like House of Nanking."

"No shit."

"Really. Best Chinese food. They use MSG, but I don't care."

"That's so funny. My last meal in SF was at the House of Nanking. It *is* good."

Ranevsky's phone purred. He looked down at the display, and picked up the phone. Carlos could just make out a deep voice on the other end. Ranevsky spoke quickly but quietly. After a couple of short exchanges, he hung up.

"So. What were you going to do to find out more about this Queen of Spades?" asked Ranevsky calmly, taking Carlos completely by surprise.

"I wasn't sure. I thought Red Square was as good a place to start as any. From the little I knew of St. Petersburg, I was hoping I might meet someone there who could point me in the right direction."

"Like me, you mean. Here I thought you were picking me up in the men's room."

"Well, you're good looking and all, but…"

"And you weren't worried about getting killed?"

"Um, well, I was told I should be."

"Not only smart, but brave. You are the only person I know who would dare to mention her name."

"Is she really all that scary?" asked Carlos, totally weirded out by that point.

Ranevsky giggled. It was very odd. Not the reaction Carlos expected at all.

"I suppose so, although I might have an unusual perspective."

"Really? You've met her?"

"Yes." He showed something of a Mona Lisa smile. "I suppose so."

At that moment, Ranevsky got up from the table and walked toward the window of the shop. It was as if he was looking at his reflection in the glass. Carlos saw the ghostly image against the darkness of the St. Petersburg early morning. Then the image moved when Ranevsky didn't, causing Carlos to jump out of his skin. The ghost moved toward the door and entered the small ice-cream parlor.

"Mr. Carlos," said Ranevsky with his now characteristic ironic smile. "Allow me to introduce Simyon. He's my evil twin."

XL

"Tell me about your family."

The dates just got better. Maddy had managed to pull herself together in time to be whisked off in Sasha's limo to the West End to see a new play at the Donmar Warehouse. It was wonderful. It was a play about a famous artist and how he created his work, seen through the eyes of his young assistant. Philosophical, deep, compelling drama. Maddy, a theatre geek, was transported by the intimate space and the star power of the actors. After a standing ovation, and a trip backstage where Sasha introduced Maddy to the young up-and-coming star of the show, they took a winding walk down Neal Street through Covent Garden and on to the Savoy for a late dinner at the Grille. Between the cozy wood-paneled room with a fire in its fireplace and a couple glasses of wine, Maddy was finding life warm and fuzzy. Sasha looked comfortable and relaxed – and ruggedly beautiful - in a black turtle-neck sweater and jeans. He was an excellent conversationalist – at least he seemed always to have Maddy talking about herself.

"My family?" she repeated. "Oh, there's not so much to tell there. We're a pretty boring bunch. No exotic travels, no artists or black sheep, not much to write home about."

"You have brothers? Sisters?"

"A sister. Austin. She's a bit of a goof, really. She's six years younger, and makes my father crazy because she has no ambition at all. She takes after my mom, I guess."

"Is she as beautiful as you are?"

Maddy blushed. I could really get used to this, she thought. "Who? My mom or my sister? They're both much prettier than me. My sister comes by it naturally, my mom, well, she's like a lot of moms in Newport Beach – she's had some work done. It was always disconcerting to go to school functions and everyone thinking that she was my older sister or something. Except she's taller, blonder, thinner and her boobs are much bigger." Maddy giggled at her joke. "I guess I'm the black sheep in the family. The one who got away. I had to get out of there – it was making me a little crazy."

"Getting into Stanford isn't all that easy," said Sasha.

"It's a miracle I got in," said Maddy, shaking her head. "I had good grades, worked like crazy, and avoided my family by getting involved in both the swim team and the drama program, so I was out the door early and home late. I guess I had just enough extra-curriculars to make the cut, but still… everyone there was much smarter and cooler than me. I mean, look at you - you're now a super-wealthy computer whiz. Jeez. Talk about putting any accomplishments I might have into perspective." She grew thoughtful, then realized that she was talking too much. "What about you? What about your family?"

Sasha stared into his wine. Maddy could just hear the gears turning in his brain. After a pause he looked back up at Maddy and sighed.

"My family is… was… complicated."

"Was? What happened?"

Another pause. "We didn't get along well. My father and mother divorced when I was very young. My mother, well, she was… unfaithful to my father, and he left her, taking me with him. For all the good that did for our relationship. He and I also didn't get along."

"I'm sorry…"

"It's okay. The fact that he was almost never around – and was an asshole when he was – made me self-reliant. I took refuge in math and computers and learned to fend for myself. I don't know…" another sigh. "It worked out okay. And I'm sure he meant well. And I'm sure it didn't hurt my college application that he wrote Stanford an enormous check for a new engineering building."

Maddy's brain was racing all of a sudden. She was trying to pull from her mental database any reference to a large donation to Stanford, but it would have been before her time. It took a long time to build a building – especially on that campus – so she decided that she shouldn't be surprised that she couldn't pull anything up.

"Is there a Borodin Engineering Hall being built soon?"

Sasha smiled an enigmatic smile. "No. I understand your confusion. I don't share the same last name as my father."

"Oh. How does that work?"

"At one point, I was so angry with my father that I changed my name. Borodin was my mother's last name."

"Wait. I thought she was the villain of the story."

"No. Well, not really. I think it safe to say that she is… I mean was… misunderstood."

"Where is she? I suppose I should back up. Where are you from?"

"I went to school in Switzerland. A pretty exclusive private school. One of those places the super-rich and powerful send their children to protect them from the outside world. Kim Jong-Il's son went there when I did. That kind of place. So that's where

I'm from."

"I mean, where were you born?"

"Berlin." After another hesitation. This was a hard pull, thought Maddy. She placed her hand on his in a show of... what? Of comfort?

"I'm sorry," she said. "I feel like I'm prying."

"No, it's okay. I guess I've buried my past a bit. It only recently came back into my life. I guess I'm still figuring it all out."

"So you're German?"

"No. My parents were... are... Russian. I told you it was complicated."

"It's very mysterious and intriguing. Sasha Borodin – International Man of Mystery."

"Sorry – don't mean to be. I'd... I'd like to have you trust me." He took Maddy's hand. The way he said that, and the way he held her hand made Maddy's stomach flip.

"I'd like you to trust me, too," she said, slipping her hand away. "There's something I haven't told you."

"What? That you're married?" said Sasha with that smile again.

"I have a boyfriend."

"Okay. Does that change anything?"

"Well, that's what I'm trying to figure out. I'm pretty confused right now. You're a really remarkable person, and I'm a little overwhelmed that you seem to be enjoying my company and all, but I find myself wondering what happens next?"

"What do you want to have happen next?"

Dang. What's the answer to that? thought Maddy.

"Maybe we order dinner?" she said with a shy smile.

Sasha laughed. "That's exactly what I hoped you would say."

XLI

"Nice shot."

Ivan Orkin turned and glared at the newcomer.

"I mean, you might look at the Owner/Player option. The Orcas could use you."

Ivan Orkin cracked a thin smile and turned back to the rack of basketballs. He drained another four three-pointers before he returned his attention to Jimmy, who applauded from the small row of bleachers within the main gym of the Orcas' training facility in Sunnyvale.

"Who are you, and how did you get in here?" asked Orkin as he wiped his close-cropped head with a towel. "This is a private facility."

"Detective James Wang of the San Francisco Police Department. I just showed my badge to the guy at the door. That has a way of getting me in places."

Jimmy approached Orkin and put out his hand. After a moment's hesitation, Orkin proffered his own. It was a powerful handshake.

"And to what do I owe the honor?"

"You seem to be the man of the moment. And not, I'm sure, in the way that you intended."

"What would you know of what I intended?"

"Not much. Except that you've made a splash on both the sporting and the arts scenes. And that you seem to be at the center of at least two, if not three, bizarre and deadly events recently."

"If not three? I don't understand."

"Then you knew of two."

Orkin's jaw muscles tensed. Then they relaxed. He was a good sport. Lost that round of chess fair and square.

"Look, as much as people tend to be suspicious of police, we're all pretty much on the up-and-up. I'm here to help."

Orkin laughed. "Can you coach basketball? I'm just about to fire the guy I've got, and I'm looking around. Other than that, I'm not sure I need any…"

Jimmy pulled out a photo of the head that was within the tank. "Do you know this man?"

Orkin looked at the photo coolly. He had obviously seen dead people before. "No, although he doesn't look as if he's in the best shape. Why do you ask?"

"Because his head was in the tank that should have contained a killer whale."

This part had been kept from the news, and Thomas Bradshaw had withheld this information from Orkin. Orkin's eyes tightened into a squint. He was not happy to hear this.

"Perhaps I should have my legal counsel present before we continue," was all he could say.

"That's more than fine, sir, although we're here to help, as I said. You're not a person of interest in this case. We know how the tank with the head was switched for the tank with the whale. And we know that the same persons who made that switch were also responsible for the… adjustment of the statues surrounding your penthouse suite."

Orkin appraised Jimmy carefully. "Go on."

"And we think we know who might have done it, or at least we have leads pointing in a certain direction."

"And which direction is that?"

"I was hoping you might help with that, sir. It's one thing for me to tell you, it's another for you to help corroborate our thinking independently. Have you ever heard of Polonium-210?"

Orkin bit his lip. "Yes. As an industrialist, I try to keep up on all my radioactive isotopes." Pretty weak, thought Jimmy. "Why do you ask?"

"As much as it may look like the man in the photograph died of being decapitated, he died first of radiation poisoning. Not something that happens every day. Any thoughts on the subject?"

"None." Orkin's eyes held fear for an instant. Jimmy knew the look. "You spoke of a third incident," said Orkin, although from his voice it sounded as if he had already heard all he wanted to hear.

"An icon. From the little Russian church on Van Ness. Painted by an apparently very famous medieval painter." Jimmy looked at his notes, and pronounced the name poorly. "Andrei Rublyev. A priest was murdered when the icon was taken. Brutally."

At this, Orkin slumped. Any defiance that might have been in his eyes or in his proud bearing slipped away. He sat down on the first bleacher. Jimmy was impressed by the transformation. When he had walked in, Orkin had the physical confidence of a man half his age, with the physique to go along with it. Now, he suddenly looked very old, and very tired.

"How can I help you, Detective?" he whispered.

"Do you know who might be behind these events?"

"Yes… and no."

"I don't understand."

"I know who should be behind these events, but I didn't think it was possible."

"Why is that?"

"Because the person who should be behind them is dead."

It was as if the temperature dropped in the

training facility by thirty degrees. Jimmy felt the shiver down his spine, and couldn't help a slight jerk of his shoulders. After a moment, he pulled out the pixilated image of the man from the thumb-drives. "Do you know who this is?"

Ivan Orkin recoiled. His face was filled with revulsion and fear. After a moment during which he collected himself, he said quietly, "Yes. Yes, I do."

"And who would that be?"

Orkin looked at Jimmy, his eyes pleading, as if he never wanted to form the words.

"That... monster is the son of my ex-wife."

*   *   *

Over several cups of coffee, it started to come together. Pretty complicated family, thought Jimmy. You needed a program to know the players. And yet there were still holes. Holes that Ivan Orkin wouldn't fill, no matter how nicely Jimmy asked, or how patient he was while waiting. Orkin had the look of someone who had been cruising along nicely and who had suddenly driven into a brick wall. But if Jimmy read his man correctly, this was a setback – another defeat in battle - but not the loss of a war. Ivan Orkin was resilient. No way he couldn't be, given all he had been through, and all he had done himself.

"So the man in this image is not Sasha Borodin?"

"No. The man in the photograph is a freak. He never should have happened. He is the worst thing in the world."

"What's that?"

"A bastard. That man is the result of a union that should never have taken place. Believe me when I say that his birth was a terrible mistake."

"Okay. May I ask what makes him so terrible?"

"Detective Wang. You look to be an intelligent young man, and probably good at what you do. I suspect you've done some homework prior to coming to talk with me."

Jimmy nodded. "I know you've worked hard to get to where you are."

Orkin smiled bitterly. "You don't know the half of it. Listen, I don't think it much of a confession to say that I've killed people."

Jimmy had read that. "Afghanistan. I can only imagine."

"You cannot imagine. The fighting was terrible. But when I killed someone, it was because I had no choice. To say the mujahedeen were a formidable adversary would be putting it mildly. These were people for whom life had little meaning. Very hard to fight someone like that. They were perfectly content to blow themselves up, as long as they took twenty of their enemies with them." Orkin sighed. "But they were not as cruel as this monster. You know how little boys can be cruel – pull the wings off insects, throw rocks at a cat? Imagine a full grown man who behaves this way with other human beings."

Jimmy shuddered. The head in the tank. The priest at the church.

"He was never supposed to have happened. He was born after his mother and I divorced. She never told me she was pregnant. I had the one boy…"

"Sasha."

"Yes, Sasha. But I didn't know about the others until much later."

"The others?"

"There were two. Twins. She had them back in Leningrad."

"St. Petersburg… Wait. Back in Leningrad… where were you?"

"I was stationed in Berlin at the time."

"And your wife... I mean your ex-wife... where is she?"

"She is dead."

"How did she die?"

"I cannot tell you."

"You don't know?"

"I know, but what is it you call it here in the States? I will not make any further statements on the grounds that I may incriminate myself."

"Did you have something to do with her death?" Jimmy figured he had nothing to lose by asking. Orkin looked into the middle distance, his finger running around the rim of his coffee cup.

"Let's just say I did the right thing."

At that moment, Jimmy's phone buzzed. Normally, he wouldn't pick up, but the number that came up on his display was from an area code he didn't recognize immediately. Hoping it was finally Maddy, he excused himself and went into the lobby outside Orkin's office.

"This is Jimmy."

"It's Francois."

"You do keep late hours – it must be two in the morning over there."

"Listen, we've ID'ed the head you found in the tank."

"Okay, shoot."

"He's a journalist. Russian by the name of Vladimir Spassky. He disappeared a few weeks ago. He was an outspoken critic of the government, and you know how that often goes."

Jimmy knew. Russia was dealing with a fundamental crisis of its nascent democracy. In the last year alone, over a dozen prominent journalists who had been investigating corruption within the government had been beaten severely or assassinated.

"What was he looking into?"

"He was investigating ties between the Federal government and organized crime."

Jimmy whistled.

"And where was he last seen?"

"Getting into an SUV in front of a Baskin Robbins. In St. Petersburg. His body was just found floating under the ice in the Neva River. Without his head, of course."

Jimmy had a moment of panic. He knew that Clarice Bryant was right.

He best get on a plane.

XXXVII

When Carlos awoke it took awhile for his vision to come into focus.

Where am I?

What is my cheek pressed against?

It occurred to him that he hurt all over – especially his forehead, which was scraping against asphalt. Better not move for a few seconds until I figure this out, he thought. His forehead felt like someone had smacked him with the handle of a gun.

Wait. That's exactly what happened. Last thing I remember.

As he lay on his side, it all became much clearer, although no less painful. His wrists were bound behind him, and he was cold in a way that he didn't think possible. His very bones ached from the cold, which was coming up damp from the pavement of what now appeared to be a garage. A large, old, garage. It looked abandoned and dilapidated. Steel columns, painted a faded and peeling light green, supported a wooden truss structure overhead. There were high windows that were letting in a cobalt blue light. It was close to dawn.

Some feet came into view. Two pairs. One pair were beautiful Italian loafers. Ranevsky was last seen in those. The others were in boots. Serious-ass Russian boots. Like in some Eisenstein movie. Carlos turned his head up and saw two faces that looked exactly the same.

Twins are creepy. Jesus, thought Carlos. They really are.

"Here I thought we were getting along so well," he croaked.

Ranevsky, looking at him sideways, smiled.

"We were. I like you. It's too bad you're a reporter."

"And Mexican," said the other twin with a sneer. "Only one thing worse than a reporter who's also not Russian would be…"

"That I'm gay? Sounds like three strikes. I think I can see where this is going."

That earned Carlos a Russian boot to the ribs.

As Carlos looked at the two men, the differences became obvious. You wouldn't be able to tell them apart if you saw them one at a time. Or on a plane. Or in line at passport control. But side by side, there were differences. The big difference was in the eyes. It was true, what Sergei said back at the restaurant. One of them was mad.

Which wasn't in the least reassuring.

Ranevsky looked mildly disappointed. "Seriously, I think you are an interesting fellow. But… my brother has issues with you. Funny thing about us. He was born a few minutes before me. Simyon always gets final say on everything, so if he decides he doesn't like someone, then we both don't like someone. He's the dominant twin. I guess I would be the…"

"The pussy." He just couldn't stop. Carlos had been picked on since he was old enough to remember. He finally learned to stand up for himself in high school, and the instinct was formed. Ranevsky looked uncomfortable. Carlos winced in anticipation of another kick from Simyon, but instead he earned a laugh. The laugh was throaty and horrible – the laugh of someone who smoked constantly, and didn't give a damn.

"You are right," said Simyon. "He *is* a pussy. I

have to smack him around from time to time," with this he put Ranevsky in a brotherly headlock. Well, brotherly would be putting it nicely. It was pretty rough. After an uncomfortable moment, Simyon released his brother and gave him a pretty fierce pat on the cheek. Carlos was profoundly creeped out by now.

"So what happens next?" Carlos had managed to sit himself up. Simyon didn't seem to mind. Instead he took the end of his almost finished cigarette and lit a fresh one with it. The pack said Marlboro, but the smoke that Simyon exhaled was blue, with a bitterness to its aroma that couldn't belong to an American cigarette. No one sane would smoke something that nasty.

"We wait for the others."

The others. Great. Carlos could often be the life of a party, but in this instance he found himself wishing he was somewhere else. He thought wistfully about the warm bed and the terry-cloth bathrobe back at the Evropaskaya. Some decisions, in hindsight, turn out to be poor ones.

They didn't wait long. A rumble was heard in the distance, growing louder with each second. A large door was thrown open behind Carlos and his shadow was thrown across the opposite wall by dozens of lights. The rumble was now a roar as a veritable army of motorcycles zoomed into the garage. Simyon laughed as the motorcycles rode in a circle around him. Eventually, they pulled up facing inward with almost military precision, their headlights blinding Carlos no matter which direction he looked.

This is super bad, he thought. Nothing like a good old-fashioned lynching.

With a pump of Simyon's fist, the motorcycles all revved their engines then switched off. As the helmets came off the riders, Carlos could only despair further. Shaved and close-cropped heads surrounded him. Tattoos everywhere, and more leather than Carlos had seen at a Village People reunion tour.

Skinheads. I hate skinheads, thought Carlos.

"Belaya Energia!" came the shout of about twenty men. A fascist salute sealed the deal. Carlos frantically searched his mental database and almost wet himself. In the little reading he had done about crime in St. Petersburg, Belaya Energia came up frequently. A white supremacist group, Belaya Energia, or White Energy, had often been identified as responsible for the deaths of many foreign students in St. Petersburg. At least the foreign students of color. Carlos looked down at his brown skin and cursed the fates.

But there were preliminaries before the main event. A certain amount of drinking, with bottles smashed against walls, a certain amount of singing, and a certain amount of physical and psychological abuse of the little brown boy in the center of the circle. A popular form of torture was the simple kick to the ribs – each skinhead taking a turn. There was spitting, which Carlos found as hateful as anything... until one especially large and ugly man with no exposed area of skin un-tattooed approached Carlos and started to unzip his fly.

This can't be one of the last images I'll ever see, thought Carlos. Anything but this.

He was spared, however. Ranevsky stepped in and told the big bruiser in Russian to keep it in his pants. The large man towered over Ranevsky and growled for a moment, but he understood his place in the scheme of things and turned and went over to the corner to pee, instead.

"I'm sorry I called you a pussy," whispered Carlos to Ranevsky after the other man had gone. Ranevsky just gave the ironic smile, looked at his watch as if he was expecting something and then moved off to the side.

Simyon then rallied the troops. He stood up onto a crate and began to speak. As crazy as he was, he had a way, even Carlos had to admit it. Simyon started calmly but clearly, building slowly to a call and response. Carlos didn't understand the Russian, but he understood the theme of the speech. Simyon would cry out some question, the response always the same: "Belaya Energia!" This built and built, with Simyon growing more and more impassioned and the men around him growing more and more inflamed and enraged, until Carlos could swear that Simyon was foaming at the mouth, and that the men around him were no more human than a pack of rabid dogs.

Finally, the spotlight fell fully on Carlos. Simyon grabbed him by the scruff of his neck and held him up. Neither of the twins was that big. Both were only a few inches taller than Carlos, and slender. But the rage that flowed through Simyon gave him almost superhuman strength, and his eyes were wild with cruel madness. Carlos had the photographic images of the Green Street Church crime scene flash through his head. He wished and wished and wished that he could click his heels together and he would be home safe in his bed.

But that was not to be. Instead a rope was thrown over a rafter and a noose was formed. Carlos was hauled fully to his feet and placed on the crate. The noose was placed around his neck and tightened. The men began to chant, slowly at first, then building in tempo. Carlos knew that the point when the tempo was so fast that the words could no longer be distinguished would be the point when the crate would be kicked out from under him.

He was not a religious boy in the least. He found that religion got in the way of who he was, or at least had a hard time recognizing his beliefs in fundamental human decency and unconditional acceptance. And love, regardless of the nature of that love. But he found religion in that moment.

Jesus, oh Jesus, oh Jesus, was all he could mumble to himself over and over.

The chant had reached its crescendo. Simyon was swinging his leg back to kick the crate. The throats of twenty men were raw from one final shout...

At that moment the screech of enormous tires on pavement broke the spell. The space was flooded by the headlights of the largest SUV Carlos had ever seen – it was actually an armed personnel carrier, painted a high-gloss black – and the crowd was momentarily blinded. The enormous vehicle roared right up to the edge of the circle and screamed to a halt. It purred there for a second, before four huge men in black suits leapt out, each with a submachine gun under his arm.

The police? thought Carlos. Thank God for Sergei...

As the circle of supremacists dissolved into panic, and Simyon stood speechless, one of the huge men moved smoothly towards the rear door of the vehicle. In a gesture that was oddly anachronistic, the man opened the door and bowed deeply.

She stepped down from the car. She was dressed in a black fur coat and hat which obscured most of her pale white face. Her boots were exquisite. There was a ripple of recognition among the crowd. What had been a vicious mob seconds before now showed a collective terror. She strode briskly up to Simyon, who stood maybe six inches taller than her. She took him in briefly, then smacked him – hard – across the face.

"Idiot," she said to him angrily. As Carlos and the other men watched in amazement, she grabbed Simyon by the ear and dragged him, howling, towards the SUV and almost threw him into the back seat. She then returned to the center of the circle. Again, Carlos wished he knew Russian, but what she said seemed clear enough. If ever a group of naughty boys was ever told off, the men, who just seconds before were about to lynch Carlos, were being sent home with their tails between their legs. "Go home before I take you over my knee," doesn't need translation, regardless of the language. It didn't hurt that four Bizon SMG submachine guns were trained on the motorcyclists as they scrambled out of the garage, but still.

The woman then turned to Carlos. Her gloved hand reached out and touched his face.

"I am sorry. Simyon gets carried away, sometimes."

Carried away? No shit, thought Carlos.

"Come, you are my guest. You look like you could use a drink." She gestured towards one of the large men, who came over quickly and disengaged Carlos from the noose and cut his hands free. As Carlos tried to step down from the crate, his legs gave out from underneath him. The last image he registered before he blacked out was of two brilliant, pale green eyes.

XXXVIII

"Are you up for dancing?"

They were waiting for Sasha's car in front of the Savoy. Another wonderful, lazy, philosophical dinner was behind them.

"You know, I'm not, really," said Maddy. She had her head on Sasha's shoulder. She felt so... comfortable... with him. She felt safe and warm. She had had a moment in the ladies' room earlier where she looked at herself again in the mirror and wondered who she was. It had been occurring to her that she had never felt so secure with someone before – not even Jimmy. She reflected that her relationship with Jimmy was more fraught than she had allowed herself to admit. He was, after all, a police detective, and, although he was responsible for great access to information which boosted her career, his interests were just as often at odds with hers. As she took in the face of the tired, but happy woman looking back at her from the mirror, she started to evaluate how often she and Jimmy were out of sync. She was quite sure she loved Jimmy, and he was as kind and thoughtful as any man she knew, but she was seeing another side of herself - and of life - with Sasha, and she found it compelling and seductive.

"I have another confession to make," she said as the car pulled up. She climbed into the back seat with Sasha piling in next to her. The driver pulled forward a bit, but hesitated to pull out of the drive, awaiting instructions. "I have slept only two hours since I landed in London. I can't imagine that I've got two brain cells functioning properly to rub together."

"So you want to go back to your hotel?"

"Eventually. What's weird is that although I'm exhausted, I don't want the evening to end. You know what I really want?"

"What do you really want?" asked Sasha with a glint in his eye.

"I'd really like to walk back to the hotel. With you. Just walk and see London at slow speed."

Sasha tapped his driver on the shoulder and said that they would walk back to the Dorchester.

"Shall I pick you up there, sir?"

"Let me call you." There was an awkward moment, and Maddy burst out laughing.

"What?" asked Sasha, pretending to be clueless.

"Just get out of the car," Maddy giggled.

*   *   *

London in the wee hours is magical, thought Maddy. Something about the fact that the Tube stopped running at midnight dictated the rhythm of the city's movements. People went home. The government stopped working. For a few hours, one of the world's largest cities slept, leaving two pedestrians feeling as if they were the last two people on earth. Maddy and Sasha walked from the Savoy down the Strand towards Trafalgar Square, a light mist causing the city to look like a stage set behind a scrim. The London rain felt good on Maddy's skin, and gave the streets a sheen. For a few blocks she and Sasha were quiet, taking in the silence which was interrupted only intermittently by cabs running people home to their beds or to off to the next club. During one moment of stillness, in the distance, the chime of Big Ben struck two.

"Kiss me," said Maddy quietly.

For a moment Sasha hesitated, his face quickly registering the momentary desire to say something clever, which he controlled. He then kissed Maddy gently, which made her kiss him back with real intensity. An excellent kiss.

As they parted, Maddy sighed. "Thank you." She took his arm again and they continued walking into Trafalgar Square. "You know the old tradition – at Stanford – of not becoming a 'Stanford Woman' until you were kissed in the Quad at midnight?"

"I remember something about that," said Sasha with his enigmatic smile.

"Now I feel like, I don't know... I know I didn't think of myself as a woman then."

"You mean after you were kissed in the Quad at midnight?"

"Yes, I mean, well, yes – I did kiss a boy in the Quad at midnight – if only to see what would happen. Who didn't? I guess what I'm trying to say is that I didn't feel anything then – I was still the silly... earnest, sheltered little girl I always was. I didn't feel any different. Now, suddenly, I do. Just now was the kiss that made the difference."

There was a moment of silence. They walked up to one of the lions at the base of the Nelson Monument.

"So your boyfriend..."

"Is not here. I'm sure that sounds terrible, but suddenly I feel the real need to be right where I am, right now. There are things I need to work out, but not right now. There will be plenty of time on the flight home to figure out what to do, and what to say."

"What happens in London could always stay in London..."

"I'm sure that's what you say to all the girls," said Maddy, trying to sound worldly.

"No, I'm sorry. I've never said that to any girl."

"What, the London part? You can't fool me. You must have more girlfriends per square inch than any boy should have a right to."

Sasha winked at her. "What if I said you were right?"

Maddy's heart flipped. "I guess I would just chalk up the last couple of days to a great life experience and... and move on." She felt that trying to sound philosophical made her just sound, well, stupid. After a moment where she found a tear escape down her cheek – godammit, I hate that, she thought as she quickly wiped it aside with her glove – she looked at Sasha full in the face. "I'm such a liar. You would break my heart. No use lying about it – I would rather you knew that. At least I would feel that I did and said something right and honest in all of this."

Sasha looked at her quizzically for a moment. "First of all, I just said that about the other girls to tease you. It's true. And second, I said that about what stays in London... because I thought that's what you wanted to hear and do. I'm not interested in breaking anyone's heart – all this time I've been thinking that you were going to break mine, and I've been just kind of hanging in there. I don't have a girlfriend, or a wife, or anybody. I've got a billion-dollar company. The whole start-up thing can suck your life up – it's a twenty-five-hour-a-day deal. Only in the last year have I finally figured out the kind of sacrifices my father made to get to where he is. He's still an asshole, but I know what it is to be consumed by one's work. You're seeing me when I've finally felt I could flex my muscles and enjoy the fruit of my labors."

"So no other girls?"

"I won't tell you that if you work hard you don't party hard. Sure there have been people who have thrown themselves at me, but that... that's what it was. I won't apologize for being single."

He brushed away a second tear on Maddy's cheek. "And you shouldn't apologize for being where you are. I liked very much the being right here, right now. Things will work themselves out. Time resolves things, and we could probably use some time. I'm not in a hurry. You've got a book to write, I've got a business to run, and..."

"I don't have a book to write."

Sasha looked at her funny for a second.

"I don't have a book to write," Maddy repeated. "Oh, fuck it. I've been lying to you the whole time. I'm on assignment." She looked at him desperately. "I'm looking for a murderer. Someone cruel enough to be capable of cutting off people's heads, and beating priests into a pulp. Someone clever enough to steal a multi-million dollar work of art... who can fly... and who can be in several places at once... and then disappear into thin air...

She gulped. "And someone who looks just like you."

She searched his face, for the umpteenth time, to see if there was anything behind his eyes that might reveal the kind of cruelty that it would take to be the person she was looking for. Instead, his eyes shifted from green to black for a second. She could still not figure out what that meant, and was never sure if it was always a trick of the light or her imagination.

Suddenly Sasha reared his head back and howled at the night sky. Maddy jumped out of her skin. It was a cry of pain and frustration and it terrified her and yet made her believe that something was truly tearing at his soul. Only after he let it out, and slumped to his haunches at the base of the lion, did Maddy have the courage to kneel down beside him and put her hands on his face. He took a moment, then looked at Maddy, his eyes back to the pale green with which she had started to fall in love.

"I'm sorry," he whispered. "It's just. I have to go. Look, there's someone I really need to talk to, okay?"

"Okay, okay," said Maddy, her mind racing to understand. "Who's that?"

He looked at his hands, which were clenched in anguish.

"My mom."

*   *   *

When she woke up in the morning he was gone. Maddy had comforted him and brought him back to her hotel. What happened next wasn't at all what she had intended. But the combination of pure fatigue, romantic excitement and real concern led her to do something that she never thought she would do. Now, with the gray light working its way through the sheers of her window, she lay on the pillow that he had slept on and took in his smell. She had a moment of blissful recollection of the few hours they spent in each other's arms, then the guilt came rushing over her. After a good cry in the shower, after barfing – yet again – she did everything she could not to look herself in the mirror. The face looking back at her was not anyone she recognized.

*   *   *

They had agreed to fly late in the afternoon. This would give Sasha time to meet with the London-based team that was working towards expanding the Infinity presence within Europe – the real reason he had come to London – and Maddy time to conduct one last interview before she left.

THE QUEEN OF SPADES

In spite of only two hours of sleep, she was ready this time when James pulled up in front of the Dorchester. It helped that she had found the Starbucks around the corner. She had her bags packed, and she had checked out. James beamed his big, sparkling smile and, once again, refused to allow her to help him as he negotiated her suitcase into the trunk of the car.

"Where to today, ma'am?"

"Oxford. By way of a mobile phone store." It was long past time for her to get back up and running, as much as she had enjoyed being somewhat "incommunicado" for the last couple of days. She was disconcerted a bit, though, when she last checked her email, that there were no new ones from Jimmy. Either he's really pissed at me, or he's giving me space, or I've been dumped, thought Maddy. Serves me right.

More worrisome in a way was that there was nothing from Carlos. It had been a couple of days.

"There's a mall on the way," replied James. "Big electronics store. You should be able to get anything you want there."

Sure enough, a few miles along the M40 outside of London an enormous retail center appeared. It was bigger than anything Maddy had seen in California, which was mildly shocking. There were ways, she thought, that England was more like the US than the US.

"Jeez. There's even a Home Depot," she said as they pulled off the highway. Less of a surprise were the McDonald's and the Pizza Hut, although the Taco Bell felt pretty incongruous. The Best Buy, though, was what the doctor ordered. After only a few minutes, Maddy left the store fully armed with the latest iPhone, capable, she thought, of not only calling, texting or emailing anywhere in the world, but making her coffee in the morning. And with a universal voltage adapter. She started to feel her inner world-conquering investigative journalist starting to come back together.

As James continued the remaining short distance to Oxford, Maddy did some preliminary programming on her phone. She was glad she had a back-up of important numbers on her laptop. Now she had the interesting task of assigning new ring tones for special people. She decided to give Jimmy the old telephone sound – the same one she had given him before. She fussed, though, over assigning a special ringtone for Sasha, now that she had his number. She came close to assigning him something dark and mysterious like "Jack the Knife" from Threepenny Opera, but then decided to leave him with the default ring tone – she wasn't sure she wanted to attach any more specialness yet. Yet.

And she downloaded her standard ringtone. "Defying Gravity" felt more appropriate than ever. It made her smile as she heard the song coming out of her little speaker. James sang along.

"You know this song?" asked Maddy, laughing.

"Of course! Glee – First Season!" Maddy smiled inwardly that an entire generation might never really know which musical a song came from – just that they heard it for the first time on a TV show. But she marveled at her driver. James had a beautiful falsetto.

"You should audition for American Idol – or whatever it is you call it over here."

"No. I could not. I am not beautiful enough."

"I disagree. I think you would have a really good chance. You're as attractive as anyone I've ever seen on the show. It's all in the smile."

James was okay with this. "I do have a good smile. Gift from my mama." After a moment of reflection he nodded. "Okay. I will audition next time. You make me feel brave."

This made Maddy blush a little, but it also made her feel good to know that she had something of the 'cheerleader' still in her.

Another twenty minutes and they were entering Oxford. James had used his map book while Maddy was phone shopping to guide them effortlessly into the town center. Maddy was awestruck at the ancient stone towers that defined the University. Being a Stanford graduate, she rarely felt envy or was impressed by someone else's academic credentials. But Oxford was in a different league altogether. This had been home to some of the finest minds in western civilization for centuries, and an essential stepping-stone for many of those in power in Great Britain - or for heads of state around the world: Saudi Arabia, Syria, Malaysia, among them. She felt the ancient energy all around her, and wondered at the faces of the students on the street. Young, bright, engaged people. It felt a bit like when she went to Harvard to visit some of her friends – Cambridge, Massachussets had a similar feel to it, but much scruffier and without the extra couple of centuries of gravitas that Oxford had.

The townhouse was only a few blocks from the center of town. James pulled the limousine up to a stone building with a bright red door. As Maddy climbed out of the car, she said that she wouldn't be much more than an hour. James said he would wait – he was working his way through the last of the Harry Potter books, and didn't mind the reading time.

"Miss Stevenson, come in," said the matronly woman who opened the door. "We've been expecting you. I'm Mrs. Hubbard. I look after him a bit. He gets around fine, but his son wants to make sure he eats properly and the place is neat, so, well, that's what I do."

"Thank you, ma'am," said Maddy taking her hand. "I'm so glad he could see me on such short notice."

"Tch. It's not like he's got a full appointment book, if you know what I mean," said Mrs. Hubbard, leading Maddy down the hall. "He'll be delighted to see you – you're a pretty thing – you'll be the highlight of his day."

Maddy wasn't sure how to respond to that. Mrs. Hubbard led her into the back of the house – into something of a sun room.

"He's out in the garden. It's too cold for me, but he loves it. I would have taken your coat, but you're going to need it. There he is, over in the corner. I'll bring you some tea in a few minutes."

"Thank you, Mrs. Hubbard." Maddy stepped out into the garden. The flower beds were filled with rose bushes, which looked pruned perfectly. She walked down the little path towards a little white-haired man who was on his knees, working diligently in the dirt. At her approach, the man straightened up, still looking ahead. It was as if he sensed her presence through feel, not hearing. He turned, and his momentary look of surprise turned to a broad smile. He started to stand up, but had some trouble. Maddy hurried to his aid.

"Oh, thank you. Knees can get stiff on this cold ground." He took an appraising look at Maddy and grinned happily. "You must be Miss Stevenson." He paused, realizing something. "Excuse me one moment." He brushed his longish hair back and fussed at his ears for a second, cocked his head back and forth and smiled again. "Hearing aids. I only turn them on when I need to. I like the quiet, you see." He removed his gloves and took Maddy's hand. "You've come a long way to talk with an old man. You said you're from California?"

"Yes, sir. San Francisco."

"You could have fooled me. You have the English Rose all over you. Beautiful, fair skin, blonde hair, a touch of freckles." He looked again at Maddy, and chuckled. He suddenly reminded Maddy of Maurice Chevalier. Thank heaven for little girls was what his expression said. Now it made some sense that he lived in a university town...

"So what can I do for you? Do you mind if we talk as I work? I want to get these bulbs in. There's a chair over there – do you mind bringing it over? Mrs. Hubbard will bring us some tea shortly, I expect."

Maddy went over to a little wrought iron chair and pulled it over. As she sat down on the cold metal, she was grateful for keeping her coat.

"First of all, thank you so much for seeing me today, Mr. Herskovin. I apologize for the short notice."

"Not at all, not at all," replied Fyodor Herskovin as he slowly got back onto his knees. Maddy started to rise to help him, but he waved her off. "As much as I like the quiet, it's good to talk to someone every once in a while. Certainly a pretty girl. Dmitri was right."

Dmitri. Oh, right. Donovan.

Fyodor Herskovin started to work his way with a trowel into the cold ground.

"Is it the time of year to be planting bulbs?" asked Maddy.

"It doesn't hurt these. These are pretty hardy. And they'll be the first things up when Spring finally arrives." He sighed. The Russian Sigh. "And, truth be told, it gets me out of the house."

"What do you do when you're not working in the garden? Which is very nice, by the way."

"I read mysteries. And watch too much television. And spend way too much time online."

"What do you do online?" asked Maddy, not sure she wanted to hear the answer.

"Research."

"Research? Are you working on a book?"

"No. It's just a hobby. Can't help myself. I like reading the news from different parts of the world and trying to put the pieces together. When you step back a bit, it's really is an enormous puzzle."

"What is?"

"Why things are the way they are," he replied enigmatically. He had laid out a series of neat rows of holes. He then turned his attention to the boxes of bulbs. He took them one by one and placed them into the holes, covering them with soil and patting them into place. "So why are you here? Not that it isn't a pleasure to spend time with a lovely young woman. It's been a while."

"I'm trying to make sense of a puzzle, myself, Mr. Herskovin."

"Fyodor, please. My few friends call me Fedya, but that seems, perhaps, too informal for a first meeting. It means Teddy."

Maddy thought that Teddy wasn't appropriate, either.

"What puzzle are you trying to work out, that you would come up from London to talk to an old man?"

"Donovan – Dmitri – told me a bit of your history. I thought you might be able to help me understand the way things... why things are the way they are."

Fyodor Herskovin sat back on his heels and hung his head. He then collected himself and pretended to review his handiwork. Another sigh. "Which part of my history are you interested in?"

"I think you know. You were an agent of the KGB a long time ago."

"A very long time ago. Thankfully. But I told them, MI6, everything I knew."

"Can you tell me?"

At that moment, Mrs. Hubbard called out from the house. "Yoo hoo! Fedya? Do you want tea in the garden or in the house?" Herskovin looked at Maddy.

"Do you really want to hear it?"

"I would be grateful."

"Then we should go into the house. It's a long story, and you are getting cold."

XXXIX

It was the nicest plane Jimmy had ever been on.

For all intents and purposes, it could easily have been the nicest hotel suite he had ever been in. After a lifetime of flying coach, with occasional forays into business class when he could use his miles to upgrade – he was, after all, a public servant, and the taxpayer dollar only went so far – Jimmy could not believe that one could enjoy the kind of space and luxury that Ivan Orkin's Boeing Business Jet 737-700 afforded. Wood paneling, plush carpeting, leather sofas that flipped into full-size beds. Several priceless works of art mounted to the bulkheads – a Chihuly chandelier over the dining room table. A full dining room table. Jimmy shook his head. It seated six, and was carved out of some exotic African wood – Bobinga. Nice. And the private sleeping quarters for Orkin with master bathroom. The interior of the plane was larger than Jimmy's studio apartment, and the view was just as striking – they were floating above Maxfield Parrish-apricot clouds. Only for take-off did everyone sit with a seat belt on. Once the plane hit its cruising altitude, Jimmy stood up and enjoyed the unique sensation of strolling around on an airplane as if he were in a living room, rather than the usual crunching of his six-foot frame into a cramped middle seat for hours on end. The Hendricks gin martini with the slice of cucumber in his hand capped the experience. Or so he thought.

"I don't usually drink on the job, but it's a long flight."

"Should take us about sixteen hours, with a fueling stop in Maine. After cocktails and supper, we can get a good night's sleep. Yoga in the morning, before breakfast."

"Yoga?"

"Of course," replied Orkin, sipping a glass of Haut-Brion. "We want to arrive fresh. Vanessa will get all your kinks out for you."

I'll bet, thought Jimmy, taking in the tight, close-cropped red-headed woman playing with her iPod before putting on her sleeping mask for a cat-nap. Vanessa, who had what looked to Jimmy like zero body fat, was Orkin's personal trainer and masseuse. She looked like she took extremely good care of herself. Jimmy could only smile to himself and think that that girl would probably be better for a cheeseburger.

"Um, supper... breakfast?"

Orkin laughed. "We'll eat very well. Michael will take good care of us."

Michael was the brisk, young Japanese-American man who accompanied them on the trip and who was already in the galley working his magic. A stint at The French Laundry as a sous-chef gave him all the credentials Jimmy could ask for. The smells emanating from the back of the plane were spectacular. Jimmy had seen several cases of food and wine being loaded onto the plane, with Michael himself boarding with bags full of that day's purchases from the Farmer's Market.

Nothing like traveling Billionaire Class. Even if I could get used to this, I couldn't get used to this, thought Jimmy. He came from a pretty well-to-do family, but this was a completely different league for him. Make that a few light years away.

Orkin watched Jimmy's face and its range of fleeting emotions with a wry smile. As if reading

Jimmy's thoughts, Orkin said, "If it makes any difference to you, I still appreciate all of this. I'm one lucky son-of-a-bitch. Dues were paid, but still." He waved his arm expansively. "But I found over the years that what might appear to be luxuries to you, have become necessities for a well-run business. I travel so much that for me to be able to perform well when I hit the ground, I need to take very good care of myself. I make decisions that mean the difference of several millions every few hours. It's sound business sense to be well-rested upon arrival. The lives of thousands of people across the globe depend on my ability to make the right choices."

"I deal with life and death decisions myself, and I wish I could travel like this," said Jimmy ruefully. He barely had time to set down his empty martini glass when it was replaced by another, frosty cold. "But thank you for the lift. There's no way I could have gotten there faster."

"We both have work to do once we arrive, and we'll have to work quickly. And it sounds as if lives will depend on us," replied Orkin. "But for now, we owe it to ourselves to unwind a bit."

Michael came out and announced that dinner was ready. Jimmy looked out the window and watched as the last rays of the sun disappeared rapidly into twilight. He realized that he hadn't eaten anything all day. The cocktails were making him light-headed. He needed to get some food into his stomach.

And he was not disappointed. Michael was a master of the fusion of French Nouvelle Cuisine and Asian refinement. From the salmon sashimi appetizer through the duck breast with port wine glaze, to the heirloom tomato and organic lettuce and artisanal cheese salad, to the rosemary and bitter chocolate bread pudding, each bite was to die for. The only thing better was the wine. Orkin was proud of his collection and enjoyed showing it off to Jimmy, who was worldly enough to know a two hundred dollar bottle of wine when he saw one. Vanessa joined them at the table, but she kept it light, with a carefully prepared meal of steamed broccoli, poached salmon and brown rice, with distilled water to drink. Jimmy reflected that she wouldn't be much of a fun date, and then had a moment of melancholy when he remembered how much he enjoyed dining out with Maddy, who seemed to have a metabolism that would allow her to eat anything, and who was young enough and open enough to find almost anything he introduced her to delightful. She was a girl who loved a good cheeseburger, and Jimmy realized that he loved her for it.

After the meal was cleared away, and Vanessa prepared for sleep, Orkin turned to Jimmy. A dark, questioning look filled his eyes.

"Speyside man?"

"Islay, myself, actually. But I wouldn't say no."

Orkin smiled. The bottle he removed from the beautiful wood cabinet was a 40 year-old Glenfarclas. Jimmy shook his head for the umpteenth time.

"That'll be just fine. But if you don't mind my asking, I haven't seen you touch a drop of vodka. Wouldn't that be more your line?"

"Vodka is just for getting drunk," replied Orkin with a look of distaste. He poured a neat finger in each glass. Jimmy noted that although the food and wine were excellent, nothing was consumed to excess and the portions were precisely controlled. He admired the restraint in the face of such luxurious options. "I like something you can actually taste," continued Orkin, admiring the label of the bottle. "Nazdarovya." He raised his glass to Jimmy, who responded in kind.

"Strategy..." he started to say.

"Can wait until the morning. We've done all we can for now, and people on the ground are in motion. Let's just enjoy a moment of quiet. Tomorrow could be a very long day." He took a sip of the gold in his glass.

"And cold."

XL

It was very tempting to believe, upon waking up, that it had all been a terrible dream and that he was back at the Evropaskaya snuggled in his bed. Carlos burrowed deeply into his pillow for a moment, then sat up with a jolt. It was so Twilight Zone. The comfy bed with the downy pillows and comforter. The fire in the fireplace was not what he remembered, but there was the terry cloth bathrobe, almost exactly as he left it. He realized that he was wearing pajamas, and was more than a little disconcerted by the idea that he had changed without realizing it. More disconcerting was the creeping suspicion that someone had changed his clothes for him.

The suspicion was confirmed when he noticed the neatly pressed and folded clothes on the chest at the foot of the bed. He crawled forward without getting fully out of bed and inspected his clothes. They were clean. Last he could remember, he was face down in muddy water, being kicked across the asphalt floor of an abandoned garage. His jeans would from now on have a real distressed quality to them – no faux rips, but real ones. But they smelled clean and fresh, even with the scent of fabric softener. Comforting and strange at the same time.

His shirt, he realized, was new, however. As he examined it, it occurred to him that his old shirt would have had too many blood stains on it to come clean properly. He sighed. He liked that shirt. He then inspected himself gingerly, slowly unbuttoning his pajama top. Sure enough, his chest was bandaged heavily. At least one rib must be broken. He feared the mirror. As he felt his face, he could tell that the image that would greet him would be someone unrecognizable. His lips and eyes were puffy, and his nose was bandaged. There was another bandage wrapped around his head.

That's the last time I do anything *that* stupid, he thought. No way could Robert smooch me now.

There was a gentle knock on the door. Before Carlos could find the wits to respond, a large man opened the door and stepped in. Carlos had a vague sense that he had seen the man before. Of course. Last seen, he had been wielding a submachine gun, bowing ceremoniously to the woman in the fur coat. The large man, who was still wearing a dark suit with a tie, approached the bed and gave a gentle smile that completely belied his size and previous formidable appearance.

"How are you feeling?" he asked quietly in heavily accented English.

"Seriously?" replied Carlos, in some dismay. "Other than being somewhat concerned that I'm going to pee blood, I'm doing okay." After a moment, he continued. "Thanks for saving my bacon back there."

"You are welcome. My mistress wanted me to express again her regret that you came to any harm. She has been worried about you."

"Oh."

"She cleaned you and bandaged you herself."

"Oh…" Carlos felt profoundly uncomfortable upon hearing this.

"Do not be embarrassed. She has some skill. She has mended me from time to time."

"Right. Must be a tough line of work."

The large man smiled. His teeth were horrible – a couple missing, the rest stained. No dental plan, though, thought Carlos. Or they just don't care.

"Yes. But it has its compensations. And it is what we know best."

Carlos had to admit that the precision with which the men had moved back in the garage had been impressive. They were good. I wonder where they get that kind of training, he thought.

"If you are able to get dressed, she would like to see you."

"She… may I ask who 'She' is?"

"You may not. I am sorry. That is for you to learn from her, should she choose to tell you."

"Security is tight here, then?" Carlos slowly stood up. He almost fell over, but the large man was there to right him.

"Konyeshna. Of course."

"So no running away?"

"After fixing you up, we would hate to have to kill you."

Carlos couldn't decide if they would really hate that, or if it would just be all in a day's work. He decided the latter. He would put running away on hold.

"Give me five minutes. I need to use the bathroom and make myself a bit more presentable."

"I will return when you are ready." The large man left the room. Carlos gingerly tried the door handle, but it didn't budge. Oh, well. Time to face the mirror.

He thought he looked a bit like Claude Rains in the Invisible Man. Hell of a way to earn a living. I'm going to have to ask for a raise… assuming I live to write all of this up. He undid his pajama bottoms to pee and was devastated by how much purple there was below the waistline. Ew. Then came the tough part. At least there wasn't any blood, but just flexing his muscles at all hurt. Thank god I don't have to take a dump, he thought. That would kill me.

I'm going to get that asshole Simyon, if it's the last thing I do. Jesus.

A few minutes of fussing at his hair – the bathroom was kitted out well for a young man, with the latest in hair care products – and some painful maneuvering to get into his clothes – bending over to put on his shoes almost caused him to pass out – and he was ready. The door to his room opened just as he turned to face it.

Nice to know that I'm under surveillance, he thought.

The large man beckoned to him. Carlos moved slowly out of the room. He entered a long corridor with concrete walls and birchwood floors. It was exquisite in its Northern European minimalism – small accent lights highlighted paintings that looked vaguely familiar. Wait, thought Carlos. He had studied just enough art history to know that these looked like Kandinskys. Who has Kandinskys just hanging in the hall?

"Are those... are those by Kandinsky?"

"I do not know," replied the large man with a shrug before he took Carlos by the arm. "It is all just blobs of paint."

There was a flight of steel stairs, cantilevered from the wall in the most daring fashion – Carlos felt like he was floating – and they descended into a large, open living area, two stories tall, with concrete walls and high windows that opened onto a snow covered birch forest. The trees were almost on fire from the final rays of a sunset, the shadows in the snow a deep blue. It looked just like an Impressionist painting, the colors so vivid and broken into their constituent parts. It was breathtaking.

Speaking of Impressionists... thought Carlos, slowing down and collecting his wits - gently shaking off his escort, who seemed willing to give Carlos a moment. On one of the tall concrete walls, above a leather sofa, was one of the most iconic paintings of the Impressionist era. That would be a Monet. Jesus. The Houses of Parliament were obvious through the sunset haze, a small boat bobbing on water composed of luminous brushstrokes. How many of those did he paint? thought Carlos - he remembered that it was something like a few dozen. It looks like one might be missing...

Shit, thought Carlos, suddenly spinning around. That would be a Picasso. And that was a Matisse.

Something was stirring in his brain. In his limited online research back at SFO he had followed up on Jimmy's mention of the art theft in Paris. Five paintings were stolen, a Picasso, a Matisse... It was the Fernand Leger that clinched the deal for Carlos. Leger, too, was on the hit list from the Museum of Modern Art in Paris. It was hanging on the opposite wall, next to an opening to what appeared to be a library.

No way, thought Carlos.

As the large man took him by the arm again, Carlos reflected on the often asked question: What happens to famous works of art when they get stolen? They can almost never resurface - the works are impossible to move without someone knowing about it. The argument went that they were buried in the private viewing lounges of the super-wealthy, who were content to keep them out of the public gaze, or who were arrogant enough to believe that no one else would appreciate them as they did.

Now Carlos knew that that was, indeed, true.

The library had a completely different feel to it as they passed through it. Cozy and clubby. There was a fire burning in a fireplace. Among the leather-bound books were niches containing more paintings, again beautifully illuminated by discreet recessed lighting. The artwork on the walls was of a different era than the Impressionist and Constructivist work he had seen so far. Old Masters.

Very. Old. Masters.

There are some painters whose work remains instantly recognizable, even to the barely initiated. Vermeer would be one of them, with his consistent viewpoint of the room within his studio with the clavichord, the map on the wall, the cool Dutch light always coming in from the window on the left side of the painting. Carlos, who felt already as if he had been led through the National Gallery, stopped dead in his tracks.

"That's a Vermeer."

"The mistress is very fond of that painting, although I cannot see what all the fuss is about," said his escort.

"No. That's a *Vermeer*." Carlos' voice cracked. "There's, like, twelve on the planet. You wouldn't happen to know where she got this?"

The man smiled enigmatically. "Please, she is waiting. We need to put you into some warm clothes."

"Why?"

"Because we're going outside. It is very cold."

They continued on to what might be called a 'mud room,' although it was really more like a large garage. There was a wall with overcoats, hats and scarves, with heavy boots in racks below. In front of a large rolling door sat several snow mobiles, and, incongruously, what looked like an old sledge.

"Please, how you say? Bundle up."

Carlos put on a coat, which almost hurt from the weight pressing down on him, and put on some galoshes. A fur hat, a scarf and a pair of rabbit-fur gloves finished the ensemble.

"Ready for my space walk," he quipped.

The other man also prepared himself, and they left through a heavy steel door on the side of the room. It was moving towards twilight outside, and the birch trees were now lavender in the waning light. As he gasped from the freezing air knifing into his lungs, Carlos took in his surroundings a bit. Behind him was a large building – extremely clean and spare in its lines – made of glass, wood, concrete and steel. The very essence of minimalist contemporary architecture. Richard Meyer would have been proud. Hmmm, thought Carlos. Maybe Richard Meyer *did* design this... some commissions you just never hear about. Surrounding them on all sides was a birch forest for as far as he could see. It was very isolated.

"Right. No running away. Got it." His breath froze in front of him. "So where are we going?"

The other man placed his gloved hand on Carlos' arm and bade him head towards the trees in the direction of the purpling horizon. As they moved forward, Carlos could discern a path through the snow. After a hundred yards or so, he could sense a clearing up ahead. A few more stands of birch trees and then...

The vista broke upon him in spectacular fashion. He was suddenly standing on the edge of an enormous ice field which was breaking away into a vast body of water. On the shore of this frozen sea sat a little wooden building, completely out of a fairy tale. It was up on stilts, like Baba Yaga's hut, with a long, raised walkway leading to it. The shingled wood was silver with age and weathering, gleaming in the last rays of the sun, which was disappearing over the horizon to the west.

"Woah," said Carlos. "Where are we? This is like

the land of the Snow Queen."

His escort snorted – as if he was in on some joke - and led Carlos up onto the raised walkway. As they approached, Carlos could see that smoke was rising up out of a chimney. The glass in the frosty windows glowed warm and inviting, while the snow on the roof gave the impression that the whole thing was covered in frosted sugar. They reached the door, and the large man opened it and pushed Carlos inside.

The inside of the cottage was small, but cozy and warm. Unlike the stark interiors of the main building, the cottage was homey and plain, with wood walls and floors of knotty pine and birch. The ceiling was low and Carlos, even as short as he was, felt as if he should stoop for fear of hitting his head. A table was laid near a wood-burning stove, and it was up against a window that looked out over the water, which was turning black against the cobalt evening sky. The table was covered with a plastic table-cloth, and on it, next to two candles, sat a plate of what looked like herring, some hard-boiled eggs, a loaf of brown bread, a stick of butter and a bottle of vodka. Carlos had just enough time to register all of this when a woman emerged from another room. She was wiping her hands with a dishcloth and wore an apron, which was covered with flour.

"Welcome! Saditzya." She gestured towards one of the chairs at the table. "The piroshki will be out of the oven in about fifteen minutes. " She tutted at Carlos and pursed her lips in a pout of sympathy. "Take off your coat, you poor dear, and sit with me a while." She turned to the large man and said, "Yuri – you may go." The man bowed his head in the same, old-fashioned way he had back at the garage and left. The woman turned to Carlos, looking at him appraisingly. Her pale green eyes sparkled in the light of the candles.

"Brave boy. No one I know would have done something so foolish." She checked herself. "Well, that's not entirely true. We often have to learn the hard way. So. Now that you've found me, what can I do for you. You are a reporter, yes?"

Carlos nodded his head. The woman was without a fur hat now, and Carlos could see her silver-white hair. It was pulled back into a small bun, but there was something odd. There was a large bald spot on one side of her head, near the hairline. Scar tissue about the size of a quarter.

"You would be…" he hesitated. Last time he mentioned her name he got the shit beaten out of him. Oh, well, couldn't hurt much worse. "You would be the Queen of Spades."

The woman looked at him, her eyes narrowing. Did they just turn black? No. That was weird, thought Carlos. Must run in the family.

"Most reporters are looking for a good story, yes?"

Carlos hesitated, then said, "Yes, ma'am. I guess that's why I'm here."

"Then sit down, and let an old woman weave you a tale."

XLI

"It was a very long time ago… more than fifty years," said Fyodor Herskovin. A fire crackled in the fireplace, and the windows of the living room were steaming up from the heat against the cold outside. "I was a station chief. I was responsible for running agents in West Berlin and passing on any useful information to my superiors in Moscow." He sighed. "It was, actually, a stupid and wasteful job. One doesn't have to spend much time in the intelligence community to realize that the layers of deceit are so many and so deep that no intelligence can really be trusted. In those days thousands of people – tens of thousands – were engaged in a game that was simply unwinnable and unknowable. At least in the trenches where *we* fought. I got to the point where I knew that the agent who was passing me information was, in fact, being fed false information by the British. But that false information wasn't false, it was true, only being told to me by that agent because the British knew that I knew that he was a double agent, so they wanted me to *think* it was false."

"Wait…" started Maddy, whose head hurt trying to follow.

"But knowing that they knew that I knew, I could determine that the truth they were feeding me was, ultimately, false.

"Unless, of course, it wasn't." Herskovin rolled his eyes theatrically.

"Madness," whispered Maddy.

"Exactly. You understand the clinical definition."

"Doing the same thing over and over expecting different results."

"When the time came, and the army was staging the equipment and material outside the city to slam the first iteration of the Wall into place, I knew what I needed to do."

"Donovan told me. You managed to be on the right side of the city."

Herskovin looked at Maddy. He had the look of someone who both dreaded what he was about to say, and yet felt the relief of finally being able to say it.

"Do you know the novel 'Sophie's Choice'?"

Maddy had seen the movie. "Yes. Why?"

"There are some choices that are so painful to make that once made, a part of your soul is lost forever."

"I understand that leaving your country was hard…"

"I left a daughter."

"What?"

"She was just a little girl – just five years old. She was ill, though. She was in the hospital, suffering from meningitis. We could not get her out – her condition was critical. Her mother threatened to stay behind, but I knew that if she did, I would never see her again. We knew that for our son to have any life in this world, and for us to save our sanity, we had to move when we did. I had been part of a security detail at Dollnsee, the government guesthouse in the woods north of Berlin, on the 12th of August, 1961, where First Secretary Ulbricht signed the order to have the wall constructed. On the drive back to the city, I could see the heavy equipment and trucks stacked with rolls of barbed wire and I knew. I wrote a report stating that I had arranged to meet one of my agents on the other side that night and I used my family as a ruse, visiting my mother in West Berlin – typical at the time - to reduce suspicion.

"You cannot imagine how terrible that next day was, the 13th of August.

"A whole city torn apart, the population in tears, wailing and screaming. Mine wasn't the only family broken into pieces. Soldiers stood with rifles drawn to prevent anyone from crossing from the East to the West. Buildings were knocked down, roads were torn up – all to keep anyone from forcing their way across the border. A border that only the previous day allowed at least the decency of families being together.

"And my decision was irrevocable. There was no way to return, there was no way to reclaim my little girl. A person of my rank and knowledge of the inner workings of the KGB would have never lived to tell the tale I tell now. So my wife and son and I were taken in by the British, and within a day we were airlifted out of Berlin."

"What was her name?" asked Maddy, her voice just above a whisper.

"Lyubov." Herskovin coughed, choking back tears. "It means 'Love.'" He took a moment and blew his nose and wiped his eyes. He looked apologetic.

"You wanted to know," he shrugged.

"What happened to her, to your daughter?"

"I learned later that she recovered, and was taken in by my adjutant's family."

"That was kind of them," said Maddy, feeling somewhat relieved. "So she was okay?"

"Yes, at least for a while. My adjutant, Sasha, was able for a brief time to use our network and system of agents to pass word on to me."

"Did you say Sasha?"

"Yes. Sasha Borodin was his name."

Maddy dropped the cup of tea she was holding onto her saucer with a crash. Tea went everywhere.

"Oh! Oh, I'm so sorry!" She rapidly wiped up as much of the mess as her napkin would allow. Mrs. Hubbard came in from the kitchen and provided additional assistance. After the shattered crockery was removed, Fyodor Herskovin took Maddy's hand and patted it in reassurance.

"A broken cup – it's lucky."

"I'm so sorry… is it really?"

"At least that's what I was told when I was a boy." He shrugged. "What can I say? Russians are weird."

Maddy laughed, then turned serious again. "So Lyubov - what happened to her?"

"I have not been sure since Sasha was removed."

"Removed?"

Herskovin sighed. "They didn't kill him when they found out, at least I don't think so. But he was arrested and sent to prison. That much I was able to learn before the network was rolled up."

"Rolled…"

"Forgive me. Those of us who worked in the profession have a tendency towards euphemism and understatement. Everyone was killed."

"Oh. Oh, gosh." Maddy sat back - she needed a moment for herself. The juxtaposition of the cozy room, and the fire in the fireplace, and Herskovin's soft, accented voice, against a level of personal sacrifice - which made her question her own commitment to… well, anything - knocked the wind out of her. She was talking with a man who lost a child and whose friends and co-workers were jailed and executed. Any problems she was dealing with paled in comparison.

This is a good job for me, she thought, as she regained her composure. Learning some perspective, if nothing else.

"So you came to England... Donovan told me that you got a raw deal from the government."

"He says that because that's what he knows – it was the only way for him to process the reality. For me to have lived to be sitting here now, I needed to be completely reinvented. Only when the wall came down did I start to relax, but if I had not become Teddy Hirsch - a little man in a little auto shop in the East End, they would have found me and killed me. I remained beneath their notice until they no longer cared...

"At least I thought so until recently."

"Why would they care now?"

Herskovin got up and went towards the window. He used the sleeve of his sweater to wipe the steam off the window. He looked out onto the street. The afternoon light was starting to fade. His shoulders slumped. "It's not 'they.' It's her."

"Her? Who?"

"Lyubov. She has found me."

"That's wonderful!..." Maddy felt a remarkable sense of relief that was quickly tempered by the body language of her host. "I mean, isn't it?"

"I have grown to doubt that," replied Herskovin sadly.

"What do you mean?"

"I mean that I have spent the last fifty years trying to connect the dots, and the picture they form isn't a pretty one." He turned back to Maddy. "Come with me. Let me show you something."

Herskovin motioned for her to follow him upstairs, and after a moment's hesitation, Maddy did so. Upstairs were two rooms – one, obviously his bedroom. A cozy little room with a large television on a dresser facing the bed. An overstuffed reading chair with a stack of mystery novels next to it filled the rest of the room. Opposite the bedroom on the other side of the landing was a little study, lined with books from floor to ceiling. Every horizontal surface was covered with newspapers and magazines and notebooks with scribbled notes - except for the large computer monitor and keyboard that occupied a small section of an old desk.

"Things got easier with the Internet. I used to have the devil of a time getting the right information earlier, in the Sixties and Seventies. Pravda wasn't so easy to get, let alone the Moscow and St. Petersburg Times. Now, if you know what to Google – or Infinity (will that become a verb, too, I wonder…), and you're good with your search syntax, you can find almost anything. In the old days, it was an art form, reading between the lines. Trying to decipher what was really happening from what the press wasn't saying, or how they turned certain phrases. Now the news is out there, one just has to know how to read it."

"I'm afraid I don't understand at all," said Maddy, although given the Cyrillic letters on half of the newspapers and Herskovin's secret agent past, if she gave it some thought she might also start to put the puzzle together, herself.

"I'm sorry. An old man can sometimes forget that the world he lives in isn't the same world that anyone else inhabits. I'm speaking of the secret world, the world where people and things disappear without a trace; where man-made disasters become 'natural' ones; where the price and availability of necessities like oil, grain or water can fluctuate just enough so that billions are made but whole populations starve; where freedom fighters are terrorists and terrorists are freedom fighters. It's a shadowy world, and its language is a fiercely nuanced one. Those that inhabit it can only be glimpsed, caught at a sideways angle, a reflection in a smudged mirror. These are the powerful ones, the ones that no one knows about, but who pull the strings, dictate the flow of guns and diamonds, traffic in drugs, human beings, stolen art…"

"Stolen art." Maddy had found something to latch onto. She had grown very nervous that she was being sucked in by a nut – a conspiracy theorist. But then, given all Herskovin had been through, who could blame him? "What about that? How does that fit into the scheme of what you're researching?"

"Do you have any idea the worth of all of the stolen art in the world? The art that is *known* to have been stolen and hasn't been returned or found? Over 30 billion pounds. Over 50 *billion* dollars. That's the art that people actually *know* is missing, which is a small percentage of the total. I'll give you an example – for decades, there was a systematic removal of small pieces of art and artifacts from the Hermitage in St. Petersburg. No one had any clue what was happening, even that the objects were missing."

"Who was taking them?"

"The little old ladies who served as docents, clerks, security guards. Millions of dollars worth of art passing through their hands."

"Into whose?"

"That's just it. Into whose? No one could find out. When the thefts were finally discovered, and the thieves' homes searched, nothing could be found. They had nothing to show for it – perhaps a little more vodka than they should have had on their salary. Maybe a slightly nicer car than they could have otherwise afforded. But that was it. Someone else ended up with the riches. But the point is that no one knew – for decades.

"Or another example – a more famous one. Have you ever heard of the Amber Room?"

"Yes, but I don't know much about it. It's sort of mythical…"

"A room that once graced Catherine's Palace. Beautifully carved and filigreed ornamentation, an entire room of walls, paneling, chandeliers – all of amber from the forests of Poland and the Baltic countries. Nothing like it in the world. Priceless."

"What happened to it?" Maddy was now rapt with attention. She had a plane to catch, but one of the advantages of flying on a private plane was that she didn't have to wait in line at the airport. She could take the time to hear what Fyodor Herskovin had to say.

"It was disassembled by the Nazis during the Second World War, when they invaded Russia. It was sent back to Germany, to Danzig. It was to become one of Herman Goering's treasures, but it never made it into his possession. Just before the Russians took the city near the end of the war, it disappeared. Never to be found. There are theories that it was destroyed in the bombing of the city, or that it was moved to a more secure location – a salt mine in Poland – but it has vanished. I know it's somewhere, and it's being kept as a sort of security."

"Security, what do you mean?"

"There are some things that are never going to lose their value. In fact, their value increases over time, better than any investment in any bank or stock exchange. And these things are liquid, in a way that even cash or gold is not. Art is one of those things. If one were concerned at all about one's future and wanted a secure investment or asset that couldn't be frozen by an angry government, then art is your answer. The Amber Room, of course, can't be rolled up and tucked under your arm, but a Vermeer could."

"Okay, I'm with you so far, except… except, well,

I'm not. The conversation started with your daughter, and then went into, well, I guess I was starting to think conspiracy theory," Maddy was a little embarrassed, but decided to go for it, "and that you were perhaps a little... nutty... and now it's stolen art."

"But that's the conversation. My daughter. Conspiracy. Stolen Art. It does all connect."

"Wait. Are you saying your daughter is stealing art as part of a world-wide conspiracy?"

"See for yourself. Look." Herskovin went over to his computer and with a few mouse clicks pulled up a map of the world. The map was dotted with red dots, significantly clustered in Europe - especially France, Germany, Italy and Poland - but there were some as far afield as Tokyo, Abu Dhabi, Boston and Hong Kong.

"This is a map pinpointing every unsolved art and jewelry theft over the last twenty years."

"Why the last twenty years?"

"I don't believe it coincidental that there was an uptick in this activity once the Soviet Union dissolved."

"What would that have to do with anything?"

"When the Soviet Union ceased to be, a vacuum was created. Or rather, a new business model developed."

"I'm falling behind again, I'm afraid," said Maddy.

"This will help." A few more mouse clicks and a different map appeared. This one was covered with blue dots. "I was a station chief. When I left the KGB, I still knew the locations of most of the other stations across the world. Most are based out of embassies and consulates, but others are in locations near borders or large ports. What do you see when I overlay the blue dots and the red?"

"That most of them turn purple. The red dots and blue dots overlap. But that's not surprising – most of the world's great art tends to be concentrated in the great cities."

"Of course, of course. But what I find intriguing is that what is revealed is a means, an opportunity. A network. Imagine you have an existing infrastructure that is capable of moving people and material around the world, capable of tight logistical coordination, which has unique tools and equipment, that a more limited, private group would not have access to. An organization that is built through training, trust, and patriotism, but is suddenly without purpose. Imagine someone had the foresight to restructure this previously non-profit organization towards new, extremely profitable ends."

Maddy's eyes grew wide. "The Pink Panthers... I thought they were mostly disaffected young men out of the Balkans."

"Sure. But who organizes them? What is the central intelligence that directs the movements of the men on the ground? Each cell has a leader, but each cell leader reports to someone above him, who must report to someone else. And the art and jewelry needs to be trafficked somehow and end up somewhere."

"What do you know about Polonium-210?" asked Maddy with a sudden inspiration.

It was now Herskovin's turn to have his eyes widen. "We discussed its use for purposes of assassination, even back in the 50's, but it was too difficult to handle, and the equipment necessary to produce it was not as prevalent as it is now. Why do you ask? I understand the FSB has been touched with finally using it, but no hard evidence."

"No hard evidence, but two people have been... assassinated with it recently. And they're not politically motivated, as far as we can tell, so I guess they're murders, not assassinations. They look to be part of a cleaning operation by someone involved in the traffic of stolen art.

"And one of them was found in a tank of formaldehyde that should have contained a killer whale. An art piece that your son created."

Herskovin was shocked by this. Apparently, the news had not been passed on to him yet by his son.

"Then she has found us."

"Lyubov?"

"I fear so."

"What has she got to do with all of this?"

"She became a ward of the state once Borodin was... disappeared. She grew up in a special school, with special training. Knowing how much she must have hated me for abandoning her, it must have been with that great sense of Russian irony that her masters made her, when she reached maturity, the chief of Berlin Station."

"For the KGB?" Woah, thought Maddy.

Herskovin just nodded, sadly. After a moment, he pulled it all together. "So what does someone, who has been trained and lived the way she has, do when the her masters no longer need her? What does anyone do when one leaves government work?"

"One enters the private sector?"

"And one can still, occasionally, consult for one's old boss - more profitable, don't you know?" He paused. "So imagine, someone with the connections, the infrastructure, the native intelligence, the training and..." here his shoulders slumped, "the anger... and you have the answer to many mysteries."

"The Queen of Spades..." Maddy whispered almost to herself. A cold breeze from somewhere ruffled the curtains, and the lights shimmered.

Herskovin closed his eyes and sighed. "Where did you hear that name?"

"My partner. He's in St. Petersburg now. He sent this text that just said 'The Queen of Spades.'"

The pain in Herskovin's face was heartbreaking, and terrifying.

"Then your partner is as good as dead."

XLII

Jimmy slept like a stone. The white noise from the engines, the forty-plus hour day, the excellent meal with the excellent wine and scotch caused him to sleep as hard as he could remember. The refueling stop in Bangor went by completely without his notice. It was the smell of exquisite coffee from the kitchen that roused him from his slumber, along with the golden light that seeped into the cabin through the slits under the window blinds.

"Good. You're just in time." Orkin was sitting across from Jimmy in sweat pants and a t-shirt. "I've got some spare work-out gear. Get yourself ready and we'll spend some time with Vanessa getting our blood flowing."

It was more than just blood flowing. Vanessa ran a pretty rigorous flow Yoga session. Although she started slowly, she cranked up the tempo quickly, so that both Jimmy and Orkin were gleaming with sweat after an hour. Jimmy hadn't done Yoga in a while, but the moves came back to him.

I'm going to be sore tomorrow, he thought. But the final ten minutes of the session were a chance for him to rest and catch his breath. Lying on his back with his eyes closed, listening to his breathing and the soft music, with the thrum of the jet engines like the waves of the ocean constantly in the background, he found his head was as clear as it had been since he could remember.

This is good, he thought. Going to need all my wits about me over the next twenty-four hours.

A shower – who knew you could take a shower on a plane before? – a light breakfast of buckwheat blueberry pancakes with a plate of kiwi to start and fresh squeezed orange juice, capped with as good a cup of espresso as he had ever had, and Jimmy was ready for the strategy session.

As he and Ivan Orkin sat down at the dining table, which had now become a conference table, Jimmy was intrigued to see the sunlight was rapidly moving through white light into golden again. He realized that between the duration of the flight and the time difference – ten hours – he would be arriving at their destination in the evening, which seemed to be approaching.

"We're being met at the airfield. We'll be interfacing directly with Interpol," he said to Orkin.

"What about the local police?" Orkin peered over his glasses, which, when he wore them, made him look especially intense.

"The Interpol agent is reluctant to get them involved at this point. It might compromise our security."

"I suspected as much. Once we triangulate, I've got my own men standing by." Orkin smiled mischievously. "We don't need no stinkin' badges."

Jimmy snorted, almost spitting his last sip of espresso.

"As a member of a local constabulary myself, I'm not sure I'm supposed to like this. By all rights, I'm supposed to be in direct communication with my counterparts."

"You would, I can tell you, only be communicating with the enemy. It's a tight arrangement…" Orkin sighed. "As a man who has had to navigate dark waters myself, I know how this works."

"Then tell me something. You know how a dog

can chase a car..."

"I know. For us, it's the dog chasing a bear. It amounts to the same thing. What to do with the bear once you've caught it?"

"Exactly. If our target is as deeply connected as it appears, then what's our exit strategy?"

"Let's just say, if we play our cards right, we'll have a bargaining chip that will purchase our passage to freedom."

Jimmy was not a card player, and didn't much like gambling. He had a moment where he reflected that that would be why he would never be a billionaire. There was a quality that those rare individuals had – certainly Orkin had – that allowed them to put it all on the line against enormous potential gain.

"I can see from your face you don't like the odds," said Orkin.

"I'm not sure what's in our favor," replied Jimmy.

"Us. A couple of smart guys. With means. And, if we don't screw up, no one will know we're coming. At least in time."

"But don't we have to get clearance to land from somebody? Someone who might pass the word on to someone else?"

"I've got a microchip plant just across the border, with it's own private airfield. We'll be landing in a completely different country, and we'll drive from there. A little cross-country. It's not that far."

"Oh. Crap. Then I better make a phone call. We're expected at the airfield outside of St. Petersburg."

"Tell him to meet us at his office. We'll need to start from there."

XLIII

"It's a beggar's life," said the Queen of Spades. "But don't tell it to a poor man." She sucked on her cigarette and exhaled out of the side of her mouth.

"Why is that?" asked Carlos. She had a way of talking that was weirdly relaxing. The purr to the Rs, the slight "sh" sound to her S's. The Russian babushka with her bed-time stories. Well, that and the constant flow of vodka. Carlos' glass never seemed to be empty. She watched him very carefully that way.

"Because he has to kill for every thrill, the best he can."

Wait a minute... She laughed and laughed. Her laugh was throaty, with a little bit of a rattle – a smoker's laugh. A touch of madness to the laugh, maybe? Carlos was more than a little freaked out all of a sudden.

"Steely Dan. Pretzel Logic. Great album. You know it?"

Carlos grimaced. He had found the album in his older sister's record collection. Listened to it once. Too odd and dark and jazzy for his taste at the time. He remembered, though, that there was an undertone of menace – even gangster slang – throughout the album. Things began to make more sense.

"I had you there, admit it." Her pale green eyes had a hypnotic quality. Carlos felt that if she wanted to, she could enchant him and turn him into a toad or something. He was falling down a rabbit hole, and was in danger of never coming out. His only recourse was to attempt some sort of journalistic professionalism.

"Queen of Spades – why do they call you that?"

The woman sighed. "I have... what do you call it? Mixed feelings about that... sobriquet. Do you know the story?"

"No, ma'am," said Carlos. His head was swimming.

"Here, your glass is empty. Not a good thing. In this weather, you need the alcohol to keep the blood pumping." She refilled his little shot glass. Whew. "A famous story by our most famous writer, Aleksandr Pushkin. It has to do with cards, an old woman and hubris. It's about a young man who thinks he's killed the old woman while trying to steal her secret to wealth, only to find out to his cost that she has one more card to play." The candles flickered momentarily. She sighed. "It makes me feel like an old woman – the nickname."

She's not really that old, thought Carlos, although, truthfully, it would be extremely difficult to place her age. She was – he checked himself – she still had *glimmers* of – beauty. She had *once* been beautiful, he decided. But one could see the hard life that she had lived in her face. It wouldn't hurt for her to stop smoking or... whew... drinking so much. He pegged her for mid-fifties.

"But it is a famous... nickname... and it inspires a certain... awe – is that the right word? She then said, "Grozny. We have a famous ruler, Ivan Grozny. In the West it translates badly. I think you call him Ivan the Terrible, yes?"

"Yes," said Carlos.

"It really means, Ivan the Awesome. Did you know that?"

"No, ma'am." Based on the painting Sergei showed Carlos, Terrible seemed a pretty good translation.

"So names, nicknames, it all can get lost in translation…"

"It's quite a place you've got here," said Carlos, by way of shifting the subject.

"You like it?" She squinted at him as she lit another cigarette.

"It's very… eclectic. And the location. It's pretty isolated. May I ask where we are?"

The Queen of Spades blew some smoke towards the ceiling and then returned her gaze to Carlos. "In round terms, we're on the Gulf of Finland. I think it would be in everyone's best interest, however, to keep it vague." She offered some smoked salmon to Carlos, who helped himself to a large piece of brown bread to place underneath. It was delicious. And he realized how hungry he had become. It was the better part of twenty hours since he last ate.

"You have quite a collection."

"Collection?"

"Of art. You look to be quite the connoisseur. If you don't mind my asking, was that really a Vermeer in the library?"

"It's nice, isn't it? The way he captures the light…" she sighed. "Glorious."

"Um… that piece has been missing for about twenty years."

"Is that so?"

"And the Fernand Leger. That must be a more recent acquisition."

"You know this because…?" She had something of a Mona Lisa smile. She was enjoying having someone with whom she could play Cat and Mouse.

"Because it was hanging on the wall of the Museum of Modern Art in Paris just weeks ago."

The Queen of Spades' eyes grew hard. Just then a little timer went off. The Queen of Spades got up from the table. "The piroshki are ready." She started towards the little kitchen. Carlos rose to follow "Oh, please, wait there, I'll be right back."

"If it's alright, I love watching good cooks at work. I love to cook, myself. Can you show me how to make them?"

The Queen of Spades paused. There was something in that moment. Was it a sense of acceptance? Perhaps an appreciation. Carlos couldn't be sure, but he realized that he might have said something that could have saved his life.

"I have some dough left over, and the filling is easy to make. Sure. Come on. You'll need an apron."

*   *   *

It really wasn't all that hard. Simple pastry dough, and the filling was just a custom blend of ground veal, pork and beef. She had a meat grinder clamped to the wooden table in the kitchen, and she fed the different tenderloins in a strip at a time.

"It tastes better when it's fresh, don't you think?"

"Couldn't agree more, ma'am."

The Queen of Spades looked at Carlos quickly, trying to decide if there was any hidden disrespect when he called her "ma'am." Carlos, though, was definitely a respectful young man when he was dealing with his elders, and she decided that he was sincere.

"I'm not sure I like you calling me 'ma'am,'" she said.

"That's what they call the Queen," said Carlos. He smiled. "Of England. I thought..." he shrugged. The Queen of Spades gave her throaty laugh.

"Call me Tyotya Lyuba."

Carlos tried it. It was hard, all the y's tight against the consonants.

"It means Aunt Lyuba."

"What do the boys, I mean Konstantin and Simyon, call you?"

The Queen of Spades looked again at Carlos, weighing the answer. In that moment, the green to black thing of her eyes happened again. A decision made. "Matrushka."

Carlos had an image of the little dolls that fit inside each other – Matrushka dolls - and it occurred to him in an instant how appropriate that image was. Layers and layers – hiding the core.

"It means 'Little Mother.' Now chop that onion up, I'll get the eggs."

In an effort to avoid mentally imploding at the confirmation of her relationship to the two hoodlums who had beaten him only twelve hours before, Carlos turned his attention to the onion, while the Queen of Spades peeled the shells off of a couple hard boiled eggs. She then slapped a chunk of lard into a hot cast-iron skillet.

"That's the secret," said Carlos. He had already eaten several piroshkis from the first batch, and was starting to feel much better.

"The lard?"

"I mean, no one cooks with lard in the West anymore. At least not in San Francisco. It's like smoking. Just don't do it."

"But it tastes good," said the Queen of Spades with a shrug. Totally runs in the family, the shrug, thought Carlos, watching the way she moved. Now he could see the family resemblance. She sautéed the onion in the lard, then added the ground meat. After it browned, she took the meat, put it into a bowl, and stirred in the hard-boiled egg, which Carlos had also chopped up. "The key ingredient is the dill." She spread a handful of chopped dill into the mixture and stirred it together. Carlos and the Queen of Spades then sat companionably at the table and put the meat into small pastry circles. She taught him how to fold the dough and crimp the edges.

After the second batch was placed into the oven, with the timer set, they wiped their hands and went back to the table by the window. The sky and the water were now black, but the snow outside was glowing blue in the light of a rising moon. The ice hanging from the eaves glistened like diamonds in a Tiffany case, beautiful, but cold. And dangerous. Carlos winced at his reflection in the glass. The Queen of Spades lit a cigarette and leaned back in her chair.

"You were going to tell me a story," said Carlos.

"I was. Now I'm not so sure."

"Why is that?"

"Because I have grown to like you." She sighed. "Neither of my boys likes to cook. It's nice to… how is it you say? 'Hang.' Hang in the kitchen with someone who likes to cook. It is… companionable." She sighed again. "I have spoiled those two." She looked out the window. After a moment of reflection, she returned her gaze to Carlos. "Do you like the fairy tales of Grimm?"

"Um, not really. Meant to scare little children, I always thought. Morals taught through fear. Why do you ask?"

"Then you probably wouldn't like my story. You know Bluebeard?"

"That's, like, the scariest one. The young wife told not to look in the room in the tower, and when the curiosity gets too much, she does and…" Carlos' eyes grew wide.

"Exactly. Once you unlock that door…" Her eyes hardened.

"You would have to kill me."

By way of a reply, the Queen of Spades casually exhaled a large puff of smoke out of the side of her mouth. She then, just as casually, poured Carlos another shot of vodka. Carlos took it, tried not to let his hand shake too much, and slammed the shot. He only hoped that all the alcohol wouldn't damage the device now working its way through his digestive system. He then set the glass down as casually as he could.

"In for a penny, in for pound. Let's hear your story."

XLIV

It was the nicest plane Maddy had ever been on. The Gulfstream V shot up and through the leaden clouds, breaking into the golden light of the late afternoon on the other side. As Maddy took in the endless field of undulating, almost cotton-candy-like fluff, she reflected on the parting words of Fyodor Herskovin.

"You cannot be careful enough. You should not go. She has earned that name. The Queen of Spades..." he sighed. "My daughter... she has buried more than a few men."

"I can't abandon either my friend, or your grandson," she replied. "I have to go. I have no choice."

Fyodor Herskovin looked at her with sad eyes. The family resemblance to Donovan was apparent.

"Wait," said Maddy. "May I see a photo of your wife? I mean, when she was young?"

This caught Herskovin off guard. "Why yes, I suppose so. Why?"

"It may help."

Herskovin took her down the hall towards the bedroom. He went in, and shuffled over to the bedside table. He lovingly picked up a black and white photograph in a small frame and returned with it to Maddy.

"My Anya. And, well, my... daughter."

Maddy saw a beautiful young woman with dark hair and pale eyes. She was holding a little girl of about two years old, resting on her hip. The woman looked nothing like Donovan Hirsch. But Maddy could see Sasha in her eyes and cheekbones – and in the eyes and cheekbones of the little girl. It all came together.

Russian families are complicated, she thought. Yikes.

Maddy turned her gaze from the window towards her companion. Sasha was asleep in the oversized chair opposite her. He is quite beautiful, thought Maddy, gazing at his features caught in the glancing light of the afternoon sun. There's something about Russian boys, she decided. It's the cheekbones and the slightly fuller lips. He was exhausted, having slept little the night before, and having had a full day of grinding meetings in the City with European investors and marketing people. He had fallen asleep as soon as he had settled into his seat.

In an impulsive moment, Maddy pulled out her new phone and took Sasha's photo. The shot was quite artistic – golden light on his sleeping face, which looked even more beautiful as his features relaxed. She then attached the image to his contact information. Her stomach did a nervous flip doing so – something about a level of commitment that crystallized in that moment.

Whew. What am I going to do?

To distract herself from her emotional dilemma, Maddy took a moment to let her eyes wander around the interior of the plane. It was simply but elegantly appointed. Soft beige leather, dark wood paneling, recessed lighting and sumptuous carpeting were seamlessly blended to create an atmosphere of calm. The glass of Sancerre on her side table, with the bottle in an ice bucket close to hand, made her feel that she was in some exclusive lounge. It *was* pretty exclusive, the billionaire's club.

She sighed, then took out her notebook and

started to draw in the family tree. It was pretty complicated, no doubt about it. But it all flowed back to Fyodor Herskovin. He had the two children, Dmitri/Donovan, and Lyuba - who had been left behind. Donovan took after his father, Lyuba her mother. Maddy stared at the photo of the mother and the daughter, which she was able to copy on Herskovin's little desktop copier. Lyuba, who had been raised by Herskovin's aide's family, had taken the name Borodina, the feminine form of Borodin. Somewhere along the way she married a man named Orkin - about whom Maddy knew nothing, except that he had been a colonel in the Russian Army - and had Sasha. She still didn't know what happened between Orkin and Lyuba – Sasha still didn't know for sure, but it was a violent separation when Sasha was only a year old. Unbeknownst to Orkin at the time, and certainly not to Sasha until recently, two more boys were born – twins – a pregnancy that had been kept secret from everyone.

So Donovan Hirsch was Sasha's uncle. Who knew?

And the explanation of who might have done what on that dark night in San Francisco, only... was it really only four nights ago? ... became clearer. Only just a little. Sasha's involvement was still vague, if there was any involvement at all. Certainly, Maddy had decided, he had taken no part in any of the violent aspects of the evening's events. Not that she had really asked – she just had to believe it to be true.

Where were they flying to? Sasha had been vague about this, too, but she knew they were flying east – the sun was behind them. All she knew was that she was willing to go along for the ride – she was working the most exciting and complex story she could imagine. And she also knew that the man across from her was as compelling as any she had ever met.

*   *   *

After they touched down, Maddy and Sasha worked their way down the rolling stairway onto the icy tarmac, where a Mercedes limousine awaited them. The door of the limousine was opened for them by a large man in a black suit wearing sunglasses – very Men In Black, thought Maddy. As Sasha handed the man in black a large package for safekeeping in the trunk, Maddy climbed into the back seat only to have one of the bigger shocks of her life.

"Hi. My name is Konstantin Ranevsky. You can call me Kostya." He was lounging in the back of the limo in a fur coat.

"But you, you look, I mean..." Maddy was sort of creeped out. Sasha climbed in after her and she took both young men in. "Well, you're not twins," she decided after a moment.

Sasha gave a tight smile.

"But the resemblance is uncanny, just the same."

"That's because we cultivated it," said Ranevsky with a Cheshire Cat grin. "It played to our advantage to cultivate the same facial hair, haircut, etc... at least for a little while."

"Our?" Maddy looked as Sasha.

Sasha looked decidedly uncomfortable. "His. Theirs."

Ranevsky giggled, and pointed to his brother theatrically. "The Smart One."

"Which one are you?"

"I'm the youngest brother, also known as The Clever One."

Maddy could see now that the man called Ranevsky was much – well not *much*, just enough –

younger than Sasha. Two or three years. And he had a mole on his left cheek. Which could, thought Maddy, be covered with makeup. His face was a little thinner and longer – more... 'feral' was the only word that came to mind. But the resemblance was indeed strong, and with enough photomanipulation and with enough people in front or behind in an understaffed and overworked passport control, no one would really notice the difference.

"Your mom must have the dominant genes."

Ranevsky cackled with laughter at this. "More than you know!" Again Sasha looked uncomfortable. Ranevsky nestled back into his corner of the limousine, snuggling in a very feline fashion into his fur. His eyes went half-lidded. "Sasha. How much does she know?"

Sasha's eyes travelled left and right before locking in on his younger brother's. "Not much. Really."

"Then why is she here? Matrushka may take issue with an outsider..."

"*Mom* will be okay with this," replied Sasha. More to himself, "I'll make her okay with this."

Ranevsky giggled. The giggling was starting to get on Maddy's nerves. "Good luck with that," Ranevsky replied with his Cheshire Cat grin, then turning to look out the window at the moonlit birch trees.

Maddy took in the landscape as well. In the distance was the glow of a great city cast up into the frozen mist. The limousine had skirted the city and was now on an arterial highway. "Where are we?"

"That's St. Peters..." began Sasha. Ranevsky put his finger to his lips, causing Sasha to bite his. Ranevsky tutted. "Sasha. She will be much... happier... for her ignorance, don't you think?" Turning to Maddy. "Let's just say we're in the land of ice and snow, from the midnight sun where the hotsprings flow..."

Maddy could just roll her eyes. There was something about Ranevsky. The world seemed to be one big joke to him, but every joke carried an undertone of menace. She decided to change the subject.

"I'm still confused by the names...."

"That's a good thing," replied Ranevsky. "If it was easy, then everyone would be figuring it out. And, as it *has* happened, figuring it out could be... unlucky... for the person who did so." Maddy shuddered, thinking of the head in the tank.

"Is that what happened to Vladimir Spassky? He figured it out?"

Ranevsky slid his eyes over to Maddy while not moving his head. He then spoke quietly in Russian to Sasha. Both men turned to Maddy, their eyes both shifting from pale green to black. Jeez, it's like they're both Slytherens, she thought.

"What do you know of Vladimir Spassky?" asked Sasha.

"Sasha, what do *you* know?" replied Maddy, her heart starting to sink.

"I only know of him as a reporter. Something of a maverick – not a big fan of the state, or of Putin. Why?"

Maddy looked at Ranevsky. The fact that his eyes retained their darkness while Sasha's lost his told her everything. She was both mildly relieved and yet more terrified. I know which one to keep my eyes on, she thought. The Clever One.

"Let's go back to the names," declared Ranevsky, now looking at the ceiling of the limousine.

"No. Sorry I asked," replied Maddy. There are some answers that aren't worth dying for, she thought.

"It's okay. I like you. And for certain Sasha does." What happens if mom doesn't, thought Maddy. I'm sure that trumps everything. Oh, well. In for a penny, in for a pound.

"Russian families can be complicated. Loyalties are interesting. It seems that in any great family, there are factions, or at least different sides to the equation. In our family, we all have staked our claims to different sides. Sasha, here, is on our mother's side, the Borodin side. As is Simyon."

sborodin@internationalx.rus suddenly made sense to Maddy. More than one sborodin. Whew.

"So Ranevsky..."

"My nom de guerre. Not that I'm *not* a big fan of matrushka's – trust me, as lieutenants go, she couldn't do much better, but it became inconvenient for me to be known as a Borodin – at least in certain circles, at least if I want to retain any... autonomy. I borrowed the name from one of the characters from my favorite Chekhov play – 'yellow into the corner pocket...'" He mimed shooting billiards, pointing his invisible cue directly at Sasha. Ranevsky grinned. This time he almost came across as charming. There has to be something there that binds Sasha and Kostya together, at least more than just the family thing. Perhaps Ranevsky really is clever – clever enough to solicit Sasha's interest, if not complete sympathy.

"And Orkin," Maddy knew almost nothing about Orkin, except from what Fyodor Herskovin had mentioned, but he was involved in the family tree.

Ranevsky slowly and meaningfully put his finger to his lips again. "Not a name I would mention. Ever. Again. Persona non grata. Just saying."

Got it, thought Maddy. She turned her attention to the window. The glow from the city in the distance had almost disappeared to her left and behind her. A large expanse of darkness lay between them and the city, glimpsed through breaks in the trees – it must be water, she thought, as the moon glinted off white caps in the distance. It must be the Gulf of Finland. She did a quick calculation. If that really was St. Petersburg, then they were north of the city and heading west. The landscape really looked like something out of a fairy tale. Birch trees stretched off into the distance, like rows of silver spikes. There was no one on the road. Where ever they were going, it was remote.

Which was not reassuring.

Suddenly, a large black SUV came roaring towards them from the opposite direction. As it passed them, Ranevsky tilted his head, as if he was trying to calculate who it might be, coming from where they were going. After a moment, he shrugged, and nestled into his fur, deciding that it wasn't worth the effort. A nap.

Sasha was deep in thought. Maddy slid her hand over towards his, and he took it. He gave her a smile – it was the kind of smile that one might call "brave." She gave it a squeeze, as if to say,

I'm in this with you.

XLV

When they hit the ground, Jimmy and Orkin were greeted by a team of men who moved with military precision, gathering them and the flight crew into a series of black SUVs. The convoy then drove towards a mammoth building – several football fields long, calculated Jimmy. It was clean and glistened in its newness. The flight crew, including Vanessa and Michael, disembarked after they arrived at the main entrance to the facility – a gleaming three story lobby with a reception desk backed by a mammoth, internally illuminated logo wall. Orkin Industries. After the others left, with orders from Orkin to be ready to fly by 0900, Jimmy and Orkin climbed into the front seats of one of the SUVs. Orkin peeled out and blew through the security gate, with a crisp salute from the guards as they passed.

"Nice operation," said Jimmy, impressed. "Looks like you've got your employees well trained."

Orkin grinned a wolfish grin. "In successful manufacturing, as with the military, discipline is everything. We're not Apple or Pixar, where people lounge around generating 'ideas.' We get things done, with clear direction from above. Different mindset."

Orkin pointed the SUV east. After less than an hour, Orkin turned off his headlights as they approached the lights of a border crossing in the distance. "This is when the all-wheel drive comes in handy," he said.

"Um, entering a country illegally isn't…" Jimmy couldn't finish the sentence as he almost bit his tongue in half. The SUV lurched off the road onto what looked to be no more than a footpath through the birches, and went flying over the snow drifts.

"Shit," was all Jimmy could manage as his bones were slammed up and down.

"Once you've had to drive like a bat out of hell through the mountains of Afghanistan with machine gun fire all around you, this kind of thing is more fun than anything. Hang on."

"Won't they find our tracks in the morning?"

"If we haven't made our way back by then, it won't really matter. We've got about eight hours to get our shit together."

After what seemed like an eternity of having his teeth rattled, Jimmy was grateful when they hit paved road. At this point Orkin put the peddle to the metal.

"Which branch of the armed forces did you say were from? The airforce?" joked Jimmy as they rocketed down the road. There was no one on the highway – it was getting close to midnight. Then, out of nowhere, a limousine came up over the hill in front of them. With both cars moving at more than eighty miles per hour, the moment of passing was the blink of an eye, with both cars buffetted slightly by the air being pushed between them.

"Must be some dignitary on his way to his dacha," said Orkin.

"How do you figure, other than the limo?"

"The government plates."

*   *   *

The Interpol office in St. Petersburg was in a run-down looking 18th Century building. Jimmy's confidence that they would find anything of value within dropped precitipitously – until he stepped through the large wooden doors. Inside, he found a gleaming office facility, with the latest in lighting and workstation furnishings.

"We're one of the newest offices in the network," said Sergei by way of explanation. "This office only opened last year, after much pressure from the international community. I guess we reached a tipping point here in St. Petersburg, where we had more crime than even Moscow." He led Orkin and Jimmy past several work stations, staffed by some of the most beautiful women Jimmy had ever seen.

Dang. Wouldn't get anything done here, Jimmy thought. It would be just too hard to concentrate.

They finally arrived at Sergei's work station, and Jimmy couldn't help but smile. He looked at the pile of papers on Sergei's desk and felt a certain commiseration. It doesn't get any more glamorous or interesting anywhere else, he thought. Police work is still all about the paperwork, and Sergei was old school.

Except he wasn't.

Sergei waved them on to a conference room. After the men were brought black tea by a stunning young blonde woman with supermodel cheekbones in a pencil skirt and five-inch heels, Sergei pulled out a wireless keyboard and began tapping away at the keys. A giant monitor came to life with the Interpol seal emblazoned across the desktop.

"So where do you want to start?"

"Carlos Rodriguez," replied Jimmy.

"Cute kid," said Sergei. "I didn't have him figured for much, but he's got balls." Sergei lit a cigarette. "We hit Red Square, and I got him situated. When he spotted Konstantin Ranevsky heading to the Gents, he went after him. That's the last I saw him. They must have gone out the back door."

"Who is Konstantin Ranevsky?" asked Jimmy.

"From what we can gather, one of the top Panthers, possibly the top, but we don't think so. He's a clever cuss, but couldn't be that clever. He works for someone." Sergei opened a file on the server. The photo that popped up caused both Jimmy and Orkin to shake their heads in wonder.

"That's Sasha Borodin..." stuttered Jimmy.

"No, it's not," interjected Orkin, sadly. "One of twins. Sasha is the fruit of my loins, but, well, the other two..."

"Two?" asked Sergei.

"I'm intrigued that you have the one boy in your database – do you have the other?"

"What other?"

"His name is Simyon."

Sergei shrugged, lit a cigarette, and worked the keyboard. A sequence of faces flashed on the screen. None of them matched the first. Sergei exhaled fiercely through his nostrils.

"It seems that, perhaps, the two brothers have allowed themselves to be morphed into one," he said. "Ranevsky is the one who is allowed to play in the light – Simyon lurks in the shadows. It can be very handy to have a twin, sometimes. It can make what otherwise seems impossible, possible."

"You can say that again," said Jimmy.

"So you have three sons," said Sergei, with the narrowed-eyed look of someone pulling the pieces together. "Only one in the database, though – a Russian, who doesn't share your last name. Then there's one who's just become a world famous American internet entrepeneur... and a third who lurks on the periphery. I think it's time you came clean with how this all fits together."

Orkin sighed. As much as he had withheld from Jimmy in their earlier conversations, he now knew that a significant piece of his past would now have to come out into the light. "The twins... they are not my boys. My wife and I met when the Soviet Union was still the Soviet Union. We were both stationed in Berlin and had a child, Sasha."

"Why's his name Borodin, then?" asked Sergei.

"I'll get to that. A year later, my wife and I had... a falling out. The collapse of our country meant for shifting allegiences, or rather, it presented opportunities that each of us followed in our own way. We didn't approve of each other's choice. That, and..." Orkin's eyes went steely, "I discovered she was having an affair with one of her agents."

"Agents... wait. What did she do?" asked Jimmy.

"She was the station chief in Berlin for the KGB."

Jimmy whistled. Sergei shook his head.

"And this agent, who was he?"

Orkin took in both men slowly, ascertaining how much they could handle. He decided that they weren't ready. "Let's just say he has moved on. He's in government now."

"So the twins..."

"I did not know she was pregnant when we parted. She left Berlin to follow her lover back to Russia. I only discovered their existence a few years later." He sighed. "It was an infamous confrontation."

"What happened?" asked Jimmy, although he thought he knew the answer.

"Won't tell you," replied Orkin.

"Pleading the Fifth again, is that it? Look, we're not in San Francisco, anymore. We can keep this between us. Right, Sergei?"

Sergei nodded. "Off the record."

A moment where, once again, Orkin took in the two men and ascertained how much he thought they could handle. A decision.

"Have you ever shot someone in the head?"

XLVI

"Have you ever been shot in the head?" asked The Queen of Spades.

"Um, I don't remember," said Carlos sarcastically, and then wished he hadn't done that. "I would think it would, well, it would hurt. At least." He stared at his piroshki.

"You would think that. It doesn't hurt at all. At least, I didn't feel a thing." She puffed on her cigarette. "It's the moments leading up to being shot that do something to you. They change your perspective."

They make you mad, thought Carlos. How could they not?

"How does one survive that?" he asked.

"A rare sequence of unlikely events." She shrugged. "I got lucky. I fainted just as I heard the sound of the trigger being pulled. It's true. I fainted." She curled her upper lip at the thought. Carlos suspected that if the moment ever came again, she would face it without fear, having gone through it the first time. That, and by becoming a serious-ass tough old lady. "The bullet came in at just the right angle and was deflected by the skull just enough. I have a hard head." She reflexively rubbed the scar tissue at her scalp line.

"What about the bleeding?"

"Like a stuck pig. That, I think, is what really saved me. I looked dead – all that blood. But I was found before I lost too much."

"Who did this to you? ...And why?"

The Queen of Spades shrugged. "Russian families are weird. Love is hard. Life can take strange twists... Let us just say that the person responsible will come to wish he had chosen differently."

I'll bet you can make someone extremely uncomfortable, thought Carlos, but kept that thought to himself. "When did this happen?"

"A long time ago. I had come home. I was pregnant. I was building a new life, a new career, and I followed my lover home, only to be.. let down gently. He could let a girl down gently. He helped me set up my new... how you say? Line of business. He took care of me. Gave me a new purpose. I had hopes and dreams – I never really thought of myself as someone's mistress - but then... I was like Anna Karenina, doomed to love this unatainable man. Then *he* came," she spat the word 'he' in a horrible way... the man who did this to me." This time she touched the scar on her forehead intentionally.

"Ivan Orkin," whispered Carlos to himself. The candles flickered, there was a cold breeze. The Queen of Spades' eyes became small slits, and Carlos knew, in that instant, he would pay dearly for the insight he had just gained. More quickly than Carlos ever thought possible, the Queen of Spades grabbed the knife next to the salmon and leapt from her seat...

"Hi, mom, I'm home!"

The breeze was, in fact, a real breeze, not a psychological one. Standing in the door of the little hut was someone who looked a lot like Ranevsky, but wasn't Ranevsky. And with him was Maddy.

"Maddy!" Carlos croaked, too freaked out to do much else.

"Carlos!" cried Maddy, who could see that her friend was in terrible danger.

Covers blown.

Oops.

XLVII

"So where is he now?" Jimmy was fearful that he was too late.

Sergei pulled up a map of St. Petersburg on the giant screen. Nothing.

"He's not in town. Anymore." Sergei tapped on the keyboard and the map zoomed out to show a larger chunk of Russia. A dot blinked on the screen. "He's about one hundred and fifty kilometers northwest of here."

"Is he still alive?"

"No way of knowing. I gave him the tranceiver, what he did with it is anyone's guess. Although I did tell him to shove it up his ass."

"Jesus," was all Jimmy could say. "Wait a second. Where was it that Spassky's body was found?"

"Bobbing in an inlet near Saints Peter and Paul."

"So there's still a chance. He's a couple hours' drive from there."

At that moment, the dot began to move. Back towards St. Petersburg.

"Christ. Can we track this as we drive? Perhaps we can head them off?"

Sergei tapped away at his iPhone. As both Jimmy and Ivan Orkin looked at him in disbelief, Sergei looked up, somewhat surprised. "What? Oh." He shrugged and said simply, "Yes. Of course there's an app for that."

XLVIII

"So what did you bring me?"

It was an awkward situation. Carlos and Maddy had their hands tied behind them with plastic zip ties. Sasha had his head in both hands looking disconsolately at the table. Ranevsky was holding a large package.

And Yuri was holding a submachine gun.

"What?" said Sasha, shaken from his despairing reverie. "Oh. Yes. I picked it up in London. I thought... well, I thought you would enjoy it."

Ranevsky tore open the brown paper. Maddy couldn't help but gasp. It was the Serebryakova. Everyone in the room took a moment, admiring the spectacular painting. Ranevsky stuck out his lower lip in real admiration. "Not bad," he said, nodding in appreciation.

"Where did you steal that from?" asked Carlos.

"Steal? I bought it, straight up," replied Sasha.

"It's true. I was with him," said Maddy somewhat defensively. "Actually, *I* bought it. I mean, I did the bidding. I mean... oh, never mind."

"Clever girl," said the Queen of Spades. "And that's my boy," she said tossling Sasha's hair. "He has learned so much so quickly. And he has good taste. I can only think that he gets that from me..."

"Mom. Do we have to have them tied to the chairs? I mean, this is spectacularly embarrassing."

The Queen of Spades laughed and turned to Maddy and Carlos. "Parents. Children. From the beginning of time, neither seems to understand the other." She placed her hand on her breast dramatically. "We make such plans for our children, we work so hard..." She looked inwardly for a moment. "We work so hard..." she whispered. Then dramatically again. "And they never understand our sacrifices..."

"Mom..."

"Matrushka..."

Both boys rolled their eyes as they spoke simultaneously. Carlos, in spite of his predicament, had to laugh. It was both too weird and yet so like any family, anywhere. Maddy kicked him under the table and gave him her best evil eye.

"Sasha! Kostya! Tisha!" 'Tisha' must mean 'shush,' thought Maddy. "I can understand your disappointment at my hospitality. She seems like a nice girl. She's certainly pretty enough."

"She's my friend and schoolmate. She's harmless."

"I don't think so. Do you know this boy?" She gestured at Carlos.

"No, never seen him before," said Sasha.

"Do you read the famous newspaper in San Francisco? The Clarion? He writes for the Clarion."

"So, tie *him* up, then, but leave Maddy alone." Maddy wasn't sure how to react to this weird chivalry.

"Idiot boy." The Queen of Spades shook her head and moved to a cupboard, where she pulled out an iPad. Maddy was surprised to see it had a pink leather cover. Black snakeskin would have somehow been more appropriate... After a few taps, she turned the screen towards Sasha. With a small gasp, Maddy saw the homepage of the Clarion's website. With the headline about the missing killer whale.

With the byline of Maddy Stevenson and Carlos Rodriguez.

"Maddyandcarlos," said the Queen of Spades. "Investigative journalists. You brought her here."

"I... I didn't know," said Sasha in confusion. After a moment, "But you brought *him* here!"

"It amused me to do so," was the Queen of Spades' somewhat coy reply. "After what Kostya and Simyon did to him, I thought..."

"What, that you would nurse him back to health and send him back to San Francisco?" asked Ranevsky.

Carlos reflected in sudden horror that the Queen of Spades had a catlike quality. She was playing with her mouse before she killed it.

"Look. I have no one to talk to." She waved her hands dramatically. "*No one.* I am so alone."

Ranevsky leaned in conspiratorially to Maddy and said, "It's her favorite play, too."

"What play is that?" asked Carlos, by way of buying some time, any time, by changing the subject.

"The Cherry Orchard," said Ranevsky.

"Our greatest playwright, Anton Chekhov," said the Queen of Spades. "He had a way with the nuances of family interaction."

"What's it about?" continued Carlos.

The Queen of Spades exhaled some smoke and thought for a moment. "It's about many things. Mostly, it's about a once wealthy family that loses everything in the face of great changes all around them. While they struggle against fate they are unhappy. Only once they embrace the loss of all they thought they held dear do they find peace, and, maybe, just maybe, happiness."

"Sounds Russian. For sure," said Carlos.

"Konyeshna," said the Queen of Spades. She went over and touched Carlos gently on the cheek. "You really are a bright boy. I will miss spending time with you."

"Why? What happens now?"

The Queen of Spades put out her cigarette and pursed her lips. It was as if she was trying to find the right way to phrase a difficult thought.

"I suppose we have to kill you."

XLIX

I'm going to kill them, thought Carey Portman as she looked out her window at the building across the way, caught in the golden afternoon light that shot straight down Mission Street. She sighed. She had expressed that thought almost from the day she took Maddy and Carlos on as interns. Those kids. They were often, in her initial assessment of any situation in which they caught themselves, not worth the trouble. But then, somehow, they got to the other side and delivered the goods. In spite of the aggravation – and she was pretty aggravated at this very moment - she found she cared deeply for them, an almost maternal instinct kicking in. She didn't have any children, herself – she and her husband, Robert, deciding that there was too much of their own lives to live without children slowing them down. But after a lifetime in the trenches, after crossing the globe countless times pursuing good stories in bad places, after adventures too scary to reflect on too carefully, she found there was still something wanting in her life. The opportunity to mentor two young people helped to fill the void. For all their faults and poor judgment, they were good kids, and to see their faces light up when they got excited about a story was enough to warm her heart.

Not that she would ever let them know that.

She rubbed her forehead. It was now almost thirty-six hours since she had spoken with Maddy – even longer since she got the email with the pdf from Carlos. She was aggravated with them, but also deeply concerned. A thought made her smile, though. Of the two of them, she found she would always worry more about Carlos. Maddy was relatively sensible, in spite of her naivete. Carlos was too brave for his own good. Jesus. The Russian Mafia. Or spies. Or both.

She was both heartened and disheartened when, in a moment of desparation, she called the Green Street station and asked for Detective James Wang and found he was on assignment out of the country. That was ominous. First, the receptionist couldn't tell her where he was. Second, she knew that Detective Wang would have no jurisdiction wherever he was headed, so it sounded more like an emergency than a diplomatic mission. But at least he was on his way.

Carey looked at the clocks on her wall. She was worldly enough to have four clocks with the local times of San Francisco, New York, London and Shanghai for immediate reference. It was coming up on three o'clock in San Francisco, midnight in London. A quick calculation - it was almost two in the morning in St. Petersburg. She was supposed to meet her husband for the members' only pre-opening reception at SFMOCA in a few hours. She hesitated, then pounded away at the keyboard of her computer. Her instincts took over and she booked the flight to St. Petersburg that was departing at six o'clock.

Her husband of twenty years would understand – it wouldn't be the first time she stood him up.

Those kids.

L

"But you promised me a story!"

The way Carlos said that, with his lower lip sticking out, made him look like a disconsolate four year old, disappointed at bedtime. Even the Queen of Spades had to laugh. Maddy just looked wild-eyed, and Sasha was fit to be tied.

"You are a funny boy." She narrowed her eyes. After the longest moment of Maddy's life, the Queen of Spades fished around into her apron pockets and pulled out her pack of cigarettes and pulled one out. She lit the cigarette on one of the candle flames, blew some smoke out of the side of her mouth, and poured herself a vodka.

"I did. Okay. A story."

"After which, you kill us," offered Maddy.

"After which, I kill you. Yes."

"Mom, that's bullshit. You're not killing anyone." There was a moment when Sasha looked around the room, searching for whatever sign would come from his mother, Ranevsky or Yuri that would offer relief from the otherwise nightmarish prospect that they were sincere. No sign came. Just green eyes shifting to black in the trick of the light. "Jesus!"

The butt of the revolver came down quickly. Sasha crumpled to the ground. Maddy screamed.

After a moment… "He'll be fine. For a Silicon Valley CEO he still just needs to learn when to shut up." Ranevsky tucked the gun into the back of his pants and motioned for Yuri to pick Sasha up and lay him out on a small sofa.

"It's true. For such a smart boy, he can be so stupid," said the Queen of Spades. "What?" She took in the two young journalists. "You've never heard of 'tough love?'"

"Tiger Mom's got nothing on you," replied Carlos, shaking his head.

"So where were we?"

"The story."

"Right. Well you two are smart young reporters, why not do the interview?"

"The what?" Maddy was still recovering from seeing her... what did she want to call him? Boyfriend? No. Lover? She couldn't quite wrap her head around that... Sasha... slump to the floor unconscious.

"You ask me questions, and I will answer them."

"This is so you learn what we know and what we don't."

"Let's just say it's more fun for me this way."

"Okay," Carlos was in. "Let's start from the beginning. Pink Panthers."

A puff of smoke. "You know, I get a kick out of that nickname. It makes it all sound relatively harmless."

"Tell that to the Russian priest at the Green Street Church."

The Queen of Spades raised her eyes to the heavens, as if she were Job, enduring one more vicissitude. "That idiot," she whispered to herself. A sigh. "He can get excited."

"Yes," said Carlos. "He sure can."

"You must break a few eggs to make an omelet," said the Queen of Spades. "Shit happens."

"So you're the one behind them?"

"Sure. It's not hard. After all, with the training we received, organizing jewel and art thefts is pretty mundane. Nothing like assassinations, running agents, supplying rebel armies."

"So you were KGB?" Maddy's turn.

"How do you know that?"

"Well, you just described the job of a secret agent, it's not much of a stretch..."

"So I did. Clever girl. I thought, perhaps, you might have heard this from someone..." Her look was casually sinister.

I did, thought Maddy, but I don't want Fyodor Herskovin in any more trouble than he probably already is.

"So. KGB. Sure. I was KGB. Worked out of Berlin."

"And you inherited a network of out-of-work agents who could then coordinate these thefts, using young men with no connection to the KGB."

"Yes. Nothing like the private sector."

"But is it private?" asked Carlos. "I mean, it must take a lot of rubles to set up such an operation. And the transportation of such stolen goods. It would be super-easy to move things around in diplomatic pouches, on government planes..."

Ranevsky stirred in his chair, a little agitated. "Matrushka..." he growled.

"What is it with you journalists?" asked the Queen of Spades. "Always looking for grand conspiracy theories." She sighed. "So pesky. So much trouble."

"So we're not the first?" asked Maddy. Neither she nor Carlos knew what Jimmy had discovered – that the head in the tank belonged to a journalist – but it would make sense.

"Let's just say that we have a robust firewall against outside interference."

"I'll say," replied Carlos.

"So we're not wrong?" said Maddy, now that she had shaken off the shock of the situation and figured that she had little to lose.

"About the grand conspiracy? Let's come back to that one." After a hesitation. "A good story has some suspense to it..." The Queen of Spades was enjoying herself.

"So the paintings, the art, the jewels... what do you do with all of it? I've seen some amazing pieces here. Some of the most valuable art in the world. I can understand that it's cool to have a Vermeer in your library, but after a certain point... I mean, what's the point? Just keeping it around so no one else can see it? It's all worth a hell of a lot of money."

"It's not about the money. You hear it from time to time, but it's true – after a certain point, money is just boring."

"Um, what could be more interesting than money?" Carlos, being an illegal immigrant's son, had to ask.

"Knowledge. Not just a little bit of knowledge, but immense amounts of knowledge. Enough to completely realign the political realities on this planet."

It was Maddy's turn to ask the stupid question. "What do you mean?"

The Queen of Spades smiled her Mona Lisa smile. "Money is only money. A billion here, a billion there, after a certain point how many tanks do you need to buy? How many missiles? How boring is that?"

"So where does it go?"

"Let's back up a bit and let me ask you a few questions."

"Okay. Shoot. No, I didn't mean that." Carlos looked at Yuri apprehensively. Yuri didn't flinch.

"Do you pay for using Google?"

"Um, no..."

"How about Facebook? Twitter?"

"No, at least not yet, anyway..."

"How do you think they make any money, then?"

"Advertising." Maddy was quite convinced of this.

"These are companies with enough cash to buy most European countries. There aren't enough advertising dollars in the world to generate the kind of profits these companies see. What is it that they have that's so valuable?"

Carlos nodded slowly. "Data."

"Konyeshna. Data. Facebook knows more about you than your parents do. Google can track your every online search, building incredible algorithms to predeterimine not just your interests, but the interests of whole demographics, whole countries. Why do you think other companies, such as Microsoft, have been trying to build their own search engines and social networks? Because after a certain point, they're otherwise just selling software and hardware. There are only so many devices that anyone wants to buy from you. But information...

"How insidious is your iPhone? Apple even makes you pay a premium for it, and yet they are continually mining information from your very movements."

"Speaking of which..." Carlos knew that something had been missing.

"It's in the trunk of an abandoned car, parked near the river. A car that you rented, remember?" prompted Ranevsky.

"I didn't..." Carlos was momentarily confused.

"As far as anyone can tell, you did." Ranevsky smirked. "The digital world. If you know how to manipulate it, what's real anymore? Anyway, it will look like you landed, went for a drive, thought it was fascinating that the river was frozen, went for a walk…"

"Shit," was all Carlos could say.

"Okay, so Infinity," prompted Maddy, desperate to shift the conversation back to the 'story.'

"It does what Google does, only faster and better," replied the Queen of Spades, somewhat proudly.

"And your connection is…?"

"It's a very different world than it was when I ran agents out of Berlin. In less than thirty years, most spy agencies have become obsolete. Think about it – who would need secret agents any longer in a world where everyone seems willing, almost desperate, to share their most intimate details with complete strangers online. Rather than run agents, I now own a search engine of tremendous power."

"Own!" Both Maddy and Carlos almost fell backwards in their chairs.

"How does any internet start-up get its initial funding?" The Queen of Spades lit another cigarette with the trail end of the first. Carlos realized that as long as she was smoking, they would stay alive. She also poured herself another shot of vodka. How does she do it? He wondered.

"Angel investors," replied Maddy. A Stanford graduate, Maddy was more than aware of the symbiosis between Stanford's business school, Stanford's schools of Engineering and Design, and the tech investment community that, conveniently, set up shop in the immediate vicinity.

"Points for you," the Queen of Spades wagged her cigarette at Maddy. "I was Infinity's Angel. I'm still the majority shareholder, even after the IPO. Rather, a company that is owned by another company that I'm the majority shareholder of is the 'entity' that owns Infinity. Let's just say that Infinity does what I tell it to do."

"And Sasha, does he do what you tell him to?" asked Maddy.

"He does. He's a good boy."

"When did he come under your... control?" Maddy was getting sick to her stomach.

"We refound each other when he was in high school. He didn't know that I existed. His father had convinced him that I was dead. He was delighted to learn that I wasn't."

"Delighted?" Maddy couldn't imagine.

"What boy wouldn't want to meet his mother? To have a mother, when he thought he didn't. He embraced me. And I told him the truth."

"What truth was that?" asked Maddy.

"The truth about his father. What an evil man he is."

"So you... manipulated your son into building a search engine for your use? How did you know he was capable of doing such a thing?"

"I didn't, but I knew he was smart enough to find the friends at Stanford who could. He's clever, but he's not the primary architect of the code. But he does make a good 'face' for the company, and he had... connections... to the startup capital. So although he's not the genius behind the technology of the company, he runs it."

"And the startup capital," mused Carlos, "came from your work with the Panthers. I see what you mean about money."

"Art is as liquid a currency as there is. And the beauty part is I get to enjoy it for a while."

"But that Vermeer, for instance. You couldn't sell that."

"Couldn't I? After a lifetime in my line of work, I know a few people."

"The people in the shadows..." murmered Maddy, reflecting on Fyodor Herskovin's words.

"But I don't have to sell it. For instance I could, through intermediaries, negotiate with the insurance companies. Or I could simply use it as collateral. It's amazing how much one can raise with a Vermeer, some Kandinskys and a Monet as insurance."

"What about Hirsches?" asked Maddy with an inspiration.

"Donovan Hirsches?" The Queen of Spades had a glint in her eye. "His work is increasing in value by the second. It's a sign of our distempered times that animals with strange things done to them are becoming more valuable than Russian Impressionists. They, at least, could paint." She wrinkled her nose. "His work is just clever."

"And has suddenly gotten more rare." Maddy was figuring it out.

"That. Yes. The pieces I own, by conservative estimate, have jumped in value by over 100%."

"So no need to recoup the investment in men, material and technology just from the Killer Whale. The notoriety of the theft has spiked interest in the rest of his work..."

"You are a Stanford girl? I thought so. A pity... Yes, there is considerable movement in certain circles. A five million dollar piece of contemporary art that cost about one million to steal, is still an enormous profit, sure, but if you hold, say, twenty million in other Hirsches, and they are suddenly worth forty million, well, that, as they say, is a killing."

LI

"Detective Wang, it's Carey Portman."

Dang, thought Jimmy. How did she get my number?

"Ms. Portman, what can I do for you?" It was not a good time to talk. His tone reflected that.

"Look, I know you're wondering how I got your number. I called Maddy's room-mate, Angelique. You're an emergency contact. Your number is on the side of their fridge... I'm sorry to be so direct, but where are you?"

"I'm honestly not at liberty to say." He had stepped out of the conference room at Interpol to take the call. He rolled his eyes thinking that all he needed was another journalist getting in the way.

"I'm on my way to St. Petersburg. I'll be landing tomorrow evening."

Double dang.

"You shouldn't have gone to the trouble, ma'am..."

"Trouble? Do you know where your girlfriend is?"

This sort of crossed the line. On one hand, he understood that Carey was Maddy's boss, but on the other, well, it reminded him of his impotence that he couldn't say where Maddy was. He didn't know. He only hoped that she was with Carlos, but then again, he also hoped that she wasn't. But even that opened the can of worms of if she wasn't with Carlos, she was somewhere bopping around the globe in a handsome billionaire's private jet. The sigh that escaped from him was soul deep.

"Again, what can I do for you ma'am?"

"You can meet me at the airport – assuming you're where the action is."

"Action? What action?" Jimmy decided that playing coy was his best tactic – at least for a few minutes longer.

"Look, dickhead, I've got two cub reporters neck deep in serious trouble from what I can make out, and one of them, if she's not your girlfriend she's still seriously liaised with your branch of the SFPD, and if you're not out looking for her, then I've got a few choice words for you when next we're face to face - if not a new asshole."

Jimmy could only pull the phone away from his ear for fear his face might get blistered. "Whew. I've heard the stories, but you live up to, if not past, your billing. Glad to have you on our team, Carey." The white flag came out.

"That's more like it. So, see you at the airport?"

"That's assuming we're still here."

"How's that?"

"I can only tell you that we have a small window of opportunity to extract our assets. We may have to be on the windy side of the law by tomorrow evening."

"And the story?"

"You'll know as much as can be told – certainly more than anyone else will ever know. You may just not be able to print it, that's all."

"Well, shit on that, Detective Wang!"

"I'm sorry, but to say this is a highly nuanced situation would be an understatement. We're all trying not to start an international incident with repercussions far beyond what appears on the face of things."

"Who's 'we'?"

"Look, I've got to go. Travel safe. And you'll be met."

Carey looked at her phone after Jimmy hung up with real frustration. She then looked out the window of her plane into the frozen darkness. She figured she was somewhere over Hudson Bay by now. She shivered, then gathered herself.

It was a really big fish. If it was going to be landed, she was the one to do it.

LII

"But it's not about the money. I don't believe the Hirsch is about the money. I mean, yes it could be, but it's about something more than that." Maddy was slowly putting all her cards on the table.

"What would make you think that?" asked the Queen of Spades with her Mona Lisa smile.

"You were sending a message, weren't you? Of all the art pieces you could steal, you chose the Killer Whale. Why would that be? And the Goddesses, what is that about, if not another layer to the message?"

"What part of 'fuck you' don't you understand?" replied the Queen of Spades casually. "If you have someone who has stood in your way in the past, who might position himself to do so again, perhaps a few gestures demonstrating the folly of that might be in order."

"The horse in the bed," said Carlos under his breath.

"So how did you do it?" asked Maddy.

"Which part?"

"I guess let's start with the whale."

"Easy enough. Take a disaffected assistant, a known route of travel and a relatively simple digital lock and you have what looks like a mystery."

"So you were right," said Maddy to Carlos.

"You figured it out?" asked the Queen of Spades.

"Yes. So did the SFPD," replied Carlos. Perhaps a bargaining chip? "So the head."

"A bonus. Part of a... larger issue."

"Vladimir Spassky. Investigating ties between the

Russian State and organized crime. Yes, that would be a bigger message." The remaining pieces were falling into place.

"A robust firewall, as I said." Maddy could see the Queen of Spades was starting to tire of the 'interview.' A few more questions to be answered, though. Maddy turned to Ranevsky.

"So the Goddesses. And the icon. Being in the same place at the same time…"

"I wasn't."

"He has a twin," said Carlos to Maddy under his breath.

"But the same fingerprint was on the door leading to the roof as was found at the church," said Carlos.

At this, even the Queen of Spades was surprised.

"Huh." Ranevsky smiled his Cheshire Cat smile.

"And the thumb drives."

"What is he talking about?" The Queen of Spades' eyes narrowed.

"And you figured that out?" Ranevsky nodded in admiration.

"Yes, but not the point of it."

At that moment, Simyon burst into the room, causing even Yuri to step into a defensive position. Whatever he said in Russian wasn't, obviously, very nice. It was something along the lines of, "What the fuck is going on here?"

Ranevsky, in his ironic way of his, said, "We're 'monologuing.'" His mother looked cross at him for a second, and he just turned to her and said, "Matrushka, you were *totally* monologuing."

She shrugged. Finally, she said, "Who could blame me?" Looking at Maddy and Carlos, she admitted, "What can I say? It's hard being a mastermind when there's no one who understands that you're a mastermind." She looked pointedly at her two twins. "It can get so lonely, sometimes... I am *always* alone..."

"It's like The Prestige," whispered Carlos.

"Times three," whispered Maddy back. "Not just two brothers..."

Sasha stirred on the sofa.

"Sasha."

"What about him?" asked the Queen of Spades.

"How much was he involved in all of this?"

Ranevsky interposed. "Let's just say that we try to protect him from the... hurlyburly of the real world of business. Let him do what he does best and leave the dirty work to those of us with a more entrepreneurial spirit."

"You borrowed his plane."

"Sure. I told him I needed a ride as far as London."

"From Denver?"

Ranevsky shrugged. "Just doing some shopping. He was on his way. Wasn't a big deal."

"You timed that really well," said Carlos.

"A small talent, but a talent, nonetheless."

"And you killed Richard York."

Ranevsky began to study the nonexistent dirt under his nails. After a moment, he glanced up at Simyon, who was staring at all of them with a feral intensity. A purr of something in Russian from Ranevsky and Simyon nodded. He then gestured for Yuri to gather up the limp figure on the sofa. Yuri slung his submachine gun behind him, went to the sofa and threw Sasha over his back like a sack of potatoes.

"Where are you taking him?" Maddy asked insistently.

"We load him up with some drugs, put him back on his plane and he goes back to San Francisco to keep Infinity running," replied Ranevsky. "Then we'll

drop you."
 "Drop us where?"
 "The Neva River."

LIII

"I now get that there are three brothers, and that explains a lot, but how does one get to the top of a twenty-three story building without anyone noticing?"

Jimmy just had to ask. By way of making conversation as Orkin weaved his way through the St. Petersburg early morning traffic. Jimmy was constantly wincing and covering his eyes as he suffered through a near-death experience at every intersection. He was glad he was in the back seat of the SUV. Orkin continued to display complete fearlessness behind the wheel. Sergei sat calmly in the passenger seat, blowing his cigarette smoke out the open window. It was freezing, but Jimmy was grateful for the cold wind which was keeping him awake. Well, that and the hair-raising driving. He paused his thought to wonder at how intense the traffic was at three in the morning.

"Who are all these people?" he interrupted himself. Sergei flicked his cigarette butt out the window.

"When it's dark twenty hours a day, people begin to drift away from their circadian rhythms. And who was it? George Bernard Shaw? who said 'Give me greater darkness, money was never made in the light…"

Wow, thought Jimmy. St. Petersburg was a city on the move, in all senses of the word.

"So back to the twenty-three story building…"

"Does it have a heliport?" asked Sergei.

"No," replied Orkin, who would know. "But the building across the street does. It wouldn't be hard to drop someone at the top of the next building."

"And getting from one to the other would be easy, because..." prompted Jimmy.

"Firing a harpoon with a cable from the roof of one building into the other, then speed-lining across – a snap." Orkin weaved onto the Troitsky Bridge, taking them across the Neva River.

"For what kind of person? Jesus, that's over two hundred feet up. And, wait a second, let's back up. Who's got a helicopter that can fly in the fog without making any sound?"

"It makes some. It's not completely soundless, but as these things go, at that hour downtown, in a City that actually *does* go to sleep, at that height, in the fog, a Kamov-50 would do the trick."

"I let my Jane's World Aircraft subscription lapse..." offered Jimmy lamely.

"Night version of the Kamov Hokum. Cutting edge technology. Only a few prototypes in existence. Pretty intense."

"And the people who would have one...?"

"Outside the Russian military, no one."

"That would tighten the list of suspects..." Jeez, thought Jimmy. Once again, I'm in way over my head. "So some serious cats."

"Serious cats. With serious connections."

"All to do what? Give you a spook?"

"Wouldn't it spook you?"

"Shit yeah, pardon my French."

"It did for a moment, but I'm here. I think it may have been forgotten what sort of man I am." He swerved past a few more lumbering trucks, made a sharp left turn and pulled the SUV to a stop. "This is where we wait." He got out and went to the rear of the truck.

"For what?"

"The cavalry."

As Jimmy scrambled out of the back seat and slipped on the frozen snow onto his butt, Orkin opened the back doors, cracked open a large chest that was nestled in the back, and withdrew the largest rifle Jimmy had ever seen. Sergei helped Jimmy to his feet. Both men looked at Orkin with dread. Orkin just shrugged.

"If you're going to hunt a bear, you need a big gun."

LIV

Something was nagging at Maddy. At least when she wasn't in abject terror at her situation. Carlos was actually pretty cool, even dozing off on the drive from the compound out towards St. Petersburg. But then, she reflected, he had had the stuffings beaten out of him and, by his own admission, he had consumed more than a bottle of vodka on his own. But the insistent nagging in her head remained. She puzzled and puzzled it. Most of the pieces were in place, but what she couldn't understand was the meaning behind the two thumb drives. And, more importantly, the meaning behind the image on them.

It wasn't Sasha. It wasn't Ranevsky. It was definitely Simyon.

Why would someone leave those clues behind? It wasn't Simyon's style. He was a brute, and straight-up crazy. She wanted to believe that Sasha wasn't involved in the deaths of Spassky and of the Russian priest, so that left… Ranevsky?

And the fingerprint. It was pretty clear that Simyon had been at the church. And that the shifting of the Goddesses had been more along Ranevsky's style. So what did that mean?

Their small caravan had Maddy and Carlos in one SUV with Simyon and Yuri. The other SUV had Ranevsky and Sasha, who was out cold due to the injection that had been administered to him. Maddy had cried out when Ranevsky plunged the needle into Sasha's arm.

"Please tell me that that isn't Polonium…"

"No. Have no fear on that score. He is still useful to us."

"For a while, right?"

Ranevsky's Cheshire Cat grin reappeared. "For a while. Right."

After that Sasha had been placed into the back seat of the car. Doors thumped closed and that was the last Maddy saw of him.

As they approached St. Petersburg, the other SUV peeled away on a different route. To the airport and the private plane. Maddy wondered ruefully how much of what happened would Sasha chalk up to a bad dream when he arrived home. And how much would he resent his manipulation by his family? Or would he at all?

Got to break a few eggs to make an omelet. Who was she, after all? A silly little girl.

A silly little girl who was in an enormous amount of trouble.

*   *   *

The industrial laser made quick work of the ice. A large rectangle had been cut out, and it bobbed on top of the freezing water coursing underneath. Yuri and another man took large ice hooks, smashed them deep into the ice rectangle, and hauled the large chunk out of the water. Simyon stood nonchalantly by, smoking his horrible cigarette, with his gun leveled at Maddy and Carlos. They stood shivering, chafing at the plastic ties that bound their wrists. When everything was in readiness, Simyon tossed his cigarette into the water. It froze instantly with a hiss.

"You won't feel anything for more than a blink of an eye," he said, breathing out the hot smoke. "It's almost as fast as just shooting you in the head, but this way, when they find you in a month, you'll be virtually unidentifiable, and it'll look like an accident." He squinted into the distance. The horizon was just starting to turn blood red under the lowering clouds. At that moment the floodlights blinked out on the spire of the fortress. "The time of day when duels were fought." He chuckled. "This river has seen more than a little blood in its time." He straightened up and gestured with his revolver for Maddy and Carlos to approach the opening in the ice. One of the men undid the ties around their wrists with a knife, the better to make it look like an accident and not a murder.

"I like the idea of you just shooting us in the head," said Carlos.

"As much as gunfire is a regular sound in St. Petersburg, I'd rather not indulge you."

"How about smashing our skulls with a candlestick, you freak," said Maddy. No holding back now.

"What did you call me?"

"I called you a freak. You heard me. You're an aberration."

Carlos, who had seen what Simyon was like when he got a wind up, whispered under his breath, "Bad idea..."

"The little boy no one wanted, the dim-witted brother, the one that your momma has to keep in the kennel..."

"Um, Maddy..."

"The one your mother hated."

This almost seemed comical to Simyon. He started to smile. Okay, that won't work, thought Maddy. Then the nagging, unresolved, puzzle pieces suddenly clicked into place.

"The one betrayed by his brother."

"What?" The veins in Simyon's temples began to bulge.

"You didn't know? Your mother didn't know. Sasha didn't know. You didn't know. Only one person would be left who would know about the thumb drives with your picture on them. Or how your fingerprint ended up on the top floor of 580 California. Face it, dickhead, you've been played for a real sucker."

This touched a nerve, which was what Maddy was probing for. At least people when they're angry can make mistakes, she thought. She just hadn't figured on how angry Simyon could get. Carlos closed his eyes, a moment of déjà vu causing him to brace himself for the worst. Maddy could see the veins in Simyon's temple begin to pop out and his eyes begin to bulge. It looked as if he was transforming into a werewolf. He snarled for a second and took a step towards them. Maybe this was a bad idea, after all, though Maddy who winced in anticipation of...

Suddenly, Simyon stopped. A small hole had opened up in his forehead and blood started to flow out of it. The rage seemed to seep out of him with the liquid running down his nose, his eyes becoming vacant and the color leaving his face. Simyon staggered for a second and then toppled forward into the water. He sank like a stone. The other men reached for their guns, bewildered.

"Freeze!" came a voice like a gunshot across the ice.

"Already half way there!" called back Carlos.

The men held their hands in the air and dropped their guns. Trotting across the ice from the fortress came a phalanx of men in black overcoats with fur hats. Two tall, lanky men led them, followed closely by a third with a rifle in his hands.

"Sergei!" called Carlos.

"Jimmy!" called Maddy.

The two leading men raised their gloved hands into the air in response. As the group arrived, the man with the rifle approached the opening in the ice, which was already starting to freeze over again. He stared into the inky blackness that was being covered by a dusting of ice crystals. His Russian-accented voice was crisp.

"I've been waiting years to do that. He was a son of bitch." He looked at Maddy and Carlos who were wide-eyed with astonishment.

"And trust me, I would know."

LV

Maddy thought she was going to barf. Again. She had never flown in a helicopter before. And this one, an Mi-35M gunship, was flying as fast as it could go, only yards above the icy water with two other gunships in tight formation on either side.

"Where'd you pick these up?" said Jimmy to Ivan Orkin over the headset.

"I know a guy who knows a guy," replied Orkin with a wicked smile.

I'll bet, thought Jimmy. "How much does one of these things cost?"

"Why do you ask?"

"Thinking of picking one up for myself. Would give a guy an edge, you know, fighting for parking in San Francisco."

Orkin laughed. "A bargain at $15 million apiece. At least that's what governments pay for them – again, I know how to negotiate the dealer down."

I *really* bet, thought Jimmy. One tough customer. Would hate to be the used-car salesman on the other side of the bargain.

"So we're about to start an international incident," said Jimmy, squinting into the dawning sun.

Ivan Orkin snorted. "What does that mean? That governments are about to posture over this? I don't think so. This is more about thieves stealing from thieves. This is the sort of thing one never hears about. If anyone complains, that means they knew about it all along. Yes, we're talking about hundreds of millions in art, but the governments involved have stolen billions over the years. I would call it 'breakage.'"

"Breakage?" gasped Maddy, inserting herself into the conversation. She was still finding it hard to breathe – her stomach was still flipping and flopping with each swerve of the gunship.

"Just like in a restaurant. Any good restaurateur allows for a certain amount of dishes to get broken, or glasses to get dropped, or tableware to walk away in someone's purse. Breakage. It's part of the equation for any businessman. You have to understand what you can accept as a loss and still make a profit."

"It's hard to imagine a Vermeer as 'breakage,'" quipped Carlos.

"You're right, there," said Jimmy. "It's been gone for over twenty years. It's moved beyond breakage to completely written off."

"So if it goes up in a fireball, no one's going to know," said Carlos from the starboard gunship, gesturing only a few yards away from them at the devastating array of firepower the helicopter had at its disposal. "This doesn't look like it bodes well for the art, if you see what I mean."

The cobalt blue water, which was iridescent under the rising sun to the east, started to get salted with ice. They were getting close.

"Baba Yaga's hut!" cried Carlos as he spotted the dacha in the distance. "We're on target!"

The hut was a black dot against the white of the icebound shoreline, with the birch forest rising a short distance beyond. It was alarming how quickly it grew as the gunships sped towards the compound.

Dang, thought Maddy. How fast are we going?

"We're going fast enough and low enough that we had better not be triggering any defense mechanisms," said Orkin, as if reading her thoughts.

"I can only hope that no one has yet learned of Simyon's untimely demise. We're counting on Sergei to keep the lid on this for at least another hour – which, in this country, could be very hard."

Suddenly, something flashed from the ground, and within a fraction of a second there was a tearing of air and a dramatic swerve of the starboard-most gunship as it avoided a missile.

"Yeeha!" shouted Carlos over the headsets. Thank god for seatbelts, thought Maddy, relieved to see a shaky thumb's up in the window of the starboard ship.

"We can only hope those are laser guided," said Orkin evenly. Everyone turned to watch the missile continue on into space without whipping a u-turn, which would have indicated heat-seaking. Orkin then shouted in Russian to his crew. At that, the gunships dropped even lower towards the icy water and split formation. Within seconds the two outboard helicopters had swooped in large arcs around the ice hut and beyond the birch grove, shielded by the forest as they closed in on the main house, removing them from the view of the two men on the deck of the dacha who were preparing another shoulder-fired anti-aircraft missle. The middle helicopter, the one containing Maddy, Jimmy and Orkin, flew straight at Baba Yaga's hut, releasing a furious cannonade as it did so. The house started to fly to pieces, the wood and ice turning into a gray mist, the two men plunging into the almost black water.

"So much for the Serebryakova…" said Maddy in awe.

The gunfire was returned, however. From the edge of the woods tracer bullets worked their way towards the helicopter. Maddy could only shudder in anticipation. As the bullets slammed into the gunship, Maddy was astonished that they seemed to skid off the surface.

"Jesus," shouted Jimmy, also having never been on the receiving end of heavy automatic weapons fire.

"Built to take it," said Orkin grimly. The gunship locked on target and blew a whole stand of trees apart. The gunfire from the ground ceased.

"Are you sure this isn't going to get the authorities on our case?"

"If they're not on our case already, they will be. But it still takes a few minutes to scramble some fighters and for them to reach us. That's about all the time we have. Let's go!"

The gunship swooped down and hovered over the clearing just before the main house. It never touched the ground, Orkin and Jimmy leaping out while it floated above the flurry of blown snow. Orkin carrying his rifle over his shoulder with a submachine gun in his hands, Jimmy armed only with his service pistol. Maddy hesitated for a second, then undid her seatbelt and tumbled out into the snow behind them.

"You were supposed to stay in the chopper!" shouted Jimmy.

"Do you think that's safer?" shouted Maddy back.

The gunfire from the roof of the main house answered that question. Maddy and Jimmy ducked behind the birch trees, bullets chipping away at the bark. The gunship lifted itself up, but tilted its blades forward, causing a blizzard of snow to be blown towards the house. Orkin took advantage of the man-made snowstorm to unleash a barrage of his own from his machine gun in the direction from which the gunshots had come. The cries that answered his maneuver indicated that he had gotten lucky.

"I'd rather be lucky than good," he shouted to Jimmy and Maddy as he gestured for them to move forward.

I hope Carlos is alright and stayed in his helicopter, thought Maddy.

*   *   *

Like I'm going to stay in the helicopter, thought Carlos after his machine set down on the roadway that led to the main house. This gunship's assignment was to seal off any route of escape. But Carlos wasn't going to watch through the icy windshield. He clambered out – well, flopped out would describe it more accurately, given his wounds – after the the helicopter touched ground. He then stumbled over towards the trees and worked his way towards the large building. At that moment one of the garage doors opened and a snowmobile leapt out, working its way cross-country. The gunship's 12.77mm machine guns swiveled in the direction of the fleeing snowmobile, but held its fire as the third gunship came swooping from around the far stand of birch trees, positioning itself directly in front of the snowmobile.

We want to keep those two alive, thought Carlos as he could descern Ranevsky in the driver's seat and the Queen of Spades in back.

After a moment's hesitation, the snowmobile swerved sharply towards the birch trees, seeking refuge from the gunship. Once amongst the trees, there would be no way for the helicopters to get to them. As the snowmobile got within a few yards of the forest, Carlos thought he heard a sharp crack over the roar of the rotor blades. Ranevsky flew off the snowmobile, causing the machine to fly straight into a tree. With the sickening collapse of its front end, the rear of the snowmobile flipped upwards, tossing the small figure of the Queen of Spades like a rag doll into the air.

Carlos then saw the familiar lean figure of Ivan Orkin, with his big rifle in his hands, running towards the fallen figures.

*   *   *

As Maddy, Carlos and Jimmy converged on the crashed snowmobile, they could see a stand-off had evolved. Ranevsky, his left shoulder split open and bleeding from the rifle shot, was still managing to clutch his mother with his damaged arm. In his right hand he held a pistol to her head.

"Back off!" he shouted. He began to drag himself and his mother slowly towards the woods.

"Or what?" returned Orkin, without any hint of fear.

"Or I shoot her!" Ranevsky didn't look too steady on his pins.

"Be my guest," replied Orkin, his eyes turning steely. "Do a better job this time than I did."

"No!" shouted Jimmy. "We're taking them with us. Who knows how much we could learn from them – how much art is hidden away…"

The Queen of Spades looked at her son for a moment and then spat on the ground. There was blood in her spit, causing the white snow to look as if it were bleeding from a wound.

"You idiot. You're not going to shoot your mother in the head. Who would tell you what to do?"

At this Ranevsky howled like an enraged wolf and threw his mother to the ground, training the gun on her. He snarled at Orkin and Jimmy to keep their distance. He then exploded with pent-up anger.

"I am done being told what to do! You have no idea what I've had to endure. You, Simyon – even Sasha. When I'm smarter than all of you put together. You live in the Stone Age, Matrushka, and your stupid egotism blinds you to what is really happening around you. My fucking brother is nothing but a stupid bully. And *I* run Infinity. Sasha thinks he does, but he doesn't have a clue what to do with the power he has. I built this empire, you stupid bitch, not you. And I'm the one who will be left standing after Simyon..."

"Simyon is dead," interrupted Orkin.

"About fucking time!" shouted Ranevsky wildly. "What took you so long?"

"So *you* put the thumb drives in the tank and the church. And left the fingerprint on the door at 580 California," declared Maddy triumphantly. "I knew it!"

"But how did you do that?" asked Carlos.

Ranevsky looked at his hands. "It was painful, and took time, but my hands are no longer my own. To have the fingerprints of one brother surgically carved onto one hand, and the fingerprints of the other brother on the other hand – it makes me almost invisible, doesn't it?"

"So you could be in all these different places at different times, but everyone would think it was either Simyon or Sasha at the same time," said Maddy in awe.

Ranevsky grinned. "And wouldn't it be perfect if, eventually, both of them vanished? Not that anyone would miss them... Once one gets high enough in the corporate world, it becomes easier and easier to isolate oneself from the prying eyes of the public – or even one's board – enough to be someone other than who they originally thought you were."

"You've been planning to take Sasha's place?" The thought made Maddy want to barf again.

"He thought it a practical joke. He was grateful to have a long-lost little brother, and got a kick out of how close a resemblence we had. What a fool."

With each word, the Queen of Spades eyes turned darker and darker. She had been lying on her back in the snow where Ranevsky had thrown her. She was slowly getting to her feet. When she spoke, it was as if venom was dripping from her fangs.

"You killed Simyon! You would kill Sasha. My boys! You. I hate you. A mother's curse on you. And you would kill me?!"

The speed with which Ranevsky pulled the trigger shocked everyone. The Queen of Spades flew backwards into the snow. She twitched for a moment and went still. Before Orkin or Jimmy could move, Ranevsky had swiveled his gun at Maddy.

"You don't want to shoot me," he said as everyone reassessed the situation.

"Why not?" asked Jimmy, ready to drop his weapon if asked in exchange for Maddy's life. Maddy was frozen with terror.

"There's several hundred million in art back in that building. And it's set to go up in flames in another five minutes unless I re-enter the code. Given that the Russian government takes its collateral very seriously, and have already scrambled several fighters to intercept you, you don't have that kind of time."

Ranevsky grinned his Cheshire Cat grin. He then seemed to levitate, to Maddy's shock, and smash himself into a tree. He then slumped to the ground.

Orkin slung his still smoking rifle over his shoulder. He looked at the others for a moment, whose jaws were slack in amazement.

"Then we better work quickly."

LVI

Ranevsky was a born liar. They actually had ten minutes left. 600 seconds. A lifetime in a "smash and grab" sense. But it was uncertain how much time they would have before the MiGs arrived, so the urgency with which they worked was profound. The possibility of being blown up one way or another has a way of kicking one into a higher gear, thought Carlos as he ran up the stairs.

It was all Maddy could do to take a knife to a Vermeer, but it was the fastest way to get it off the wall, given its mounting within the library niche. The frame was valuable, but the painting was priceless, so she followed Jimmy's instructions and made the leap. She rolled the canvass up and stuffed it under her arm. Carlos had run down the hall upstairs and grabbed all of the Kandinskys. These he was able to grab with frames intact, but he had his hands full as he tried to find the balance between running down the stairs in sheer terror of being blown to pieces and not tripping with his priceless cargo.

Jimmy had to take a moment in front of the Monet. "Move, you idiot!" shouted Orkin, shattering Jimmy's reverie. He grabbed the painting off the wall and stacked it with the Leger and the Matisse. Jeez, he thought, nothing like running out the door with a hundred million in art under your arm.

"Move, move, move!" called out Orkin as Maddy, Carlos and Jimmy, along with two of Orkin's trained men, ran toward the waiting helicopters. Carlos tripped in the snow, landing face first onto his stack of Kandinskys. He was horrified at the potential damage, but the urging of Orkin got him back on his feet. "They'll be fine!" A big hand grabbed Carlos by his waistband and hauled him into the back of the Mi-35M. Blankets awaited – mostly for the treasures the team off-loaded – and the barely damp Kandinskys were gently wrapped. At least as gently as possible, given the sudden vertical jump the gunship took. Carlos almost fell out the door, but the same, strong hand grabbed him and pulled him back into the cabin and threw him, with no shortage of pain, into his seat and strapped him into a seatbelt. The Mi-35M arced up and away, with Maddy and Jimmy's chopper right behind. Orkin clambered into the third helicopter once he was sure that all was secure. Just as his gunship banked westward, a sequence of deep rumblings were felt behind them. The windows of the house blew out and balls of flame erupted into the surrounding woods. As Maddy watched in horror and fascination, the roof of the large main building collapsed, with flame shooting out of the roof.

"Hope we didn't miss anything," called out Carlos, having put his headset on.

"Probably only the data on every cell the Panthers have," replied Jimmy. "Dang."

"Are you sure this won't be an international incident?" asked Maddy. "I mean, it looks like a war zone back there…"

"It's only an international incident if you get caught," replied Orkin. "We're about two hundred miles from the nearest military airbase. At a thousand miles per hour, any MiG coming after us would be here in about ten minutes, if what Ranevsky said was true."

"How far are we from Finnish airspace?" asked Jimmy, more than a little tense.

"About fifty miles. At our current rate of speed, we should get there in about seven minutes."

"Nice to have a three minute cushion..." replied Jimmy, trying his best not to panic.

"I mean, plus or minus," said Orkin. Jimmy could just imagine the twinkle in his eye. "Assuming my math is correct..."

At that minute, all three gunships were buffeted by the blast of air generated by two MiG fighters blowing past them. It was a maneuver designed to intimidate the gunships into aborting their flight.

"They don't want to shoot us down – they must know what our cargo is!" shouted Carlos. "That totally seals it! The Russian government has known all along!"

Orkin shouted something in Russian. If it were at all possible for the helicopters to go faster, they did.

"Wait, we weren't going top speed before?" asked Carlos incredulously.

"Didn't want to risk permanent damage to the rotors," replied Orkin evenly.

"Oh, I guess getting blown to pieces or arrested for grand theft art was less risky!" shouted Carlos.

"Uh, Carlos..." Maddy just wanted him to be quiet for a minute.

"10-4, chica!" Maddy could look over at Carlos and could see him zipping his lip through the window of his chopper.

Meanwhile, the MiGs were doing an elaborate swoop around in order to come up behind the gunships again. Maddy could only watch the water and pray that the ice got thicker as quickly as possible. "Are we there, yet?" she asked plaintively.

"In five, four, three, two, one!" shouted Orkin. The MiGs did their best to peel up in time, but they still blew past the three helicopters, causing them all to wobble in the afterdraft. There might have been a slight infringement of Finnish airspace, but not so's anyone would notice. The jets pulled away, with a wag of their wings. They knew they had been beaten, and their orders took them only so far.

"Yippeekiyay, mother..." Someone switched off Carlos' headset. But his middle finger in the direction of the disappearing fighter planes said it all.

LVII

As Carey turned on her cell phone upon passing through passport control, she received a cryptic text:

St. Pete too hot. Explain when we get home. Say hi to Sergei for me. C

That Carlos. I'll kill him.

At that moment a tall, slender man with a wolfish grin and terrible teeth approached her.

"Ms. Portman? Sergei Potemkin. I understand you're here for a story?"

Carey looked at her phone and then at Sergei. "You must be Sergei…"

"*The* Sergei, ma'am," he said with a laugh. "Sorry your protégé had to depart in such a hurry, but he left quite a trail. It would be a great story – *if* it could be told."

"*If*?! So what the fuck am I going to do here?" snapped Carey, more than a little put out. "Next flight back to SF doesn't leave until tomorrow morning."

"Tell you what. I know a place where we can get a very interesting dinner…" Sergei bowed and offered her his arm. After a moment's hesitation, Carey sighed, put on her best smile, and took it.

LVIII

The flight home was awkward and strained. Neither Maddy nor Jimmy had had a moment since the rescue at the fortress for a quiet conversation. Maddy wasn't ready for one now. She had hoped to have a long flight home on some commercial airliner to collect her thoughts. Instead she was almost trapped within Orkin's jet with everyone watching her. At least that's how it felt. Jimmy just looked at her closely, she looked away, and, in an effort to keep his pride intact and his emotions in check, he climbed into the lounge chair opposite Carlos for a long debrief. Maddy spent the bulk of the flight in Orkin's master suite, sleeping an exhausted, but stressful, sleep. She had, after all, been the better part of a week without rest, and it caught up with her heavily. It was only as the plane was making its final descent into San Jose airport that she stirred, accepted a cup of espresso from Michael, and strapped herself in for landing. Again Jimmy searched her eyes. This time she looked at him pleadingly.

He understood. He remembered Clarice Bryant's admonition.

But it didn't make him feel any better.

LIX

"Ready for your 'perp walk' Mr. Borodin?"

They had been expected. Security at reception had led Jimmy and FBI agent Johnny Hernandez, along with the rest of the FBI team, straight to the board room. Sasha sat with his legal counsel, a very sharp-looking young woman in a charcoal-gray suit with heavy-framed black glasses. Sasha, who had an internet mogul's reputation to maintain, was wearing jeans, sneakers with colorful socks, and a hoodie. A very expensive hoodie, but a hoodie, nonetheless. Jimmy could only roll his eyes.

"It's a ritual more than a few successful men have had to go through," Sasha replied with a wry smile.

He really is good looking, thought Jimmy. And he's super-rich. Jimmy kept his composure, even as he came to fully understand what he was up against.

"Should we also, perhaps, go through the 'ritual' of having the charges read?" asked the attorney.

"Ready when you are," replied Agent Hernandez. When everyone had settled, he began. "We have Grand Theft... What? What's so funny?"

The attorney had already started laughing. "It's only misappropriation – a prank." She turned to Sasha. "Nothing to worry about."

"A five million dollar prank, with the attempt at price manipulation across the art market..." The laughter subsided. After a moment, Hernandez continued. "Then we'll give you something harder to work with. How about Accessory to Murder?"

At this Sasha's face went white. "Murder? What

murder?" His attorney put her hand on his arm – a signal to refrain from speaking further.

"We've got three: Vladimir Spassky, Russian national; Richard York, Britsh national; and Sergei Arkadin, Russian émigré and U.S. citizen."

"But I don't know any of them!" Sasha's attorney's effort at restraint failed as her client rose in real dismay.

"Tell it to the judge, Mr. Borodin."

"Anything else?"

"Odds and ends – transportation of stolen goods across state lines and international borders, traveling with false documents..."

"I never!"

"The smuggling of a high-tech Russian military aircraft into the United States for criminal purposes. It will be a real pleasure to impound that, by the way... And the real kicker..."

"Sorry I'm late," said an earnest looking, balding man in a dark suit who just entered the room. "James Randolph, SEC."

"You want to tell Mr. Borodin why you're here?" asked Agent Hernandez.

"Right. Falsification of filing documents during your IPO. We don't take it kindly that a foreign government owns a majority share of Infinity without proper disclosure."

At this Sasha sat back down. He started to speak but then thought better of it. Jimmy could tell his mind was racing, trying to determine how this information became public.

"You have the right to remain..."

"Yes, yes, yes," said the attorney impatiently. "Let's get this over with."

The handcuffs were applied. "Is this really necessary?" asked Sasha.

"It's all part of the 'ritual,'" replied Jimmy. Then, after a moment, to the assembled, "May I have a moment with Mr. Borodin – alone?"

"Not without me present," replied the attorney.

"It's okay, Denise."

"One. Minute." said Agent Hernandez holding up a single finger for emphasis.

After the boardroom door clicked behind them, Jimmy gestured to a painting on the wall. It was of a naked blonde woman brushing her hair. "Russian Impressionist, yes?"

"Full marks, Detective. Serebryakova. Bought it in London, only recently."

"An investment?"

"A memento. Of a wonderful few days with a lovely young woman while I was there. A dalliance, really, but a great distraction."

"I see. So you have nothing you would like me to pass on to Miss Stevenson, seeing as how it was only a brief romance?"

"Wait…"

"Good luck in prison, Mr. Borodin."

LX

The Boston police who descended on the old, rusty white van that rested in an abandoned industrial parking lot under the turnpike would later describe the sensation of discovering the lost masterpieces as akin to entering the presence of some power greater than themselves. The objects radiated a certain energy, despite the layers of dust and grime that encased the crates that contained them.

Detective Ryan Dowling, who took the anonymous call, was at first dismissive of the umpteen-thousandth tip in the over twenty-year-old case. But it was the accent of the speaker, with a deep and convincing Russian roll to his words that made him register the information with more than the perfunctory response.

"It had to have been the Russians all along," he said later to the throng of reporters, who jammed the hotel conference room that had been prepared for the press announcement. "The crime had their fingerprints all over it." The masterpieces were unveiled one at a time, with the Vermeer eliciting a gasp and a special ovation.

"Is there any evidence of their involvement, other than the accent of the speaker who called in the location of the van?" asked the reporter from the Washington Post.

Detective Dowling paused for a moment. "To be honest, not really. Just instinct, I guess."

"And instinct solves many crimes that otherwise would remain unsolved," said the Commissioner, stepping in, clapping Dowling on the shoulder.

It was a great day in Boston.

* * *

The mood was just as jubilant at the press conference in Paris, where four of the five stolen paintings were arranged on large easels in front of a huge throng of reporters from every news agency in the world. The paintings had been discovered the day before in a shipping container that had been stacked behind a warehouse near a railway siding outside of Marseilles. The tip had come anonymously, but the voice on the phone, when played back for the hundredth time by the forensic analysts, indicated a slight Asian inflection. As much as the French unit of Interpol remained silent on the subject, the press latched on to the potential connection.

"The work of the Japanese mafia," declared Le Figaro, and the suggestion rippled throughout the rest of the world. No other evidence was offered.

But the art world rejoiced.

* * *

The box with no return address was waiting for her when she returned to her desk after lunch on Monday. It had been a brutally long week for Katya Medvyedeva, church secretary, starting with her discovery of poor Deacon Arkadin the Monday morning before. The ceremony over the weekend had been beautiful and moving, but contrary to tradition, the casket had to remain closed. She shivered when she thought about it. The poor man's face – there was nothing the mortician could do…

The box on her desk, though. She hesitated to touch it. It radiated such energy, such mystery. She wanted a witness for when it was opened, so she went and got old Gennady, the custodian, to be with her. Her hands trembled when breaking the seal, but she managed to get the box open. As the priceless icon slid out onto her desk, both she and Gennady fell to their knees.

God had not forsaken them.

*   *   *

As the truck backed into the loading dock of the Museum of Contemporary Art, Thomas Bradshaw got tingles down his spine. He missed that sensation, and savored this brief reappearance. It took some time to position the enormous crate onto the dock out of the refrigerated truck, but Bradshaw wouldn't take his eyes off it.

"You're sure this is the right tank," he whispered to Jimmy.

"Locked the truck myself," replied Jimmy. He too, remained focused on the crate, avoiding eye contact with the press. One member of the press in particular.

As the crowbar did its work and the wood panels fell away, Bradshaw covered his face with his hands. The last time he went through this, he had received the shock of his life. He didn't want to see another head floating in front of him. He'd had enough bad dreams from that to last a lifetime.

The shouts of approval from the crew and press caused him to open his eyes and peer through his fingers. There, in all its glory, was as fearsome a creature as any human ever gazed upon. The killer whale was majestic. The sound of the cameras clicking away elevated the moment to one of a Hollywood premiere.

Thomas Bradshaw's star had arrived and was ready for its close-up.

LXI

The mood at the Clarion was despondent. As far as Carey Portman was concerned, the whole thing was a disaster. Nothing like being a day late and a dollar short on your own scoop. She and her team of young reporters could only stand in the background with the other correspondents - or worse, read in dismay - as the various art pieces were returned, with no way to lay claim to the real method of discovery without causing an international incident, or irreparable damage to their relationship with their best source at the SFPD. Although damage *had* been done there, much to Carey's chagrin. Following the Borodin investigation was now assigned to Carlos, seeing as how a certain line of journalistic professionalism had been crossed by Maddy.

"Nothing like being the apex of a love triangle," she said bluntly as the two cubs sat miserably in her office.

"I'm so sorry..." stammered Maddy. She looked positively green.

"Don't. Speak." replied Carey. "We're moving on, okay? Although, to be twenty-five again..." she trailed off whistfully, recalling her own misadventures as a young journalist. After collecting herself, she took off her glasses, set them neatly on her desk, and said evenly. "There's still a lot of news out there. Now go get some! But don't expect me to be handing out any hall passes anytime soon." As usual, Maddy and Carlos were too frightened to move.

"Go!"

LXII

"Hi sweetie! Come on in, come on in! To what do I owe the pleasure?"

"Oh, Mrs. Bryant, I guess I just needed someone to talk to, and you're the best. I hope I'm not disturbing you." Maddy gave Clarice Bryant a gentle hug and followed her into the house. Clarice Bryant was wearing an apron and was holding a dish towel with which she had just wiped her hands.

"You couldn't possibly disturb me – I don't have too much going on, as you know. Except getting this stew together. Come with me into the kitchen and talk to me while I put a few things into the crock pot. Charelle's just about to head off for her evening shift, and this will be ready for her when she gets home."

"You're awesome, Mrs. Bryant."

At that moment a pretty young Asian woman entered the kitchen. She was wearing black slacks and a white blouse with a Barnes and Noble name tag.

"Hey, Maddy," said Charelle, giving her a hug and smooch. "Great to see you!"

Maddy could feel the difference. Six months earlier, Charelle was skin and bones, dangerously ill with HIV, and living on the streets. Now she had some meat on her bones and radiated health and confidence.

"Great to see you, too – you look amazing!"

Charelle wiggled a bit at the compliment and tucked a lock of her shimmering black hair behind an ear.

"I owe it all to Mrs. B." she said. "She makes sure I'm well fed, that's for sure."

Clarice Bryant tutted, but smiled all the same. She came over to Charelle and gave her a hug. "And this one keeps this house together. Couldn't manage without her. Now what time you gonna be home?"

"Late, Granma. I got to close up tonight." Maddy smiled at the term of familial endearment.

"Well, there'll be some stew in the pot when you get home – you be sure to eat some."

"Yes ma'am." Charelle gave her a kiss on the cheek and waved to Maddy. "I've got to run – I'm a little behind. Hope to see you again soon!"

After she left, Clarice Bryant shook her head. "That girl's all right."

Knowing that Charelle was really a Filipino boy, and knowing that Clarice Bryant knew that too, only made Maddy shake her head in wonder at the magic that Clarice Bryant possessed.

"Have a seat, I've got some carrots and parsnips to chop up"

"May I help you?" asked Maddy.

"No, thank you. Once I get planted in one place in front of the counter, I'm pretty good." She began chopping away at some carrots. "So what do you want to talk about?"

"I don't know where to begin…"

"Do you love that boy or don't you?"

Maddy burst into tears. A bony, firm, but kind, hand on her shoulder, and a deep sobbing fit into Clarice Bryant's apron helped Maddy pull it together. Only just.

"That's just it, Mrs. B. – I'm no longer sure which one!" She began to cry again.

"Now why are you crying so hard, girl?" Clarice Bryant had a way of cutting through it.

"I guess… I guess because I'm afraid."

"Afraid? Afraid of what? You're a brave girl. Been through a lot for someone so young. Been shot at, if I remember correctly."

"More than once." Maddy managed a weak smile. "I guess I'm afraid of making a terrible mistake and of hurting someone I care about deeply."

"Your detective man."

"Yes, ma'am. I love him, but I'm no longer sure if we're meant for each other."

"Because you met this other boy."

"How did you know that?"

"I have my methods. Truth be told, it wouldn't take Sherlock Holmes to figure it out. I hear this other boy is quite the charmer."

"You're spooking me, Mrs. B."

Clarice Bryant went out of the kitchen for a moment, then returned with a Wired magazine. *The* Wired magazine. "Charelle is trying to keep me current. She brings 'em home from work. I read the interview. Certainly a smart young man. And very wealthy now, it seems. Could set a girl up for life, if he gave her the time of day. Do you think he's got time for a girl in his life right now?"

"I wonder that. And it's all so new. Too new. And Jimmy's the best, you know?"

"But..."

"But we've been out of sync lately. I guess I've been feeling... I don't know what I've been feeling."

"You've been feeling like you need some space, haven't you? Like you need to spend some more time learning who you are. You were just a little bird six months ago and now you're starting to spread your wings. Your work is exciting and getting more so. You've got a lot of ground to cover, a lot of people to meet."

"You're amazing Mrs. B. That's just it. I feel terribly lucky having met such a wonderful man so early in my life, but it *is* early in my life. How do I balance the security and kindness he provides me with the growth I know I still have to go through?"

"You mean the growing *pains*. 'Cause it's going to hurt. Life is like that. As much pain as there is joy. Almost no getting around that."

Maddy looked into Clarice Bryant's sparkling eyes. Clarice had been through as much pain as anyone Maddy knew, and yet she still had a light in her eyes that spoke of love, trust, confidence and kindness.

"So what do I do?"

"The truth is always going to be right thing to do. The truth about everything. Even your fears - and your mistakes. Almost everybody wants that, deep down. Especially a man. Especially a man like Jimmy Wang. He's strong enough to know what to do."

"I slept with the other boy."

"That won't make things easier, that's for sure." Clarice Bryant squeezed Maddy's shoulder. There wasn't any judgment, though. "But Jimmy should know, and he should know it from you."

"I know you're right. I guess that's why I was crying. I'm so afraid to do it, though. I've been avoiding him for the last couple of days."

"You'll feel better afterwards. Not right away, though, from what I can see, but much better than if you lied to him. To someone you care about."

Mrs. Bryant went back to her carrots. There was a flap at the kitchen door and the gray cat pushed its way in. It sidled up to Maddy's ankles and gave them a rub. Purring filled the kitchen.

"That cat's all right. Curls up on the end of the bed and keeps my feet warm at night. Thank goodness I'm deaf enough – otherwise who could sleep through all that purring?"

Maddy stroked Robin for a few minutes. It was

warm and cozy in the kichen, the smells beginning to eminate from the crockpot giving Maddy a sense of home. She was glad to have someone like Clarice Bryant for a friend.

"You hungry?"

"No, well, yes ma'am – who wouldn't be with that stew you got going on there. But I don't think I should. I've been having some trouble keeping food down lately."

Clarice Bryant gave Maddy a look. A long look.

"When's the last time you been to a doctor?"

"It's been a while…"

"I think you better get to one, and soon."

"Yes, ma'am. I mean, I guess so… um, I'm okay. Just nerves and stuff…" Maddy stood up to go. Clarice Bryant just came up to her and put her hand on her tummy. After a moment…

"You get yourself to a doctor right away, young lady. From what I can tell, you're going to have more than one tough decision to make."

LXIII

He switched on the light and sat bolt upright clutching his heart in sheer terror. The dream had come to Darryl Richards once again.

"It's okay, baby, it's okay," cooed Agnetha as she rubbed his back and coaxed him into lying down again.

"I don't know, baby, I'm going to have to get another job. I can't go back to that one. I'm done, there, I'm done…"

"Don't you worry about that now," Agnetha whispered. "You just rest. Do you need another pill?"

"No, just need to to get that image out of my mind. Jesus. What evil things. What the fuck does San Francisco need with monsters like that?"

"They're odd, that's for sure. But they're only fiberglass. You know that, right?"

"My head knows that, but my soul…"

"The Masters starts tomorrow…" she was now rubbing his forehead.

"Don't I know it…" he smiled, beginning to relax, his eyes closed. Thirty-two hours over four days of uninterrupted, commercial free coverage. His idea of heaven. Before he lapsed back into sleep, he opened his eyes and looked at his wife.

"I love you, baby."

"Now you shush, and get some sleep." A minute more of having his forehead rubbed and Darryl Richards was snoring lightly. Agnetha Richards leaned across her husband to turn out the light.

"I love you too, you silly man." She curled up

against her husband and fell asleep in spite of the snoring.

LXV

Half a world away, it was already early morning. But that didn't stop the old man from working in his garden. It was cold, but promised to be a fine, clear day. Perfect for some time with his roses, thought Fyodor Herskovin.

Perfect for some time to work through some complicated feelings, too.

He was deep into pruning and didn't sense the tread of the boots on the ground behind him. A hand on his shoulder caused him to start suddenly.

"You got here early," he said as he turned around to face the tall, bald man with heavily rimmed glasses, who kneeled down beside him. The leather jacket worn by the newcomer creaked.

"So you got my text," replied Donovan Hirsch.

Fyodor Herskovin fished into his pocket and pulled out his phone. "Don't know what I would do without this thing. Texting is a wonderful way to communicate. I mean, if you're deaf…"

"Are you okay?"

"Oh, yes. I mean, this is hard on my old knees…"

"Are you *okay*?"

Fyodor Herskovin looked at his son for a moment, then at his roses. He took his pruning shears and trimmed a branch back.

"The decision was made so long ago. I've carried it with me for over fifty years. If I had known how terrible the price was…"

"You gave me my freedom."

"Yes, although you would have never known the

difference. I find freedom more than a little overrated. Freedom can mean fear. And it can mean loneliness."

Donovan Hirsch put his arm around his father's shoulders and pulled him close. "I know, Dad. If it helps at all, I love you."

Fyodor Herskovin turned back to his son and embraced him fully. A tear ran down his cheek, staining the leather jacket.

LXVI

"Have there been any ramifications?"

The man stood in the muddy clearing. A few days of April rain had started to turn the snowy ground to slush, the weather turning suddenly warm, almost tropical. The scene before him was of complete destruction. At least there wouldn't be much evidence left. It was now a job for one of his special contractors, those with the highest clearance, to make the site look as if there had never been buildings there at all. The trip out to the Gulf of Finland was something of a formality, although truth be told, he shouldn't have come at all.

"On our side or on theirs?"

The first man squinted in annoyance. The second man understood. He took up again.

"We're not in any trouble... yet. No issues with our distribution system. Although talented, they are being replaced."

The first man shivered momentarily. The second man went on. "I understand, though, that the Securities and Exchange Commission will be doing an investigation."

The first man shrugged. Nothing a few dollars in the right hands couldn't solve. Even then, an investigation that complicated would take months, if not years. By then more than enough information could be mined from the operation. Finding a new CEO would be a challenge, but he knew a few people. He picked up a stick.

"There's the issue of the helicopter..."

"How could they have been so stupid?" He threw the stick into the woods.

"Emotions can blind people."

"Yes, but letting one out of our sight…"

The second man made a face. "Subcontractors. Most of the assembly takes place in Romania. What can you do?"

There was a pause. Finally the second man went on.

"What are your orders regarding ramifications on their side?"

"For what? Nothing happened here. Here doesn't exist."

"Yes. And, if I may say so…"

"I know. More than anyone in the world, I know."

"We should head back. You've got a meeting with the Mayor at 3."

"Give me a moment. Have the car brought round."

The second man bowed slightly, then tapped his phone as he moved away. The first man made his way along the small path through the woods. The Gulf of Finland opened up before him, black and forbidding. He shivered. He had long ago learned to limit any diplay of emotion, but he felt a certain sense of loss, and he was glad that he was alone. As his cold blue eyes stared towards the horizon he chided himself for letting his eyes begin to water.

How can one mourn people who didn't exist?

LXVII

The knock on the door of his penthouse condo at the late hour didn't surprise Ivan Orkin. He was expecting it, and answered the door himself, having dismissed his staff earlier, and having put his girlfriend to bed. He was relaxed about it even, answering the door with a glass of wine in his hand.

"We had a deal," said his guest as soon as the door opened.

"We did?"

"There were only four paintings in that container," said Jimmy as he entered the palatial, loft-like residence. The view from the top floor of the Four Seasons was spectacular, taking in the entire City. It was a clear night, so every light from every window and street light and boat in the Bay sparkled. It took Jimmy's breath away. "The Matisse. What happened to the Matisse?"

Ivan Orkin shrugged. Russians have a way with shrugs, thought Jimmy.

"Oops?" suggested Orkin. "Perhaps it fell of the truck on the way?" After a moment, "I'm enjoying a very nice Lafitte Rothschild. Care for a glass?"

"I'm still working," replied Jimmy evenly.

"Listen. Call it what you want. I call it a 'finder's fee.' As we discussed on the plane, with great risk comes great reward."

"Where is it?" asked Jimmy.

"Could be anywhere. Sure you don't want a glass?"

After a moment when Jimmy tried to hold on to

being the toughest detective in town, he gave in. "A Lafitte Rothschild? Really? Must be nice."

"It is. Having tasted wine ranging from Two Buck Chuck to this, I've learned that I prefer this." After pouring Jimmy a glass, and raising his own, "Nazdarovye. So, you're not going to arrest me?"

Jimmy tasted the wine. He let his body react to the quality instinctively. He let a certain amount of tension go. "You know as well as I do that I have no evidence whatsoever but my own knowledge of events."

"I do. Checkmate."

"You play a good game of chess, Mr. Orkin." Jimmy took another sip and sighed at the pleasure of it. It was a cold night in San Francisco and the red wine was helping him shake off the chill.

"Ivan, please. After one has been in the trenches with a comrade, the niceties can be dispensed with."

"Speaking of those trenches, I have to ask… I saw you kill two men with my own eyes. The circumstances were certainly mitigating…"

"Your young friend's life was threatened in both instances…"

"Yes. And for that, I owe you, certainly. But I am curious as to how it feels to do that. I have, fortunately in my career so far, never had to take someone's life. I hope I never do – I've seen how it can change a man. But you didn't bat an eye."

Orkin sat down on a minimalist black leather sofa, gesturing for Jimmy to take the armchair next to him. "In moments like that, one can't. The first time I had to do so, back in Afghanistan, I found that the math of the equation was simple: it was him or me. I certainly never enjoyed it, but given the alternative, I prefer to be the one still standing." After another sip of wine, "Making hard decisions quickly is what I do.

One doesn't become a colonel in the army without either developing that quality, or being born with it."

"One also doesn't become a billionaire without it, too, I suppose."

"No," replied Orkin simply. After a moment, "Have you ever considered the private sector? You're a smart guy. I could use someone like you."

"Doing what?"

"Anything. 'Trouble-shooting.'"

"Thank you for the vote of confidence, but I've got cop in my blood. Literally. And, truth be told, I don't have the... 'killer instinct,' I suppose. I do what I do to help people, and to keep them safe. Not one for confrontation, really. Mediation is my thing."

Orkin nodded with understanding. "Anyway, Detective... Jimmy... it's been a pleasure. Stay in touch." He rose.

"And the painting?"

Orkin smiled. "If it makes you feel any better, I have no plans to keep it. Stolen goods isn't really my style. I prefer to work for my prizes – they feel better that way. It'll turn up in a bit."

"I'm holding you to that." Jimmy looked Orkin straight in the eye. The two men understood each other. "Thanks for the wine, I'll remember the taste of that for a while."

"I'll have a case sent over." Before Jimmy could protest, "A gift from a friend."

After enough of a hesitation to be decorous Jimmy let it go. "Thank you." Just then Jimmy's Blackberry vibrated. A text: *We need 2 talk - bench* Jimmy set his jaw. "I've got to get going. Good luck with everything."

After Jimmy shook his hand and left, Ivan Orkin turned out the lights in the living room and took in the lights of the City. They were breathtaking. After a long moment of appreciation, he broke from his reverie and worked his way towards his bedroom. He entered the room to hear the soft breathing of the beautiful woman in his bed. He then turned to gaze at the beautiful painting on the wall and smiled.

All was right in his world once more.

LXVIII

As Carlos lay on the sofa, his head in Robert's lap, he sighed. How lucky was he? Once Robert saw Carlos, with his face and ribs all bandaged, his maternal instinct kicked in. Carlos had never been so pampered in his life. It was a cold San Francisco evening, one of those nights that were crystal clear and super cold. But with a fire in the fireplace and a blanket over him, and the warmth of Robert – and Smash on TV – Carlos thought he had died and gone to heaven. He stirred slightly to look up at his lover. Robert looked down at him and smiled.

"Everything okay?" he asked.

"Never better," purred Carlos. A pang. "Well, when this rib heals, it'll be better, but for now… I'm so glad to be home. And with you."

"Shhhhh… the commercial break is over…" Robert winked at Carlos and Carlos knew.

He had found true love.

LXIX

It was really cold. And starting to get damp. Fog was creeping in, racing in front of the stars overhead and starting to pull a scrim across the Bay. Maddy was going to wait on the bench, but chose to lean against the railing, instead, avoiding a wet butt. Nothing like physical discomfort to support the misery of emotional discomfort, she thought.

The "bench" was situated along The Embarcadero. At the beginning of her relationship with Jimmy, she had adopted this location as a "neutral site," a place where really difficult conversations could be had. She had just forgotten how bleak it could get.

She saw him walking down The Embarcadero, the click of his shoes echoing off the concrete sidewalk. It was a long walk, and he didn't wave or anything. It felt to Maddy as if this was the longest moment of her life.

"You okay?" he asked when he finally reached her. There was concern, but also a hardness to his expression.

"Cold," she replied. "This can be such a cold town..."

"We don't have to do this, you know. I get it." He leaned against the railing, staring out at the Bay. He didn't look at Maddy.

"We do. We owe it to each other." After a moment's hesitation, "I owe it to you." She tried to put her hand on his shoulder, to get him to look at her, but there was something in the tension he carried in his shoulders that made her think that it might not be a good idea.

"So what is it you want to say?"

"Just that I did something that I'm supposed to regret, but because I don't regret it, I feel terrible. I feel like the worst person ever, but what happened happened really naturally and that must mean something."

Jimmy didn't say a word. He wasn't going to help. Maddy found the absence of his ironic sense of humor frightening. He could almost always be counted on for breaking the tension. The tension remained.

"But I don't know what it means. I've worked it over and over in my head..."

"How about in your heart?"

"That, too..." A tear started to work its way down her cheek, but she didn't bother to brush it away. "...And I just find myself questioning. If I can fall apart so quickly, then there must be something either wrong with me, or us, or... or right with... with..."

"With Sasha Borodin? Other than a billion dollars, a killer smile, a funny trick with his eyes and a long rap sheet, what's he got going for him?"

"I think he made me feel more like *me*, rather than someone I was trying to be. I didn't have to be tough or hard or smarter than I am. I guess I grew up in a place and a family where I was just, I don't know, I guess taken care of. I felt taken care of."

There was a silence for an uncomfortable amount of time. The lights continued to play off of the water. A fog horn went off in the distance, sounding like a mournful whale.

"Who saved your life?" asked Jimmy quietly. Finally. "If that isn't taking care of you, I don't know what is."

Maddy could only look out over the water.

Jimmy took a breath and went on.

"Once - I don't know what it was that my dad did, but my mom was so angry with him. She didn't speak to him for I don't know how long. When she finally did, all she could say was, 'I love you, but I don't like you very much right now.'" Jimmy finally looked at Maddy. "I love you, but I don't like you very much right now. I am unhappy being with you at this moment. I think I would rather be somewhere else. That might change, with time, but I'm not going to lie to you. Right now, I'd rather be on my own. It would hurt a lot less."

Another tear worked its way down Maddy's face as she continued to look out over the Bay. She couldn't form the words she needed to form. In spite of everything that had happened, there was something she needed to share with him. There was glue in her mouth.

But she had to tell him.

"Jimmy… I… I'm…"

At that moment her phone rang. Defying Gravity.

And with it the image of Sasha asleep in the golden sunlight appeared on the screen.

Jimmy sighed and pushed his way from the railing. For a moment, he reminded Maddy of Humphrey Bogart in Casablanca. There was just enough fog, and with the lights along the Embarcadero stretching off into the distance looking like an airfield landing strip, and with his trench coat pulled up around his face, all that was missing was the hat.

And the final speech.

But there was no final speech, the phone instead supplying the soundtrack to her heartbreak. Jimmy just turned and started walking, his shoes clicking along the sidewalk, each step like the tap of a hammer on a nail. Maddy stood up to call after him, but her voice was dead in her throat. After a moment, she sat down on the bench, defeated, and watched him continue northward down the Embarcadero towards Telegraph Hill. He didn't look back, and after the third streetlight he began to blur, shimmer, and finally disappear into the gathering mist.

The foghorns around the Bay began a slow keening. Maddy burst fully into tears.

> *I'm through accepting limits*
> *cause someone says they're so*
> *Some things I cannot change*
> *But till I try, I'll never know!*

She wiped her nose and stared at her phone, the cool light of its screen taunting her.

> *Too long I've been afraid of*
> *Losing love I guess I've lost*
> *Well, if that's love*
> *It comes at much too high a cost!*

Her thumb moved to hit the little green phone-shaped Answer button. It hovered there.

> *It's time to try*
> *Defying gravity*
> *Kiss me goodbye*
> *I'm defying gravity*
> *And you can't…*

The phone hit the water with a slap.

The foghorns continued keening, the lights of the Bay blinked in and out of the streaming fog. Sometimes you *can* fly too high, thought Maddy. The wings can melt when you're too close to the sun…

And there's nothing like hitting the earth falling from that height.

Acknowledgments

Writing is, for me, the most organic process in which I engage. The words just come, the characters are who they are, and they surprise me constantly. I have no idea when I start a book, a chapter or even a sentence, where it's going to take me. That being said, I was fed a lot of fuel during the writing of this book, material that I gravitated toward due to my strong interest in the subject and would read for pleasure, but which would then help the flow of the writing move in a certain direction. I owe great debts to Sarah Thorton for her funny and illuminating book Seven Days in the Art World, Ulrich Boser for his great dissection of the Gardner Museum heist, and David Samuels for his fascinating article in The New Yorker about the Pink Panthers, who do, actually, exist, although I made up the St. Petersburg cell - and the people behind them. At least I think I made them up…

I am grateful to Mr. Stephen Schwartz for allowing me to use his lyrics for Defying Gravity. The title of his song was the working title for this novel during its early development – as you can see, I felt the song captured perfectly the struggles and desires of a young woman seeking real freedom for the first time in her life.

Those to whom I also owe a great debt are those who have supported and encouraged my efforts, in spite of the little I offer in return: Maryvel Firda, Lauren Dandridge, and, bless his heart, my father, who asks me on every meeting, "How goes the writing?"

And, always, the love of my life, Eileen, who puts up with me when I have an inspiration, or when I ask for a few hours on a weekend to write, and grants me the time and space to do so. I love her madly.

Made in the USA
Charleston, SC
28 May 2013